The City of
DARKNESS

Book Two of The Watchers Chronicle

Nakeisha,
Enjoy the
book!

"Open your
memory..."

Evan Braun
and Clint Byars

THE CITY OF DARKNESS
Book Two of The Watchers Chronicle

Word Alive Press
131 Cordite Road, Winnipeg, MB R3W 1S1
www.wordalivepress.ca

WORD ALIVE PRESS
Just Write!

MIX
Paper from
responsible sources
FSC FSC® C016245
www.fsc.org

Printed in Canada.

ISBN 978-1-4866-0304-6

Cataloguing in Publication information may be obtained through Library and Archives Canada.

www.thebookofcreation.net
www.facebook.com/thebookofcreation
sherwoodbrighton@gmail.com

Cover illustration by Bradford M. Gyselman (http://occamite.com).

ACKNOWLEDGEMENTS

Once again, the first person who has to be recognized is my co-author, Clint Byars, who invited me to play in this wonderful sandbox and to whom I will be forever grateful.

No book can go to print without careful and attentive editing, and so I must express gratitude to Leigh Galbreath, who has gone above and beyond. If there's some aspect of this book that works exceptionally well, it's probable that Leigh helped to make it so.

Thank you also to the many people who advised and proofread the manuscript, holding nothing back—Tom Buller, Colette Black, Nancy DiMauro, and Frank Morin. I have also been supported and inspired by a fantastic group of fellow writers who are too numerable to be named here, but they know who they are. Beyond my writing buddies, I've been blessed with so many wonderful advocates since the release of *The Book of Creation*. If you're one of these people, know that this book wouldn't exist without your contribution.

—E.B.

CONTENTS

PROLOGUE

Cairo, Egypt
SIXTEEN YEARS AGO

He was married, and she no longer cared.

Elisabeth Macfarlane crossed her legs and flipped a lock of brown hair over her shoulder. The object of her desire, Doctor Emery Wörtlich, didn't give her a second glance. In fact, none of the men on the rooftop terrace seemed to notice her at all. The problem with these work gatherings was that they didn't see her as a woman, but rather as another man, another colleague. Except for Emery. But tonight the Egyptologist was embroiled in his own brand of inner turmoil, of which Elisabeth had so far been afforded just the barest taste.

The last vestiges of daylight—blotches of purple and orange splashed against the desert horizon—slowly sunk out of view, forcing the garden lights to switch on. They bathed the terrace in a soft electric hum.

Zahi Menefee, a fat Egyptian man with jowls that danced and swayed with every syllable, held the others' interest. He was project overseer and commanded attention even during off-hours like these, at least to the degree that any time spent amongst this group could be considered "off-hours." Their discussions invariably returned to work.

"A joke is what it is," Menefee spat. "The books, they say! Where are the books? Well, I keep looking. What else can I do? They are out there. Somewhere, I am so certain. So certain."

Elisabeth stifled a smile. She had visited Cairo's Archaeological Institute six times so far this year, and Menefee always railed on the same subject—the lack of books in the library sites. If the Library of Alexandria had contained half the intellectual and academic marvels it was purported to have had, *some* books must have survived the various fires and floods. Menefee had made it his mission to find them, but the Institute's board of directors—never mind the Egyptian government—had little patience and even fewer resources to keep him on the scent.

Beside her, Max Holden shifted in his seat. He looked the way he always did—bored. No doubt this beautiful garden terrace, embraced by descending twilight, was the last place he wanted to be. The one thing Holden seemed to hate more than any other was being in Cairo. If he had his way, he would never leave the field. In his first year at the Institute, he had logged more than a thousand hours in the Valley of the Kings alone.

"You can't rush it, Doctor."

Elisabeth smiled as she glanced at the speaker, twenty-five-year-old Noam Sheply, the youngest member of the team by a good decade. Well, he was hardly a full-fledged member. More of an intern.

Sheply's English accent made him sound even more pretentious than his light brown, barely grown-in goatee already implied. If Elisabeth was certain of one thing, it was that Menefee wasn't looking for sympathy or support—especially from a man more than thirty years his junior.

Menefee turned to Sheply with smoldering eyes. He didn't say anything. He didn't have to. Sheply, the little twit, blanched and pressed himself into the beige cushions of his chair.

Without looking, Elisabeth felt a distinctive mental tingle and knew someone was gazing in her direction. Her gaze shot across the terrace to find Emery giving her a once-over—not quite as appraisingly as she had hoped for, but still, any attention was good attention. Perhaps he just didn't want to appear too forward in front of his colleagues.

Or perhaps I've imagined the whole thing.

No. She hadn't imagined the way he had rested his hand on her inner thigh when they shared the back seat on the drive to Luxor last March. His hand had rested there for nearly ten minutes without comment; she'd been so shocked she hadn't known what to say. She also hadn't imagined their growing chemistry over the preceding year. How many evenings had they spent together in hotel bars? She'd lost count.

She was certain Emery wanted to be more than friends. He just hadn't quite worked up the courage to say so.

And of course, there was the matter of his wife.

"Emery, how's your paper going?" Max asked.

Emery's eyes drifted away from her but didn't quite settle on Max. Whatever he was staring at, it was far off in the distance.

Max chuckled. "Earth to Emery!"

Emery snapped back to the present, a smile flitting across his lips. He leaned forward and plucked up his half-finished glass of beer. He swirled it for a second, then took a long drink.

"The paper? Not done yet," Emery said, wiping foam from his

upper lip.

Menefee's belly shook from laughter. "I stopped holding my breath, as you English speakers say."

Everyone knew Emery was working on a theory, though he refused to talk about it. Elisabeth had tried to get him to open up about his new ideas, but he wouldn't. Not with her. Maybe not with anybody.

Menefee reached down for his empty glass, then heaved himself out of his chair. He stood in place for a moment, pretending to admire the view, but Elisabeth knew he was really catching his breath.

"Turning in?" Max asked.

Menefee nodded. "These late nights of ours... well, I am not the young man I used to be. See you all in the morning." He shuffled toward the door leading into the penthouse apartment he shared with his wife. Before going in, he called back, "But stay as long as you like."

With Menefee gone, the remaining four drew their chairs closer together.

"Max, have you made your decision yet?" Emery asked.

Max ran a hand through his graying hair before answering. There was a good reason Emery had waited for Menefee to retire for the night before broaching the subject; Menefee had worked long and hard to convince Max to join them in Egypt, and he studiously ignored all evidence that Max wasn't happy here.

"I think so, yes," Max said. "My plan is to stay until the end of summer. Two years in Egypt is enough. My research may bring me back from time to time, but I'm eager to be home."

For Max, home was Australia. His work on hieroglyph translation was legendary, but he insisted he could do the bulk of his work remotely. He didn't like to be so far from family, and Elisabeth gathered he had a very large family.

"When does it become official?" Sheply asked, looking a bit more relaxed now that their leader had left them for the night.

"End of the month." Max raised an eyebrow at him. "Eyeing my spot?"

Sheply shrugged. "If there's an opening, why shouldn't I?"

"No reason," Max said. "Just be warned: you'll have to work a lot of hours with Emery here. And he's the cantankerous sort."

Elisabeth let out a chuckle and all eyes turned to her.

"Please excuse me," she said. "Cantankerous! Hardly the word I would use."

There was a glimmer of amusement in Max's eye. Did he know something? Had Emery told him? She hoped not. This field was difficult enough for women, never mind for those who were seen to be flirting with their colleagues. She had to be more careful.

Sheply lowered his head and peered at her over the rim of his glasses. "What word would you use?"

Trapped.

She bit her lip, pretending to put thought into it. "Argumentative," she said, feigning conviction. "Yes, there you have it. Argumentative."

Max tilted his head, thinking it over, then nodded in appreciation. "Very perceptive, Doctor Macfarlane. I believe you have hit upon the perfect word to describe our friend here." He turned to Emery. "What do you think? You are argumentative, aren't you?"

Emery gave them a cunning smile. "I am not."

The response was good for a smile or two. The men talked shop for a few more minutes, but eventually everyone stood to go. Menefee had offered them the terrace as long as they wanted it, true, but they operated under an unspoken curfew. Failing to adhere to it would only bring trouble with the boss come morning.

They gathered their things, rode the elevator to the parking garage, then said goodbye before advancing toward their respective cars.

"Need a lift to your hotel?" Emery asked her.

She fell into step behind him. "Please."

Elisabeth slipped into the passenger seat and waited for Emery to sit down and start the engine. She looked across the garage toward the street exit. Max's car waited to turn left and Sheply was just behind him.

A minute later, they were alone.

Emery drove her to the hotel in silence, but instead of pulling into the service loop in front of the lobby entrance he found an empty space in the parking lot.

Her heart pounded, knowing exactly what the man intended. This time, she would let her heart take her wherever it wanted to go. Tonight she would finally ignore her conscience, her inhibitions, that dreaded voice inside that shouted "Married man! Married man!" at the top of its lungs.

They took the stairs up to her room, Emery leading the way while Elisabeth fished through her purse for the room key. She found it just as they arrived at her door and she slipped it into the lock.

"After you," she said.

Emery entered first and headed straight for the bed. He perched on the edge of it, looking slightly uncomfortable while Elisabeth shut the door.

She cleared her throat. "I need to use the bathroom."

Elisabeth half-closed the bathroom door and turned to look at her reflection in the mirror. She made fists and leaned forward on her knuckles.

Maybe I should have had a few more drinks. To prepare.

She shook her head and sat down on the closed porcelain lid of the toilet. No, she wouldn't allow herself to go through with this unless she was completely clear-headed. She'd made that decision weeks ago and she would stick to it. The last thing she wanted was for them to fall victim to a drunken night of passion, a night only to be regretted in the morning.

She was determined to give him no cause for regret.

With one last glance at the mirror to instill confidence, Elisabeth swung open the door and walked toward the bed. She sat next to Emery and reached down to remove her shoes, tossing them into a corner. "How are you feeling?" she asked. He had been in his own world all night. Something was eating at him.

Something usually was.

He took a deep breath and let it out. "I am fine."

"I can tell when you lie to me."

"That is the problem with letting people get to know you," he murmured in that stilted German accent she'd come to adore. "You cannot get away with nearly as much."

She put an arm around his shoulders. He stiffened. A moment later, he relaxed again.

"Is it something at home?" she asked.

Emery's grin was both involuntary and authentic. "There is always something at home. Catherine is upset that I spend so much time at the Institute. She is right."

"You're working on your paper."

"That is not the reason." He turned to her, his eyes filled with longing. "You know the reason."

Enough beating around the bush, she told herself. Without hesitation, she brought her hand up behind his neck and held it there, leaning in for a kiss. He didn't stop her, but neither did he reciprocate.

She pulled away, mouth open, reveling in the scent of his warm breath caressing her cheek. Her other hand went to his chest, where she could feel his heart racing at least as hard as her own.

He wants to. Oh how he wants to …

This time, he took the lead, moving in and gently teasing her lower lip. She closed her eyes tight and kissed him back—

—but it didn't last.

He turned his head away and lay down, his back pressed against the freshly made bed. His forehead creased.

"This may not be a good time for this," he groaned. "You were right. There is something on my mind."

"Catherine—"

"Not Catherine." He let out a sigh. "Well, yes. But not *just* Catherine."

Elisabeth lay down on her side, her brown hair forming a pillow beneath her head. She reached out and rested her hand on Emery's chest. He didn't pull away.

"Tell me. Is it work?"

A glimmer came into his eye and he pushed himself up onto his elbows. "You should move to Cairo."

She frowned. "Me?"

"You already travel here every month, or nearly so. Ask the university for a year-long sabbatical. Tell them Cairo's Archaeological Institute needs your help on a translation project."

"What translation project?"

Emery sat the rest of the way up. "With Max leaving, I will be encouraged to conduct more fieldwork. As much as possible. It would be helpful to have an assistant—no, not an assistant. A partner. An equal. Someone working at my side." He took her by the hand. "How does a week in Memphis sound?"

"Sounds romantic," she said. "But anyone could take that job. You don't need me."

"You have skills nobody else can offer, believe me."

She let out a laugh, wondering which set of skills he was referring to.

"Once I publish my paper, nobody will want to work with me," Emery continued, looking dejected. The forehead crease was back.

Elisabeth held her breath, wondering whether or not he would finally talk about what he was working on. A shared secret would solidify their bond. As far as she knew, nobody at the Institute—nobody anywhere—knew about his secret theory.

She debated whether or not to prompt him about the paper. If she did, he might shut down. If she said nothing—

"You know that I have been avoiding field excursions the last few years, right?"

"Yes," Elisabeth said. The word came out strangled from her having held her breath too long.

"Well, I think the time has come to go back, see a few monuments in person." He hesitated. "To confirm some suspicions that have been on my mind lately."

Suspicions? This was definitely related to that damned paper.

"I have been trained to evaluate all my findings in terms of symbology. My peers insist that religious texts don't provide a clean sense of history; they're full of myth and metaphor. Is there more to it than that? Take the histories of the ancient kingdoms, for example. The people worshipped the gods, but more than that—the people *interacted* with them."

Elisabeth straightened up, sitting next to him. "What are you getting at?"

"Maybe we cannot evaluate everything in terms of metaphor. Perhaps some of those tales hold kernels of truth, literal elements, and perhaps somewhere out there I will find evidence of just that, evidence which might have previously been missed because nobody was looking for it." He gave her a winning smile. "How would you like to look with me?"

Her emotions churned at the suggestion. Among the many things she had expected to come out of this night, a job offer hadn't been one of them. In the context of their mounting relationship, it was practically a marriage proposal.

What would it mean to accept?

"I realize you cannot just uproot yourself," he said after nearly a minute of silence passed. It was one of the longest minutes she could remember.

"Like you said, I'd have to take a sabbatical. I'd also have to apply for a visa."

"The Institute can take care of all that."

Well, that was one roadblock out of the way. Why was her mind so desperately trying to find another to replace it? Didn't she want this? To travel with Emery, to work with him? To be alone with him?

"Where does Catherine fit in?"

His eyes turned dark. "The same way she has always fit in. She remains at home and knows nothing of my life. Does she care about it? No. She should go back to Dresden, for all I care. That would make things easier for both of us."

For someone who claimed his marriage was over, he spent an inordinate amount of time worrying about his wife. He cared more than he claimed. Of course, he cared for Elisabeth, too. He had shown her on many occasions; he wouldn't have made this offer otherwise. He wanted her more than he wanted Catherine.

But he still wanted Catherine a little bit.

And that "little bit" was too much.

Elisabeth stood up and ran a hand through her hair, pushing it behind her ears. She didn't know what to do. If only this night had been just about sex. Instead he had made it about so much more.

"I'll have to give it some thought," she said, but there was more weariness than excitement in her tone.

He picked up on it. "You are unhappy with me."

She walked to the window and looked out at the view of the waterfront. The waters of the Nile slipped by silently under the city lights. That water was fortunate; it only flowed in one direction.

"Unhappy?" She could sense him studying her reflection in the windowpane. "Mostly confused. But yeah, a little unhappy."

"Why?"

Because all I came for was something physical, but you want more. I wish I knew for sure that I wanted more.

Instead all she said was, "I think you should go. We'll talk in the morning."

Emery gathered his things and walked to the door. She turned just in time to catch his momentary hesitation, but then he was gone and all she was left with was the sound of his retreating footsteps.

Careful, Elisabeth. One of these days he'll be gone for good.

ONE

Tiahuanaco, Bolivia
JULY 17

Cheers and catcalls, accompanied by a lively samba, spilled out of the cafeteria and wafted down the tent-lined avenue. The cold winter wind whistled and snapped against canvas walls; even the stars twinkled and danced to those Latin rhythms.

The volume intensified as a man and woman stumbled out of the dining tent, both clutching bottles of amber liquid. A gust of wind caught the alcohol's acrid scent and made the journey to the twitching hairs on Dario Katsulas's upper lip some five meters away. Dario didn't step out of the way in time to completely avoid them as they lumbered toward one of the four dozen or so virtually identical tents behind him.

As Dario watched them giggle and duck into the privacy of one of those tan-colored homes away from home, he caught sight of the Pyramid of Akapana, the tallest of the ancient city of Tiahuanaco's remaining structures, its stepped outline vague against the purple wisps of sunset sinking over the snow-capped western Andes. Come morning, he would be atop Akapana, tools in hand and ready for another day of mapping the contours of that earthen marvel.

But not tonight.

He brushed back his mop of thick black hair. Tonight was about socializing. It was about "fitting in," something Dario had never been adept at, as his more effervescent siblings had constantly reminded him. Steeling himself, he pushed a pair of circular-lensed glasses up the bridge of his nose and stepped into the dining tent to join the revelry.

Someone had moved the array of tables to the tent's periphery to make space for a dance floor. A dozen or so bodies swung to the music pouring out of a pair of speakers on the counter usually reserved for fried empanadas and strong coffee.

Familiar faces greeted him with friendly nods followed by the occasional slap on the back, though he knew only a handful of names to attach to them. In moments like these, he longed to be back among the steep, comforting slopes of Italy's west coast. He had friends there—well, if not friends than at least longtime colleagues. In his experience, the difference was marginal.

The song ended, and before the next began he heard gales of laughter coming from the far corner of the tent. A smile crept onto his lips. As he drew nearer, a mass of blond hair stood out like rays of sunshine among dark clouds.

Rhea Dunford wore a wide grin as she leaned over the table she sat at and gathered up a pile of silver coins, stacking them neatly in front of her. The others at the table—all Bolivians, and all men— evinced pained expressions. Dario didn't think they were too pained, however; he would have bet most of them had only joined the card game as a pretense to spend time with Rhea, whose fair complexion set her apart.

Rhea's facial features and bright personality marked her for a first-worlder in a way that Dario's didn't, and perhaps that accounted for why they had bonded so well since her arrival the previous week from Canada. Both were outsiders, though she was an infinitely more popular outsider than he.

Between card deals, Rhea looked up and spotted him. She smiled and gestured to an open chair. He waved her off. Poker wasn't his game.

To her left sat two young interns from the university in La Paz. Dario didn't think they had any archaeological training, but the government had insisted that the Tiahuanaco restoration team be comprised of as many locals as possible. They made useful gofers.

Next to them sat Marco Salvatore, a man with long hair, thick arms, and a generous circumference. His gregarious personality was somewhat muted this evening, though. Three bottles of Paceña were lined up in front of him, their contents as depleted as his stack of coins. The slump of his broad shoulders told Dario the man was in a dark mood, though he seemed to at least feign high spirits when meeting Rhea's gaze. Her gaze had an uplifting effect on just about everyone.

Dario secured a drink, and then a chair in a relatively undisturbed corner. He leaned back and watched the dancing, not tempted in the least to join in. Today was someone named Fareed's birthday, he gathered from the snippets of conversation around him. Dario wouldn't have been able to pick Fareed out of a lineup.

He wasn't quite sure how much time passed, but eventually the tent emptied. Even the poker game had come to an end, the only remnants a few stray cards lying in a pool of alcohol where a half-empty bottle had tipped over.

The fact that Rhea had slipped away without saying goodbye saddened him a great deal.

Quietly, he escaped into the fresh air. The wind had slackened somewhat, but it was still cold enough to make his teeth clack. He wasn't accustomed to the experience, having never ventured far from the Mediterranean before this job. The cold didn't suit him.

Instead of returning to his tent, though, he rubbed his hands together and walked toward the edge of the tent city, which had been erected east of Tiahuanaco's newly restored city walls. Grotesque faces carved from ancient stone blocks stared down at him from those walls, lit by the ever-shifting light of swinging lanterns.

Above loomed the Akapana summit, where he'd spent most of his week. Even from this vantage, he could make out the tall ladders leaning against the eastern slope. So much of this city had crumbled to dust, but Doctor Wallis Christophe, the site coordinator, had taken a week to install the ladders, the only means of ascending the pyramid, in such a way that they wouldn't dislodge so much as a single pebble.

Though he couldn't see it from this angle, there was a depression in the rock atop the summit deep enough for a man to stand in without being able to see over the edge. Local legends and human remains spoke to the horrors that had taken place at Akapana, where the residents of the city had gathered to witness dedications to the gods.

Dedications, Dario thought grimly. *Sounds sterile. Like the sprinklings of water Catholic priests daub over newborn babies.*

The priests of Akapana had viciously torn apart the victims of these dedications, ritualistically disemboweling them and laying out their entrails as sacrificial offerings. The summit depression may very well have held the spilled blood of foreign trespassers—or perhaps misbehaving children. Those bloodthirsty priests could have bathed for a week in the resultant pools.

Dario shuddered, reining in his imagination.

What am I doing here?

Fresh off unearthing the index to the Library of Alexandria, he now found himself sifting through a city that had boasted no written language whatsoever. These ancient illiterates hadn't deigned to write down so much as a to-do list in a thousand years. Herculaneum felt very far away, indeed.

He shored himself up against the wave of self-pity that threatened to wash over him. It wasn't as though there were no advantages to being here; the project offered great pay and connections. Coming to Tiahuanaco had been his own decision. Just because exploring the world hadn't turned out quite as he'd hoped was no excuse not to make the most of his opportunities.

Dario turned and walked quickly through the maze of tents, coming at last to his own. He unzipped the front opening, dipped his head to fit through the low entrance, then secured it behind him.

He slipped his shoes off and sat on the edge of his single bed, its metallic hinges squealing in protest. The small rug's thin bristles itched against the soles of his feet. The only other furnishings were a wooden table and chair, and a low bedside stool just large enough to hold an alarm clock and stack of hard-backed books. His shirt came off, then his pants, and before he could register the cool air against his chest he dove beneath the covers and pulled them up to his chin.

"Dario, are you in there?"

He lifted his head and stared at the tent entrance. Sure enough, a silhouette stood against the translucent material. His heart beating faster, he swung his legs over the side of the bed and reached for his pants. A few moments later, he pulled back the flap, giving Rhea enough room to come inside.

She settled into the wooden chair, folding her hands in her lap.

"What are you doing here?" Dario asked.

He wanted the words back the moment they slipped out, but wishing didn't make it so. Fortunately, her response was a sardonic smile, one he had seen her wear countless times.

"Really, Dario," she said, "sometimes you have all the grace of a toddler. Why didn't you join us at the poker game? We had an open seat."

Dario slid his bare feet into a pair of slippers. "I don't play cards."

"You don't dance, either. I think there are a lot of things you don't do, huh?" She laughed. "Sorry. I'm not trying to mother you."

"Are you just here to … talk?"

Her eyes flared. "Talk?"

"Well, it's one o'clock in the morning. Don't get me wrong, I'm happy to see you, but it's a little—"

"After your bedtime?" Rhea leaned forward, clasping her hands together. "Anyway, it may very well be the middle of the night, but I don't think anyone's getting much sleep."

He froze. What did she mean by that? His mind flashed to the couple who had stumbled past him a few hours earlier to disappear into a tent together. Was that what Rhea had in mind? Was she angling to "not get much sleep" with *him?* Could he be so fortunate?

"The truth is, I did come to talk," she continued before he had a chance to stick his foot in his mouth. "I'm sure it's nothing."

"What's nothing?" he asked, his heart resuming its normal rhythm.

"Well, after the game, I went back with Marco for a nightcap."

"Please, I don't need to hear the details."

She gave him a lopsided smile. "Believe me, that's not where this story is heading. I *wish* it was something as uncomplicated as that."

That perspective—that sex could ever be "uncomplicated"— served to illustrate the many differences between them.

"I noticed something was up with Marco earlier," Dario said.

"You have no idea. After having a few too many, he told me a secret."

She paused, perhaps weighing whether or not to share it, but she wouldn't have come to him if she weren't already resolved to break the confidence. And that meant it was something serious. Rhea was nothing if not loyal.

"Apparently, two interns from La Paz went missing on Thursday," she finally said, looking him in the eye. "Nobody has heard from them and the disappearances haven't been reported."

This took a few moments to sink in.

"Was Marco being serious?" Dario wondered. "I mean, he wasn't playing a joke on you?"

"This was no joke, Dario. The look in his eyes…" She bit her finger nervously. "He was afraid."

"They went missing three days ago? If they were on Marco's crew, why wouldn't he report it?"

"He didn't say. As soon as I started asking questions, he clammed up."

Dario kicked off the slippers and reached for his shoes.

"Dario, just hold on. Think first."

"What's to think about?" He stood up, looking for a sweater. "For all we know, those two interns are dead. It gets cold at night in July, and if no one's heard from them since Thursday."

"But I don't think we should—"

He wouldn't let her finish. "No, stop. We both know that the only reason you told me about this is so that I would do something. You want to do something, too, just not alone."

She let out a long breath. "Well, yes."

"Okay, so we'll talk to Marco." He stepped up to the entrance and waited for her.

Rhea hesitated only a moment before taking the lead, since Dario realized he didn't know which tent belonged to Marco. It turned out to be on the other side of the camp—and was almost twice the size of Dario's, he noted with mild annoyance.

There was no obvious place to knock, so Rhea settled for grabbing a flap on the front of the tent and shaking it.

"Marco," she said. "Marco, it's me."

They waited for almost a minute, but nothing happened.

"He's probably sleeping," Dario whispered.

"Not likely, in the state I left him," Rhea said. "Marco, I know you're in there."

Still nothing.

"Marco!"

Dario was considering the ramifications of forcing his way into the tent when they finally saw some movement inside.

"Go away," Marco growled. The words slurred together. However many drinks he'd had at the party, Dario was pretty sure he'd since helped himself to a few more. Maybe a lot more.

"I can't do that," Rhea said, leaning her head forward and lowering her voice.

"Oh, I think you can." Marco unzipped the top of the entrance and peered out at them. "Go away, or I'll call camp security."

Dario wasn't intimidated. "Yes, you should do that. And when they come, you can explain to them about the missing members of your crew."

Marco looked daggers at Rhea. "Why did you bring *him?*"

"You weren't doing anything, so I had to," she said.

Marco unzipped the tent the rest of the way. "Keep your voices down and get in here."

Dario smiled in satisfaction, following Rhea inside. The tent had two chairs, which Dario and Rhea took. Marco sat on the ground, cross-legged with an almost-empty bottle of tequila.

"I told you not to talk about this," Marco said.

"What were you thinking, Marco?" Rhea said. "Those kids could be in trouble, and you let three days pass!"

Marco brought the bottle to his lips and drank long and deep. "You should have left well enough alone," he said when the bottle came down. He wiped his lips.

"You're the one who got her into this," Dario reminded him. "What happened?"

Marco eyed him with as much menace as a drunken man could manage. Dario met the look with determination.

"Jorge found me after lunch on Thursday," Marco said. "He and Yasmine had stumbled onto a narrow tunnel entrance a half-mile north of the city. I assumed it was nothing. A sinkhole, maybe. They insisted it was something more, but they couldn't explore the vicinity without permission. So I gave it to them, telling them to do it quickly and report back before nightfall."

Dario bit his lip and exchanged a look with Rhea. The site was strictly administered by the Bolivian government, meaning all archae-ological activity conducted outside a few hundred meters of the city ruins was prohibited. If it was discovered that Marco had approved an excavation without anyone's knowledge, even a minor one, he would be swiftly fired.

"Why did you let them do it?" Rhea asked.

Marco's eyes were hollow, resigned. "I never imagined something like this would happen."

"And you've told no one?"

"Only you." Marco picked up the bottle again, pretending to be interested in the printing on the label. "What am I supposed to do? I have a family to support."

Dario stood and walked to the front of the tent. He peered outside. All was quiet.

"You said they went a half-mile from camp," Dario said, turning back. "Do you think you could find the spot?"

Marco's mouth dropped open, then snapped closed. "I went out this morning, crossed the road, and walked as far as the river."

"Nobody saw you?" Rhea asked. "You would have had to cross several farms to get there."

"No one was awake that early," the Bolivian said. "Jorge said the tunnel entrance was near the river, but I walked almost two miles of the riverbank. I couldn't find anything."

Dario noticed a flashlight sitting atop the small desk tucked into the corner. He grabbed it and flicked the switch. Light poured out.

"It may have been easy to miss in the dark," Dario said.

Marco rubbed his bleary eyes. "Are you suggesting we go looking now, at this hour?"

Dario gritted his teeth. "If we wait another day, it may be too late. After three days, I would already expect the worst."

That shut Marco up.

After arranging to meet back in a half-hour, Dario and Rhea headed to their respective tents.

"There may be nothing to find," Rhea remarked just before they parted ways.

"If that's true, Jorge and Yasmine would have made it back by now."

Unless it was an animal attack of some kind, Dario thought, but he didn't voice it. A quick exchange of looks with Rhea told him the idea had occurred to her at exactly the same time.

*   *   *

Dario pulled the hood of his jacket across his face. It was several degrees below freezing and the gusting southerly winds made it seem even colder. The camp was finally quiet when they snuck out, avoiding the main paths and picking their way through a forest of green and brown tents. The quarter-moon was half-obscured by swiftly moving clouds. He aimed directly toward the mountains to the north. The river passed through the valley about halfway between the camp and the foot of those slopes. The half-mile trek hadn't seemed like much at the outset, but as his boots trudged through thick grass it came to feel interminable.

"You can use the flashlights," Marco whispered once they were far enough from camp. "Just point them at the ground and not the sky."

Maybe twenty minutes later, Dario heard the telltale gurgle of slow-moving water. The riverbank was just ahead, its narrow course meandering off to the west, toward the southern shores of Lake Titicaca.

"They wouldn't have crossed the river," Marco said. "They found the tunnel by happenstance while on a walk, and there's no way they just happened to swim the river."

"Take the course west," Dario told him, nodding. "Rhea and I will head east. Set your watch for one hour, and I'll do the same. When the time's up, head back. We'll meet again here, whether we've found anything or not. Understand?"

Another grunt.

Marco's dark form turned, his flashlight already scanning the muddy ground.

The mud got stickier the farther Dario and Rhea walked, forcing them off the riverbank and into the grass. He stepped carefully, sweeping his light along the ground. The last thing he needed was to step into the very hole they were looking for and break a leg.

The night was louder here than in camp, the chirping of crickets and other insects so overwhelming that the noise drove him to distraction. From time to time, he felt something brush against his legs. He kept telling himself it was nothing but shifting blades of grass, though it didn't set his mind at ease; if a predator prowled nearby, as he feared, the tall grass would make for perfect cover.

Dario cursed himself for not bringing a tranquilizer gun. There was at least one in the camp's security tent… but what excuse could he have come up with to sign one out at this late hour?

He navigated around an outcropping of large rocks in his path, continuing to scan the riverbed, but found only mud and beached sediment. Maybe in the daylight they'd be able to better inspect the grasses—

"Dar—"

Rhea barely managed to get out his name before cutting herself off with a strangled gasp, followed by the distinctive sound of flesh slapping into mud.

Dario got to his knees next to Rhea, who was already sitting up and picking mud out of her hair.

"Are you okay?"

"I think so," she said. "I tripped on something."

He brought his flashlight up to her mud-streaked face. She used her free hand to clear the muck out of her eyes. It did nothing to dull her Nordic beauty.

"Get that out of my face. Haven't I suffered enough indignity?"

"Did you trip on a rock?"

Rhea shook her flashlight, then cursed. "The batteries must have died." She hesitated. "Sorry, no, not a rock."

"A hole? A tunnel entrance?"

"It didn't feel big enough for that."

"Marco called it a narrow opening," Dario said. "It wouldn't have to be big—"

He stopped and swung his flashlight back. Rhea had been walking along the water's edge, and indeed there was a spot lower than the surrounding ground. He moved to get a closer look. There was a crevice, hardly visible unless you ventured into the muddy riverbank. He came to the lip of the hole and pointed the flashlight into it.

"I found something," he said. "It's barely wide enough for a child to slip through, but if you'd been walking a foot to the right, you would have stepped right into it. Could have twisted your ankle."

Rhea got down on her knees and traced the edge of the hole with her hand. "It looks like the beginning of a sinkhole." She glanced out at the river. "The course of the river may have drifted over the years. This opening was probably covered by about a meter of topsoil before the river eroded it."

Dario had to agree. Rivers like this one, traversing relatively flat valleys, often moved over the decades. Was it possible this was a tunnel, as the interns had claimed, freshly discovered after centuries of hiding? His heart beat faster at the thought.

"This has to be the entrance they found," he said. "But where are Jorge and Yasmine?"

"You think they went down?"

If they did, chances are they're not coming out again, he thought. *Not after three days.*

Water from the river had recently passed right next to the hole, maybe even close enough for some to pour in, smoothing the surrounding mud. From the top lip, however, Dario thought he could make out the remnant of a footprint.

"Someone else was definitely here," Rhea said, as though reading his mind.

"One of us needs to go back for Marco."

"Well, we only have one working flashlight and I don't plan to be left alone in the dark." She shook her head. "I have a better idea."

"Oh?"

"We don't have the equipment to properly explore this area. Not tonight. We should return to camp. Tomorrow, we start fresh."

"Yes to returning to camp, but coming back tomorrow?" He let out a low whistle. "If anyone finds out, we'll be stripped of our credentials and sent home. I don't know about you, but that's a mark on my reputation I could live without."

"What choice do we have?"

He was silent, considering how best to answer. "Marco should accept responsibility for his actions and report the missing interns. When the truth is known, and this tunnel discovered, there's a good chance a team will get permission to excavate here."

"Only three problems with that," Rhea said. "One, there will be obvious evidence that we came out here. We haven't even tried to cover our tracks. And two, Marco is unlikely to leave us out of it at this point. That means we're going to get in trouble either way."

She was probably right. They didn't know Marco well enough to ask him to cover for them, even if the result was just a slap on the wrist.

"You said three things," Dario said. "What's the third problem?"

"Oh, it's not a problem exactly. It's just that… well, even if a team does excavate here, it won't be us. Don't you want to find out what's down there?"

He grinned to himself. Of all three points, that was by far the strongest.

TWO

O*nce something is in your memory, it is possible to access it."*
The bartender dropped a mug of dark ale on the wooden bar. The wood was pockmarked with the rings of previous mugs, a marker of the hours Sherwood Brighton had occupied this creaky stool. His clumsy hands brought the mug to his lips, tipping it back and feeling the frothy head cling to his moustache as the sweet ale went down.

Brighton ignored the bartender's judgmental gaze, but worried it might mean he was close to being cut off. He was certain it was too early for that. He focused on the clock hanging above the beer taps and waited for the three clocks to merge into one.

One-thirty, he determined as the clocks separated again.

Brighton put his head down. The hours had come and gone faster than one of those god-awful trains that had shot him through the chunnel. His eyes hurt and his head hurt. In fact, most of his body had suffered miscellaneous aches and pains long before he'd sauntered in.

"Once something is in your memory, it is possible to access it."

He shut his eyes tight and willed Ira's voice away, to disappear as thoroughly as the rabbi himself had. Even so, he could never forget those words; they would dog him to his deathbed—that, and the sight of Emery Wörtlich's broken body, drowning in blood caked with dust and fallen stone—

Another swig of ale made that image dim a little around the edges. How many more beers to make it fade entirely? He'd experimented heavily these last few months and still hadn't reached a conclusion, except that common ale likely wasn't enough to achieve such magic. He might need something a little stronger.

"It takes discipline and reflection," Ira's voice continued, ringing maddeningly somewhere deep in his head. *"It takes patience."*

He gritted his teeth and felt another wave of pain roll from one side of his head to the other. More ale.

"It does not happen by accident. It happens through intention."

Fed up, Brighton pushed back his stool and stood—or attempted to, anyway. He almost tipped over but managed to throw his right arm against the edge of the bar in time to catch himself. What would Ira Binyamin think of him now, staggering through a pub, barely able to keep his own feet?

"I'll be back," he mumbled at the bartender, but he wasn't sure the words were coherent enough to understand. He didn't care.

This was his third straight night here and his feet knew the way to the loo. After doing his business, he stood at the sink, staring at his reflection in the mirror. The bruise over his left eye—or was it his right eye? Intoxication rendered him easily confused. Well, the bruise over one of his eyes was dark brown… an improvement over the purple color he'd sported the night before. It hurt worse than almost anything he could remember, but passersby gave him a wide berth when they saw it—and that's exactly what he needed.

Everywhere he went, he memorized the faces of the people around him, paranoid that he was being followed, being pursued. Ira had absconded with the Book of Creation, and Wörtlich had died, leaving only one target for their enemies: him.

In truth, he couldn't afford to get this drunk.

He splashed water on his face, then watched as the drops streaked down his cheeks, mingling with facial hair. He yawned, dismissing the ache in his jaw, and returned to his stool.

Instead of sitting down, he pulled a stack of bills out of his wallet and left them next to his final half-finished mug of ale. The amount was too much, he was sure, but he didn't trust his ability to count; besides, the bartender deserved a reward.

Brighton pulled on his jacket and stepped out into the muggy night. The humidity was out of control and he could practically feel drops of water squeezing out of the air around him. From everything he'd heard of England, the one consistent fact was that it rained almost all the time, and yet not a drop had fallen since Brighton arrived.

I need a plan, he told himself, repeating the mantra that had stalked him all day. His first trip to Stonehenge had yielded nothing. Of course, he wasn't quite sure what he'd expected. Just something.

There had to be something. This was a hotspot, just like the Giza pyramids and the bone field in Antarctica. He and Ira and Wörtlich had had dreams in those places. No, visions. When they'd been lost, those visions had helped them figure out where to go, where to search for the Book. They had provided direction, and if anyone had ever needed direction...

Brighton looked up at a group of young people chatting and gesturing animatedly a block up the street. He tried to walk in a straight line as they passed. He might look and sound like a drunk; no use in walking like one, if he could help it.

They hardly noticed him.

Brighton looked both ways for traffic—there was none so early in the morning—then steered across the cobblestone street toward his hotel, a narrow sliver of a building with a bright blue door. That door shone like a beacon, making it impossible to get lost in his wanderings.

He approached the door, reaching into his pocket and producing a skeleton key. He admired it for a moment under the streetlight; it was quintessentially old-world, the sort of thing nobody would have ever found in North America, so caught up were they in new technology and modern amenities. It only took three tries to unlock the door.

The green-shaded lamp atop the front desk lit the tiny lounge, lending everything a green tint. Nobody was on duty at this hour. Brighton's shoes clicked over baby blue ceramic tile as he crossed from the door to the staircase, which spiraled upward. He gripped the metallic railing and began to climb.

He paused on the second floor, where several tables waited to accommodate the morning's continental breakfast.

A man sat at one of the tables, still as stone, face mostly hidden by shadows, his back to the window overlooking the front stoop. A well-worn book lay open in front of him, and next to it a pen.

The stranger lifted his head and stared right at him. "Are you okay?"

Brighton furrowed his eyebrows, mustering all possible sobriety, and took a step toward the mystery man.

"Yes," Brighton answered. "You must be a night owl."

The stranger craned forward into the light. He was smiling. "I'm not the only one. Smells like you've had a few."

Brighton froze. It hadn't occurred to him that the scent of ale wafted off him. He sniffed his jacket appraisingly and cringed.

"As most people have who are up past two o'clock," the stranger acknowledged, his long hair swaying. He gestured to an empty chair across from him. "Sit? Unless you're on your way someplace."

Like my bed, Brighton thought wistfully. *And my air conditioner.*

Instead, he pulled out the chair and sat.

"Have we met?" the stranger asked.

Brighton fought his instinct to run. He'd been running for months, moving from one city to another, never staying long, always worried someone was after him. Never had he allowed himself the luxury of considering himself safe, that no one cared about his whereabouts or what he was up to.

"I don't think so," Brighton replied. "Maybe I just have one of those faces."

The stranger looked down at his book and shrugged. "Could be, could be."

Brighton gazed at the pages of the book—a notebook. There was a sketch on the nearest open page in black ink, a number of squares and rectangles arranged in a rough circle with lines of scribbled text in the margins, the writing connected to the diagram via crudely drawn arrows.

"Stonehenge," the stranger answered before Brighton could ask the question. "I was there today."

"So was I."

The stranger lifted an eyebrow. "Perhaps I spotted you on one of the tours."

Brighton doubted it. He hadn't been part of any tours.

"You're mapping out the blocks of stone," Brighton said. Just looking at the diagram gave him the shudders. They were almost exactly the same as the sketches in Olaf Poulson's notebook, the way the Norwegian had mapped out the bones of the giant skeleton...

The stranger nodded, closing the book. "This place... it's special, you know."

"*Once something is in your memory—*"

Brighton shook his head and, mercifully, Ira's voice fell silent.

"You okay?" the stranger asked again. "You look like you have something on your mind."

Brighton smirked. "More like *someone.*"

The stranger regarded him quizzically.

"Never mind," Brighton said. "So, what's special about Stonehenge?"

"The energy, mostly. But the history intrigues me, too. Who built it and why? It's one of my favorite mysteries."

"One of?"

A grin split the man's face. "Oh, there's too many good mysteries to choose from. Could you feel the energy when you were there today?" The stranger's face slackened and his eyes glazed over. "It infused every rock, every stone, every blade of grass. Even the air, it sizzles, like a frayed wire, like electrical current loose in the sky."

Brighton fiddled with the cuffs of his jacket, not looking up. He'd had no such experience, sensed nothing extraordinary even though he had been so certain he would. He'd traveled a long way only to come up empty-handed.

"Don't worry," the stranger said. "It's all over the world, in many places, but it's strong here. One day you'll know what I mean. You'll find it, whatever you're looking for."

That took him by surprise. "I'm looking for something?"

"Everyone is, didn't you know?"

His heart was beating fast now, and the faster it beat the more clear-headed he became. He didn't want to become clear-headed.

"I shouldn't have disturbed you," Brighton said, standing up. The chair legs skipped against the floor tiles.

The stranger looked as though he might protest, but Brighton didn't give him a chance; he was already halfway up the stairs.

Brighton shut the door to his room and leaned against it. His breath came short and his headache flooded back, stronger than ever. He put his hand to his head, his palm brushing against the bruise over his eye. He winced, feeling the bump from where he had been hit two days ago. The swelling had gone down by half, but it still had a long way to go.

That was a foolish risk, he told himself, not of the bar fight but the conversation with the stranger downstairs. *I might have compromised everything.*

He walked into the bathroom and poured water into a flimsy plastic cup. He took a few sips, feeling the pain in his head subside, albeit only slightly. He filled the cup again and carried it to the nightstand.

Brighton pulled off his shirt and was about to undress the rest of the way when a panicked thought occurred to him. If that stranger had been working for either Raff Lagati or Noam Sheply... Brighton cringed. He left his pants and shoes on, just in case he had to leave in a hurry during the night. He had to be prudent.

Brighton rested his head into the too-soft pillow and turned to look out the window. There weren't as many stars as there had been out in the street. Had clouds rolled in?

And with them, perhaps some blessed rain.

THREE

Tiahuanaco, Bolivia
JULY 18

D ario managed to score a couple hours of sleep, waking later than was his custom. Still groggy from the night before, he dressed and walked out of his tent into a clear, cool morning. He shielded his eyes and wished the sun brought a bit more warmth to this high-altitude plateau.

He walked through camp, greeting those faces that were familiar and nodding politely to those that weren't. Remnants of last night's party were everywhere in the dining tent. The tables were still pushed to the tent's margins and a stack of speakers remained next to the serving dishes. Despite this, most of the workers had already come and gone, leaving just enough breakfast scraps for dawdlers like him—and Rhea, who was pouring coffee into a styrofoam cup. She spotted him over the top of dark sunglasses. The two said good morning, then sat together at a corner table.

"Aren't you hungry?" Rhea asked, taking off her glasses and folding them.

Dario glanced at the assorted muffins and juices.

"Strangely, no. Any sign of Marco this morning?"

"I passed him earlier. He was headed toward the ruins." Rhea smiled. "He didn't so much as glance in my direction."

"That's good," Dario said. "It's best no one suspects what's going on."

She sipped from the cup in front of her. "What *is* going on, exactly? Tell me we're still going out tonight. I couldn't sleep last night. Not a wink."

"We just need a bit more equipment," he said. "A couple of shovels. Industrial flashlights with backup batteries. A tranquilizer, in case we run into animals. Did it occur to you there could be something living in that hole? We could get down there only to find a pack of wolves and a pile of intern bones."

Rhea made a face. More coffee down the gullet.

"Who should sign out the equipment?" Rhea asked.

"It will have to be Marco. He started all this, so it's only fair he takes the biggest risk. Hopefully we come back in the morning with Jorge and Yasmine, all of us alive, and with some fresh discovery to distract the powers that be."

"That would have to be some discovery."

"I think saving a couple of lives will be distraction enough."

*   *   *

The day passed more quickly than Dario would have liked. He anticipated the night's activities with a tight balance of excitement and trepidation; he couldn't tell which was stronger.

He ignored Marco when they crossed paths at lunch, and then again at dinner. Afterward, he returned to his tent to change. He packed three flashlights into a red duffel bag, slung it over his shoulder, and left the tent.

Marco paced from one corner of his tent to another. Dario could offer no comfort. The most likely outcome was that they would all face disciplinary action after this, and maybe even lose their positions. Dario could afford the setback, but Marco's circumstances clearly weren't as secure.

Dario held back a look of relief when Rhea, carrying a pair of shovels, poked her head into the tent. Her blond hair was pulled into a short ponytail and she still wore sunglasses, though the setting sun would soon render them useless.

Unzipping the bag, Dario showed them the flashlights. Both he and Rhea then turned to Marco, who walked to his folding bed, got down on his knees, and reached underneath. He extracted a wooden box and unclasped a pair of metallic hooks.

Dario held his breath as Marco pulled out a long-barreled rifle.

"Well, that's no tranquilizer," Rhea murmured, a smile tugging at the corner of her lips.

Dario wasn't sure he was so amused. "What's that?"

"What does it look like?" Marco asked. "We couldn't sign out a tranquilizer without someone asking questions." He picked it up by the barrel and aimed at an empty spot on the canvas wall. "Got it from my grandfather twenty years ago. It should do the trick."

"If we have to use that, everyone within a two-mile radius will hear," Dario said.

Marco shrugged. "Then let's hope we don't have to use it."

Dario made no further objection. In truth, it comforted him to know they were heading into the unknown well-armed.

The three left camp at sundown, each shouldering their own burden. By the time the last vestiges of twilight faded, they were crossing fields on the way to the river. As they got close to the bank, they veered east.

Rhea led the way. After forty minutes of hiking through knee-deep grass, she stopped and pointed.

There it was. From this vantage, it looked like a harmless hole in the ground. Only from the right angle did its width become apparent.

"This is it?" Marco's voice sounded uncertain. When he crossed to the low side, though, his uncertainty passed. "Yes, this is exactly what Jorge described to me."

The Bolivian shoveled away the overhanging dirt at the edges of the hole, widening it even further. By the time he was done, two of them could drop into it side by side.

Marco lowered his shovel straight downward and smiled when it clanked against something solid. "The river is surrounded by clay, but whatever this is, it's older and harder."

Dario handed him his flashlight and peered where Marco pointed it. Indeed, the tip of the shovel had struck a flat stone surface—too flat and even to be natural.

"What do you think it is?" Dario asked.

"Jorge said he thought they had found a tunnel. If so, maybe this is the entrance?" Marco's uncertainty was back. "They were here."

Rhea squeezed into the hole with Marco and knelt over, studying the hard surface.

"Do you see these carvings?" She leaned back enough for the beam of Marco's flashlight to find its target. She used her fingers to clear away dirt that had nestled in the carvings' stone grooves for centuries.

She gasped, then stood up.

"What is it?" Dario asked.

She met his gaze. "It's a Grey."

Dario looked down and realized she was right. The face of the carving stared back, its alienness unmistakable.

The walls in and around the Tiahuanaco ruins were studded with faces—faces of warriors, faces of women, faces of children, and a few faces with wide, pear-shaped eyes and elongated skulls that looked uncannily like the images of Grey aliens so common in pop culture. They were easy to account for; the elongated skulls had been the fashion in this and many other cultures in the central and southern Americas—including the Mayans and the Aztecs. And those eyes were spooky but not unheard of; most of the available carvings demonstrated a penchant for exaggerated facial features. Conspiracy theorists loved to speculate about alien involvement in such sites as Tiahuanaco and the Giza Pyramids, but there wasn't a shred of evidence to lend those speculations any credence.

"Well, well," Dario breathed. "That carving proves it. The people who placed this stone are the same as the ones who built the city. It's a new site." He threw Rhea his best grin. "You think this is enough of a distraction?"

But she was back on her knees, her fingers probing the edges of the stone. Before Dario could ask what she was doing, she put down her flashlight and asked Marco to step out of the hole. Marco lifted himself out and waited next to Dario.

A moment later, Rhea let out a whoop. She settled her feet just off the stone and grasped it by an exposed corner.

And lifted.

Dario thrust his hands toward her to help, and together they lifted the stone free from its casement. Beneath was a deep, dark opening.

Blackness.

A musty smell drifted up, making Dario cough into his hand. This tunnel had been sealed for a long time.

The three archaeologists stared down at the hole in silence for several minutes, not sure what to say or do. Nothing like it had ever been unearthed in this valley, never mind in the furthest reaches of the territory thought to have been under the influence of the former Tiahuanaco Empire.

Marco put his hands on his hips and cocked his head. "Go figure."

Dario moved the stone door far away from the opening. "Any sign Jorge and Yasmine went down there?"

"I'd say so," Rhea called up, her head hovering over the opening. "The edges of the stone were already uncovered. We weren't the first to lift it free."

"Maybe they were trapped," Marco said. "Maybe the door closed behind them and they couldn't get it open again."

It was a reasonable guess, Dario thought. And after four days, they had no doubt given up waiting for rescue.

Or maybe they were dead.

"Well, we didn't come all this way just to look down a hole, did we?" Rhea asked.

Dario handed his shovel to Rhea. "Use this to see if you can reach the bottom."

She took it from him and lowered the spade as far as it would go, and then extended herself until she was about to topple in headfirst.

"I can't reach the floor," she said, pulling herself out. She perched on the edge of the hole, dangling her legs into the darkness. She plucked up a stone from the dirt next to her and dropped it in the hole. After a long moment, it skittered against a surface.

Dario pointed his flashlight down, fighting nerves to hold it steady.

Rhea dropped a few more stones, counting how long each of

them took to fall.

"Must be at least six or seven meters," she guessed.

"Too far to jump," Marco said.

Rhea cast the shovel aside and accepted Dario's flashlight. She aimed it down, angling it to the sides.

"One of the edges slants, and there appear to be handholds." She stuffed the flashlight into her back pocket and positioned herself over the hole. "I'm going to climb down."

The woman was fearless. Dario fought his instinct to grab her by the wrist and pull her to safety.

Afraid of the dark, Dario? He shook his head as if in answer to his own question. *Embrace the unknown.*

Soon the only part of Rhea still sticking out of the hole was a few blond hairs. And then, a moment later, not even those.

"What do you see?" Dario called down after more than a minute had passed.

Rhea's voice drifted up out of the hole. It had a singsong quality. "Come see for yourself!"

Obviously she felt none of the reservations coursing through his blood, pounding into his extremities. He looked down and confirmed that his fingers were shaking of their own will.

Fear.

He swallowed it as Marco, too, disappeared from sight. Dario grabbed his duffel bag and stepped to the edge of the hole. Counting to three, he lowered himself into the opening.

The tips of his shoes found the various holds easily, each one deep enough for him to gain solid footing. After one of the longest minutes of his life, the heel of his shoe scraped loose stone and he realized he had hit bottom. Stepping away from the wall, he looked up at the tiny patch of stars visible through the hole high above his head.

Drops of blood fell from small cuts on his fingers where the flesh had dug into the stone grooves. He made a fist and held it, hoping the bleeding would stop.

Marco gruffly pushed the third flashlight into Dario's chest. He flicked it on. The tunnel proceeded south, back toward the city. Maybe all the way.

"The tunnel moves in a straight line," Rhea's quiet voice echoed back. "Wait, I see something."

Marco slowed in front of him. The tunnel was more than wide enough for all three of them to walk abreast, yet it seemed natural to proceed in single file.

Rhea stopped in front of the smooth tunnel wall where a metallic strut protruded about a foot. Attached to it was a perfectly round globe of rock.

Dario swept his light further into the blackness. The rock globes continued down the length of the tunnel.

"They almost look like light fixtures, don't they?" Dario reached up, having to stand on his tiptoes to graze the bottom of the globe with his fingers. Its surface was as smooth as glass. Much too smooth for the level of technology evidenced in the city.

"They may look like lights," Rhea said, "but they're made of solid rock. They could be distance markers."

They made slow but steady progress for a few hundred meters. The uniform dimensions of the passage amazed Dario. The tunnel was more of a long gallery than a tunnel, really. From time to time, he almost felt like he was inside a building instead of deep underground—

Rhea stopped in front of him, causing him to almost run into her.

"What is it?" Dario asked.

She stepped aside, their flashlight beams revealing a thick mass of cobwebs glistening across the full width of the passage. Amongst the webs were tiny—and some not so tiny—white masses. Hundreds of them. Maybe thousands.

Spiders.

Dario let out a groan. "There's no going through that."

"We can't turn around," Rhea said. "Are there any signs that the webs have been disturbed recently?"

Marco took a closer look. "Well, there's a space along the floor that's wide enough to crawl through without getting in the spiders' way."

It wasn't a crawl Dario was especially looking forward to—the hard-packed ground covered in an inch of dust, spiders dropping from above.

"Too bad we don't have a torch," Rhea remarked. "We could have burned straight through these webs."

Dario got down on his hands and knees and peered along the floor. There was maybe two feet clearance, maximum, and the distance they would have to crawl was difficult to determine.

"I'll go first," Dario volunteered, hearing his own overcompensating bravado the moment the words slipped out.

He had been in worse situations. He couldn't think of any examples offhand, but he was sure they existed.

Lowering himself to his belly, he slid forward, wincing as his shirt was pulled down and the collar dug into the back of his neck. He pressed his palms flat to the ground and grunted as he heaved himself forward.

He swore he could hear spiders tittering above, all those tiny legs working their silken tightropes.

"Better hope there's no snakes down here!" Marco called loudly from the rear. "Last place you'd want to be with a deadly snake is trapped under a cloud of deadly spiders."

"Thanks," Dario deadpanned through gritted teeth. "That puts me right at ease."

Nobody said anything for a while after that, though each scoot forward now came with equal parts haste and dread.

Dario clawed forward, his eyes scanning for the clear passageway ahead. Several times he thought they'd reached the end only for the darkness to reveal more of the same. It wasn't inconceivable that the spiders filled the entire passage, that there was no end.

Scarcely had the nightmarish thought occurred to him than the webs receded toward the ceiling, creating more and more headroom until Dario was able to push himself up onto hands and knees.

"Almost there," he called back.

Soon, he stood and looked back the way they'd come. Rhea and Marco emerged from beneath the enormous web, dusting themselves off as Dario reached into the duffel bag for the water bottle. He drank deep, then spilled a few spare drops on his hands to rub the grime off his face.

They proceeded in silence for several minutes before Marco said, "How far do you think we've gone?"

"Feels long. Five hundred meters?" Rhea guessed. "Six?"

"If I'm right, this tunnel will lead right back under the city," Dario said. "That's a half-mile, and I bet we've covered half the distance so far—" He broke off, slowing.

"Dario?" Rhea asked. "It's not more spiders, is it?"

"No."

They stood at an intersection. The passage they had been following continued straight ahead, but now there were passages to the right and left. Both paths were equally dark. The same strange fixtures marked the walls.

Rhea let out a whistle. "Perhaps we've uncovered a whole network of tunnels."

Dario groaned. If that was true, Jorge and Yasmine could be anywhere.

FOUR

Amesbury, England
JULY 17

Brighton snapped awake a couple of hours later from a deep sleep. He caught his breath at the labored rumble coming from the air conditioner, remembering where he was. His chest rose and fell as he stared wide-eyed at the dark ceiling.

His mouth parched and dry, he reached for the cup of water and accidentally tipped it over with outstretched fingers, slopping its contents on the tiled floor. He got up to clean the mess before finding that his discarded shirt had already soaked up most of the spill.

Only in Europe would a hotel room not come with carpet.

Perched on the edge of his bed, his fingers tangled in the knots of his bedraggled hair, he realized he would get no more sleep tonight.

Brighton wandered to the window where the air conditioner, turned up to its highest setting, blew cool air into his face. He turned down the dial and looked through the rain-pelted glass. The rain had stopped, so he lifted the pane and stuck his head out into the fresh nighttime air. A clean, sweet fragrance—foreign to these trash-ridden and urine-soaked English streets—had replaced the oppressive humidity.

Craving more of the fresh air, Brighton pulled on a long-sleeved shirt and stepped out of the room, leaving behind the jacket that still smelled vaguely like the pub's restroom.

Brighton emerged from the blue door and breathed in, feeling more energized than he had any right to after the preceding night. Energized enough to tackle a two-mile walk.

He avoided the deepest puddles and kept to the sidewalks—at least, until he left the town behind and ambled over the highway's gravel shoulder. The stars were bright enough that it didn't much matter that the moon was only a slim crescent. He could make out every detail of Salisbury Plain's rolling hills.

Brighton approached a fork in the road and veered right, knowing he was less than a mile away. Downhill from him, he could make out Stonehenge's mysterious columns. He left the roadway and continued through tall grass, giving the monument a wide berth. Surely the site had security to prevent off-hours trespassing.

Growing tired from the long walk, he dropped to the ground. A combination of cold morning dew and rainwater soaked into his pants. He didn't mind. With the slight slope to the ground, he could lie on his back and still have a clear view.

Stonehenge. Everything he'd heard about it, everything he'd read, had told him this was an important place. An energetic place? What did that even mean?

He had found the Antarctic bone field with Ira and Wörtlich by searching for the earth's magnetic pole. He supposed that made it energetically significant, in a sense. Some texts he'd read used that same characteristic to refer to a number of locations around the world, locations with unusual energetic properties. Some people called them vortexes; others called them hotspots. Whatever you called them, almost everyone put the pyramids on the list, and Brighton understood why. When he had been there, the air beneath the Great Pyramid had felt otherworldly, as if he'd been standing on an alien planet.

That stranger from the hotel had felt the same way about Stonehenge, one more indication that Brighton had come to the right place.

"Once something is in your memory, it is possible to access it."

He rolled his eyes and turned his head to the side, getting an eyeful of starlight. "Damn it, Ira, get out of my head."

But he knew Ira's words held significance. When the rabbi had said those words, he'd been referring to the technique of walking into one's own memories, reliving and even interacting with them in ways Brighton would have thought impossible if he hadn't seen it for himself. Perhaps more importantly, the technique had been used to delve into the strange dreams all three men had experienced while in these "energetic" places.

Perhaps if I close my eyes and fall asleep here, I'll have another of those dreams…

Instead of drifting off, other memories plagued him. Ones he didn't want to revisit. He'd spent so many months accumulating them.

"Hey, you!"

Brighton's gaze snapped forward, drawn to a dark figure approaching from the direction of the Stonehenge parking lot. A flashlight's beam danced over the waving blades of grass.

A security guard.

"This is private property, sir." The guard stopped a few feet away and pointed the flashlight in Brighton's face.

Brighton shielded his eyes. "I'm sorry. I didn't realize—"

"Come back in the morning, sir. The site is closed."

Brighton pushed himself up, pressing his knuckles into cool earth. Satisfied, the guard made his way back down the hill; he looked over his shoulder only once to make sure Brighton really was leaving.

Brighton circled up to the top of the hill, then descended again, finding a more discreet spot to view the ancient stones. He soon found a spot that ironically was a bit closer, but not as visible from the guard's position. Every once in a while, the flashlight switched on and roamed over the broad side of the hill, but as long as Brighton lay flat it wouldn't detect him.

A week ago, he'd been sitting at a computer kiosk in Barcelona when he came across a drawing of Stonehenge. Purported to be the earliest depiction of the famous site, he had found the image in a thousand-year-old manuscript dedicated to the myth of King Arthur. The picture showed the wizard Merlin overseeing Stonehenge's construction, and next to the wizard a giant twice Merlin's size lifted the enormous stone blocks into place.

Brighton knew it was just one picture, and perhaps nothing more than the musings of a tenth-century painter's overactive imagination, but still…

The notion that Stonehenge was built by giants gripped him. Like the pyramids. Like the bone field. Like the enclosure on the bottom of the ocean, where they'd finally unearthed the Book, which Wörtlich had paid for with his life—

Brighton's eyes roved across the incredible stones, trying to gauge the weight of the crossbeams. Giants had to have helped in its construction. How else could it have been done five thousand years ago?

Most people could dismiss such fantasies, but Brighton no longer had that luxury. Nobody knew better than he that giants were no myth. They *had* existed. He'd seen one with his own eyes.

It had tried to kill him.

He closed his eyes and breathed in the scent of summer rain. The longer he lay in stillness, the less inclined he was to sit up again—which bothered him not at all. Lying in this open field, the sky above and the earth below, the full weight of his exhaustion hit him hard, pinning him to the ground.

In the stillness, all irritations vanished. Ira's voice. His paranoia about being chased. The headache that four hours of sleep had not yet managed to dull. Rarely had he ever felt so at peace.

"Why are you here?" a voice asked.

Brighton blinked, surprised he hadn't seen the guard come back. But there he was, a dark figure standing a short distance away. Too dark, though. Where had the man's flashlight gone?

"I'm sorry," Brighton apologized again. "I just had to—"

Brighton propped himself up on his elbow. The guard wasn't moving. By now, Brighton should have been escorted back to the road under threat of police involvement.

The dark figure moved closer. "The rabbi was wrong."

The four whispered words roared in Brighton's ears. He sat up even straighter.

"Who *are* you?" This was no guard, Brighton realized. "Who are you and what do you know about me?"

He knows about Ira. What other rabbi could he mean?

"Step closer," Brighton said. "Show me your face."

The figure stepped backward.

"Stop." Brighton came to his feet, but the figure turned its back and walked away. "I said stop!"

To Brighton's surprise, the figure did stop, but he didn't turn around.

"The rabbi was wrong," the figure said again, louder this time.

Brighton gasped, hearing the accent for the first time. That voice suddenly sounded *very* familiar. Could it be? His heart beat too fast for him to think straight.

"Emery?"

"You should wake up now."

Before Brighton could ask another question, light poured in from all around, at once blanketing the world in white-hot luminosity. Frustration seized him as the light softened into the amber glow of morning sunshine.

It was a dream, he realized.

Daylight cascaded over him. The ground beneath him felt stony and worn. The rugged stone columns of Stonehenge towered around him, their tips piercing the dazzling azure sky like spears striking at prey. Each cast a long shadow, one of which crossed his legs. He shivered from the cool morning air, realizing that his clothes—at least the undersides—were soaked with moisture.

Something wasn't right. He rolled over and came face to face with another stone block. Any faster and he could have broken his nose.

Something *definitely* wasn't right.

He braced himself against the stone block and sat up. The columns closed in around him like prison bars.

How did I get here?

He turned his eyes toward the road and found the slope where he had settled down the night before. He had fallen asleep on that slope, still within view but afraid to come any closer.

And yet here he was, at the center of Stonehenge, with no guard in sight.

There's someone watching you, he told himself, his sixth sense tingling. *You're not alone.*

He flipped himself over, but saw nothing. No one.

At least, not with his eyes. He couldn't put his finger on the reason, but his heightened senses told him there was someone there, someone close. A presence, watching him.

"Emery?"

He didn't know why he said it, why he felt it. Emery Wörtlich was long dead and his dream had been just that—a dream.

But there *was* a presence, and it seemed familiar to him. Benevolent, even.

"What's next?" Brighton said to himself. "I believe in ghosts now?"

He took a deep breath to stabilize himself, but the horizon pitched to the left and a wave of dizziness knocked him over. He lay down again, disoriented. His head felt strange—and not in the same way it had the night before. He knew well what the effects of alcohol felt like, and this wasn't it.

Gravity felt strong, like the ground was magnetic. As he stood, leaning against a fallen stone, the grounded feeling spread up his legs. He felt as though he were part of the earth, as though jumping with both feet would separate him from something wonderful. Something strong.

And the air… it was just like the stranger at the hotel had described it: *Even the air, it sizzles, like a frayed wire, like electrical current loose in the sky.*

Again he felt the presence. He looked to confirm there was no one with him. He was alone.

In the stones, anyway. He was about to walk out of the inner circle when he realized there were people staring at him. Visitors had arrived, their cars lining the side of the highway. Why hadn't they used the visitors' parking lot?

The answer hit him when he glanced down and saw the body of the guard sprawled on the ground. The guard had not opened the lot because he'd been knocked unconscious…

Panic rose in Brighton's throat as he leaned down, fighting dizziness, and pressed his index finger to the guard's neck. He let out a prayer of gratitude when he detected a pulse.

Did I do this? he asked himself. *No, I couldn't have. All I did was fall asleep—I was nowhere near the guard, nowhere near the stones.*

Nervous whispers passed between the arriving onlookers. Their pointing fingers all aimed at him. Brighton took a few steps and saw a second guard on the ground, his face pushed into the grass, green and lush after the previous night's rain.

I didn't do that, either.

But there were now dozens of witnesses placing him at the scene. A glance toward the highway told him the number of witnesses was only going to climb, and some of them already had phones pressed to their ears.

Brighton did the only thing he could think to do. He ran.

*   *   *

The houses of Amesbury crept closer and closer and in a few minutes Brighton was running through the cobblestone streets like a madman. He did his best to allay suspicion by narrowing his wide eyes, closing his open mouth, and slowing to a controlled pace. Perhaps he would be mistaken for an early morning jogger.

He made it the hotel unmolested, though he expected the sound of sirens or running footsteps behind him at any moment. He tried the knob on the blue door and found it open. He slid inside and immediately made for the stairs.

"Is everything alright, sir?" the desk clerk asked, watching him with concern.

Brighton put on a fake smile. "Yes, thank you. Just a little chilly this morning."

"Nice change of pace, don't you think?"

"Very."

Brighton took the stairs two at a time before the clerk could ply him with further insights about the weather. He paused for a moment when he swung open the door of his room, just long enough for panic to strike again.

This time, twice as hard.

In any other circumstance, Brighton was sure that his upended suitcase, bed sheets heaped in the corner, and furniture pulled back from the walls would have discomfited him. But at the moment his panic was focused wholeheartedly on the man reclining on the mattress (no longer squared to the frame), showing mild startlement at Brighton's sudden entrance.

Brighton had only seen this man once before, but that day's harried chase still haunted him.

"Mr. Brighton, how delightful to bump into you. And in your own hotel room, of all places," Noam Sheply deadpanned, swinging his legs off the bed and coming to his feet.

Brighton took a backward step into the hallway.

"Your first instinct is to run," Sheply said. "I understand, given our last encounter. Another hotel room, not much different than this one, I recall. How quixotic. But from the sweat of your brow, it seems you've already had your fill of running. Please, come in and close the door. We have much to discuss and, given your current state, perhaps little time to accomplish it."

Brighton fought a surge of adrenaline. How likely was it that he could escape both Sheply and the authorities… and if he had to choose one or the other, which was preferable?

Brighton closed the door, but waited at the threshold.

"A fine choice." Sheply extended his arm in hospitality. "Come in, make yourself comfortable."

"What do you want?"

Sheply feigned surprise. "What do I want? What color is the sky? What is today's date? Who constructed the pyramids of Giza?" He waved off the perplexed look on Brighton's face. "All questions we both know the answers to. What I came for is patently obvious. I want to know the location of your cohorts... and, of course, I want the Book of Creation, though I never expected you would be so foolhardy as to carry it with you. I looked, anyway. One can never be too careful." He surveyed the tangle of clothes and overturned furniture, sighing heavily as though it couldn't be helped.

His cohorts? It amused Brighton to know Sheply was five steps behind this time. Ira and Wörtlich were beyond Sheply's grasp; this one small consolation warmed Brighton's heart.

"Get out," Brighton said.

"No." Sheply sounded almost apologetic. "No, no, no. We have so much to talk about."

Brighton took a few steps closer. "Not as much as you'd think. I can honestly say I have no idea where the Book is. Wish I did. You seem to think we found the thing. And I haven't seen either of my 'cohorts' in over a year."

"That's difficult to believe."

"Your ability to accept the truth is of grotesquely little interest to me." Brighton stepped just far enough forward to peer into the bathroom and confirm that no one waited for him there. The only thing he saw was his own reflection looking back from the mirror. "How did you find me? It can't have been easy."

"Indeed, you've led me on a long chase, but you've been using the same aliases, and everywhere you go has one feature in common—an ancient monument. A man with Lagati's resources can use that information to track you." Sheply straightened the mattress and sat back down. "You're a little out of breath. Had a busy morning?"

Brighton narrowed his eyes at the man, and his cheeks flushed. Could it be a coincidence, the strange events of the night before and this ambush, occurring within minutes of each other?

"That bruise above your eye, I hope you've been icing it." Sheply rubbed the same spot on his own forehead, wincing. "Must have hurt like hell."

You needn't worry on my account, Brighton thought. *Alcohol helps numb the pain.*

"So you have me where you want me. I'm man enough to admit when I've been outplayed," Brighton said. "You need answers, and I need to get out of the country. Problem is, I've given you all the answers I have."

"Even if that were true, what makes you think I could get you out of the country?"

"You want information. Unless you're planning to torture me, you must have come with a carrot to dangle."

Sheply sighed. "I don't need to offer you a thing. Perhaps I'm here to simply take you in."

That didn't ring true. If Sheply's plan was to take him to Lagati, he would need some muscle. And yet Sheply really did seem to be alone.

"I could choose to leave you to whatever trouble you're in," Sheply continued. "Or I could help the authorities locate you, assuming they're looking."

The look on Sheply's face was controlled, but Brighton read it well enough to confirm that Sheply had had nothing to do with the incident at Stonehenge.

"So, are you going to give me what I want?" Sheply prompted.

Brighton raised his hands. "Don't get ahead of yourself. First, I surrender. Should I call the police or should you?"

It was a bluff, and he worried Sheply would see right through it. Given the choice between Sheply and the police, he would take Sheply. In the hands of the law, life as he knew it would come to a quick end. The fact that he'd been traveling the world on aliases wouldn't reflect well on him, and if he was charged with assault on those hapless Stonehenge guards—well, he wasn't eager to pay for another man's crimes. With Sheply, he would have a chance. Sheply wasn't a killer, despite what he might want Brighton to think. Besides, after all this time, Lagati didn't have the Book, and Brighton was his only link.

Sheply hesitated. Had he bought it? Then the man fished a phone out of his pocket and held it up.

"Gather your things." Sheply gestured to the scattered contents of Brighton's suitcase. "I need to step out and take a call. But I'll be right outside the door, so don't try anything."

The moment Sheply was in the hallway, Brighton hurtled to the window and looked down. Would he be able to survive the three-story drop onto a cobblestone street? Best case scenario, he was looking at a broken bone or two.

Brighton listened for a minute. Sheply's low voice whispered in the hall, but he couldn't discern any clues from Sheply's side of the phone conversation except that he was asking for instructions. Was it possible Sheply really was on his own in Amesbury and had no one to assist in taking Brighton in?

Sheply didn't expect to corner me, Brighton thought. *He was waiting for backup when I came in.*

Brighton returned to the window and cranked open the single pane. The cool morning breeze spilled in, but instead of refreshing him, it chilled him to the bone. He punched out the screen and watched as it tumbled to the ground almost in slow-motion.

He turned over an upended chair and placed it next to the window, using it to climb up onto the sill. He balanced himself and looked down again, reconsidering. His options were few, and most of them bad—going with Sheply, jumping and injuring himself, falling into police custody…

The sound of the door opening drew him back to the present.

In that moment, all considerations went out the figurative window as Brighton took a deep breath, settled himself, and jumped out the literal one.

FIVE

Tiahuanaco, Bolivia
JULY 18

Should we split up? Each take a path?" Marco asked.

Dario shuddered. He didn't think it safe to wander these passages alone. They had already lost two people to this maze, and nobody back at camp knew where they were.

"I vote we stay together," Rhea said.

Dario nodded. "If we run into any trouble, we stand better odds as a group."

But that didn't help determine which way to go. The three dark passages gaped, rebuffing their flashlights, which could pierce no farther than a few meters. All passages looked the same: dark, dank, and possibly full of spiders.

"We should head straight," Dario said. "We don't know where

Jorge and Yasmine went, but if we're right and this passage leads back toward Tiahuanaco, it makes sense to follow it to its terminus."

He looked from Rhea's face to Marco's. Both nodded. After taking a moment to gather their courage, they left the intersection behind.

As they went along, jagged cracks became visible in the walls. The air wasn't quite so dry and when Dario put his hands to the stone, he felt a hint of moisture.

"Can you smell that?" Rhea asked. "Mold. Water has trickled down here recently."

Dario concentrated the light on his feet, watching for puddled water, but he didn't encounter any. If Rhea was right, the water must have drained someplace—perhaps down the passage in one direction or another, or perhaps farther underground.

The cracks cut across more than smooth, unadorned stone walls. Just above their heads were massive carvings.

"Faces," Marco said quietly. "Just like the ones in the Kalasasaya Temple walls."

"Only much larger," Rhea noted.

Dario strained to make out the detail. The faces lined both sides of the passage. The first was of a man with hardened features, a stony jaw, and narrow, angry eyes. A warrior, or perhaps a priest. The next was of indistinguishable gender, with wide eyes and a pointed chin. On and on they proceeded—a gallery of faces standing watch over this long-abandoned crypt. Men, women, children, and even a few of those maddening Greys. Dario counted ten faces on each side before the line ended.

"I'd love to study these," Rhea breathed, still halfway down the gallery. She stood back from each one as though inspecting a painting. "This will take months to document."

"For now, we should continue," Marco reminded her. "We

shouldn't stop too long."

Rhea stepped away, her shoulders slumped in disappointment.

"Don't worry, we'll be back for a closer look," Dario assured her.

He hoped that was true.

For the next twenty meters, the cracks in the wall grew wider, longer, and more frequent. Entire pieces of stone had broken free and crumbled on the floor.

Dario tripped over a large block in the middle of the passage. The others stopped to look at him and he tried to mask the momentary anguish.

Rhea stopped just ahead. "There was a cave-in," she called back. "The passage is blocked."

"Can you tell when it happened?" Marco asked.

"Not recently," she said. "I wouldn't worry. These walls and ceilings have been stable for hundreds of years."

"We should double back," Marco suggested. "If we return to the intersection, we can choose a different route."

"Agreed," Dario said, grimacing as he put weight on his foot.

Get over it, he told himself. *You have bigger things to worry about.*

Dario could see it was hard for Rhea to pass under the gallery of faces again without stopping. She only slowed for a moment; Dario knew her just well enough to notice.

When they reached the intersection, Marco gestured to the right and neither Dario nor Rhea could think of a reason to argue the arbitrary choice.

"What time is it?" Rhea asked after a few minutes of walking.

Dario looked down at his watch and flicked on its green backlight. "Almost three o'clock. How long will it take for our absence to be noticed?"

"Midmorning, but that's not our biggest problem," Rhea said. "The camp will already be awake by five-thirty, making it difficult for us to sneak back in without being seen. Do you think we should head back?"

Dario's instinct was to say yes. And yet—"It depends."

"On?" Rhea asked.

Dario glanced at Marco, who walked silently ahead of them. "On how likely it is we'll find the interns alive. They've been here four days. A person can die from dehydration after three and survive no longer than five."

"Assuming neither of them brought water."

He shook his head. "If they did, it was maybe a bottle or two. Not enough. My point is, if this is a salvage mission, then yes, we should return to camp. If this is a rescue, another day and they'll be dead for sure."

"I'm not leaving them," Marco said. "You can turn back, but I'll press on. My career is on the line. Perhaps more than that if I'm deemed responsible for their deaths."

Dario hadn't thought of that. Marco had broken camp rules, but had he committed a crime? He didn't know enough about Bolivian law to answer that.

"We won't need to decide for at least another hour," Dario said.

No one spoke for a while. Dario realized that Marco's mistake could just as easily have been his own; if an intern had requested a few minutes to investigate something out of the city, he might have done the same thing. Who could have guessed the "something" in question was as big as *this*?

He looked at the towering walls and ceiling, marveling at how this had gone undiscovered for so long. How had it eluded them when modern technology could do so much?

The walls and ceiling…

Dario frowned. The walls here weren't quite as uniform as they had been in the first passage.

"We're not headed in a straight line," he said. "The first passage headed due south, but this corridor is taking us on a southeasterly arc. Can you see it?"

"It's very gradual," Marco said.

"Do you think these passages are set up like a wheel, with Tiahuanaco in the epicenter?" Rhea asked.

Dario thought about it for a moment. "If you're right, the first passage was like a bicycle spoke. That suggests there could be others, all converging beneath the city."

A moment later, they came upon another intersection.

"It crosses at a right angle," Rhea said, confirming her theory. "It's heading for Tiahuanaco. We've come no more than twenty or thirty degrees around the wheel, meaning there must be a dozen or more spoke lines."

Marco immediately started down the new passage. "Come on!" he called over his shoulder.

Dario and Rhea followed, more slowly.

"If this network really does circle the city on all sides, there are miles of passages to explore," Rhea said.

Dario shrugged. "That only makes it more difficult to find Jorge and Yasmine. They could be anywhere by now. For that matter, they could have found another exit."

But if they'd gotten out, they would have returned to camp. Dario was more certain than ever they were dead. Rhea obviously wasn't optimistic, either. She said nothing.

Looking up, Dario saw that they had fallen behind Marco. Had Marco sped up, or had they slowed down?

"I came to Bolivia for a change of pace," Dario said after a while. "Nothing like this, that's for sure. Don't get me wrong; this is more than I could have hoped for, but I didn't expect anything so earth-shattering. On paper, this assignment sounded almost mundane."

"After the excitement of Herculaneum, I can see why you might have looked for something quieter."

For the first few days they'd known each other, Rhea had been obsessed with the discovery of the Alexandrian index. She'd been full of questions, able to speak of almost nothing else. Dario had been grateful when that settled down; feeling out of place here, he had been more interested in making a friend than a groupie.

"In fact, don't you think this might be bigger?" she asked.

His head came up. "Bigger?"

"I mean bigger than the index. An entire network of unexplored caverns below what is arguably the oldest city in the New World? We still know almost nothing about this culture, and yet it formed the basis of all the civilizations from the southern Andes to northern Mexico. That's a big deal."

"I hadn't thought to compare this to Herculaneum."

"Really?" Rhea sounded genuinely surprised. "That's the first thing I would have done. To be involved in two so significant finds in less than two years… you live a charmed life, Dario Katsulas."

He hadn't put much thought into it before now, being so preoccupied with the search. Was it really just good fortune? Being in the right place at the right time?

"I found him!" Marco shouted from ahead.

Dario broke into a jog, his flashlight beam dancing across the floor. He ignored a new line of stone faces set into the walls. There was no time for that.

He came to a sudden stop, Rhea practically launching into him from behind, when he saw Marco on his haunches, leaning over a body.

Dario had only seen Jorge a handful of times, and he was embarrassed to admit he would have had difficulty telling the young man apart from the other two dozen interns. Jorge's eyes were closed and his skin pale, coated with sweat.

"My God, is he alive?" Dario got down and probed the boy's jugular, searching for the telltale signs of... there it was. A slow pulse. Very, very faint.

"We need help," Marco said, panic creeping into his voice. "We have to get him out of here."

"Are the three of us enough to carry him?" Rhea asked, joining them on the ground.

Dario pulled out his water bottle. "Hold this to his lips. See if you can get him to drink."

Marco's hand shook as he dripped the water against Jorge's lips. The young man didn't respond. He was out cold.

"What about Yasmine?" Rhea placed a hand against Jorge's chest, feeling for a heartbeat.

Dario turned his flashlight farther down the passage. Nothing. That was strange; they would have stuck close together. Wherever Yasmine was, she was probably in no better shape.

"There's medical equipment back at camp," Dario said. "Instead of moving him, what if one of us goes back for help? We can bring back a search party to cover more area."

Marco seemed on the verge of protest, but Dario silenced him with a glare that hopefully came across a lot tougher than he felt.

"It's too late to worry about breaking the rules," Dario said. "Besides, we won't be able to keep this place secret for long."

"I want to stay," Marco said. His tone said it wasn't up for debate. "I'm responsible. I have to stay by his side."

Dario turned pleading eyes to Rhea, who sighed and pushed a strand of blond hair out of her eyes.

"You go," she said to Dario. "We'll stay and look after Jorge. Go directly to the site director and tell him what's going on. And tell him we don't have much time. Jorge could die in a matter of hours."

Dario got to his feet, aimed his flashlight, and took off the way they'd come without so much as a backward glance. Whereas he had dared nothing faster than a jog earlier, he now broke into a full-out run.

He barely gave any conscious thought to navigation as he ran headlong down the passageways. No more than ten minutes seemed to pass before he reached the giant mass of cobwebs, even though he was sure it had taken an hour or more for them to cover the same ground earlier.

Five minutes later, by his frenzied reckoning, he scrambled out of the hole in the riverbank. Mud clung to his clothes as he clawed his way to ground level. He took a moment to orient himself, his eyes adjusting to the starlight.

Light was beginning to appear on the eastern horizon as he rushed into camp. Sheets of beige canvas blurred together as he sprinted through the main avenue. He passed the cafeteria tent and smelled fresh bread inside; breakfast was already on the way.

He ignored the confused looks of the few early risers who hurried out of his way.

In a few moments, he was standing in front of the tent belonging to Doctor Wallis Christophe. He hesitated before making his presence known, opening and closing his fists, sweat burning in his eyes.

"Doctor Christophe." The words came out in more of a strangled whisper than a full-throated cry. Perhaps it was habit, but he couldn't quite bring himself to yell.

No answer came from within, and he searched for a hard surface to knock against. There was none.

He raised his voice a few decibels. "Doctor Christophe?"

A small crowd of onlookers gathered. He groaned. The last thing he needed was to draw a crowd.

"Doctor Christophe!"

At last he heard grumbling and the creak of bedsprings. The on-lookers were closer now, calling out to him, asking what was going on. He shut them out and waited for Christophe.

"What is it?" a voice came from inside the tent.

"Doctor Christophe, it's Dario Katsulas. Can I come in?"

"Do you know what time it is?"

"Yes. It's an emergency. Please, I just need a few minutes to explain myself." Silence. "Doctor?"

The tent flap opened and Doctor Christophe's face appeared, tired and bleary-eyed. Greying bristles clung to his jaw. His eyes were dark and impatient. "This better be important."

"Two lives are at stake," Dario said in a rush. "How's that for important?"

Christophe waved him in.

The tent was lit by a plastic lamp on a fold-up wooden table next to the cot. There were two crates of books on the ground, and another stack of them atop the black-topped desk in the corner. The chair in front of the desk was the same as the ones in the dining tent; a second chair rested in the opposite corner, on the edge of a colorful area rug which had the effect of humanizing the otherwise austere space.

Doctor Christophe, dressed in sweats and a white undershirt, shuffled toward the desk and flicked on a second lamp. He pointed to the desk chair. "Sit down. Whose lives are at stake?"

"Two interns—from the university in La Paz," Dario said, catching his breath and failing. "All I know are their first names. Jorge and Yasmine."

Christophe's stared back with vacant eyes. "I don't know of them."

That wasn't surprising. The director didn't know everyone personally, least of all the interns.

"They're part of the Bolivian contingent," Dario said. "Do you know Marco Salvatore?"

"Of course."

"Four days ago, Marco gave them permission to investigate a site half a mile north of here, along the riverbank."

"Off-site!" Christophe's face grew cloudy. "Four days ago? Two interns have been missing for *four days* and nobody brought this to my attention?"

"Marco was worried about losing his job," Dario said. "But that's not important. What's important is that together with Rhea Dunford, we've located one of the interns. Jorge."

Christophe sat on the edge of his cot, trying to digest all this. "Where?"

"That's the part you won't believe."

"This is no time for guessing games."

"Yes, of course. The interns located the entrance to a tunnel near the river. We went looking for the entrance last night and found a network of previously undiscovered passages. There's miles and miles of them, Doctor, filled with carvings which clearly connect its builders to the inhabitants of the city."

Christophe's jaw worked, but no sound came out.

"That's where we found Jorge. Salvatore and Dunford are still with the boy. He's been down there for four days, sir, and could die of dehydration at any moment. He had a pulse but was unresponsive."

The director pulled a chest out from underneath the cot. "Give me a few minutes to dress, Katsulas. Find Doctor Perez and meet me in the dining tent."

Dario straightened and exited the tent. A crowd had gathered, everyone whispering questions to him, but Dario brushed past them and half-jogged, half-ran across camp to Perez's tent. He called for the dark-complexioned medical doctor, who soon came out looking as disoriented and surprised as Christophe had been. Perez raised an impatient eyebrow at Dario, who rushed to explain himself. Hearing the full story, Perez ducked back in to get her equipment together.

Five minutes later, Christophe, Perez, and a third man Dario didn't know walked into the dining tent, almost in unison. Christophe carried a flashlight and Perez held a black bag at her side.

Christophe briefly made introductions. The third man was one of Christophe's assistants. His name was Guy.

"Let's go," Christophe said brusquely. "We could be too late already."

"There's just one other thing we need," Dario said. "A torch."

The director glared at him. "A torch?"

"For the spiders."

SIX

Amesbury, England
JULY 17

Four days ago, Brighton had enjoyed a leisurely afternoon stroll through the streets of Amesbury, taking on the eight-block walk from the train station to his hotel. Today, he hurtled along a similar route, zigzagging through side streets and alleys like a pinball on its way up a slanted playfield. His chest burned. Each agonizing breath felt like swallowing a razorblade.

He badly wanted to sit down and catch his breath. He tried to disregard the sharp ache in his knee where he had fallen badly on the way out the hotel window. His shoulder throbbed, too, and he could differentiate between at least three separate, near-crippling abdominal cramps. No matter which muscles moved, which joints pivoted, they all felt like the beginnings of death.

Four blocks down, four to go.

He turned left into an alley. He couldn't risk stopping.

Sheply will guess I'm headed for the train station. He doesn't need to chase me down. All he needs is to get to the station and wait for me. I have to get there first.

Brighton reached the end of the alley and emerged onto a wide street. The entrance to the station was three blocks up. As soon as traffic cleared, he zipped across the street and hit another alley.

Three blocks to go.

He didn't intend to slow, but his body started to veto his decision-making process. He lost some speed when he stumbled over a high curb. Still, his momentum propelled him beyond logic, beyond reason.

He took a sharp corner, then another.

Two blocks.

One.

Brighton decelerated to a trot for the final few hundred feet. He hoped walking through the station's front doors instead of sprinting would be less likely to raise alarm bells, though even at a walk his heavy breathing was conspicuous. He didn't stop to buy a ticket. He hurried straight to the departure quays and boarded the only waiting train. He collapsed in the first empty seat he could find, a window seat, and rested his head against the glass, exhaustion taking over.

He raised his head and blinked back tears of pain. He had to remain vigilant.

The rail personnel didn't check every stop, so with luck he might be able to hop a few towns over and get off without being flagged. Brighton glanced at the list of stops above the compartment door. Salisbury was the next station. He could get off there or press his luck as far as Southampton.

The good news was that there was no Sheply. At least, not yet.

Five minutes later, the train lurched out of the station.

Brighton's instinct shouted for him to avert his eyes from the other passengers, but doing so would only make him look stranger than he already did with his damp, sweat-soaked clothes, unwashed hair, and breath that no doubt still contained traces of last night's ale. He felt like the equivalent of a street person on a New York subway, its other riders giving him a two-seat berth in every direction.

Just as his brain authorized his heart to slow down and take a breather, movement in the car ahead brought it back up to full speed. A woman in a blue-and-white striped uniform was checking tickets. By his calculation, she wouldn't reach him for a few minutes, but Salisbury was at least ten minutes away.

He stood up and steadied himself by grabbing the metal bar bracing either side of the walkway. Trying to look as dignified as circumstances allowed, he walked to the next car back and hoped for an available seat.

"Hey, I know you," a voice called toward him as the glass door slid shut behind him.

A man in the third row, seated next to the aisle, was staring at him. Brighton's first impulse was to run, but he had nowhere to run on a moving train, plus he didn't think his body could take the strain. Instead he kept his head down and kept walking, pretending he hadn't heard.

But the man's arm snaked out and grazed Brighton's jacket. Brighton twisted out of the way, then grimaced from the resulting chest cramp.

"You look like you need to sit down," the man said.

From where he stood, Brighton saw the ticket checker coming into his car. She was working faster than expected; in another five minutes, he'd be caught.

Uncertain what to do, Brighton claimed the vacated seat the

stranger had cleared for him.

"Must be fate, huh?" the man asked.

Finally giving the man his attention, Brighton realized this wasn't just *a* stranger, but *the* stranger, the same man he had shared a late-night conversation with at the hotel.

"It's you!" Brighton exclaimed.

The man stuck out a hand. "Trevor Barnes. I don't think I got your name last night."

Brighton hesitated before shaking his hand, then realized he didn't have much choice. All he could do was wait for the train to stop.

And if it doesn't stop in time?

Brighton didn't want to think about that particular outcome.

"Jason," Brighton said absently.

Trevor waited for a moment, then gave Brighton a slow smile when he offered no last name. "Good to meet you, Jason. You seem... like you've had a rough morning."

Brighton's attention flicked back to the ticket checker. "You could say that."

"Anything I could do to help?"

Brighton gave Trevor his full attention. Perhaps bracing honesty would do the trick. "I need to get off this train before that ticket checker gets here. Any ideas?"

Trevor's eyes shifted to gaze out the window; Brighton followed them, his heart leaping as the passing hills slowed their mad left-to-right dash. They were stopping! Had they arrived in Salisbury so quickly?

"I don't think you'll have a problem," Trevor said, turning back.

Brighton bolted out of his chair, even though it would be another minute before the doors opened. Even then, he might not be out of harm's way. Had he travelled far enough to escape Sheply's reach?

He didn't think so, but it was a start.

Brighton bounded onto the black-topped quay, having momentarily forgotten his fatigue. Those few minutes off his feet had enlivened him. His mind was clearer than it had been all morning.

"Who are you running from?" Trevor said from behind him.

Brighton pivoted and saw with a sinking feeling that Trevor had followed him. For the first time, it occurred to him that this man wasn't here to help.

"Leave me alone," Brighton called, already racing up the stairs toward the station entrance.

Trevor kept pace and Brighton noticed how tall he was. And muscular, too.

"Well, I would, but you look like you could use a hand," Trevor said bluntly.

"I'm fine. Is this even your stop?"

"It is now."

Brighton pushed through a glass door and emerged into a busy terminal. To his right, a bank of televisions spied down at him. Ticket agent booths lined his left side. Before him, the exit beckoned.

Trevor's voice stopped him. "Hold on a minute."

Brighton looked back as Trevor pointed at the televisions. They flashed several phone-snapped pictures of Stonehenge at dawn—and in the center, looking like a caged animal, was Brighton, hovering over the body of the fallen guard. Another shot showed him wandering through the blocks of stone as a caption crawled across the bottom of the newsfeed: "One dead, another injured: Fugitive on loose in Wiltshire County."

Brighton's heart dropped. One dead?

I couldn't have done it, he told himself. *It wasn't me!*

Before he could decide on a course of action, Trevor grabbed him by the arm and pulled him toward the doors.

"You can't be seen in public," Trevor whispered into his ear. "You need to clean up and change your clothes. As word spreads, your presence on the train will be reported. You got lucky moving so quickly, but the police will have already expanded the search area. My guess is that the trains will stop running any minute now."

"The police," Brighton grunted. He shaded his eyes from the bright morning sun as they emerged outside and walked along the sidewalk. "The police aren't the worst of those chasing me."

Trevor raised his eyebrow but asked no questions.

Who was this man? Why was he helping him? What did he want?

"I didn't hurt that man," Brighton said in a low voice.

"I believe you."

"You don't even know me."

Without answering, Trevor steered him around the side of the building toward a lawn shaded by towering oaks. No one was around as they crossed the park, their shoes slipping through fresh dew.

"We shouldn't stay here," Trevor said, peering across the park.

"Seriously, who are you?"

"A friend. A suspicious guy like you probably doesn't have too many of those, huh?"

The comment hit hard. Brighton had once had lots of friends. Friends from his Caltech days, colleagues, a girlfriend or two along the way… but not anymore.

He missed the girlfriends in particular—not the sex, but the company. The last girl, Rachel, had stuck by him for almost two years, despite the fact that he'd spent half that time travelling from one corner of North America to another, trying to further his career by getting assigned to as many digs as possible. He'd stayed in New Mexico and southern Utah for five months once, never returning to his apartment in Virginia. The Christmas before that, he'd asked Rachel to move in with him; she'd ended up being little more than a house sitter.

All this time on the run had revealed how much he *wanted* to share his life with someone and hoped he could one day stop running long enough to find that again.

Perhaps that was too much to hope for.

"You coming?" Trevor asked, holding open the door to a taxi he had flagged down.

Brighton crept into the back seat and waited for Trevor to get in. To his surprise, the man shut the door and tapped on the passenger window. The driver rolled it down.

"Take my friend to Southampton," Trevor said. He fished in his pocket for a pen and then jotted down an address on a slip of paper he got from the driver.

Brighton leaned forward. "What's waiting for me there?"

"I'll meet you in a few hours," Trevor told Brighton while sliding a few bills into the driver's open palm.

Brighton had no time to argue. In seconds, the window rolled up, Trevor stepped away from the curb, and his taxi pulled out onto the road. The train station receded behind him.

"I don't suppose you'd stop the car and let me out," Brighton called to the driver.

The driver waited a moment, and when he spoke he sounded confused. "Is that what you want?"

"No," Brighton said, only really believing the word as it came out of his mouth. He settled into the seat. "Never mind. Just keep driving."

Brighton didn't like giving up control, putting his fate in another man's hands. He'd been his own man since leaving Tubuai, making his own decisions, taking his own risks.

And where has that led me? I'm running, I can barely afford to stay in one place more than a night or two, I haven't slept soundly in months—

unless I drink myself under.

They left the town behind and drove through hilly countryside. Everywhere he looked was verdant. England was so often characterized as dreary, but this place looked straight from a dream.

He briefly surveyed the inside of the taxi. There wasn't much legroom, the seat fabric was worn thin and ripped in spots, and bulletproof glass separated him from the driver.

Not as plush as Lagati's Bentley, but it would do.

SEVEN

Tiahuanaco, Bolivia
JULY 18

Dario perched on the edge of the opening before descending. Once at the bottom, he looked up and made eye contact with Doctor Christophe. The site director seemed unable to believe what he was looking at. Christophe, Perez, and Guy obligingly climbed down behind him.

They hurried through the tunnels, Christophe holding a flashlight in one hand and a kerosene-doused torch in the other. When they got to the cobwebs, Guy lit a match and nestled it against the side of the torch. The blaze caught immediately, bathing the stone passage in an eerie, flickering glow. The webs disintegrated like cotton candy. The tiny white spiders twisted, writhed, and scurried away.

"There's something I don't understand," Christophe said as they reached the intersection. "Well, the truth is there's a million things I don't understand, but from your description, all this started when Salvatore let those kids dig around where they didn't belong. How did you and Dunford get involved?"

Dario hesitated. Christophe was giving him an opportunity to absolve himself. All he had to do was tell the truth. He and Rhea had only gotten involved in order to save two young lives. Was it possible to do that without implicating Marco? Why was he even concerned about that?

"Do you want to mar the official record of this find by firing the man responsible for it?" Dario gestured to the towering cavern walls. "Accidents happen. They happen all the time. Every once in a while something good comes from one. In this case, something magnificent."

Christophe was quiet for the rest of the journey.

Dario soon saw flashlights ahead. Rhea was coming toward them while Marco remained next to Jorge, his head lowered.

"Is he still alive?" Dario asked.

Rhea nodded. "Just barely. I don't think he's going to make it."

Doctor Perez hurried to the young man's side. Marco stood back, giving the doctor room to work. Perez opened her bag and withdrew a stethoscope. She held it to Jorge's chest and listened as the others kept their silence, watching and waiting.

"How is he?" Marco asked.

Perez placed the back of her hand beneath Jorge's nose to ensure he was still breathing. "Four days without water is pretty bad."

"We gave him water," Marco said. "Or at least, we tried."

Perez reached into her pack and pulled out a blood pressure gauge. She wrapped it tight around Jorge's arm and gave the latex bulb a few squeezes. She continued to listen through her stethoscope, then placed her fingers under the boy's neck to confirm the results.

"Well, it's not just the dehydration," Perez explained as she worked. "We're beyond water loss. He's hypernatremic, and probably hyperkalemic." She noted their blank expressions. "Low sodium and potassium, which can be fatal. Has he had any seizures?"

Dario was about to say no when Rhea nodded. "He shook for a few minutes. We held him still, pinned him down so he wouldn't hurt himself any worse."

"That's good," Perez said. "Depending on how long he's been unconscious, I suspect he's already suffered some muscle breakdown, which can lead to kidney failure. We have to get him out of here. There's a portable cardiac monitor back at camp. I need to check his heart rhythm, and of course he needs fluids right away."

Perez dug around in her bag and removed a handheld blue device, only slightly larger than the typical remote control, and a bag of clear fluid, the two attached via a series of clear tubes. She then produced a needle and held it up to the light.

"Hold him down again, just like you did during the seizure," she said. Dario got down on his knees and grasped Jorge's legs while Marco took his arms. "I'm going to install a PICC line. Under normal circumstances, this hurts. A lot. Maybe enough to rouse him to consciousness, and I can't have him moving around."

Dario was just squeamish enough about needles that he couldn't watch the procedure. He looked down at the ground, closed his eyes, and counted to himself. He got to fifty and wondered how long it was going to take.

For Jorge's sake, of course.

"Okay, done," the doctor finally said. "Looks like he isn't waking up. That's a bad sign."

A short blue tube protruded from the newly installed catheter in Jorge's left arm. As Dario watched, Perez wrapped the arm tightly with gauze to secure the line. Next, Perez attached the clear bag of fluid and hit a few buttons on the blue device. Numbers appeared on the small analog screen as the clear fluid raced up the tube.

Perez stuffed the rest of her equipment back into her bag. "When you lift him, be sure you don't let that catheter move. Not even a millimeter."

Christophe pointed to Marco and Guy. "You two, get his arms and legs. You're going back with the doctor."

"And you?" Guy asked. "You're not coming back with us?"

Christophe exchanged glances with Dario and Rhea. "There's a second one, right? A girl?"

"Yasmine Delgado," Marco said. "Please, keep looking."

"We will," Christophe assured him. "The three of us will stay behind and keep up the search." He turned to Perez. "When you get to camp, have Doctor Kincaid look after the boy. I want you back here. If the boy was this bad, the girl can't be much better."

She nodded. "Will do."

Marco unslung his rifle, gripped it by the middle of the barrel, and held it out to Dario. It took Dario a moment to realize he was supposed to take it.

"You might need it," Marco told him.

Dario took the rifle by the wooden stock, almost dropping it. He regained his grip at the last moment and pulled it to his chest. He had never held a gun before, never mind fired one.

Marco smiled. "Take care of that. It's been in my family a long time."

Dario nodded as he lowered the rifle to his side.

Struggling under Jorge's weight, Marco and the others disappeared into the darkness.

The damp, breezeless passage seemed especially quiet now. Dario's shoes shifted as he waited for instruction. With Christophe present, there was no question who was in charge.

"How far have you explored this corridor?" Christophe asked.

"No further than this," Rhea said and explained the theory that these passages were shaped like a wheel, with a dozen or more spokes spreading out from the hub.

Christophe seemed to chew on that for a few moments. "And what do you suppose is at the hub?"

"Whatever it is, it's almost certainly below Tiahuanaco," Dario said. "But we're not here for science. We have a girl to find."

Christophe gave him a withering look, perhaps annoyed that he'd implied the director was more interested in archaeology than saving Yasmine's life.

Dario didn't especially care.

Without saying a word, Christophe turned toward the unexplored passage and began walking, slowly at first and then more confidently with each step.

"You should tread carefully with him," Rhea whispered to Dario as they continued closer toward the hub. "When people are assigned to explore these tunnels, you may not end up being one of them."

Dario grunted. "How long do you think it's going to take the Bolivian government to open this site up to international inspection? How many years? There's a good chance that after we leave these tunnels tonight, we'll never be welcome back in."

Rhea was silent on the point, but he thought he caught something in her eyes. An emotion he couldn't decipher. Maybe it was nothing but professional trust. He hoped it was more.

Dario was keenly aware that he wasn't the only man she spent time with. She was quite flirtatious and often kept late hours drinking with the other archaeologists. Like Marco, for example. Many people were interested in her. Then again, a blond-haired, blue-eyed Caucasian woman in the third world was bound to pick up a marriage proposal or two.

Lost in thought, he walked straight into a spiderweb. He grimaced, clawing the silky threads off his forehead and the contours of his nose. Rhea glanced his way and smiled as he spat out a moist string of the fine, silken substance.

"Try not to swallow spiders," she remarked, picking up her pace to catch up with Christophe, who had almost passed out of view.

Minutes later, Dario found Christophe and Rhea stopped in the middle of the passageway. The site director's palm was pressed flat against a smooth wall blocking the way forward. Dario had to look twice—then a third time—before realizing the wall wasn't made of stone.

Dario stepped closer and pressed his hand against it.

Metal.

"What the hell is this?" Dario asked.

Christophe felt along its edges, where the metal seemed to slide in behind the rock, as though this metal barricade passed straight through it.

"It's impossible, for one thing," Christophe said mirthlessly. "The people of the city couldn't have refined metal this smooth. Look at it. Feel it! It's glossier than my stainless steel refrigerator back home."

Dario had to agree. "Obviously Yasmine didn't come this way. We should turn around. If there are as many spokes as we think, we can try the next one over."

It was as good an idea as any. The three turned back, though all of them lobbed glances back toward the metallic barrier, unable to put it out of their minds. What was behind it? Where had it come from? Dario worried they would never find out. This time, even he had to remind himself that finding Yasmine was more important than investigating this strange place's many mysteries.

The next spoke didn't take long to find. They passed several more galleries of faces but gave them no more than a moment's glance. They encountered another nest of cobwebs, too, but Doctor Christophe's torch made short work of it.

Dario didn't feel his heart racing until it panged from the disappointment of seeing yet another metallic barrier blocking the way.

"Is it worthwhile to try another spoke, or are they all going to be like this?" Rhea asked.

Dario glanced at her, then swept his eyes back to the metallic sheen that was so smooth, so shiny. He could see his own reflection in its surface.

"That barrier will block every path," Christophe spoke up. "I'm sure of it. Just as I'm sure there's something worth protecting behind it. If not, why go to such elaborate lengths to conceal it?"

Christophe slapped his palms against the wall in frustration.

"Here, now, control your temper," said a female voice. It came from behind the barrier.

No one said anything for such a long time that Dario started to think maybe he had imagined the voice. But if that were the case, why did Rhea look like someone had reached down her throat and detached her esophagus from her stomach?

"You heard that, too, right?" Rhea asked.

Dario nodded. "Uh-huh."

"Good. I thought I was going crazy."

"I'm not sure 'good' is the word to describe it," Christophe said. He took several steps away from the reflective metal which moments before he had gazed at as intimately as one gazed at a lover.

"That's better. Nobody approaches me with violence in their heart."

The disembodied voice sent shivers up and down Dario's spine. It was silky, feminine.

"Who are you?" Christophe asked.

"You came all this way and don't know who I am?"

There was also a trace of superiority in the tone, Dario decided.

Rhea stepped forward. "We're looking for a girl who's badly hurt. Have you seen her?"

There was a chuckle, too deep-throated to suit the saccharine voice. The laughter contained no humor.

"You need not concern yourselves over the girl."

"What does that mean?" Dario said. "Why shouldn't we be concerned? We found her companion earlier. He lay near death."

"Yes. You took him away. I wish you hadn't done that."

"Like I said, he would have died." Dario couldn't believe what he was hearing. "Who are we speaking to? We believed these tunnels were uninhabited."

Another laugh, an ugly, hostile sound. *"The city is empty, but it has never been uninhabited. Why do you ask who I am? I cannot believe you don't know."*

"We don't," Rhea insisted. "Tell us your name."

"My name?"

"Yes, your name. And also what happened to the girl—"

Rhea jumped as the metallic barrier seemed to ripple. It didn't, it surely couldn't, but for a moment its surface … undulated.

Dario scrambled away. He lost his footing and winced as he fell, his knee scraping over a rock on the ground. As he struggled to get up, he heard Rhea gasp.

"It's her," she said, barely above a whisper.

Once the pain subsided, Dario saw how close to the barrier Rhea stood, her nose almost touching its surface. Dario got to his feet and came up next her.

"Rhea?"

She didn't react to him.

"Rhea, you're scaring me."

"It's her," Rhea whispered, her eyes glazing over.

"Who?"

Her mouth fell open and she leaned her forehead even closer, the skin resting against the cool metal. Her eyes wouldn't focus on him.

"It's her. It's Yasmine."

EIGHT

Southampton, England
JULY 17

The sunshine that had opened the day had vanished by the time the taxi arrived on the outskirts of Southampton twenty minutes later. Dark clouds raced across sky.

Brighton rolled down the window. Not too far in the distance, he heard lonely foghorns from the cargo ships as they made their way to and from the Solent. The ships were so large that Brighton could make them out from high points on the expressway, their bulks sliding through the choppy harbor waters.

The taxi turned into a dreary neighborhood with an endless grid of streets fronted by identical two-story brick townhouses. Brighton could hardly imagine living in such tedious and tightly packed housing. He wondered how even a slightly rotund person would manage to squeeze through some of the narrower doors.

"This is the place," the driver said as he stopped. He pointed to the building to the left of the idling car. Etched in the glass of its front window was a mug of beer with foam bubbling over its side.

Brighton hesitated. "But this is a pub!"

The driver pulled out the piece of paper Trevor had given him and held it up for Brighton to see. "Albany Road, it says right here. And the street number. There's no mistake."

Brighton opened the door and stepped outside. Without hesitation, the taxi sped off through the tiny street as though being chased.

The first thing Brighton noticed was the salty air. The taste was strong, but not unpleasant. He breathed deeply, then turned to the door with just two words scrawled across it: "Public House." He smiled, never having realized where the term *pub* came from.

He tried the door handle and found it locked.

Not surprising, he mused, looking both ways down the street to see if anyone nearby had witnessed his foolishness. *Not surprising at all that there'd be no one at the pub at nine-thirty in the morning.*

Brighton raised his hand to the wooden frame and knocked. There was no answer, so he walked around the building to check for a second door. Only garbage bags waited to be collected in the alley, and a fence preventing passersby from this street wandering through the alleys.

He returned to the front door and knocked again. This time he heard the scuffling of shoes and the sound of a man—or deep-throated woman—coughing loudly.

The door opened a quarter of the way and a woman peered out from the crack, her squinty eyes full of sleep.

"Who are you and what do you want?" she demanded.

He hesitated, wondering why he hadn't planned this out. All that time in the taxi and he'd never given a thought to how to identify himself.

"Trevor sent me," he said.

The woman's eyes lit up, changing from tired and ill-humored to full and vibrant in an instant.

"Trevor, you say," she said cheerfully. "Very well! Very well, indeed. Come in."

She swung the door wide and stepped out of the way.

"Don't mind the mess. I wasn't expecting company."

"I'm sorry for disturbing you," Brighton said.

"No, no, you mustn't be sorry. If Trevor sent you, you must be very important. What did you say your name was?"

The words blended together so quickly that Brighton almost missed the question. "Uh, Jason," he answered, remembering his pseudonym de jour.

The woman closed the door and the room darkened. Brighton's eyes needed twenty or thirty seconds to adjust.

He was in a common pub, reserved for common folk on their way home from long days working on barges. Well-swept planks stained black from soot comprised the floor. Half a dozen tables were surrounded by more stools than there was room for. Empty beer casks lined one wall, and next to that wall was the bar itself, modest but clean. Brighton got the feeling this woman kept her establishment as tidy as possible, under the circumstances, and was proud of it.

"Oh, my manners!" she said. "I'm Celeste Hodges. I run this place."

"A pleasure."

Celeste took a moment to appraise him. "You look in a bad way, and smell worse. You need a change of clothes?"

"If it's not too much trouble."

"Not for a guest of Trevor's." She bustled toward the back room, gesturing for him to follow. She led him around a tight corner and pointed up a narrow set of stairs. "Up you go. You can rest in the parlor while I find you something to put on."

"Thank you."

She waved him off and disappeared into the back room.

What on earth am I walking into? Brighton asked himself as he proceeded up the steps. The only light was a single, dim wall sconce so high that it seemed almost impossible to reach. Half its tiny bulbs were burnt out, but it would've been too much trouble to replace them.

When he opened the top door, he was relieved to see light pouring in through two windows facing the front street. In the living room—or parlor, as Celeste had called it—rested a pair of armchairs and a pillow-laden couch long enough for him to stretch across. Old hardcovers with frayed spines crammed a bookshelf. Either Celeste read a great deal or not at all. Brighton took the lack of a television for a good sign; she might have missed the ubiquitous news bulletins about his flight through Wiltshire County.

It wasn't until he sat down in one of those armchairs that Brighton realized how hard it was to keep his eyes open. But he had to stay awake. He still wasn't sure if these people were trustworthy. He glanced backward at the window and prayed he wouldn't have to jump through it in the near future.

Part of his resistance to sleep was that he didn't want a repeat of the previous evening. He hadn't been imagining things; he'd fallen asleep outside Stonehenge and woken up inside. Had somebody moved him? It didn't seem possible. As tired as he'd been, that was something he'd be sure to remember. But what other explanation was there?

He must have dozed off for a few minutes because the next thing he knew Trevor stood in front of him with a stack of folded clothes. The man's long hair was pulled back into a ponytail emphasizing his strong features.

"Celeste said you were tired," Trevor said, putting the clothes down in front of Brighton's chair and sitting on the couch.

"Thanks," Brighton mumbled, reaching for the clothes. "Is this where you live?"

Trevor seemed to think about that a few moments. "Sometimes."

"And your relationship with Celeste?"

"Hard to explain," he said, a slight smile growing.

Brighton rubbed his eyes. "Right."

"Celeste and I go way back. We have an arrangement. I'm welcome any time and my guests are free to come and go as they please."

Brighton still had so many questions. Trevor was either being intentionally vague or Brighton wasn't phrasing his questions right. He was tired, but he wasn't *that* tired.

"You should make a plan," Trevor said, clapping his hands together. "You're safe for now, but you can't stay forever. You must have someplace you need to go."

Funny thing was, he didn't. Not really. He'd had a number of destinations—Japan, Indonesia, South Africa, Spain, and now here. His first priority had been to keep moving, to evade pursuit, though that had turned out to be a colossal failure. The second had been to visit ancient monuments, conduct research, gather evidence … and all for what?

Ira, where did you go? You said we'd find a way to stay in contact, but it's been more than a year and not a word.

Brighton held Ira responsible for the situation he found himself in—at least, in part. Together, they had found the Book of Creation, which shouldn't have existed at all. The fact that it was real had profound and disturbing implications. Was Ira right about its origins? Had his Hebrew God written it? That didn't seem possible, yet Ira had demonstrated power and knowledge beyond ordinary human comprehension.

Never mind the questions he had for Trevor, the questions he had for Ira would have been enough to overwhelm a Mensa convention. Ira had made certain assurances—and instead of honoring them, he had vanished.

Their last conversation plagued Brighton. Ira had been so circumspect about his plans, but they had involved the Book. Returning it, perhaps? Returning it where?

Brighton's head spun.

"Jason?"

Trevor watched him, somehow infusing his gaze with casual benevolence.

"Sorry, I have a lot on my mind," Brighton said.

"Like I said, you're safe for now. You can rest."

"How do you know I won't be tracked here?"

Trevor shrugged. "The best anyone can do is link you to the train, but after that you could have gone anywhere. The police will try to figure out if you had help, any contacts in the area. Fortunately, there's no reason for them to connect you to me."

"What about surveillance video on the train?"

"Well, no *immediate* reason." He put up his hand to forestall Brighton's next question. "I know what you're wondering—why I'm doing this. Isn't it enough for one person to help another, even a perfect stranger, when he is in such obvious distress? There aren't enough Good Samaritans in this world."

"You're either incredibly generous or incredibly stupid," Brighton said. "Maybe it's because I'm three-quarters delirious, but I choose to believe the former."

"Wise choice." Trevor stood up. "Why don't you take a shower? After that, there's a guest bedroom. You can sleep until you're rested, however long that takes."

That sounded divine. Brighton's only concern was staying awake long enough to shower, though the thought of crawling into fresh sheets smelling like a street person turned his stomach.

"If I haven't thanked you—"

"No need." Trevor stood and pointed toward a small hallway Brighton hadn't noticed until now. "The bathroom's down that way, second door to the right. There are fresh towels beneath the sink."

Brighton rose slowly, steadying himself.

Trevor hesitated before heading back down to the pub. "Come downstairs when you're awake and we'll discuss your plans."

*   *   *

The pub didn't look any more respectful when Brighton came down that evening to the sight of packed booths. Celeste, in a white shirt with ruffled sleeves and black pants two sizes too big, stood behind the bar pouring drinks.

Celeste saw him standing at the bottom of the stairs and called to him over the din. "In the back."

Brighton gave her a slight nod, then stepped around a large man in greasy overalls and entered the back room.

Kegs lined a brick wall, and a rickety wooden desk sat across from it. Manila folders stuffed with receipts and slips of colored paper waited in a pile next to a decades-old desktop computer.

Trevor stood in front of a narrow window, his hands in his pockets. The light through the window was failing. Sunset. Finally, an end to this interminable day.

"You slept long," Trevor said, turning.

Brighton sat on the edge of one of the kegs. The way it wobbled told him it was empty.

"I can't stay," Brighton told the tall man. "Maybe enough time's passed for me to take the train."

"And go where? London?" Trevor shook his head. "Not a good idea."

"And you're full of good ideas, I presume?"

Trevor sighed. "You are very suspicious."

"It hasn't been an easy year for me."

Trevor sat on the edge of the desk. "The safest mode of travel is by car. Public transit is too dangerous."

"And where am I going to get a car?"

Trevor dismissed the question with a wave. "Celeste. If you leave tonight, you can drive north and cross the border into Scotland by sunrise tomorrow."

"Scotland?"

"Unless you want to swim the channel."

Brighton smiled crookedly, shutting out the raucous noise streaming in from the pub. "I hear even an amputee can do it."

"Even if you don't drown, the Strait of Dover is the busiest stretch of water in the world. May not be as low-key a departure as you would hope for."

Brighton ran a hand through his hair, now blessedly as close to sweat-free as it had been in days. "So, Scotland?"

"Glasgow, preferably. A seven-hour drive, maybe less. There won't be much traffic at night."

From the pub, Brighton heard a loud bang (something or someone bumping into a table, most likely), laughter and cheering, followed by the beginnings of a slurred drinking song. Brighton looked wistfully toward the half-open door.

"How about a drink before I leave? One for the road?" Brighton felt disappointed when Trevor didn't crack a smile. "You have no sense of humor."

The man treated him to a blank stare, then walked out into the pub. Brighton was about to follow when the tall man reappeared in the doorway. He dropped a set of car keys into Brighton's hands.

"Leave the car in long-term parking at Glasgow's airport," Trevor instructed him. "Lock the doors and leave the key on the floor under the front seat. Make sure it's out of sight."

Brighton put the keys in his pocket.

"Do you need anything else before you leave?"

"Money and a passport?" Brighton asked.

Trevor led Brighton into the flat's second bedroom. Brighton stood in the doorway as Trevor rummaged through one of the drawers, removing bits of clothing and placing them on a neat pile atop the faded yellow carpet.

Hidden at the back of the drawer was a plastic bag, and from it Trevor drew a stack of bills held together with a rubber band and a passport with a blue leather cover embossed with an eagle crest.

An American passport.

"Where did you get that?" Brighton asked in a strangled voice. "Who does it belong to?"

"It belongs to whoever needs it." Trevor held it out to him.

Brighton flipped it open. "What about the picture? It's not of me."

"Don't worry about that."

"Don't worry about that?" Brighton repeated back. "I'm worried as *hell*. Do you know what happens to people who get caught using fake passports? Bad stuff, and after the trouble I've gotten into these past couple of years, I'm due for some *really* bad stuff."

Trevor sat on the edge of the bed. "I know it sounds implausible, but you're going to get out of the country without any problems."

Brighton flipped the passport to the photo page. The face looking up at him was dark-haired and brown-eyed, like him. The height and weight was close. But it wasn't him. No border agent in the world would be fooled if they took even half a glance at him, and in this day of heightened security they were extra careful.

"It doesn't look like me," Brighton said.

Trevor closed his eyes and leaned his head backward. Brighton wondered whether this strange man was losing his patience. If so, it would be a rare human moment from someone who had so far kept himself closely guarded.

"You'll get through," Trevor said, emphasizing each word. "You need to trust me. After everything I've done for you, surely you can see that I'm trustworthy."

"Unless you've gotten me this far just to set me up."

"If I wanted to set you up, I would have stopped you at the train station and turned you over to the police."

Well, Brighton couldn't argue with that. If Trevor's plan was to send him into the hands of the border police, it was an unnecessarily complicated one.

"Problem is, you're not giving me much reason to trust you on this," Brighton said. "Apart from faith."

"Now you're just being dramatic. Come on, you've got money, you've got a passport, you've got a car and keys to start it. I, on the other hand, have a job to get back to. Don't make me argue with you all day."

Brighton stood his ground. "I'm sorry, I can't trust you."

Trevor stood without speaking and walked out of the room, but he didn't tell Brighton to follow this time. Brighton walked to the hallway and found Trevor in the kitchen, looking through a black book next to the phone.

Trevor ripped off the corner of a page and scribbled something down on it. He held the paper up as Brighton closed the distance between them.

"What's this?" Brighton asked, taking the paper.

"You won't get out as quickly, but I know a guy in Manchester who can get you a fake ID. The money should cover it, but you'll be stuck in Manchester for at least another day. Is that a risk you want to take?"

Brighton looked down at the digits.

"There's no name," Brighton pointed out.

"The man who answers the phone doesn't have one. Very discreet. You know how it goes."

The piece of paper reminded Brighton of the simple white business card he had once received from Lagati. Calling that number had changed his life for the worse. Could this number reverse his bad fortune?

Not even Ira's meditations could calm his nerves. They weren't just frayed; they were shredded.

"Is there any way for me to let you know I made it out safely?" Brighton asked.

Trevor shook his head. "Probably not a good idea."

"Is Trevor even your real name?"

"Is Jason yours?"

Brighton grinned. The smile felt good, even if it was sardonic. "Well, thanks again. If it wasn't for you, I don't know where I'd be."

"Don't mention it."

Brighton pocketed the keys and walked toward the stairs.

"No, really," Trevor said behind him. "Don't mention it. I insist."

NINE

Tiahuanaco, Bolivia
JULY 18

Rhea, how do you know? Do you recognize her voice?"

Dario's words reverberated loudly in the passage, but Rhea didn't appear to hear them. She remained with her forehead pressed against the metallic barrier.

Frustrated, Dario found Doctor Christophe standing a few feet behind them. The site director eyed Rhea with suspicion, his features pinched together.

"Something's wrong with her," Dario said.

Christophe offered a slow nod. "Maybe we should go."

"Nonsense!" the voice crowed.

Rhea stumbled backward as if pushed. She fell to her knees and let out a gasp. She clutched her forehead, groaning.

Dario came to her side and draped his arm over her shoulders. "Rhea, you appeared to be in a trance. Do you remember what you said?"

"I think so," she said. "I have the worst headache."

"You were staring into the barrier, your forehead pressed against it."

The disembodied female voice laughed again, a cold and uncomfortable sound. *"It's a glam, that barrier. Stare into it too long, too hard, and you'll never come back. Never, never. But I can help with that."*

Dario tried to shut out the voice, focusing on Rhea. She needed his help.

"You said it was Yasmine," Dario said. "I didn't realize you knew her well enough to recognize her voice."

Rhea looked up with a pained expression. "I don't."

"Then how did you know—"

"Enough. This girl you mention, Yasmine. She passed this way."

Dario stood, favoring his good foot. "You mentioned that you could help. What did you mean by that?"

"I can bring you through."

"Through the barrier?" asked Christophe.

A few seconds of silence passed.

"Yes."

Christophe took a step closer. "Tell me how."

"Put your head to the barrier."

"Don't," Dario warned him, gripping the rifle still at his side. "The same thing that happened to Rhea could happen to you."

Christophe nodded to him, but spoke to the voice. "You said it was a glam."

"Not so foolish, this one. The secret to passing through is simple. All you must do is speak the key."

"The key?" Christophe asked. "You mean a password?"

With great effort, Rhea came to her feet. She teetered. "Doctor, this is wrong. Yasmine is lost. We should get out of here."

But Christophe was entirely intent on the barrier now. Why was he acting so bizarrely?

"We don't know the key," Christophe said. "You have to tell us."

"*Tell you?*" Another chuckle, almost lighthearted. "*It's not something you tell. No, you don't understand at all.*"

"Then educate me."

"Doctor," Rhea warned again. "That voice is dangerous, and so is whatever's on the other side of the barrier. We're not prepared to deal with what we'd find."

"Listen to her," Dario said.

"*Quiet!*"

Dario shrunk back at the voice's authority. Nobody spoke for a long time, afraid to move.

"*I apologize,*" it said after a minute. "*I don't know your customs. You may speak amongst yourselves. I am ready to assist when you're ready.*"

Rhea reached out to Christophe and took his arm. "Come, Doctor. We should return to the camp and report our findings."

"What about Yasmine?" Christophe asked.

Dario didn't think it was spoken out of a concern for the missing girl's wellbeing. The doctor seemed to be looking for an excuse to humor the voice.

"I sincerely believe it's too late for her," Rhea said. "And that voice … well, it doesn't feel *right*."

The director shook his head. "No, you're wrong. At first I was afraid, but whoever's there is going to help us. This is an opportunity to make a great discovery. Isn't that why we got into this business in the first place?"

Dario took Rhea by the hand. "I'm ready to go."

But Christophe had turned back to the barrier. "We await your instructions!"

"*Excellent choice, my friend. I will provide the key, but you must then choose to enter.*"

"And the door will open?" Christophe touched the wall again. He sounded almost mesmerized.

"*When you hear the sound, walk into the barrier. You'll pass into it like a pebble through water.*"

And then they waited. Dario felt the heft of the rifle, but it offered little protection. What could he do, fire it at the barrier?

The voice soon began to sing, taking Dario off-guard. The look on Rhea's face told the same story. For the first few beats, the voice wavered, uncertain, as though whoever it belonged to was unaccustomed to the sound. But the woman—if it truly *was* a woman—soon found what she was looking for, striking a note in the middle of her range and latching onto it, holding it, carrying it. The sound of her voice reverberated through the cavern, bouncing off the walls and flowing away like an outgoing tide.

Dario lost track of time, the beautiful sound filling his head. He could not help his disappointment when the note faded away, its echo still ringing in his ears.

"*Now,*" the voice called almost warmly. "*Come to me.*"

Christophe approached the wall, testing the apparently solid metal with his fingers.

"*Don't think. Close your eyes and imagine you are walking through an open doorway.*"

Christophe did as he was told, closing his eyes and breathing in and out, readying himself.

Rhea pressed up to Dario. "Should we stop him?"

"How do you recommend we do that?" he whispered back.

"You could point that gun at him."

"He wouldn't take me seriously." Dario looked down at the barrel, gleaming faintly in the beam of Rhea's flashlight. "Hell, *I* can't even take me seriously. Besides, you must be curious."

Rhea brushed her hair behind her ear. Even with dirty clothes and grime on her face, she was exquisite.

They both glanced toward Christophe at the same time. He was as still as a Tibetan monk.

"I'm more than curious," Rhea said, turning back to Dario. "But when I was in that trance, I sensed something hypnotic. Powerful."

"It wasn't so powerful that you couldn't overcome it."

Rhea looked down at her feet. "No, Dario, I didn't. It let me go."

Christophe stepped forward slowly, approaching the wall bit by bit, and just when Dario expected him to collide with it, he passed through, calm as Gandhi, without causing so much as a ripple in the barrier.

Dario ran forward and touched the wall where Christophe had disappeared. "I didn't just see what I thought I saw."

Rhea touched him on the shoulder, but he didn't turn. He couldn't.

"Did you see that?" Dario was almost frantic.

"Yes."

"We have to go after him."

Rhea pushed herself between him and the wall, forcing him to look at her. "Are you crazy? We have to get the hell out of here, that's what we have to do."

Dario dropped his hands to his sides and slowed his breathing.

"What are you doing?" Rhea asked.

"Shhh. It's hard to relax when you're talking to me."

"Good. That's the point. This is a bad idea."

He put his arms around her waist and bodily moved her aside. "All I have to do is close my eyes, like Christophe did."

Breathe in, breathe out. He rubbed his sweaty palms together, the rifle heavy on his shoulder. He tried to shut out any distractions. *Just relax. It's no big deal, you're just going to walk through a solid wall. Like the lady said, don't think about it.*

He heard Rhea talking to him but shut her out. That in itself was difficult. Her instincts weren't wrong; this *was* a bad idea, wasn't it? But they'd already lost two of their people to whatever was behind that barrier.

Maybe three.

Determined, he opened his eyes and walked forward. He thought he heard someone crying, but it was distant. Faraway. He took another step.

Another.

And another.

Dario blinked, then whirled around. He was through! Rhea stood just a couple of feet behind him, her eyes roving back and forth as though she couldn't see him.

He ran his hands down his chest to make sure all his various parts were still where they were supposed to be.

Dim light surrounded him, but it didn't come from his flashlight. The corners of the room were darker than dark, but ahead of him was a snake of light seeming to spike through the air like the filament inside a light bulb.

It was the strangest, most unexpected sight. Extending from a monolithic block of gold—or at least something plated in gold—was a long bulb-like protrusion three times his height and half as wide. It came within a meter or two of grazing the high ceiling. The filament gave off an unhealthy pale glow.

Dario stepped around the unusual apparatus. The room had at least a dozen entrances, all of them evenly spaced around the periphery. They had been right about each spoke leading here.

To whatever this thing was.

Up ahead, Christophe knelt next to a lifeless body. Dario came closer and realized it was a girl in beige work clothes. She had long dark hair and high cheekbones. Yasmine.

"How is she?" Dario asked.

Christophe didn't acknowledge him.

"Doctor Perez will be back soon," Dario said, trying again. "We can get her help."

Yasmine's body was limp, so weak Dario doubted she could move. But the girl's eyes were open, her face alive with expression.

"I am touched by your concern, but as you can see, I am quite well."

Seeing the prostrate girl's mouth move nearly made Dario jump out of his skin.

"This body is very weak."

Dario hesitated. "Then Yasmine is dead."

The girl grinned. *"Yes, of course she's dead. Was that not clear?"*

That grin made him feel uneasy.

"Are you a spirit?" Dario asked. He couldn't believe he was lending the theory credence, but it looked like whatever this being was, it had possessed the girl.

The idea sounded like one of the horror stories his grandmother used to tell him and his sister after returning home from Mass. He could practically hear her shrill "I told you so" beaming down from heaven—or up from hell, wherever the old woman had ended up.

"Not a spirit," Christophe whispered to him. "A god."

Dario's eyebrow shot up.

"Yes. A god."

The sight of Yasmine's limp body was utterly disturbing, yet Dario couldn't bring himself to look away. She was dead!

Not much of a god, he thought. *She can't even move.*

"I have been here a long time. A very long time."

"How did you get here?" Dario asked.

"You're worried," it said. *"Worried that I'm dangerous. Baseless fears."*

"If you're a god, then what are you doing here?" Dario rocked on his heels, ready to grab Christophe by the cuff of his shirt and drag him out of there. He caught a glimpse of the strange light bulb and its unearthly glow. "And what is that?"

"The machine? You might call it… a generator."

Christophe looked at Dario. "Stop with the questions. She doesn't owe us answers."

"I offer them freely. My people once lived in this place."

"Here, in the tunnels?" Christophe asked.

"This city was the center of a great empire, and I was their god of many faces, dwelling among them."

Dario released a long breath. "The faces on the walls of the city, and in the caverns… they depict you?"

"I have walked in many bodies. Many shapes. Many faces. A woman, a man, a child. Those of the city worshipped me, gave their lives for me."

His memory flashed back to the depression atop the Pyramid of Akapana, used to collect the blood of human sacrifices.

"They sacrificed their own people," Dario said in a low voice. "And you took their forms."

"I inhabit the willing and the dead." It fell silent for a long minute. *"Tell me. What happened to my great city? My people?"*

"If you're who you claim to be, shouldn't you know that?"

The girl's face smiled ghoulishly. *"I have been asleep a very long time."*

Dario's stomach twisted in knots at the girl's fate. "Her name was Yasmine, and you could have helped her. Instead you let her die."

"It was necessary if I was to communicate."

"Do you have a name?" Dario asked.

Christophe shot him another impatient look.

"*You are preoccupied with names.*" The creature's face went blank, as though the being had fled the body, leaving her in peace. A moment later, the eyelids fluttered and it was back. "*I am Ohia of the Rephaim, son of Samhazai and father of Sihon. Tell me, do you know the whereabouts of my sons?*"

Dario stared at the creature, puzzled. "Can't say that I do."

"*My father sent me to this place, to gather a people. I was master of this city.*"

"The city is called Tiahuanaco."

"*This place was known by another name. It was sacred, ordained from the beginning of time, from the time of the creators… the time of our fathers.*"

Dario took a moment to look back toward the passage he had come through. The machine's bulk obstructed his view. Was Rhea still waiting for him on the other side of the barrier, or had she fled? He hoped she had fled.

"*What has become of my city?*"

"It has passed into ruin," Christophe said. "I am the leader of a team whose job is to restore the city to its original condition. Unfortunately, there is very little left. Only platforms and the footprints of long-destroyed buildings." He paused. "We don't know what happened to the civilization here. If you have some memory of those times, it would be helpful to—"

"*Enough.*"

Christophe flinched. "I apologize—"

"*I have been asleep too long. My memory is not…*"

Dario waited with apprehension, expecting something more, but as the seconds ticked by, the being was silent, Yasmine's face inanimate.

"Where did it go?" Dario asked.

Before Christophe could respond, it returned.

"Someone is coming."

Dario looked behind him. Rhea stood just on the near side of the barrier, her pale face a picture of bewilderment. She approached the machine, resting her hands on the golden base.

"It's a generator of some kind," Dario explained.

She nodded. "Yes, I know. I was listening."

"Then you know—"

"There's no such thing as gods, Dario." She completed her appraisal of the machine and turned her attention to Yasmine. "Whatever its powers, it doesn't seem able to move."

"I cannot move because this body has deteriorated. In the days of greatness, my people provided me with fresh specimens to avoid the effects of deterioration."

Rhea took Dario by the arm. "How many times do I have to tell you we need to leave?"

"But the things it's saying," Christophe protested. "Everything we know, things we never suspected about the purpose of the temple ..."

"Yes, the temple. This room is part of the temple."

"You're saying we're inside the Kalasasaya Temple?" Christophe asked, looking up at the high ceiling. "The earth has been scanned repeatedly for evidence of an interior. None has ever been found."

"The barrier protects this sacred place against intruders."

"The barrier," Dario said, drawing the word out. "You mean it extends through the ceiling?"

"It extends all around us."

Once again, Yasmine's eyes drifted upward and lost focus, staring emptily at a darkened corner of the room. Dario followed the gaze, but saw nothing.

"This is the third time it's happened," Dario explained to Rhea. "It only speaks to us a few minutes at a time."

"This being… it's treacherous," Rhea said.

Yasmine's eyes snapped wide. *"Treacherous? You are a fool. My father was leader of the Twenty, one of the Grigori. A god of the highest order, a Creator."*

Rhea whispered into Dario's ear. "It's further weakening, less and less able to inhabit the body."

"Not as weak as you imagine."

And then it moved, quickly, as though it had been conserving its energy for just such a burst. One minute Yasmine's body was slumped against the wall and the next it was on its feet, rushing Dario like an enraged bull.

He let out a gasp, then realized his shoulder felt lighter than it had a moment earlier.

The rifle!

He turned only in time to see the creature raise the rifle, one hand on the trigger and the other on the wooden grip. Dario took a moment too long see where it was pointed. He flung himself toward Rhea with enough speed to knock her over.

The explosion of the rifle's discharge rang in his ears as he collided with Rhea and flattened her. In the same instant, he heard Yasmine's body crumple to the floor in a heap of dead tissue.

Dario looked down, hoping to find that Rhea was alright—

A trickle of blood rolled down from Rhea's open mouth. She drew shallow breaths.

Dario jumped off her and watched a pool of blood spread across her chest.

"No," he murmured. "No, Rhea… "

With one hand, Dario put pressure on the wound to staunch the bleeding.

"Hang on." He stared into her eyes. "The doctor's coming back. You'll be okay."

She shook her head, more blood gushing out of her mouth. He leaned his ear to her mouth and felt the faint tickle of a whisper.

"Run," she said. "Run…"

Rhea's head lolled to the side and the light went out of her eyes.

Dario stumbled to his feet and brushed a hand across his face. His fingers came away wet and he realized that tears were running down his cheeks.

Run.

He took a backward step as a rush of air blew past.

Just as Rhea's eyes snapped open, he flung himself at the nearest tunnel entrance, the cackle of laughter in his ears.

TEN

Tiahuanaco, Bolivia
JULY 18

Dario hurtled over the vast fields separating the entrance to the caverns from the tent city. He slowed only when he reached the first line of tents, barely registering the newly reconstructed temple walls—and the chamber of horrors he now knew languished beneath them.

The sun had risen, and with it the camp. The men and women he passed looked at him strangely, no doubt wondering what had spooked him into a sprint so desperate, so furious, that rivers of sweat poured down his face, stinging his eyes.

"Dario?"

He turned and found himself face to face with Doctor Perez with the now-familiar equipment bag in her left hand.

For a few seconds, he was speechless. His brain seemed incapable of forming thoughts, never mind words.

"Dario, what are you doing here? Did you find Yasmine?"

He wanted to tell her, but a woman of science like Perez surely wouldn't believe a word of it. Was there anything more implausible than a malicious spirit capable of possessing dead bodies?

"Are you feeling alright?" Perez pressed.

He'd been standing still too long and his legs collapsed out from beneath him, the muscles shrieking in agony from extreme exertion.

Perez sank down and placed her hand against his forehead. "You're burning up."

He nodded almost involuntarily.

"Damn it, I'm not a mind-reader," she said. "What's gotten into you? Why aren't you with the others?"

Dario breathed, heaving air into his lungs. "You can't go back."

"Christophe instructed me to—"

Dario brushed her hand away. "Tell me about Jorge. Is he going to make it?"

Still confused, Perez said, "He's on his way to La Paz with Marco and Kincaid."

At least there was some good news.

Perez stood up. "Perhaps you should lie down. I have to get back to the caverns."

"No."

"Why? You're not making sense."

Dario swallowed down a throatful of bile. "Rhea is dead."

Saying it aloud brought on a surge of pain that started in the back of his head, winding downward until it settled in his gut.

"Rhea's dead," he repeated. Unbidden tears blurred his vision.

Perez's mouth fell open. "You can't be serious. What happened?"

"You won't believe me. It's not... rational."

Dario saw that people were stopping to watch. He couldn't stay in this terrible city. Rhea's last command had been to run, and nothing was going to keep him from obeying it.

"I have to go," he mumbled, standing up.

"You're not going anywhere." Perez held him in place by the shoulders. She didn't need to exert much force to pin him. "You just told me that one of our colleagues is dead, and as far as I know you're the one who did it."

Dario's eyes shot up. That hadn't even occurred to him. His thoughts were muddy, cloudy, incoherent; he had to force himself to think clearly.

"Where's Doctor Christophe?" she asked.

"Still in the caverns." At least that's what Dario assumed.

Perez called for some help, and soon there were two men on either side, helping him up.

"Take him to his tent," Perez instructed. "Restrain him if you must."

Dario opened his mouth to protest, but no sound came out.

Perez picked up her black bag from the dusty ground and broke into a trot, heading north toward the river.

Dario walked back through the tents, trying his best to appear nonchalant. He didn't know the man on his left, but the one on his right was named Peter. Or maybe Pietr. Either way, they weren't good enough friends to make a difference.

"Somebody was carried away on a stretcher earlier," Peter/Pietr said. "Do you know anything about that?"

Dario said nothing. It was better that way.

With Rhea dead and Marco out of the picture, he felt very alone. If he'd known he would need allies, he would have tried harder to make friends these past two weeks.

Rhea would have told him being friendly was its own reward.

Soon he was back in his tent, considering his next move. He took only five minutes to come to a firm decision. He pulled a suitcase out from under his bed and began packing—quietly, to avoid the attention of the two sentries outside his tent. The last item to pack was a leather satchel of tools, from which he removed a small knife. He held it up under the dim light of the lantern. The blade was narrow but sharp.

Dario advanced toward the back wall and slipped the blade through the canvas. He sawed downward, pressing hard. He gritted his teeth from the effort of cutting through the thick material with such a small blade. Inch by inch, he worked his way downward until the tear was large enough for him to step through.

He picked up his suitcase and exited into the tight space between his tent and his backdoor neighbor. He carefully avoided tripping over tent lines and steel spikes as he picked his way toward the edge of camp. More than once, he waited for people to pass before crossing the more well-travelled paths.

The camp employed a fleet of three excursion vehicles, one of which was missing from the gravel parking lot next to the highway. Marco and Kincaid had most likely used it to transport Jorge.

Dario had to get the keys to one of those vehicles, and they would only be in one of two possible locations—the security tent, or Doctor Christophe's tent. The security tent seemed his likeliest option.

He hid the suitcase in the space between two tents, where no one would see it unless they expected to.

The security tent was located near the main route into the camp, on the other side of the parked vehicles, and held everything worthy of being kept under guard, including tools, medical supplies, and various keys. The camp dwellers came and went most frequently here, and from the tent's entrance one had a clear view of the important nearby landmarks. To the northwest was the town—named Tiahuanaco, for the ruins—which was home to most of the region's eight thousand Aymaran residents. To the south, the camp's widest avenue proceeded all the way to the dining tent. The rest of the view was dominated by the east-west highway.

A security guard was always assigned to the tent, making it hard to get in and out unseen. But Dario had to try.

As he approached, a dark-skinned man in jeans and a bright green t-shirt stood up from a fold-up chair just outside the security tent.

"Can I help you?" the guard asked.

Dario lifted his chin and put on a mask of total confidence. "Doctor Perez sent me over to pick up a medical kit."

"She was just here ten minutes ago to get supplies," the man said. "Are you sure you understood her correctly?"

"Yeah, we were just leaving camp when she realized the kit was missing a roll of sterile gauze."

"You need a requisition from the site director, or from one of the doctors."

Dario's face fell. "But Doctor Christophe is out of camp, and so is Doctor Kincaid. Please, this is an emergency. You can ask anyone. I've been with Doctor Perez all morning."

Dario was impressed by his quick thinking. It sounded more plausible than he'd anticipated.

The man managed a conflicted frown. "I don't know…"

"Perez and Christophe will both be back in an hour, no matter what happens," Dario said. "You can confirm it then. Anyway, I don't even need a whole kit. Just the gauze."

The man gave him a begrudging nod. "Alright, come with me."

Dario had never been inside the security tent, but it looked just as he'd imagined it. A portable cabinet stood along one of the walls, probably to hold various guns. On a table were rope, sledgehammers, picks, and a bin brimming with flashlights.

Next to the flashlights, a row of hooks affixed to a plywood board held several sets of keys. Many were small and meant to open lockboxes. The last two, however, were attached to bulky remote starters.

As the man opened the cabinet and fished around for a medical kit, Dario used his free hand to slip one of the bulky keys off its hook.

The man only took a few seconds to turn around and hand Dario a roll of gauze. "Tell the doctor to come herself next time."

Dario offered an easy smile. "I'll do that."

He retreated to the spot where he'd left his suitcase, hoping he still had enough time to get away before the men outside his tent noticed his absence—and before Perez and Christophe returned to camp. *If* they would return.

He waited a few minutes, then walked back toward the parked expedition vehicles. Unfortunately, both of them were plainly visible to the man in the security tent.

Good fortune struck when a pair of women arrived at the security tent, presenting the man with a piece of paper. The three of them exchanged words, then stepped into the tent. Out of sight.

Dario sprang forward. He pressed the unlock button on the remote starter, hesitating just long enough to see which of the two vehicle's lights responded. He jumped inside and inserted the key into the ignition.

The engine purred to life.

He slammed the gear into reverse. With a glance into the rearview mirror to see if anyone was watching, Dario stomped on the accelerator. The sound of spinning gravel overwhelmed the beating of his own heart.

ELEVEN

Syracuse, New York
JULY 19

Temple Emmanuel stood tall and proud in the heart of the city, its towering edifice no different than most Catholic churches Brighton had seen. The exterior walls were brown sandstone and featured wide arcs over evenly spaced windows and doors.

Brighton hurried across the square, hoping to avoid the torrent of rain that was coming. The sky had darkened in the last hour. Low-hanging clouds had swept in fast, grazing the tops of the synagogue's tallest tower. Brighton reached the heavy wooden doors just as the first drops began to fall. He pulled at the handle, unsure if the synagogue welcomed visitors midweek. Thankfully, the door opened.

Massive stone columns featuring intricate carvings along their bases lined the long central aisle. Light shone down from a stained-glass

Star of David at the far end of the church, bathing the sanctuary in a blue afternoon glow.

Brighton took several tentative steps forward, his shoes clipping against the tiled floor. The sound echoed throughout the cavernous room, bouncing off stonework and glass. Never had he felt more like an intruder. He felt watched as he passed beneath the broad domes that blossomed like flower petals from the tops of each column. Upon those lofty stone arches were ornate paintings. God's imposing and angry face glared down from the central panel, surrounded on all fronts by stern men with long beards.

Brighton slowed as he reached the front, where an immense wooden box sat upon a stone platform, its sides plain and smooth and draped in a purple cloth. He stopped, his instinct telling him not to approach.

"Hello," a female voice called down.

Brighton glanced up to find a woman with long brown hair watching him from the balcony.

"I'm here to speak with the rabbi," Brighton called.

She backed away from the railing, disappearing from view. Brighton found a hard wooden bench to sit on.

A few minutes later, he heard a door open and turned toward the east wall. The woman crossed the front platform toward him. She wore a gray robe over a white shirt and long black skirt. She stopped next to the giant wooden box.

"The rabbi isn't here," she said. "Best return on Saturday."

"I'm afraid I can't wait that long," Brighton said. "Maybe you can answer my questions, though. Do you work here?"

She nodded. "What do you want to know?"

"I'm a friend of the rabbi who used to minister here. Ira Binyamin. I'm trying to find him."

"Rabbi Binyamin hasn't been here in a year and a half."

"And you don't have any forwarding information?"

The woman paused, pressing her lips together. "I'm very sorry that I can't help you. The rabbi was a good man."

"Was? Did something happen to him?"

She didn't reply, which Brighton took to mean she didn't know anything. He rested his arm against the back of the pew and leaned back. He had avoided coming here, avoided exposing himself, but he had believed this was the path to Ira. If not here, where?

Ira, I need you now more than ever. I can't do this on my own.

But there was no answer. There never was.

"Thank you," he said.

He stood up and turned to leave.

"Wait," she called, coming down from the platform. Her robe swished against the floor. "How did you know the rabbi?"

Brighton stopped. "He was my friend."

"He was mine as well," she said. "My name is Janene. I didn't catch yours."

"Jason." He turned to find her right behind him. "Ira and I… we travelled together."

She gave him a small smile. "You must be very special. Everyone Ira touched was special in some way."

The silence between them hung heavy. Outside, the wind whistled through the building's stone arches. The rain pelting the windows grew into a dull roar.

"Come with me," she said.

Janene walked up onto the platform and vanished through a door hidden from the front rows. Brighton found himself stepping out of one world and into another, as the corridor here led past offices and meeting rooms not much different from most office buildings. They came to a room at the end of the hall and turned inside.

They entered a large office with a single bookcase next to the room's only window. There was a heavy oak desk, a chair of worn leather behind it and a simple wooden chair in front. An austere couch rested beside an end table with a stack of books neatly arranged on it.

"This was Ira's office," Janene explained. "No one ever comes in here. The Temple president has instructed that it remain undisturbed. Rabbi Feynman, Ira's replacement, occupies another office."

Brighton walked to the bookshelf and scanned the titles. "Surely that isn't standard procedure."

"Of course not."

"It's almost like someone expects Ira to come back."

Janene inclined her head. "Seems that way."

Brighton ran his fingers over the book spines, all of them perfectly in line with each other, as though someone had used a ruler.

"The last time I saw Ira was in this room," Janene murmured. "It was just after a Saturday service. He left the following day."

Brighton's finger came to a book sticking out a quarter-inch from the others. Frowning, he pulled it out and studied its cover for a moment. The book was a translation of the *Sefer Yetzirah*.

"Is something the matter?"

He showed it to her. "This book. It was one of the rabbi's favorites."

Janene opened it to the first page. "He never spoke of it. Is it important?"

She handed it back to him. He made sure the spine lined up with the others when he slipped it onto the shelf.

"It was slightly out of place, that's all," he said, trying his best to sound casual. "Perhaps it was the last book he read before going away."

Brighton turned his attention to the desk. On it was a pad of stationery, a couple of pens, and a few file folders. Ira didn't seem to have owned a computer. Which was just like Ira, when Brighton thought about it.

"You mentioned that you two travelled together," Janene said. "When was that?"

Brighton sat in the leather chair and lowered his arms onto the armrests. The leather was worn and comfortable.

"Quite some time ago," Brighton said, dodging the truth. "Thank you for bringing me here, but I don't see any clues to his whereabouts. Were you hoping I would know something you didn't?"

Janene's face fell. "I don't have any information, but there is one other person who might be able to help."

Brighton sat up straight. "Who?"

"Someone Ira knew from his seminary days. He claims not to know where the rabbi disappeared to, but—" Janene's voice cut off as though someone had flipped a switch. "I shouldn't be telling you this."

"Tell me."

"The day before Ira went away, he left a message with me explaining that he was visiting a friend in Vermont. He could only have been referring to one person. If my suspicions are correct, this man, Aaron Roth, was the last man to see Ira alive. And the two were not on good terms."

"Who's Aaron Roth?"

Janene leaned over the desk, uncapped a pen, and wrote a couple of lines on the bottom of the stationary pad. She ripped it free and handed the piece of paper to Brighton.

"This is where you can find him," she said. "Just one thing."

"What's that?"

"Tell him the truth, and don't leave anything out. He'll see through any lies."

Brighton put the paper in his pocket and got up from the chair. "Who's to say I've been lying?"

Janene raised an eyebrow as though to say, *How stupid do you think I am?* She walked to the open doorway and waited for him.

"You coming?"

Brighton gave the office one last sentimental look. He could almost imagine Ira sitting in this office composing sermon notes by hand, flipping through dusty tomes, and squinting overtop a pair of twenty-year-old reading glasses. It was the closest connection to Ira he had felt since they'd parted ways.

Tamping down the sadness, Brighton followed her out.

*   *   *

The burly man at the nurse's desk initially wouldn't let Brighton into the palliative care wing of the hospital, but changed his mind when Brighton told him he had come as a representative from Temple Emmanuel.

"He's been in and out of consciousness the last few days," the nurse explained. "He may not be up for much talking."

Brighton nodded, then walked past the desk into the hospital corridor. The bright orange walls glared under fluorescent lights—an inappropriate style choice, given the serenity that permeated the hallway. Patients came here to die; couldn't the hospital give them something more pleasant to look at in their final hours?

He stopped in front of the door to Aaron Roth's room and found it half-open. Inside, the lights were off except for the amber glow of a bedside lamp. The window was closed and only narrow strips of light slipped through the downturned blinds. A monitor next to the bed hummed but didn't beep. The only other sound was the rhythmic suction of the ventilator.

Brighton walked in and stopped when he got a peek at the gaunt-looking man in the bed. He was skin and bones, thin as a rail, his chest rising and falling sporadically with shallow breaths. A breathing mask covered his mouth and nose and his eyes were closed.

Brighton located a chair next to the window and sat. Perhaps this had been a bad idea. The man was clearly on his deathbed; maybe it was best to leave him to die in peace.

Five minutes passed. Then ten, then twenty. Perhaps an hour later, Brighton heard the man stir.

"David, is that you?" Aaron asked in a strangled voice.

Brighton leaned forward, realizing that although the man's eyes were closed, he was awake. Who was David?

"No, Mr. Roth. My name is Jason—"

Aaron slid off his breathing mask and coughed. He laid the mask on the sheet next to his pillow, then struggled to look up. Brighton stood and approached the bed, making sure the man was able to see him clearly.

"That's not your name," Aaron rasped.

Brighton hesitated, surprised. Then he remembered Janene's warning. Even without opening his eyes all the way, Aaron was able to see through him.

"Sherwood Brighton." He felt unsettled revealing his name; he hadn't spoken it aloud in a long time.

Aaron somehow managed a chuckle, even though Brighton couldn't imagine what a man in his vulnerable position could possibly find funny.

"You don't need to tiptoe around me," Aaron said. "I may be dying, but I'm not as frail as I look."

"Yes, sir."

But he certainly *looked* frail as he struggled to sit up. Brighton helped him lean forward, then stuffed an extra pillow behind his back. Aaron thanked him as Brighton pulled the chair closer to the bed and sat down.

"It's my hundredth birthday this weekend," Aaron mused. "Not sure I'm going to make it."

"A hundred years? Very impressive."

"What's so impressive about not having died?"

"What are you dying from?" It felt like an insensitive question, but he got the impression Aaron Roth was a man who disavowed sensitivity in favor of blunt honesty.

"At my age, it's a little of this, a little of that. Some cancer in the bowels, some emphysema." Aaron coughed as though to demonstrate the latter condition. "A hell of a lot of arthritis, too. That's a new development. Nothing to worry about, though. It would be hard to distinguish joint pain from all the rest of it, except for medication. Do you know how much medication they give me? I tell them I don't need it. I'll go when I'm ready and not a minute sooner." More coughing. "But you're not here to talk about my health. You're here to talk about Ira."

"How did you know?" Brighton asked.

"A friend whispered it to me. He also told me you came a long way to get here."

That's an understatement if I ever heard one.

"And that you have a long way to go," Aaron finished.

Brighton's heart fell. He didn't know how Aaron divined these truths, but Ira had exhibited similar prescience at times.

"I'm very tired," Brighton said, making a surprisingly personal admission to a complete stranger. Of course, the only people he had in his life now were strangers.

"Of course you are. The world is a tiring place if you choose for it to be."

Ira had uttered that same brand of doublespeak all the time. The trouble was he had almost always been right.

"I can't tell you where Ira has gone, because I don't know. Not for certain." Aaron blinked his deep-set eyes, then left them closed for a minute, resting them. When they opened again, they were red and rheumy. "But I have my suspicions. If I'm right, where he's gone, he will be in no hurry to depart. No one is in a hurry to depart that place, though a few have."

"How do you know Ira?"

"We taught at seminary together." The old man's eyes sharpened, becoming more alert. "Ira taught you as well. What did he teach you?"

"Teach me?"

"Oh, come now. There was something, wasn't there?"

Brighton put a hand to his head just as Ira's voice filled it: *"Once something is in your memory, it is possible to access it."* In his mind's eye, he saw himself sitting on the Norwegian scientists' couch in Antarctica, Ira next to him. Even though it was nothing but a memory, he could almost feel Ira's hand in his, holding it in a determined grip. Ira had led him on a meditation, something about a river, reaching down and anchoring to the bottom before being swept away by the current.

See the possibilities. It's a choice. You have to choose.

Brighton pushed it away. "He showed me how to reach into my memory."

"I see," Aaron said, his voice soft and contemplative. "That is a powerful gift."

Brighton didn't answer. He wasn't sure it was a gift, and even if it was, he hardly knew how to use it properly. Ira hadn't stuck around long enough to finish the lesson.

Aaron's eyes closed again. Had he fallen asleep?

"There is a reason you are here," the old man spoke in a stronger voice than Brighton thought he was capable of. "A glorious and disastrous coming is about to take place, and you are to play a part. The black awakening is soon upon us. You, Sherwood Brighton, a beacon of light in a dark place…"

Brighton stood up, startled. "What did you say?"

All he heard was the hiss of the ventilator.

"Mr. Roth?"

Brighton placed his hand on the man's arm. Aaron's skin was clammy and he didn't respond.

In and out of consciousness, indeed.

Brighton stepped out into the hall just as a nurse walked by, carrying a stack of patient charts.

"Excuse me," the nurse asked, making eye contact. "Are you a family member?"

Brighton shook his head and told the same lie that had worked earlier. "I'm from the synagogue."

"Only family is allowed into this wing," she said. "I'll have to ask you to leave."

"The nurse at the main desk…" He gestured down the hall, then lowered his hand, realizing it didn't matter. "Never mind. I already got what I came for."

Or at least, everything you're going to get.

"That man, Aaron Roth," Brighton said as the nurse escorted him to the door. "How much longer does he have?"

"Days. A week at the outside. He's strong, but his health has rapidly declined."

Brighton sighed. "He told me he's almost a hundred years old. Sound like he's a good man."

"Yes, a very good man. I've been caring for him since the end of April when his son brought him in."

"David?"

She nodded as they got to the end of the corridor. "Before you go, do you mind answering a question?"

He turned to face her.

"You had a conversation with him, yes?" she said. "Did he have anything unusual to say?"

"Unusual?"

She frowned, shifting her stack of charts from one hand to the other. "He's been mumbling a lot the last few days about waiting for someone to visit. I haven't seen you before, so I thought…" She shook her head. "Never mind. Have yourself a good day."

She walked behind the nurses' station and went about whatever task had brought her there. Brighton left the ward, unsure what to make of his encounter with Aaron Roth. He'd come looking for answers, but he left more confused than ever.

TWELVE

Alexandria, Egypt
JULY 19

E lisabeth Macfarlane slipped a pair of sunglasses over her eyes. She didn't ordinarily care for the glasses, but they were a necessity in Egypt, where the mere act of making eye contact with a man could be mistaken for an unwelcome advance.

After just a couple of minutes under the hot summer sun, sweat collected underneath her bulky clothes. She longed for a pair of shorts and a t-shirt, but instead she was covered head to toe, a black, wide-sleeved *abaya* draped over her shoulders and hanging to her ankles. Even her hair was pulled back underneath a black headscarf. How the locals accustomed themselves to such discomfort, she would never know.

Tall hotels and apartment towers glistened white along the eastern harbor road, waving palm trees standing between them like sentinels. A group of young boys scampered along the seawall. A minor slip and any one of them could tumble onto the rocks buttressing the highway, but they scurried over it as though they had done it a hundred times before. They probably had.

That rocky shore soon widened into a sandy beach. She briefly imagined casting off her black robe and throwing herself into the surf.

Five blocks down the road, she came to a yellow building with wrought-iron balconies overlooking the sea. She climbed the front steps and entered through the glass-paneled door.

The building's cramped lobby was mostly empty; she bypassed it, turning left into a café. Half the tables were occupied by businessmen with cigars hanging out of their mouths. She brushed past two men crowding the doorway and spotted Zahi Menefee waiting at a table next to a large front-facing window. The corpulent man was impossible to miss; he was more than three hundred pounds and wearing a hideous shirt with an orange and green floral pattern.

Elisabeth pulled out the chair across from him and bowed. "Mr. Menefee, I appreciate you agreeing to include me this afternoon."

Menefee thrust out his right hand and she took it. "My pleasure, Elisabeth. Lovely to see you back. How long has it been?"

"A long time," she said, sitting down. A soothing breeze from an open window brushed the brown curls matted to her forehead. "I don't believe I've had the chance to congratulate you on your progress with the library."

Menefee flagged down a waiter, allowing Elisabeth to order a cup of tea. A couple of minutes later, the server placed the cup in front of her on a light green saucer. Steam curled up from it, dissipating in the warm afternoon air.

"The library, yes!" Menefee leaned back, his chair creaking. "You had a lot to do with that. If it wasn't for your efforts, half the scrolls found in Herculaneum would still be waiting to be digitized. Your team has done a marvelous job."

"You're too kind," Elisabeth said. "When does construction get underway on the new wing?"

"End of summer. We are very excited about it. Half the Herculaneum scrolls are staying in Italy and the other half are coming here. It's going to be marvelous. Just marvelous." He paused, his face turning from jovial to solemn. "Sorry to hear about Emery Wörtlich. It's hard to understand why he turned against us."

Elisabeth held her tongue. She knew the truth, of course, that Emery had stolen the index to the Library of Alexandria on the orders of Raff Lagati before coming to his tragic end. But all Menefee knew was that Emery had taken the index and fled. The two men had been colleagues for more than twenty years, and no doubt the development puzzled Menefee more than most.

"It's a mystery that may never be solved," she allowed.

Elisabeth took the lull in the conversation to peer around the café. Menefee was pleasant enough to chat with, but she hadn't come all this way to renew an old acquaintance.

"I don't know what's keeping him," Menefee said, as if reading her mind.

The clock above the door to the lobby read a quarter past the hour. Just as Elisabeth was about to turn her gaze back to the fat Egyptian, Noam Sheply strolled in wearing a white jacket and fedora. It was a ridiculous outfit, a callback to colonial times.

Sheply approached their table and shook each of their hands. He ordered a Turkish coffee before settling himself down in the last chair.

"Good afternoon, Noam," Elisabeth greeted.

He raised his eyebrows. "Elisabeth. I heard you were in town, though why on earth that is, I haven't the faintest notion."

"Elisabeth has played a part in the library effort from the start," Menefee said.

Sheply's coffee arrived in a ceramic cup. He stirred in a pinch of sugar before gently lifting the cup to his lips.

"A part that is finished," Sheply said, setting down the coffee. "Not that I object to seeing you, Elisabeth. As always, you are a sight for sore eyes. Lately, my eyes have been especially sore."

He's bitter, Elisabeth thought. *He was always bitter that I liked Emery more than him.*

It wasn't that Elisabeth hadn't noticed Sheply so much as Emery had completely outclassed him. Sheply had claimed to be Emery's best friend—or the nearest to one he had found in Cairo during the old days—but Sheply had made a hundred passes at her, knowing full well the burgeoning romance she shared with Emery.

She sighed, forcing herself to remember that their "romance" had hardly been the bastion of purity she sometimes pretended. Emery had been a married man and she had pursued him relentlessly. Not that he hadn't wanted to be pursued.

Elisabeth glanced out at the waves rolling over the beach. "Not sure how your eyes got so sore. The view from Alexandria is nothing short of breathtaking."

Sheply smirked at her. "It's not the beach I care to look at, my dear."

Was it her, or was he smarmier than usual? Though he had always been smarmy. After Sheply's initial internship sixteen years ago, Menefee had gotten rid of him as fast as he could arrange. But the Englishman had continued to show up over the years, finally getting a full position four years ago. She had never understood how he got the assignment when Menefee professed to despise him so much.

Now she knew the answer, thanks to Sherwood Brighton. Brighton had been able to explain so many things. It pleased her to know

Emery had died for something meaningful, that he had at long last found the thing he had spent a lifetime searching for—

Menefee pulled out a flash drive and placed it on the table next to Sheply's coffee cup. "These are the latest plans. Construction starts at the end of the month, and we're already behind schedule."

Sheply stiffened. "If that's a subtle dig at my recent absence…"

Menefee held up a hand to stop him. "Family emergency, I understand. I was sorry to hear about your mother."

Sheply nodded, then glanced at Elisabeth. "A stroke. It was bad timing, what with everything that's going on, but I had to return to England for a few days. To arrange for her care." He picked up the flash drive and dropped it into his shirt pocket. "I'll take a look and file my notes this afternoon."

Menefee peered out the window. "You see the Citadel?"

Looking east, Elisabeth caught sight of the distant wharf, and upon it the Citadel of Qaitbay. The fort had rested on the tip of Pharos Island since the late 1400s, a critical defensive stronghold erected on the exact site of the former Lighthouse of Alexandria, one of the seven wonders of the ancient world. The Citadel was no more than a tourist attraction now, though soon it would be repurposed.

"The plan is to annex the Citadel to the Bibliotheca Alexandrina, the modern city library," Menefee continued in a faraway voice. "It's going to be glorious."

Menefee had played a critical role in the planning of the Bibliotheca. A modern architectural wonder all its own, the library sported bold stone edifices and graceful curves, all of it surrounded by an enormous reflecting pool—a contrast in styles appropriately echoing the confluence of cultures and learning that the library represented. The building also featured one of the country's most well-furnished antiquities museums. Menefee himself had unearthed many of its artifacts.

Elisabeth finished her tea as Sheply and Menefee exchanged details about the exact scrolls the Institute was going to formerly request from the Italian government. Menefee expressed annoyance that they were only entitled to half the discoveries, but a fifty-fifty split was perhaps more generous than Italy had needed to be. After all, the scrolls had been discovered on its soil.

The discussion soon turned to transporting the scrolls from where they currently rested in a vault at Brigham Young University in Utah. The petrified scroll remains were unbelievably delicate, so there were a myriad of special considerations. Of course, that transport couldn't begin until their Italian counterparts signed off on the exchange.

Menefee soon heaved his giant frame out of the too-small chair and brushed crumbs off his shirt from a plate of biscuits he had enjoyed earlier.

"Elisabeth, are you flying out from Cairo?"

She smiled up at him. "That's my plan."

"Wonderful. Stop by the Institute before you go."

With that, Menefee hauled himself out of the café. He was sweating profusely long before he made it to the lobby door.

Elisabeth watched him go, then turned to regard Sheply, who had moved over to the window chair. He took off his preposterous hat and placed it flat on the table.

"Well, should we catch up?" he asked, a lilt in his voice.

Despite his caustic words earlier, he really seemed pleased to see her. He was all smiles. Or maybe he was just happy to see a familiar face. She suspected he didn't have many close friends in Alexandria—just colleagues, acquaintances. Sheply wasn't the type of man to make friends easily.

Besides, she'd come all this way for exactly this reason. Brighton's last message to her had been cryptic and brief: Sheply had tracked him down in southern England—and would have caught him if Brighton hadn't acted quickly. Something about jumping from a window… knowing Brighton, the details might have been exaggerated.

"Too bad your visit to England didn't happen under better circumstances," she said carefully.

Had his mother really suffered a stroke, or had that merely been an excuse to escape Alexandria for a few days? Or maybe Sheply's real employer had taken some part in it. Elisabeth shuddered to think what a man like Raff Lagati might do to an innocent like Sheply's mother to motivate him to do his bidding. All she knew about Lagati was secondhand, but every bit of it terrified her.

"Indeed," Sheply remarked. "But is there a good time for one's mother to have a stroke?"

She considered trying to get Sheply to admit that his mother's illness had only been a pretense for his trip to England, but doing so would only expose her alliance with Brighton—and that was one thing Sheply *couldn't* know.

Sheply reached out his right hand and placed it atop hers. He made it appear casual. "But to tell you the truth, I feel energized. Everything is coming together now."

"I only wish Emery was here to see it." She caught herself. "I hope he gets to see it one day, if he's ever allowed to return to Egypt."

A look of annoyance flickered on his face, but he masked it quickly. "Emery never cared about the library project. All he cared about was his ridiculous ideas. Giants in ancient Egypt? God-like creatures? Human-animal hybrids? The man lost his mind. The supposed proofs he clung to are self-evidently mythological."

"His research was more thorough than you give him credit for."

"Far be it from me to speak ill of the departed—"

She caught her breath. Did he know?

"—but if he ever comes back, he'll never work again. Not as an archaeologist, anyway. After what he did, he'll spend what's left of his life in a jail." Sheply withdrew his hand. "But he won't come back. I wouldn't."

Elisabeth pushed back her chair and stood. "Emery Wörtlich is many things, but a crackpot is not one of them."

Sheply tossed her a lopsided grin. "I think we may be quibbling over the definition of 'crackpot.'"

She dropped a few coins on the table and made her way to the exit. She sped through the lobby and emerged outside, the heat of the afternoon hitting her square in the face.

Before she reached the sidewalk, Sheply appeared beside her, keeping pace.

"Don't be angry at me for speaking the truth," he said.

She laughed. "Oh, I'm not angry. And for the record, you don't know what you're talking about."

"Easy, now." He tried to take her by the arm, but she swatted him away. "Don't you think all this tension between us means something?"

She regarded him with amusement. "Sure. It means you're an idiot."

"Perhaps so," he said. "But Emery isn't much better."

"Oh, I think he is."

"He had a chance to be with you and he threw it away. Doesn't sound so smart to me."

She felt a pang in her chest. The words stung, but Emery *had* changed his mind. At the end, he'd been a changed man. That letter he'd written, his last words to her…

"What happened at the end of your year together?" Sheply asked. "I've always wanted to know. The two of you gallivanted from one corner of the country to another. A night in Luxor, the next in Sinai, then Edfu, then back to Cairo. All that time together, and you expect me to believe nothing happened?"

"I never said nothing happened."

They stopped at a crosswalk and waited for cars to whiz by. Even once it was safe to pass, they were careful; drivers often disregarded signals.

"So, you were sleeping together," Sheply said.

She was glad for her sunglasses; they helped contain her mounting fury. "Is this your idea of seducing me? Dredging up painful memories of the man I love?"

"So, you were *more* than sleeping together. You loved him."

I always will, she admitted to herself. But her feelings for Emery were none of Sheply's business. Though that would never stop him from prying.

"Emery and I were doing research that year," she told him flatly. "And yes, there was a little more to it than that, but that's not news. Our affair was, at best, the worst kept secret at the Institute. Everyone knew about it."

"Except Catherine Wörtlich."

She sighed. "She found out eventually."

"At which point it was over." Sheply tipped his fedora to protect his eyes from the sun. "But I don't think that's the whole story."

"Why on earth do you even care?"

"Because I think we have undeniable chemistry, you and I." He pulled her to a rest next to him. "And there's another reason."

"And that is?"

Sheply looked behind him, a conspiratorial look on his face. "When Emery returned to Cairo after that year abroad, he was more determined than ever to finish the paper he was working on. It took him a few years, but we all eventually found out what kind of insanity he had taken to believing."

Elisabeth almost protested, but he raised a finger and placed it against her lips. She startled back but allowed him to continue.

"The timing is suspect," Sheply said. "Something must have happened to tip him over the edge, and I'm dying to know what it was."

A beep sounded from the general direction of his white pants. Sheply pulled out a cell phone, threw her an insincere smile, and walked a few paces away. He spoke into the phone while using his free hand to cover his other ear from the street noise.

Elisabeth could have walked away at that point—probably should have—but she didn't. She had told Brighton she would try to learn anything she could that might help them.

Brighton hadn't told her the specifics of what had happened in England, not over email, but he'd alluded to something big, a mission-altering event. Something had taken place at Stonehenge before his confrontation with Sheply. Whatever it was, it had caused Brighton to go off the grid for a couple of days only to resurface in New York.

He should have told me more, she thought. *How can I mine information from Sheply when I don't know what's going on?*

It felt more like Sheply was mining her than the other way around. After all these years, why was Sheply suddenly so interested in her year with Emery? The things they had uncovered were well-documented; Emery had written exhaustively on his findings, to the detriment of his career. What did Sheply hope to learn?

She felt a hand on her shoulder and looked up to find Sheply standing next to her again. He still held the phone in his hand.

"Who was that?" she asked.

"Nobody important." He shrugged. "Well, nobody you know, anyway."

He tried to look nonchalant, but whatever news he had just received, it had disturbed him.

"As much as I've enjoyed our little chat, I'm afraid I have to get going," he said. "There's been a development."

"What kind of development? Is it serious?"

Sheply tipped his fedora again. His false sincerity was back in full force. "A pleasure, Elisabeth. I can't tell you how much I've enjoyed this."

He flashed a smile and jogged away.

And I can't tell you how relieved I am to see you go.

THIRTEEN

La Paz, Bolivia
JULY 19

Dario couldn't believe the dark-haired boy was a day over four-teen. His scrawny build could barely fill out the dress shirt tucked into pants that were at least three inches too long. His big brown eyes stared over Dario's shoulder into the hotel room.

Nothing to see here, Dario wanted to say, fishing into his pocket for a handful of bolivianos. He thrust the wad of bills into the boy's hands, hoping it was about the right amount; he still didn't fully grasp the exchange rate. The boy took the money without blinking. Given the speed with which he took off down the hotel corridor, it had probably been far too much.

Dario shut the door and looked at the tray of food resting on the edge of the bed. An empty glass was downturned next to a bottle of water, and alongside it a plate with two large humitas, their golden brown color shining like gristle. The wheel of soft white cheese made his stomach lurch. It was quesa fresco, and Rhea had introduced him to it just two weeks ago. She had gone to some length to have it imported to camp, where the food tended to be bland and unremarkable. They had decided to make wine and quesa a Saturday ritual, though they'd only gotten to partake on two occasions.

Somewhere overhead he heard the roar of a plane taking off. With the airport right next door, the sound recurred once every ten to fifteen minutes.

He put the quesa aside and took a few bites of humitas—soft and sweet. It was prepared better than he'd had before, but he was in no state of mind to enjoy it.

He sat on the bed, staring at the wall. He wasn't sure for how long, exactly, except that by the time he remembered where he was and what he was doing, the constant buzzing of airplanes had slowed considerably. Taking his shirt off, he got under the covers and lay on his back, eyes open, breathing steady… awake as all hell.

When his eyes did eventually slip shut, he was so tired that he didn't notice.

"Run!"

Rhea ran through darkness, her blond hair pulled back in a ponytail that whipped from one shoulder to the other, the beam of her flashlight bouncing off the stone walls. He knew instinctively that if he stopped, if he tripped and fell, he and Rhea would be dead.

The tunnel went on forever. Smooth walls passed in a blur, the faces carved into them laughing, their stony jowls shaking in hilarity. The sound was rich and deep, and no matter how fast or how far they ran, it was always in his ears, coming from every direction at once.

He bolted awake amid clammy sheets. He'd had the same nightmare the night before, and probably would have it every night for the rest of his life.

I have to get out of here, he thought as he looked toward the window where La Paz's lights shone back at him. Somewhere out there a siren wailed. If he closed his eyes, that wail sounded uncannily like laughter…

"Let him go."

This time it was Marco, standing outside Dario's tent. Dario hurriedly packed his bags. Recklessly. There was so much to take with him. Clothes. Books. Tools. By the time he got to the bottom of one pile of folded shirts and work pants, another pile appeared behind it, and another one after that. He kept stuffing clothes into the bag. There was always room for more.

"Stay," Perez's voice drifted toward him. "We need you."

"No. He failed us," Marco said, his voice deep and gruff and angry.

Dario refused to look at them; he put all his energy into packing. Another shirt. Another pair of pants. There was room for a book or two; he stuffed them in. A hammer. A flashlight. In they went. In everything went.

"The boy's dead. Jorge's dead."

"Yasmine. Dead."

"Rhea. You killed her."

"Christophe. You left him behind."

The accusations came at him in a rush, so quickly he couldn't distinguish between the voices. They were right, all of them. He had tried to save two lives and instead given up four. Their blood was on his hands.

"It wasn't your fault," Rhea said, reclining on the bed behind the piles of clothes. She was bleeding, and he lunged for her. He knew she'd be dead before he reached her, and the piles of clothes only grew higher, towers rising in front of him like bread in an oven.

Soon, he couldn't see her at all. There was too much in the way.

It's not your fault.

Of course it was.

Marco was next to him, that damned rifle slung over his shoulder. He longed for Marco to point it at him, to nestle its long cool barrel into the moist recesses of his mouth and mercifully blow his brains out.

"You could have stopped it," the Bolivian man whispered into his ear.

I know.

"Why didn't you stop it?"

I don't know.

"Didn't you love her?"

I might have.

Hadn't he, though? Hadn't he felt something deeper than friendship? How many wheels of quesa, how many bottles of wine would it have taken to drag it out of him? Two more weeks' worth? Maybe three?

"You."

The sound of *that* voice made him freeze. But only for a moment. Ignoring his packing duties, he turned and fled through the camp, following Rhea's instructions in his ear—*run run run run*—and not looking back.

"You."

People dove out of his way, didn't try to stop him, couldn't have stopped him if they tried.

Yasmine's face, that insidious smile, those dead eyes…

Too late, he realized he was running in the wrong direction. He was back in the tunnels, barreling toward the metallic barrier.

"Stay away," Rhea said, running beside him. She hardly broke a sweat. "It's dangerous. Just go. Run."

He tried to stop, but his feet had lives of their own. Possessed.

They skidded across loose stone. His toes crashed into strewn rocks and burned in pain, unimaginable pain. Toe broken, will broken, heart broken—

The barrier grew closer, closer, ever closer.

"You. I know you."

Tears streamed down his face—not sadness, but terror. Unrelenting hysteria.

"Don't go in. Run! Run!"

No, don't make me. Don't make me go in there. I can't do this, I can't live through it again. Not again.

The barrier gleamed. It shone. It beckoned.

"Come to me," said the voice. Not Yasmine's, but another's. Cold, calculating, and very, very old. Older than time.

His heart beat so fast he thought for sure he couldn't take the strain, that it would give out, that it would burst from his chest and vault to the ground, blood spurting from its ventricles like fountains. The muscle continued to beat, flexing and contracting, but slower, then slower still, each spray of blood weaker than the one before until it stopped completely, growing cold, dead. Dead. And not alone, for there were other hearts nearby, ripped and tattered as though an animal had gotten to them.

He wanted so desperately to stop watching, to look away, to close his eyes forever and never open them again, but they were wide and dry and unable to blink.

"You can't escape."

And then laughter, terrible peals of laughter all around him, inside him, pounding through his skull, and reverberating in his ears.

Dario lurched awake. He sat up and gasped for breath, grabbing his chest as pain arced through him. His heart galloped against his ribcage, the blankets and pillows twisted into sweaty tangles.

He forced himself to stay awake by turning on the TV, but he grew frustrated by his inability to follow the Spanish. He tried reading, but nothing held his interest.

At last the first rays of daylight lit the sky outside his window. He showered, dressed, and gathered his bags. Even though his flight didn't leave for another five hours, he couldn't spend another minute in this hotel room.

The taxi ride was short, and soon he was waiting at the front of a nonexistent queue at the airline's ticketing station. A few minutes after six, a woman appeared behind the computer and beckoned him forward. She confirmed the flight and printed off a couple of boarding passes.

Dario headed for the security checkpoint, looking over his itinerary. He had connections in Miami and London. He wouldn't be back in Italy until the following morning, but at least he would be half a world away from this place.

He located his gate and waited in a blue chair next to a window overlooking the runways. The departures lounge slowly filled up. Men in business suits soon surrounded him, nobody giving him a second glance. Just the way he liked it.

He knew they were close to boarding when the woman behind the boarding station began calling the names of specific passengers. He stuck his hand in his pocket, feeling for his passport; it was right where he'd left it.

Time to go.

"Passenger Katsulas," the attendant called.

He looked up, wide-eyed. Tentatively he stood and walked toward the counter.

"Passenger Katsulas?" the woman asked again in accented English.

"That's me."

"Security would like to have a word with you."

He gripped the edge of the counter. "No, no, no ... " He looked up and saw two security guards standing nearby, waiting.

His throat caught. Between them was the last man he wanted to see.

Doctor Christophe looked like a new man compared to the last time Dario had seen him. His dark hair was combed to the side and his face clean-shaven. His eyes were thoughtful and attentive. Rational. They showed no trace of whatever spell had gripped him down in the caverns.

This wasn't the same man.

Dario backed away, feeling lightheaded, but the security guards were soon at his side, taking him by the elbows.

"Mr. Katsulas, please come with us," the guard said, gripping tighter.

Dario struggled against the guards' hold. "What do you want?"

"Dario, don't make a scene," Christophe said. "Just come with us."

"Who are you?" Dario asked.

Christophe balked. "Who am I? Don't be ridiculous."

"The last time I saw you ... " He shook his head. "No. Whoever you are, you're not Wallis Christophe. You're *her*."

Christophe shifted his weight from one foot to the other. "Please, Dario, not here. Not in front of all these people."

Indeed, all eyes were on them. Onlookers stepped back, giving them a wide berth. No doubt they were gauging whether Dario posed a terrorist threat. Without saying a word, the guards led him and Christophe down the long terminal.

Dario's mind went through all his options, grimacing as each one brought him to a hopeless end. He could make a run for the gate, but he wouldn't be allowed to board. He could try to escape into the city, but he was currently in a secure area.

He was taken into a small interview room and pushed into a red plastic chair. The guards stepped out into the hall while Christophe took a seat across from him.

"First of all, I'm not *her*, as you crudely put it," Christophe said. "The god doesn't have gender, but it's easiest to call it male. And his name is Ohia."

Dario folded his arms. "Why should I believe anything you say?"

"Because what happened was a terrible tragedy, but it wasn't your fault. The god needed a body."

Dario felt his eyes getting wet, but he steeled his jaw. He refused to show emotion in front of this man. "If it wasn't my fault, it was yours. Rhea wanted to leave the caves, but you wouldn't go."

"Of course not!" Christophe leaned forward, his palms flat against the steel table. "Ohia is a god!"

"Not mine."

"He doesn't require worship. Not mine, not yours. But I offer mine freely."

"Then you're a fool."

Christophe let out a long sigh. "That's because you wouldn't listen to what he had to say."

"He killed Rhea. Forgive me if I didn't stick around long enough for an explanation."

"And you say I'm a fool!"

Dario clenched his fists together. "Yes, that's what I say. This being... this *creature*..."

"This god," Christophe finished. "He has knowledge of history unlike anything I've ever encountered. His accounts explain the archaeological evidence in Tiahuanaco. All of it. We could have spent another ten years digging up those ruins and come nowhere near to understanding the culture. Ohia changes everything. You must see that."

"I see that he's a murderer."

"He had to find a way to communicate with us."

"He could have found someone else!"

Christophe raised an eyebrow. "Oh? Would you have been happier if it had been me? Or Marco?"

There was no reasoning with the man. "Fine. Even if everything you say is true, what do you need with me?"

"Word of Ohia cannot leave the camp," Christophe said. "At least, not yet. It's not the right time."

"You're organizing a cover-up."

"Not a cover-up. Ohia wants nothing more than to reveal himself to the world, but first we have much work to do at Tiahuanaco."

Dario stood up and turned away, blinking back tears. His nightmare from the night before was still fresh in his mind, the terror of what he'd witnessed, the warning Rhea had given him... and which he had ignored. It was too much.

"I'll never go back," he said through clenched teeth.

Christophe didn't answer right away, but when he did his voice was compassionate. "I understand your anxiety. But there's really nothing to be afraid of."

Tell Rhea that, he thought, but he didn't say it. There didn't seem a point.

"I'll ask again," Dario said. "What do you need me for?"

"For all appearances, it must seem as though this never happened, as though life at camp has been proceeding normally."

Dario turned back, pushing the red chair into the table. "Maybe you didn't hear me. I'll never go back there. Never."

"And neither can you stay here. Someone might notice and ask questions."

"How do you know it isn't already too late for that?"

"We know."

The implications of those two words set Dario on edge. How far were they going to contain the situation, and who was in on it? He swallowed those questions.

"Where is 'the god'?" Dario said after a short pause.

Christophe sat back and crossed his legs. "Still in the caverns, of course."

"Why didn't he follow us out?"

"He chooses not to."

Dario almost laughed, but it caught halfway up his throat. "Not much of a god, if you ask me."

"I think it has something to do with that machine," Christophe mused. "Whatever the reason, he believes it best to stay where he is until all the preparations are made."

"What preparations?"

Christophe smiled. "He's going to help us return the city to its former glory."

FOURTEEN

Provo, Utah

JULY 21

Brighton faced a sparsely forested mountain slope where a row of diamond-shaped orange signs warned drivers to turn back before reaching a dead-end. This subdivision was new, half the houses on the street unfinished. The occasional freshly mown lawn stood in sharp contrast to the tall brown grasses that grew on a nearby parcel of land set aside for agricultural purposes. A low picket fence ran the length of the sidewalk, its white slats standing out against evenly spaced saplings held in place by cords to protect their fragile trunks from strong winds.

The house next to him had two stories and its back door exited onto a concrete pool deck. The hollow poles of emerald green patio umbrellas chimed against the metal confines of the tables through which they sprouted.

Suburban living at its finest. A faux-wood-paneled jeep in the driveway completed the picture, its tinted windows reflecting the sun. *Rachel would have hated this; she always told me she dreamed of living in a Manhattan loft. Can't get any farther from Manhattan than Provo.*

He climbed the stone steps and tapped the brass knocker against the red door, a bold color choice if he'd ever seen one. He waited about ten seconds, then knocked again. He heard footsteps pounding down a staircase and readied himself for the door to swing open.

It didn't.

Sighing, he looked into the peephole in the door. No doubt there was an eye on the other side of that lens right now, scoping him out, making sure he wasn't a salesman or a Jehovah's Witness.

Or something much more sinister.

He reached his hand to knock again, but before his fingers brushed the handle, the door opened—just a crack. A girl of five or six with blond hair stared out at him, her eyes squinted in suspicion.

Brighton cocked his head. "I'm Mr. Smith. Who are you?"

The girl opened the door the rest of the way. "I'm supposed to let you in."

Brighton stepped inside, put down his newly acquired suitcase— mostly empty though it was—and studied his surroundings. The hardwood floors gleamed, either from being freshly polished or recently installed. There wasn't much furniture in sight and the only decoration, apart from the five-candled light fixture swinging down from the tall ceiling, was a mirror on the wall next to the staircase landing.

He studied his reflection, no longer surprised by how disheveled he appeared. The bags under his eyes had grown larger in the past week, and the remnants of bruising still remained on his forehead. Sweat stains marked the armpits of his blue polo shirt; he could smell them as well. He needed a shower and change of clothes.

When he looked back, the girl was gone, having padded off some-place, her socks whispering silently across the smooth floors.

Deciding to explore, he turned left and walked into the living room—or at least, that's what it would be in time. For now, a stack of unopened boxes waited next to the stone fireplace. A downturned couch, covered in a mover's tarp, waited beneath a large bay window. The only ready-to-use piece of furniture was a brown-upholstered armchair missing its seat cushion and an accompanying ottoman still covered in plastic.

Beyond the living room, toward the back of the house, the kitchen awaited. Dirty dishes were piled neatly in the sink and a frying pan rested on the front burner of a stainless steel stove.

Brighton approached the sink and washed his hands under the cold water. He then looked up and studied the pool deck through the window. The unpacked kitchen and furnished pool deck spoke volumes about the homeowner's priorities.

"I see Daphne told you to make yourself at home, hmm?"

He turned to face Elisabeth Macfarlane, her hair wet and dripping onto the shoulders of a light blue bathrobe. She held a tube of toothpaste in one hand, the other tangled in her hair.

"Well, not exactly. I presumed that part."

"She's shy around strangers." Elisabeth put the toothpaste down on the countertop. "My sister will be by to pick her up later, so you won't have to worry."

Brighton lifted himself onto the counter, his legs dangling against the cupboard doors. "She seems sweet. But if I'd known she was stay-ing with you, I would have come later. My presence here could put you in danger, and everyone who sees me, Daphne included."

"You're being paranoid."

"Am I? I refuse to underestimate Lagati."

She moved to the fridge and pulled out a carton of orange juice. She plucked up a glass from the edge of the sink and filled it halfway.

"Speaking of," she said, "I met Sheply in Egypt."

Brighton spotted Daphne standing in the doorway to the living room. He silenced Elisabeth with a look, then changed the subject to something more innocuous.

"I love the new place," he said. "Must have cost a small fortune."

Elisabeth waved the girl inside. "Daphne, are you thirsty?"

Daphne came the rest of the way into the kitchen, hugging the far wall to avoid proximity with Brighton. Her reaction to him made him feel like a monster.

Elisabeth poured her a glass of juice, then opened the back door and let her into the yard. Brighton watched through the window as the girl sat by the edge of the pool and dipped her toes into the water.

"What was I saying?" he mused. "Oh yes, a small fortune."

Elisabeth remained near the sliding door, keeping an eye on her niece. "You know I don't like to talk about money."

That much was true, even though he had tried to broach the subject on more than one occasion. People with money so rarely wanted to talk about how they had accumulated it.

In any event, Elisabeth's money had probably saved his life. He could never have afforded his recent travels on his own dime.

"I can't thank you enough," he said. Never had five words felt so insufficient. Would ten words have been enough? Twenty? A hundred?

"I do it for myself as much as for you." Elisabeth walked into the living room and sat on the plastic-covered ottoman. "Sit down?"

He approached the armchair and stared down at the flat wooden braces where the cushion should have been.

"I get the impression you don't entertain a lot of guests," he said with a smile on his face.

"Indeed, the floor might be more comfortable."

"This hardwood? Not likely."

He lowered himself awkwardly into the chair. Without the cushion, he sat too low for his elbows to comfortably reach the armrests.

"How long have you been moved in?" he asked.

"Almost a week. Don't judge." She crossed her legs. "So, I met with Sheply, but before I can evaluate what's important and what's not, I need you to tell me what happened in England."

Brighton looked away to gather his thoughts. He didn't understand it himself. Even after four days, he had a hard time summarizing the trip.

"The last time we spoke, I was in Spain," Brighton said.

"Right. Barcelona."

"I came up empty. There were a lot of old churches, dusty crypts, that sort of thing. Same story all over Europe, but nothing of the age we're looking for." Brighton brought his finger up and ran it along his parched lips. "I could use a drink."

Elisabeth lifted herself from the ottoman and returned to the kitchen. "Water, juice, or something a little harder?"

He paused, censoring himself. It was barely three o'clock. Did she know something about his recent drinking?

"Water's fine."

She brought him a glass of water and he gulped it down. Lukewarm but refreshing.

"You have a bruise," she said, gesturing above her own right eye.

Brighton instinctively felt the spot. The swelling had gone down so much in the last few days he'd almost forgotten it was there.

"Believe it or not, I got into a fight."

"A fight?"

He grimaced. "A bar fight. You don't want the details. They're perfectly mundane."

"Still, it worries me that you may not be keeping a low profile, as we discussed."

"It's nothing like that."

"Well, I *am* worried," Elisabeth said. "You're out of contact for long periods of time, leaving me little recourse but to follow the receipts you leave in your wake. You're getting into altercations. And frankly, on this last trip, you came dangerously close to being captured." She met his eyes and held them in her gaze. "And what was in Syracuse?"

"Let me start with Stonehenge." Brighton waited for a moment, putting words together silently. Elisabeth prompted him with impatient eyes, but there was no way to rush this. "I visited Stonehenge more than once and found nothing. After all the hype, I stood around with reams of tourists, avoiding people's cameras, trampling the grass in wide arcs, looking at the stones from every angle… and everything was perfectly ordinary. I mean, yes, the stones themselves are mysterious. They're very large, and based on the dates and the history I read, they must have been constructed by the same giants and supernatural beings responsible for the pyramids."

He stumbled briefly over the word *supernatural*. He hated thinking it, never mind saying it aloud. But what other alternative was there? Angels? Demons? Those terms were even worse.

"But you didn't find any evidence?" Elisabeth asked.

He tapped his foot against the hardwood. He found the slow rhythm relaxing, reminding him how badly he needed a rest and a shower.

"I wouldn't exactly say that," he replied. "On the last night I was there, I went back. I knew the site would be guarded, so I didn't get too close. I sat on the side of the grassy slope and just… I don't know, I just looked at it."

"And that's when you had your… experience?" she prompted. "Your email was pretty vague."

"I fell asleep. It must have been three o'clock, maybe four in the morning. I couldn't have slept long, because when I opened my eyes, the sun was coming up. Except—and this is the part I can't sort out— I wasn't on the slope anymore. I was *inside* Stonehenge, in the inner ring of stones, flat on my back. It took me a few minutes to realize where I was and what was happening…" He snorted. "No, I take that back. I *still* don't know what happened.

"Now, this is the strangest part." He saw her raise her eyebrow at that, but he pressed on. "I felt like someone was with me, but there was no one there. At least, no one I could see. I can't even say for sure *how* I sensed this presence, and Elisabeth, that presence… it was familiar."

That was as far as he was willing to go. He wouldn't tell her he had dreamed an encounter with Wörtlich. She had been in love with the man, and Brighton didn't want to go there.

"When you say 'a presence,' do you mean a ghost? A spirit?" she asked.

More words he wasn't comfortable with.

"Maybe," Brighton said. "It reminded me of the dreams I had when I was with Wörtlich and Ira."

She leaned forward. "It's called dreamcasting. I've been looking into it. Apparently some people have discovered a way to share dreams with others, to meet them in a mutual dream space."

"Well, it wasn't quite like that," Brighton said. "It was more like we were sharing each other's *consciousness*, as though I could sense the others' thoughts and share their memories."

Elisabeth's eyes gleamed at the mention of that. "To have been inside Emery's mind, even if incompletely, and only for a short time—"

She broke off and blinked. Brighton wondered if she had been on the edge of tears.

"Give me a minute," she said. "I want to check on Daphne."

Daphne was fine, it turned out, wading in the shallow end of the pool. Elisabeth walked slowly back into the room and resumed her place on the ottoman.

"Sherwood," she said thoughtfully. "Do you believe in ghosts?"

Two years ago, he would have unequivocally said no. Now? Those visions he'd shared with Wörtlich and Ira, they hadn't *just* been visions. They had been memories of a living person. Someone named Barakel. Someone who had lived thousands of years ago. How could those memories have survived on their own if the spirit of Barakel didn't also exist someplace, perhaps following them, haunting them?

"Sherwood?"

He glanced up, unaware of how much time had passed. "Sorry. I was thinking. I wish my answer was no, but I think it might be yes."

She nodded. "It's hard to accept, but when we die, I think some of us stay behind. We don't move on, at least not right away. Maybe it's because we have unfinished business. Who can say?" She stood up, anxiously rubbing her neck. "Excuse me. I should be keeping a better eye on my niece."

They both returned to the kitchen. Brighton placed his empty glass by the sink as Elisabeth stood by the screen door, watching Daphne, who now stretched out on a patch of grass next to the water, her eyes closed as she soaked in the sun.

Elisabeth opened the door and poked her head out. "Come inside!" she called. "You're going to get sunburn if you stay out too long."

The girl jumped up and ran to the house.

"Go upstairs and make sure your things are ready," Elisabeth told her. "Your mother will be here soon."

Daphne fled the room, her footsteps racing up the stairs.

"So, when did Sheply come into the picture?" Elisabeth asked once the room was quiet again. "And why did you run?"

"After I woke up, I found the bodies of two guards on the ground near me. I checked on them to make sure they weren't badly hurt, but tourists were already showing up. Some of them took pictures." Brighton's heart raced just thinking about that trauma. "I took off before the authorities could connect me to the crime."

Elisabeth stared at him, incredulous. "What happened to the guards?"

"I have no idea, but Sheply was waiting for me when I got to the hotel. He had broken into my room and searched my luggage."

"Do you think he had something to do with what happened at Stonehenge?"

Brighton was loath to believe in coincidences, so he wanted to believe Sheply was somehow responsible. But even if Sheply had somehow found him sleeping, drugged him, and dragged him into the circles, could he also have overcome both guards? Sheply was neither a large man nor particularly strong. And what would have been the goal of it? Why would Sheply have wanted him to wake up amongst the stones?

It's not possible. Plus, how could Sheply have orchestrated that familiar presence?

"That's when you jumped out the window," Elisabeth said.

"That's right."

Elisabeth let out a low whistle. "I'm not sure I could have done that."

Brighton sighed and walked to his luggage in the foyer. "I'd like to clean myself up and get some sleep."

"Of course!" she said, following him. "I should have let you do that right away instead of drawing you into a long conversation. We can talk shop later. Head upstairs and put your stuff in the first bedroom on the right. There's an adjoining bathroom."

He picked up his suitcase and started up the stairs, already anticipating the feel of hot water washing over him.

"I could be a while," he warned her, pausing on the landing.

"From everything you've said, you've earned some downtime."

He was almost out of view from the foyer when she moved to the
bottom step and called his name again.

"Sherwood, one more thing."

"Yes?"

"In Alexandria, Sheply got called away," Elisabeth said. "He took a
phone call, then had to leave. I think it was something important. Perhaps something that involves this whole mess we're in the middle of."

"You think it was Lagati, don't you?"

She let out a long breath. "Yeah. I mean, maybe." She turned
away, waving him off. "Sorry, I shouldn't have brought it up before
you got some sleep. We'll talk later."

He hefted his luggage. As far as he was concerned, they'd talked
enough for one day.

FIFTEEN

Provo, Utah
JULY 21

The top floor of Gayle Voss's home was surrounded in glass and filled with telescopes. A spiral staircase corkscrewed up the center of the house and ended here, in the observatory. Elisabeth looked about in fascination. Her friend Gayle, dressed in a yellow cloak which complemented her long and straight blond hair, followed Elisabeth up the stairs and immediately walked toward a shiny black telescope aimed at the eastern sky.

Gayle usually didn't bring guests to the observatory when her husband wasn't home, but after hearing Elisabeth's story she had deemed this a special occasion. The view was enchanting. City lights spread out to the north and west, and to the east an ocean of stars peeked out from behind the highest ridges. The sky wasn't quite clear;

thin wisps of cloud passed over the stars, never enough to blot them out but enough to make them sparkle and dance.

"You're sure Henry doesn't mind us being up here?" Elisabeth asked.

Gayle pressed her eyes tight against the telescope's side-mounted eyepiece, twisting the focus knob. At last, she stepped back, satisfied. "It's ready. Have a look."

Elisabeth brushed back her hair and leaned over the eyepiece. Stars covered the view from one side to the other, more stars than could be seen with the naked eye.

"Do you see it?" Gayle asked.

Elisabeth scanned the view, frowning. "I'm not sure what I'm looking at."

"The star in the middle, the really bright one."

"Yes."

"That's Saturn."

"And why am I looking at it?"

She felt Gayle move to the next telescope in the row. "Because it's very active. Do you see the fluctuations coming from it?"

"It's twinkling, if that's what you mean."

"Yes, exactly. It's more than an atmospheric effect. While Saturn does sometimes have storms that cause minor flickering, it doesn't usually do it so strongly."

Elisabeth pulled her face away. "So it's flickering more than usual. Does that mean something?"

"Oh yes," Gayle said, pulling focus on the next telescope. "I'm sensing an incredible amount of energy from that sector of the sky, and I'm not the only one. I've been getting messages from a dozen other sensitives like me. There's definitely something going on. Something cosmic."

"What does that even mean?"

Gayle looked away from the telescope, a lopsided grin on her face. "My dear Elisabeth, so skeptical."

Elisabeth shrugged. "I can't help it. I'm sorry. You know I don't understand this world of yours."

"It's not a special 'world,' Elisabeth. We all share the same one." Gayle walked toward a couch facing the eastern window. "But what I'm picking up, it's big. Like someone suddenly pointed a fan right at my face and turned it on the highest setting. As for what it means, well… in fairness, this is new to me. Normally I detect node energy from the earth. Without a doubt, something's going on out there in the solar system. Something extraordinary. Unprecedented."

"Does this have to do with those ley lines you talk about?" Elisabeth asked.

Gayle had explained the concept of ley lines many times, channels of energy crisscrossing the planet's surface and intersecting at certain nodes. Except ley lines weren't fixed and often fluctuated in relation to movement of the magnetic poles.

Elisabeth had always treated this with natural skepticism, which Gayle took in good humor.

Gayle's eyes brightened. "Yes! Very perceptive. Saturn's energy is being absorbed by the earth, drawn to the nodes at ley line intersections. And I have a guess why it's started up now. The Starseed people may be stirring."

"Starseed people? You mean aliens?"

"Please, sit down. You're making me nervous." Gayle put her legs up on the coffee table and stretched out. "My network is reporting all kinds of activity. It's interfering big-time with radio signals all over the southwest. You might have noticed some disruptions these last few days."

Instead of sitting, Elisabeth wandered along the line of telescopes, admiring them. "My car radio was cutting in and out yesterday. I figured it was my antenna."

"I doubt it." Gayle stood to follow. "When Henry comes home, you'll see what I'm talking about. All the extra energy is wreaking havoc on him. His hair has gotten two shades grayer since the beginning of the week. And you should see his eyes!"

Henry self-identified as a channeler. This wasn't quite the same thing as a medium, Elisabeth had come to learn. Henry's specialty was to harness spiritual energies. Elisabeth didn't put much stock in all this mysticism.

"What's wrong with his eyes?" Elisabeth asked.

Gayle chuckled. "How come you know so little? We really should spend more time together. Anyway, his eyes have changed color. Usually they're brown, but I swear they've gone blue."

Elisabeth found it hard to concentrate when Gayle started talking this way. Her attention swung to a row of four paintings on the wall between the eastern and western observation areas, one for each season of the year. They all depicted the same meadow under a star-studded sky, with a young woman sitting on the ground, her expectant eyes upturned.

"What do you think is causing the energy?" Elisabeth asked. "These Starseed people you mentioned?"

"You'll think I'm crazy, but yes."

Elisabeth smiled at her friend. Gayle had always been a little crazy. Her free and uninhibited spirit was one of the qualities that had drawn them together. Gayle's only real fault was that she had the tendency to be a little too open-minded; as far as faults went, Elisabeth counted it a rather good one.

"Only a little crazy," Elisabeth agreed. "Have you heard of the Drake equation?"

"No."

"It just means there's probably a lot of life in the universe. So you could be right about aliens."

Gayle nodded vigorously. "Oh, I'm right about them. And they've been to Earth. You know who built the pyramids, right?"

Elisabeth finally completed her circuit of the room, bypassing the two telescopes pointing west. The city lights were much brighter from this vantage.

She sat in the spot Gayle had vacated on the couch. "I think I have a vague idea."

And it wasn't aliens, she told herself.

Emery had flirted with the idea of alien pyramid builders for a while. During the year they'd spent together in Egypt, they had encountered all kinds of evidence suggesting alien origins. Especially at the Edfu Temple. Only after a lot of consideration had Emery discarded the theory, focusing instead on more terrestrial possibilities.

"The story you told me about your friend," Gayle said. "You said he was at Machu Picchu?"

"That's right."

Stonehenge, actually. The only way Elisabeth had been able to share Brighton's story was to change a few details.

"I've always suspected alien involvement there," Gayle said.

As much as Elisabeth wished she could write off Gayle's out-of-this-world notions, she couldn't. Perhaps there was something to it.

Elisabeth shifted to make room for Gayle on the couch.

"You said that he felt something," Gayle continued, sitting again. "A presence, or something close to it. You think it might have been a spirit?"

"He wasn't sure what it was. Only that it was familiar."

"A spirit, then."

Gayle was distracted for a moment by the sound of a door opening downstairs. It was probably Henry coming home.

"Does your friend know anyone who has passed away recently?" Gayle asked, returning her attention to Elisabeth. "A friend? A family member? Siblings, especially those a person is close with, often linger after the point of physical death."

Emery.

The thought struck like lightning, stunning her.

"It could be anyone he was close with, really," Gayle said. "The truth is, ghosts don't usually haunt the living without good reason, and it needn't be malevolent. Horror stories have trained us to fear spirits, but most of the time they're friendly, here to pass on a message, to finish something they started. Hauntings, in the negative sense, are very rare. I've only heard of a couple of real-world examples... Elisabeth?"

Elisabeth was only half-listening, so preoccupied had she become with this new possible identity of Brighton's mystery spirit.

Could it be? she asked herself. If Gayle was right, and such a spirit had attached itself to Brighton—

"Elisabeth? You look pale."

She brought her head up. "Your words got me thinking, that's all."

The sound of footsteps on the stairs prompted both women to crane their necks. Henry, a slim man in an argyle sweater, appeared at the top landing, resting his hand on the railing. His hair really *was* several shades grayer than Elisabeth remembered; when she'd last seen him a few months ago, his hair had been mostly chestnut brown, with only slight streaks of gray.

If that's the direct result of this energy from space, maybe Gayle really is on to something.

"Evening, ladies," Henry said. He walked slowly, dragging his feet as though he'd had a long day.

Gayle stood to make room for him on the couch, then came

around the back and began massaging her husband's neck.

"Still feeling the effects?" Gayle asked.

Henry let out a long groan. "I constantly feel the need to lie down. I've never felt this drained." He peeked an eye open. "Have you told her?"

Gayle nodded. "About the energy? It's all we've talked about."

Elisabeth started when Henry turned his eyes to her. His eyes were light blue, and they practically glowed.

"I told you," Gayle said. "His eyes have changed."

"Is there no way for you to shut it out?" Elisabeth asked.

Henry stiffened as Gayle's hands probed an especially sore point behind his left shoulder. "There are techniques, but I've never been so inundated before. It's all I can do just to think straight. If I let down my barriers, I'm afraid it would be akin to dropping a toaster in a bathtub."

Elisabeth rose. "I should leave you two alone."

"Oh, don't be in a hurry," Henry said. "I'll rest downstairs. You can keep visiting."

"That's alright," Elisabeth said. "It's late and I should be getting home. Besides, I want to share what Gayle said with my friend."

Gayle frowned at her. "That's not a bad idea, but perhaps I should consult with you both. If you're going to try contacting the spirit, there could be dangers. Consequences you're not aware of."

"What kind of consequences?"

"Well, for one thing, it might not be a friendly spirit. I know I said the other kind is rare, but they're not unheard of." Gayle hesitated, biting her lip. "And there's another possibility."

"I don't know about this," Elisabeth said.

"Listen, just promise me one thing," Gayle said. "Before you do anything, come back to see me, so we can divine whether your desired course of action is the best one for all involved. We can choose to do anything, but it's our responsibility to choose wisely."

That gave Elisabeth pause. As frivolous as Gayle could be, some-times she came across as positively grounded.

"Promise me, Elisabeth."

Elisabeth nodded, knowing it was a promise she might not be able to keep.

Gayle and Henry saw her out, waiting on the front stoop as Elisabeth slipped behind the steering wheel of her car and pulled away from the curb.

Back at her house, Elisabeth found Brighton stretched across a lounge chair on the back patio, his fingers playing the keys of his laptop like a piano. Three lights lit the deck from the back wall of the house, their faint glimmers reflecting off the calm waters of the swimming pool.

The air was dry, the temperature warm. Perfect for a late-night swim. She slipped back into the house without Brighton noticing, returning a few minutes later having changed into her swimsuit. She sat on the edge of the pool, pulling her hair into a ponytail, then dropped into the water with the barest splash.

She swam five lengths. Once finished, she propped her elbows onto the concrete pad next to the pool, watching Brighton in the dim light.

"Have you made any headway?" she asked.

The young man looked up, his face lit by the screen. "Yes, actually. That call Sheply received while you were in Alexandria? Well, I think you were right about it coming from Lagati."

"Did you hack into his phone records?"

"Essentially, yeah. The signal seems to have come from a satellite phone. From the satellite, it's impossible to track, but who else would be so paranoid?"

Elisabeth waded to the pool stairs and climbed out. She dried herself, then wrapped a towel around her before dragging a patio chair closer to Brighton.

"You want to see?" he asked.

She waved him away. "No, I trust you. I wouldn't be able to make heads or tails of it anyway. But there's something else I wanted to ask you about."

He closed a few computer windows. "Yeah?"

"It has to do with that familiar presence you felt at Stonehenge."

Brighton closed the lid of his laptop and placed it on the deck beside him. "I just read that the second guard died."

"The second guard?"

"At Stonehenge. The other man I supposedly attacked. I'm starting to think whatever the familiar presence was, maybe it was responsible."

Elisabeth narrowed her eyes. "I had a different idea."

"Does this have something to do with the friend you went to see tonight?"

"Don't worry, I didn't tell her anything that could be traced back to you." Elisabeth felt a slight chill and folded her arms across her chest. "I think I know who it was, Sherwood. It was Emery."

Brighton's eyes grazed over the pool, then landed on her.

Elisabeth shivered again. "Do you remember what you told me a few months ago about the hotspots? That they were energetically significant? My friend Gayle calls them nodes, places where ley lines cross. From the research I've done on my own, a lot of the ancient megalithic sites you've visited are built on nodes. The pyramids of Giza, the Antarctic bone field, those coordinates off the coast of Tubuai… and Stonehenge. Probably others. Machu Picchu. The Nazca Lines. Easter Island. Gayle says there are plenty of nodes here in North America, too. A popular one is near Sedona, Arizona. Some people claim these nodes have healing powers which can be harnessed if the energy is channeled."

She paused, gauging whether or not Brighton was taking her seriously or dismissing her crackpot claims; his eyes were stormy, but she thought the effect came from his own uncertainty, not her information.

"Gayle told me the energy in those nodes is stronger now than ever," Elisabeth continued. "Her husband is a channeler and he's suffering extreme physical effects from the strain. Ordinarily I take Gayle's assertions with a grain of salt, but I saw some of those effects for myself. If what she says is true, there could be a lot of power at those sites."

She decided to leave out the part about aliens from Saturn.

"What are you saying?" Brighton finally asked.

"Well, Emery died on a node. Isn't it possible you were able to sense his spirit at another node, given the amplified energy it's being subjected to?"

He rubbed his eyes. "He's dead, Elisabeth. You have to accept that."

She knew there was no verifying it, but the idea felt right. If Emery could somehow come back, he would.

She hadn't been part of Emery's life in his last years, but something in him had changed at the end. She had a letter in her nightstand to prove it. He *did* have unfinished business. With her.

"Gayle might be able to help us contact the spirit," she said.

"No." Brighton's response came fast, definitively. There would be no debate.

Elisabeth wanted to argue, but it might be better to let him sleep on it. "I'm concerned you've stayed too long in one place," she pointed out, changing the subject to safer ground. "Maybe it's time to move before Sheply connects us. The longer you stay, the more likely it is that he'll come calling."

Brighton spared a quick glance for his computer. "Oh, I wouldn't be so sure about that. Unless I miss my guess, Sheply has bigger fish to fry."

*   *   *

"You're not going alone," Elisabeth said.

Brighton reached for a stack of newly purchased t-shirts and placed them inside the suitcase. Elisabeth stood behind him, her hands folded over her chest. If he looked up, he could see her in the bathroom mirror.

"I have to." He tossed in a pair of jeans. "I've been at this a lot longer than you. I know the risks."

"The risks of traveling overseas? You think I haven't gotten on a plane before?"

"The risk of being on the run. And we can't let Sheply see us together."

Sheply's call logs clearly showed that he was in Bolivia, and there was only one archaeological site in that part of the world that made sense for him to visit. Tiahuanaco.

She sat on the edge of the bed. "You forget that I know more about Sheply than you do."

"And we both know that isn't the real reason you want to go."

Elisabeth pressed her lips together. "Do I only get to have *one* reason?"

He rolled up a pair of socks, ignoring her. She was letting her heart get in the way of the mission. Wörtlich was dead, and she needed to accept that he was never coming back.

"Tiahuanaco is a hotspot," she reminded him.

"We don't even know what the hotspots are, except that they exist."

"I already told you. They're nodes, and they're energetically active. Emery tried to contact you at the one in Stonehenge—"

He looked up, silencing her with cold eyes. "Enough about that."

"Oh, so you'll believe in giants and these Nephilim you've been gathering evidence about, but not ghosts?"

Brighton closed the lid of the suitcase. "I saw a giant with my own eyes."

"Can't you open yourself to the possibility that the spirit was Emery? That Emery is somehow still alive, somewhere, in some form?"

That sounded like something Ira would have told him. *See the possibilities…*

"And if it was, what do you suppose he wanted to tell me?"

"No clue," Elisabeth said. "But if he has a message from beyond the grave, don't you think it's worth knowing?"

He zipped the suitcase closed and lifted it off the bed. "I don't believe in anything beyond the grave."

"After what you've seen?" she asked, getting up. "Maybe you're forgetting that the Nephilim are mythological beings from the Torah. Now that you know they're real, haven't you considered that other aspects of the scriptures might be real, too?"

In the months following Ira's disappearance, Brighton might have agreed with her. But now? After Ira had been missing so long? There was only one explanation—Ira was dead, which didn't lend much credibility to his strange religious ideas.

"The truth of certain Jewish myths doesn't necessarily point to the truth of the Jewish god, or an afterlife of any kind," Brighton said. "The only thing proved by the existence of the Nephilim is that a powerful race of beings walked the earth thousands of years ago. Some of them were giants. Others might have been aliens." He stopped, then picked up the suitcase and headed out of the guest room. "I don't know what to believe. No matter where I go looking for answers, I end up empty-handed. Perhaps the best explanation is that there *aren't* any answers."

"I know what I know," Elisabeth insisted, following him down the stairs. "Emery is still a part of this somehow. He may have died, but—"

"He *did* die. I saw it happen."

Brighton reached the foyer and put down the suitcase.

"I'm not saying he didn't," she said. "But how else do you explain the spirit?"

"Dreamcasting. You're the one who suggested it. And who knows? Maybe you're right. Maybe the energy at these hotspots somehow allows it to happen. When I was with Wörtlich and Ira, we experienced memories of the distant past. The sensation I felt at Stonehenge is probably no different."

Elisabeth shook her head. "It was Emery. I know it!"

"And if it was, who killed those two guards? Did he do that, too? I spent three weeks with Wörtlich. He was no killer."

"I don't know," she admitted. "But I'm going with you to Tiahuanaco, Sheply be damned. Whoever tried reaching you at Stonehenge might try again at another hotspot. I'm entitled to answers just as much as you are."

Elisabeth positioned herself in front of the door.

"And don't forget, Sherwood, I'm the one who's been financing these adventures of yours, on the expectation that there would be a return on my investment."

Brighton could have moved her aside. He could have merely used the back door. He could have done any number of things to leave her behind, but the ferocity in her eyes told him there was no way to stop her. She would find a way to Bolivia with or without him, but without him she would be more vulnerable.

"Fine," he grumbled. "But pack light."

SIXTEEN

Tiahuanaco, Bolivia
JULY 20

The camp was rife with subdued whispers behind turned backs, probing questions spoken through silent gestures. Conversation was short in public, often exchanged in winks and nods, and long in private, where friends gathered in tents and bartered snippets of gossip.

Dario longed to take his place atop the Akapana and shout the truth to anyone near enough to hear. But there were consequences to breaking Christophe's rules.

There was to be no discussion of underground caverns or the mysteries they contained. Jorge and Yasmine had succumbed to injuries on an offsite excursion, despite the camp doctors' best efforts. Their bodies had been taken away.

Rhea had quit the project and returned to Canada. A filthy and unsatisfying lie, but Rhea had been popular and no explanation could suffice to dampen interest in her sudden absence.

Despite these stories, people still speculated, and it pained Dario not to be able to elucidate the confusion. Whenever people asked him about Rhea, he shrugged and repeated the party line. Once he had felt so nauseous afterward that he emptied his stomach on the floor of the dining tent—not that there was much in his stomach to begin with. He barely ate anymore.

Yes, there were lots of rules. He wasn't allowed to leave camp for any reason. To ensure his cooperation, Doctor Christophe had assigned a shadow to keep tabs on him. Dario couldn't go two steps without tripping over Guy; the assistant had all the subtlety of a wrecking ball. The only way to achieve any kind of privacy was to shut himself in his tent, and even then it was hard to relax knowing that Guy was just outside, doing his mediocre best to appear inconspicuous.

Dario had spent most of the day atop the pyramid, sifting sediment. The ordinarily painstaking task had become unbearable. All he could think about was getting the hell out of here, but like it or not he was a prisoner.

The indignity of the way Rhea's body was being desecrated filled him with horror. Not only could she not rest in peace, but her bones were now being dragged around the earth by the one who had murdered her in cold blood. There truly was no justice in this world.

"I'm done here," Dario called down the pyramid slope. Guy, sitting in a lawn chair at the bottom of the ladder, nodded without saying a word.

Dario packed his tools carefully into the satchel next to him. He climbed down and headed toward camp. Guy scrambled to his feet and followed close behind.

Dario stopped briefly by his tent to change and then proceeded to the dining area. He wasn't hungry, but if he spent too much time out of sight people might start asking questions—and Christophe wouldn't like that.

Dario found a table in the corner. Gratefully, nobody but Guy joined him. He wasn't up for small talk. A group sat huddled around the table next to him, however, and Dario was just close enough to make out what they said.

"Did you see cars pull in this afternoon?"

"Men from the government. That's what I heard."

"They disappeared into Doctor Christophe's tent and haven't come out for over two hours."

"You think it has to do with the missing people?"

"They're not missing. They're dead."

"If you believe that—"

"Okay, okay, but whatever happened to them, we aren't being told the whole story. Have you seen Marco walking around camp like a zombie? I think he saw what happened."

"I heard Marco was drinking with Rhea the night of the party. You think that's a coincidence?"

"Doubt it."

Dario stood and walked to a fold-up table holding coffee and a stack of styrofoam cups. He poured himself some and returned to his original seat. He settled himself down to continue eavesdropping when a shadow fell across the table.

He lifted his head to see Marco towering over him.

The conversation at the table behind him dried up, and Dario felt their eyes on the big Bolivian man. Marco shot Guy a contemptuous look.

"Hey Guy, why don't you get in line for food? Dario and I are going to have a private conversation."

Guy didn't get up. "Not hungry."

"No, huh?" Marco's tone was angry, but he was smart enough not to make a scene. He looked down at Dario. "Maybe later then."

Silence reigned for a few minutes after Marco walked way. The conversation behind him resumed, this time in whispers too soft for Dario to hear.

Dario finished his coffee and left the tent. At first he had no particular destination in mind, but before long he found himself standing outside Christophe's tent. The chatter in the dining area hadn't been his first clue about the site director's mysterious visitors.

"You can't go in there," Guy said behind him.

Dario stood in place, wondering if he should barge in and see what was going on for himself.

And what would I do after that? He had to admit it would be stupid and impulsive. The only way to get through this was to think rationally.

"Did you hear me?"

Dario spun around. "Yes, I heard you. Why are you even here? It's not like I have anywhere to go."

That much was true. As badly as Dario wanted to escape, security closely monitored the camp's only excursion vehicles. Lookouts were placed around the camp's perimeter.

Frustrated, Dario returned to his own tent. He closed the flap behind him. There was no more privacy, but the illusion comforted him.

He lay across the narrow bed and looked up at the ceiling, rippling in the slight wind. Even getting into bed filled him with stress, given his recent nightmares. He didn't dare close his eyes until he absolutely had to—until he couldn't stay awake a moment longer.

Dario bolted upright when he heard a scuffle outside the tent. It sounded like a fight, though an oddly quiet one.

"Dario, let me in," came a whisper.

Dario crept toward the door. "Who is it?"

"Marco. Let me in, damn it, before someone sees me."

Dario's fingers fumbled to unzip the opening. He barely had the chance to get out of the way before Marco's husky frame burst in, dragging something heavy behind him.

It was Guy.

Dario gasped. "What did you do?"

Dario knelt next to Guy and checked to make sure he was still breathing.

"He'll be fine," Marco said. "Don't worry about him."

That's when Dario noticed the rifle slung over the big man's shoulder. He cringed, remembering the last time he'd seen that weapon.

A moment later, the rifle was in Marco's hands, pointed straight at him.

"Instead, worry about this," Marco growled. "You have one minute to start telling me what the hell's going on before I do something I might later regret."

The irony of the situation overwhelmed Dario, and a smile broke out across his face.

"It would be my pleasure."

*　　　*　　　*

Marco's face turned ashen as Dario led him through the events of that fateful night. Afterward, they sat in silence, Marco cross-legged on the ground as the lantern swung from its hook, casting ominous shadows over his dark features.

"I need a drink," Marco said.

Dario pulled a half-empty bottle of tequila from under his bed. He swished the golden liquid around in the bottle a few times before twisting off the cap and handing it to Marco.

"Got it in the city," Dario explained. "I bought three bottles. This is the last one."

Marco took a swig, then dried his chin with the back of his hand. He put down the bottle and took a deep breath. "I can see why."

Marco took a second drink before handing the bottle back to Dario.

Dario drank deep and felt the liquid scorch his throat. He didn't really care for the smoky taste; it was about as palatable as battery acid, but it got the job done.

Three more shots and he had to lie down.

"I'm so sorry," Marco whispered. "It was my fault."

Dario's instinct was to placate him, but he kept his mouth shut. If blame could be assigned, Marco deserved a large part of it.

Marco let out a short laugh. "She was quite a woman. I had my eye on her, you know."

"Me too," Dario said, rolling onto his side. Unlike Marco, he didn't laugh. He felt a profound ache in his stomach; it could have been the tequila or the heartbreak. More likely it was both.

"What was the machine for?" Marco asked.

"Damned if I know." Dario put his hand to his forehead to wipe away the sweat. "What about the men Doctor Christophe is meeting with?"

Marco took another drink. "I heard they were from the government, but there may be more to it. I saw them arrive. Two of them looked Bolivian, but the other was whiter than snow."

"You didn't recognize them?"

"Maybe one. The shorter of the two Bolivians was dressed like a businessman. He may have been here before. Perhaps from one of the corporations sponsoring the restoration."

The lantern creaked as a gust of wind caught the tent's roof. Dario's eyes shot up to the swinging beam of light, then back down to Guy's body.

"You hit him pretty hard," Dario murmured.

Marco glanced at Guy. "The boy's just taking a nap."

"Good. The body count's already up to three. No reason to raise it."

The Bolivian handed back the drink, but Dario refused. Marco twisted the cap back into place and rolled the bottle under the bed. "Not sure that's true."

"Not sure what's true?"

"The body count may not be up to three. I didn't see the boy die."

Dario sat up, ignoring a wave of dizziness. "You mean Jorge?"

"Who else? We got him up here and Doctor Kincaid said he might pull through if we got to the hospital in time. He was stable enough to be taken to La Paz. I saw the doctors take him out of the emergency room."

"He still could have succumbed to his injuries."

Marco shrugged. "True, but we never heard anything from the doctors who worked on him. Doctor Christophe picked us up that evening and told us that Jorge had been too far gone for the hospital doctors to do anything. But I was there, and that's not what it seemed like to me."

While Marco was talking, a shadow appeared against the front of the tent. Dario put a finger over his lips.

Without making a sound, Marco crept to the door. He then pulled the flap apart in a fluid motion, catching the eavesdropper by surprise.

"You almost gave me a heart attack!" a voice said from outside the tent.

Marco excused himself, leaving Dario alone for two uncomfortable minutes with Guy's body. Dario reached over to pinch the poor sap's arm; the man flinched just enough to reassure Dario he hadn't died.

Marco ducked back in.

"Who was that?" Dario asked.

"Not important. The meeting in Doctor Christophe's tent is over."

Dario swung his legs over the side of the bed and slipped his shoes on. His head swam, but he fought it off. "Did you see the men? What did they look like?"

"I'm told they were on their way to the dining tent."

Dario and Marco hurried out, leaving Guy behind. The wind had picked up outside, causing the canvas tents to twist and snap. Near gale-force squalls tore through the valley from time to time. Dario pulled his sweater tight and picked up the pace.

He was the first into the dining tent.

There were actually five men in total. Three sat at one of the round tables while the other two stood nearby. Doctor Christophe sat with a thermos between his hands. Next to him was a short man in a gray suit—the businessman Marco had mentioned. There were two other brown-skinned men.

But Dario's attention was drawn to the fifth visitor, dressed in dark pants and a beige polo shirt with a pair of sunglasses perched overtop his receding hairline. Sunglasses in the middle of winter… he wasn't from this hemisphere.

Dario's breath caught in his throat as the man's eyes swept over him. Dario recognized him.

SEVENTEEN

Bogotá, Columbia
JULY 22

The plane dropped through heavy clouds, navigating between rugged mountains covered in trees. The sky was too dark at this early hour to make out much beyond the sprawling city carpeting this high-altitude savannah. Brighton's eyes were glued to the window, taking in as much as he could.

Beside him, Elisabeth awoke from her nap. She rubbed her eyes, then put away the magazine that had been lying open on her lap.

Bogotá's airport was small for a city of over ten million people. The two terminals stuck out on either side of the main tower like raised jaws, with their plane taxiing straight into the airport's gullet.

Disembarking took a long time once the plane came to a stop, and Brighton couldn't figure out why. His restlessness must have been apparent to the other passengers; an older woman leaned across the aisle and told them that long wait times were to be expected here.

When they were eventually freed, Brighton bounded down the plane, anxious for an opportunity to stretch his legs. Instead of exiting into the terminal, they made their way across the tarmac to a secluded entrance where they flowed into the customs area. Only one official waited at the end of the long line.

Brighton leaned against the wall and settled in for what looked like an extended wait. They still had over an hour to get to their connecting flight, but this could easily take that long, and if there was any trouble...

Near the front of the line, detection dogs roamed around the passengers, sniffing at their legs. Brighton stiffened as one of the dogs paused at his feet and stared up into his eyes. Though the red-coated Doberman never bared its teeth, Brighton felt certain it could have overpowered him without much effort.

"*Pasaporte,*" the rotund customs official asked from behind bulletproof glass when Brighton reached the front of the line.

Brighton handed his passport to the man, who scowled at the American crest. He briefly looked backward and exchanged a few words with another official passing through the hallway on the other side of the customs barricade. Brighton thought he heard the word *Americano.*

"*Hablas español?*" the officer asked.

Those were about the only words of Spanish Brighton knew. He shook his head. "English."

The man gave the passport another cursory glance, then stamped it. "Proceed, Señor Hastings."

Brighton held himself in check at the unfamiliar name, forcing his outward appearance to remain impassive. He stumbled away from the booth as the official waved for the next person in line. Along the way, he passed another Doberman, though it barely gave him a second glance.

He flipped open the passport in his hand, turning to the picture page. He nearly gasped; the man's face looked nothing like his own. He had mistakenly used the passport Trevor had given him.

That could have been it, Brighton realized, raising a hand to wipe away the sweat on his forehead.

A nearby guard eyed him, so Brighton straightened and stuffed the passport back into his pocket. Fortunately, Elisabeth crossed into the hallway right at that moment and the two of them marched toward a wide flight of metal stairs leading to the main terminal.

"You look like you're going to be sick," Elisabeth said softly.

Without explanation, Brighton darted into a nearby bathroom and spent a few minutes locked in the stall, his head in his hands.

How could I have been so careless?

Trevor *had* said not to worry about using the passport. What was it? A magic passport?

Brighton washed his hands and left the bathroom, falling into step with Elisabeth as they proceeded to a monitor with gate information scrolling across it.

The first leg of the journey had been lively, with Brighton recounting stories from his travels. When those stories ran out, Elisabeth spent an hour reminiscing about her year in Egypt with Wörtlich, but then the mood grew somber. Surprisingly little conversation had passed between him and Elisabeth since their Miami connection.

He didn't feel particularly chatty now, either.

"Did you see a place where I can recharge my computer?" he asked her, looking around the terminal.

She hadn't.

"I think I saw a kiosk by the bathrooms." He consulted his watch.

"We have at least a half-hour. I'll be right back."

After selecting the most private kiosk with an electrical outlet, he breathed deeply and opened his computer. He accessed the internet, activating his IP scrambler. Nobody on their trail could trace them to Colombia, but this was no time to let down his guard, especially after his passport screw-up.

You have to get a hold of yourself, he thought. *You got away with it this time. Don't let there be a next time.*

He checked his email and found only two messages. One was a days-old message from Elisabeth, and the second came from an address he didn't recognize. The subject line said only "jkaplan." He almost excised it to the junk mail folder when he thought twice and opened it.

> Jason:
>
> I know that's not your real name, but Aaron wouldn't tell me anything more. Sorry for contacting you this way.

Aaron Roth? How had the old man gotten his email address? Brighton certainly hadn't shared it with him.

> I'm afraid I have some bad news. Aaron passed away last night. I was at the hospital when it happened, and so was his son, David.
>
> This probably sounds like it's none of your business, but I'm writing because Aaron mentioned you in his last hours. Every time he opened his eyes he talked about the young man who had come to visit him. That was you, right?

He repeated several phrases over and over, and David thought it was important enough to give them to you. Aaron was even lucid enough for a few minutes on the last day to give us your email address. This is what Aaron had to say:

"A glorious and disastrous coming is about to take place, and he is important, part of the battle, a beacon of light in a dark place. The black awakening is upon us. Tell him to listen. Tell him to heed."

Does that mean anything to you?

—Janene

Brighton's heart pounded as he read words almost verbatim to what Aaron had spoken to him in the Syracuse hospital room earlier in the week. Except for the last part: "Tell him to listen. Tell him to heed."

He closed his eyes and tried to relax. He had far too many voices in his head lately. Just like Ira's shapeless, nebulous words of wisdom, Aaron's words were confusing. But Aaron's were stronger, laced with turmoil. And most important of all, they had been his last.

Of all people, why were his last words aimed at me?

*   *   *

Elisabeth reclined her seat back the three inches it was allowed, not much caring if the passenger behind her didn't like it. They were back in the air, passing over the densest regions of the Brazilian rainforest. She sipped a ginger ale and leaned in toward Brighton so her voice wouldn't carry in the tightly packed cabin.

"We should come up with a plan," she said. "For when we get there."

He turned away from the window. "What did you have in mind?"

"We might run into Sheply at the Tiahuanaco site, and if that's the case we don't want to travel together."

"Sounds reasonable."

"It will be easier to explain my presence, so I should go alone." She saw his mouth open and cut off the objection. "At least at first."

To Brighton's credit, he didn't argue. Perhaps on a subconscious level he felt relieved to let someone else take point.

In fact, he was almost too restrained. Elisabeth couldn't say she knew him well enough to read his moods, but she could have sworn something was bothering him.

They finally arrived in La Paz, just in time to witness one of the most beautiful sunrises Elisabeth had ever seen. Sunshine poured over the city's eastern peaks like water cascading over the walls of an immense cistern. Misty clouds drifted above the city, a blanket of white pierced by the craggy Andean summits. The razor sharp edges of the Choqueyapu Canyon dazzled in the early light—though even those sheer cliffs paled in the shadow of the glacier-topped Illimani, looming like an immovable guardian over the city, its triple peak so altitudinous the clouds failed to contain it.

Within forty minutes they stood outside in the chill morning air, wide palm fronds whispering over their heads. From this vantage, the vast Altiplano plateau lay before them.

Fifteen thousand feet up, and flat as a board, she thought in amazement. *A geological marvel.*

A fierce gust of wind picked up her mass of curls and blew them from her face. "I wonder if it's always this windy."

"Just in the winter, I think," Brighton said.

They kept moving, though they turned away from the wind as best they could. The sidewalk led to a clearly marked visitors center.

"We'll find a hotel somewhere nearby," she suggested. "Tiahuanaco is less than fifty kilometers from here. The main highway will take us right to it."

"I don't want to just wait at the hotel while you visit the site," Brighton said as they reached the visitors center.

She lifted her suitcase, then dropped its wheels to roll over the room's gray tiles.

"Are you sure it's a good idea to come along?" she asked.

"There's a village near the site. I can explore without anyone knowing I'm there."

Elisabeth didn't want to make a case out of it, so she nodded her agreement.

The car rental went fast, and soon she was in a hotel room, staring at herself in the bathroom mirror. She didn't feel worn out by the long trip. She couldn't wait to get moving.

She took a quick shower, got dressed, and applied just enough makeup to cover a few lines here and there. The last thing she wanted was for Sheply to think she was trying too hard.

After securing some breakfast, they jetted west down Highway 1 with Brighton in the driver's seat. The view was incredibly scenic, with snow glistening off distant mountains in all directions. The original settlers here must have felt like they'd reached the top of the world.

Sometime later, they came to an intersection marked by three rectangular towers that reminded her of grandfather clocks. Each was supported by four columns of stone, and from their centers dangled slabs of blasted rock that swung like pendulums; these were paving stones harvested from the ancient city just a few miles north.

Despite their proximity, Elisabeth didn't spot Tiahuanaco until they were nearly upon it. The ruins of the city sat low to the horizon, save for the remains of an earthen pyramid. As they drove closer, Elisabeth made out the walls of the Kalasasaya Temple, behind which hid the vast sunken courtyard she had read about. She looked forward to seeing it for herself.

A city of beige tents, almost as large as the ruins themselves, stole her attention. Aligned along two main avenues, the tents housed an international team of archaeologists.

Sheply probably waited in one of those tents at that very moment.

Brighton steered them into the village to the west of the site. Two blocks into town, they found what promised to be the largest square. He stopped the car along the side of the road and shut off the engine.

"I'll wait here." He got out of the car and glanced toward an old brick church across the street. "Pick me up just after nightfall. Say, at eight o'clock. I'll be waiting on those church steps."

Without another word, Brighton turned and headed up the street, his shoes kicking up clouds of dust as he receded into the distance.

Elisabeth slid into the driver's seat, started up the car, and drove back to the main stretch of road. The sun hung above her as she headed east. To the left, the land was parceled into small farms, and to the right she beheld what they had traveled half a world to see.

She located a dusty parking lot next to the tents. Several men and women stopped what they were doing to watch as she pulled in next to a line of black Suburbans caked with dirt.

Elisabeth opened the door and stepped into the daylight. She dropped a pair of dark sunglasses over her eyes and walked toward a group of three workers clustered around the entrance to tent city.

"Can I help you?" a short but well-built woman asked as Elisabeth got closer.

Elisabeth peered over the top of her glasses. "I'm looking for the site director."

The woman removed a pair of gloves and rubbed her hands together. "Doctor Christophe is in meetings all morning. Do you have a name?"

"Doctor Elisabeth Macfarlane. Is there somewhere I can wait?"

Furtive glances passed between the group, then settled after a few uncomfortable moments on a brawny man with dark skin who looked more like a guard than an archaeologist.

"This way," the man volunteered.

The man led her into the labyrinth of tents. Their path veered close enough to the edge of the camp that she got her first close-up view of the Kalasasaya walls, studded with curious stone faces.

"What is your specialty, Doctor?" the man inquired.

"Spectral imaging. Mainly creating digital copies of badly damaged scrolls and ancient texts recovered from archaeological digs around the world. I work with anything that's too badly scarred to be legible to the human eye."

"A strange specialty for a visitor to Tiahuanaco. This civilization had no written language."

"I'm not here to offer my services," she said.

"Then why are you here?"

"To visit an old friend. And to see the city."

They continued in silence, coming at last to the largest tent. Beyond the scattered tables inside, two cooks set about preparing lunch.

The man indicated a table.

"Have there been any other visitors recently?" she asked, pulling out a chair to sit.

He hesitated. "Yes, as a matter of fact."

She waited for him to elaborate, but nothing came.

"I apologize," she said. "I don't mean to pry. Do you know how long Doctor Christophe will be?"

"Hard to say. Lots of meetings lately."

"Would you have any objection to me visiting the site?"

"Not without supervision," he said. "There are several delicate excavations underway. You understand."

"Of course. But I'm no stranger to archaeological sites. I worked with the excavators in Herculaneum, where they unearthed the Alexandrian index."

That got the man's attention. "Herculaneum? The former director of that project is stationed here."

Elisabeth's mouth hung open. "Dario? Dario Katsulas?"

"You know him?"

Her eyes lit up. "Very well! I had no idea he was here. What a delightful coincidence. Do you know where he is? I'd love to see him."

"I believe he's at the Akapana. I'll take you to him."

Elisabeth jumped up and followed her guide back through the maze of tents. They soon broke through the outer edge, tracking along a well-beaten path leading straight into the ruins.

Everywhere she looked, workers paused from their labors to note her passing. She avoided making direct eye contact. She had no need to draw attention to herself.

The pyramid of Akapana rose several meters above the rest of the ruins, its stepped slopes lined with regularly placed ladders. Only one ladder climbed to the top of the pyramid's flattened top, where they seemed to be heading.

The man stopped at the base of the ladder and pointed up. "Watch your step."

Just as he said it, a familiar face appeared at the top of the ladder. Dario's dark features turned confused, and then excited.

"Elisabeth Macfarlane?" Dario called down.

She removed her sunglasses and peered up at him. "The one and only."

"What the hell are you *doing* here?"

"I could ask the same of you."

He swung his foot onto the first rung of the ladder, but then stopped himself. "Come up here. The view's great."

That turned out to be an understatement. From atop the pyramid, she could see the entire dig—the semi-subterranean temple, the heart of Kalasasaya with its many-faced gods depicted in scattered obelisks, even the ancient planning site to the east where the city's original architects had built crude models of the final structures.

Her eyes turned down, falling on the depression in the center of the pyramid.

"I've read about this," she said, squatting along the ledge of the excavation. "For human sacrifices?"

Dario's face slackened and he looked away. She had touched on a sore point, apparently.

"That's been confirmed," Dario said in a quiet voice.

"It sounds like these excavations have yielded new discoveries. That's good news. Tiahuanaco has famously been a tough nut to crack."

Dario wiped sweat off his forehead and sat on the ground. "It's as good as cracked."

"Really?"

Dario put his finger to his lips, and a hundred questions flitted through Elisabeth's mind. Confused, she turned just as another man joined them from the direction of the ladder—a lanky young man with brown hair and a long face. A goose egg marred his forehead, bright red around the edges, its shiny mound catching the midday sun.

The newcomer hung back, far enough not to get in their way but close enough to catch their conversation.

"That's Guy," Dario said, his voice dripping with scorn.

The derision took Elisabeth by surprise. She had only spent time with Dario on a few occasions, with their work on the Herculaneum scrolls largely carried out on different continents, but she had come to know him well enough to get a sense for his kindly disposition. Whatever Dario held against Guy, it went deep.

Elisabeth realized Guy was here to keep an eye on Dario. For what purpose, she could only begin to guess, except that it seemed to prove something was, indeed, amiss.

"Looks like your friend got into an altercation," she said, tilting her head toward Guy.

"You might say he rubbed someone the wrong way." Dario leaned in, taking her by the shoulder and turning her away from Guy's watchful eyes. "I don't know what brought you here, but your timing is uncanny."

"I'm getting that," she whispered. "Do you remember Doctor Noam Sheply, from Alexandria? I have reason to believe he's been digging around."

Together, they stood up and strolled close to the edge of the pyramid, trying to look casual as they put more distance between them and their watcher.

"Sheply got here the day before yesterday," Dario said.

"Did he recognize you?"

"I don't think so. Why?"

"He works for the wrong kind of people. And these people…" She took a deep breath. "They're very dangerous, Dario. Whatever has brought them here could have global consequences."

Dario's lack of surprise told her that he was already right in the thick of this mess.

A quick look over her shoulder confirmed that Guy had inched closer. She turned her back to him.

"Elisabeth, can I trust you?" Dario asked, scanning the land north of the site. All she saw in that direction was a patchwork of farms, and beyond that the meandering course of a river.

"Of course you can."

"Good. Because I need you to do me a favor."

EIGHTEEN

Tiahuanaco, Bolivia
JULY 22

B right blue light poured into the ramshackle cantina through a
pair of dingy windows facing the street. Wooden floorboards
creaked as Brighton walked over them. Overhead lights,
dimmed by dirty red lampshades, swung from his approach.

A fat man sat on a tall stool behind the bar, his elbows resting on
the counter. He was adding up a stack of coins, barely giving Brighton
a glance even though the bar was empty except for one other customer. A row of green bottles lined the shelf behind the fat man, arranged
from tallest to shortest.

"Something to drink?" Brighton asked, hoping the man spoke English. A far from certain prospect; this didn't look like a tourist haunt.

The man pushed back his stool and faced the row of green bottles before selecting two. One was tequila, another something homemade called *chicha*. Neither sounded appetizing. Seeing Brighton's indecision, the man opened a cooler hidden by the counter and produced a can of beer.

"Paceña?" the bartender asked.

Brighton took it and dropped a few bolivianos on the countertop. The fat man swept the coins into his open palm and returned to his stool.

This bar was perhaps not the friendliest establishment he'd found himself in—and he'd found himself in many—but neither was it the worst way to spend the remainder of the afternoon.

The village of Tiwanaku, named for the nearby ruins, didn't have much to see. The church, complete with working belfry, proved the town's most interesting feature, but even this held limited interest; it wasn't old enough to matter, having been established by the invading Catholics only two hundred years earlier. There was a museum, but it was located too close to the dig site for Brighton to risk visiting.

Brighton found the darkest corner and sank into a straight-backed wooden chair. The beer wasn't half-bad, though sweeter than he would have liked. He drank three before the bar's only other occupant glanced his way. Brighton hoped the young man would read his standoffish body language and leave him be.

Instead, the man came closer. In reality, he was little more than a kid.

"You speak English?" the young man asked.

If there existed a polite way to avoid talking to the man, Brighton didn't know it. He simply nodded. The memory of his latest black eye ached slightly where he'd been punched for getting better acquainted with locals.

"You must be here to visit the ruins, yes?"

Brighton put a great deal of attention toward setting down his beer. "Yes."

The young man didn't say anything for a while, then mercifully returned to the counter.

Brighton retreated into his own head, running through the words of Aaron's warning. Ira would have called it a prophecy, or something else overtly religious. The words were probably no more than a dying man's senile ravings.

It made him feel better to think so, but it did nothing to explain how Aaron had intuited his email address.

Brighton's head shot up when he heard raised voices. The bartender shouted at the man who had tried to sit next to Brighton; apparently he wasn't happy about something. The bartender gestured to the door.

Shaking his head and muttering under his breath, the customer walked away.

"He thinks I'm crazy," he said loud enough for Brighton to hear. "They all think I'm crazy."

The bartender shouted again, but the young man ignored him.

"You heard the stories?" the young man asked Brighton, his hand on the doorknob.

Brighton hesitated, debating whether to get sucked into whatever dispute was going on. But if there were stories floating around the village, they might just be the kind of thing he wanted to know.

He had waited too long to answer, though, for the young man walked out, the rickety door slamming shut and bouncing in the frame.

Brighton got to his feet and followed the stranger out of the bar. The man was crossing the road.

"Hey!" Brighton called.

The man looked over his shoulder, confused and surprised.

"You said something about stories?" Brighton caught up.

"Everybody talks, but nobody believes." He pointed east, toward the dig. "The visitors found something. Something secret."

Brighton let the man set the pace as they reached the other side of the road.

"I'm Jason," Brighton said.

"Ricky."

"Sorry if I was rude before, Ricky." They took a right turn and headed toward a row of old houses. "Your English is really good, by the way. Where did you learn?"

"Everyone has to learn in the army."

"What did the archaeologists find?"

Ricky gave him a hard look. "Not here."

The young man shifted toward a narrow alley between buildings. When they got there, he turned to Brighton.

"For two days, everyone's whispering about some secret, but nobody says what it is. I've heard so many different things. A new temple maybe. Some writing. Bones." Ricky shrugged. "My grandmother says something else, and always she is right. She is Machi."

"Machi?"

Ricky scrunched up his face. "Machi... kalku. Don't know the word. Shaman?"

Brighton groaned inside, but didn't let it show on his face. "Shaman, yes. A healer. Or an oracle?"

"Yes."

Just what he needed—more superstition. "What did she tell you?"

"The old gods..." Ricky's cheeks flushed at whatever he meant to say. "You will not believe. Like the others. But she is always right."

"Try me."

Ricky took a breath to compose himself. "She says the old gods are coming back."

"And that's what the archaeologists found? Evidence?"

"Not evidence," Ricky said. "They *found* old gods."

Brighton realized his mouth hung open and slammed it shut. It didn't matter where he went; madness followed.

*   *   *

Elisabeth repeated Dario's instructions in her head as she returned to the tent city. She came to the first tent, took a left, then counted off six tents before taking a right. She recognized the cafeteria, but continued past it to the end of the row. Along the way she passed a tent slightly larger than the rest—presumably, this belonged to the site director. She quickened her pace.

She finally came to the one she wanted. She carefully maneuvered around a tent pole and lifted the canvas flap, holding her breath in anticipation of what she might find inside.

Her breath whistled out in relief when she found the tent empty. She dove to the fold-up bed. Her arm snaked underneath, grasping as far as she could reach. Nothing. She lowered her head and peered into the darkness.

Pushed all the way to the back was a long wooden box. Elisabeth pulled it free and ran her hand over the smooth case before unhinging the two brass hooks keeping it closed. She lifted the lid and stared at the rifle cradled inside, its barrel gleaming. She hefted the weapon, a part of her fearing the merest touch would cause it to discharge.

Her grandfather would have laughed if he were alive to see her. Flashbacks of shooting empty soup cans behind his ranch house came to mind. She tried to remember what he'd taught her, but she could only recall the proper way to hold the weapon. She secured the forestock with her left hand and placed her right hand on the trigger; the butt burrowed into the crook of her shoulder as she brought it up, closed one eye, and used the other to stare down the barrel's natural line of sight.

Once she felt comfortable, she put it down and made sure the magazine was loaded. She then placed the rifle back in the case and closed the lid.

This is stupidity itself. She stood at the open flap, clutching the nondescript box, but didn't make any move to leave. *What have you gotten yourself mixed up in? This is one hell of a big favor.*

*   *   *

Dario stood at the edge of the pyramid, nervously scanning the camp for Elisabeth. Fifteen minutes had passed for a trip that should only have taken ten. If anyone had stopped to question her, she'd be hard-pressed to explain herself, an unauthorized visitor to the site walking through camp with a loaded rifle. Worst case, she was tied up with Marco in that makeshift holding cell.

Ordinarily, knocking Guy around should have gotten Marco kicked off the dig, but he knew too much. Dario could only speculate what horrible fate awaited his friend; the creature would soon be hungry for a new body to devour.

"Who was that woman?" Guy asked from behind him.

"An old friend," Dario said without looking back. "We worked together last year."

"You're waiting for her to come back."

"I forgot some of my tools in my tent, and she offered to get them for me."

Guy narrowed his eyes. "Does Doctor Christophe know she's here?"

Dario's heart quickened at the sight of Elisabeth weaving her way around the edge of the Kalasasaya. He breathed a prayer that she was safe.

"That box is a little too big for tools, if you ask me." Guy pursed his lips. "This has something to do with those tunnels, doesn't it?"

Dario shook his head absently, not particularly worried about whether Guy believed him. He wondered how much Guy knew. Surely, Christophe hadn't told him the truth—a fiction would have been easier to accept and more likely to inspire loyalty to Christophe, however misplaced.

"What did happen in the tunnels?" Guy asked.

For the first time in days, Dario really stopped to evaluate the man charged with spying on him—and realized he didn't have anything against Guy. All the anger and frustration he'd directed at Guy had better targets, like Christophe, who wasn't around to take the brunt of it.

By now, Elisabeth was climbing the ladder, balancing the box in her right hand. When she got near the top, Dario reached down to help her up.

"Did you have any problems?" Dario asked.

"No," she said. "People mostly gave me space."

Dario took the box from her. "The atmosphere's so tense around camp these days, nobody wants to stir things up. And that's wise. I believe Doctor Christophe has lost his mind."

Guy inched closer, wide-eyed, perhaps surprised they were speaking so openly.

"Lost his mind?" Elisabeth asked.

"Completely," Dario said. "He believes he has discovered a god in the caverns beneath the city. It calls itself Ohia and plans to re-establish Tiahuanaco to its former glory."

Elisabeth suddenly sat down—no, fell down, as though her knees had buckled from disbelief.

"What you say can't be true," Guy cut in. "I've worked with the doctor for months."

Dario put the box down, opened the lid, and pulled out the gun.

"Tools," Guy muttered under his breath.

"These days, this is the most useful tool of all," Dario said, pointing the gun at Guy. "I feel bad about this, especially after what Marco did to you. Nothing that's happened is your fault, but Doctor Christophe is using you to spy on me, and I can't let it go on."

"What are you going to do?" Guy asked. "March me out of camp at gunpoint? Shoot me?"

Dario closed the distance between them and tapped Guy on the chest with the rifle's barrel. "Take off your shirt."

Guy flinched, but did as he was told.

Dario passed the gun to Elisabeth, who leveled it at Guy, holding the weapon far more handily than Dario would have guessed. He took Guy's shirt in both hands and ripped from the collar to the waist seam. He created three strips of equal length, one to bind Guy's hands, another for his ankles, and the third for a gag, the remains of the shirt balled up in his open mouth.

Guy shouted unintelligible profanities, but Dario ignored them as he and Elisabeth lowered his struggling body facedown into the depression.

"Is he going to be okay?" Elisabeth asked, dusting herself off.

"It won't take long for someone to notice he's missing," Dario assured her. "He checks in with Doctor Christophe three times a day, and seeing as he spends most of his time watching me, it'll be one of the first places they look."

Elisabeth handed back the gun and followed Dario to the ladder.

"How do we get out of here?" she asked once they had climbed to ground level.

Dario looked off into the distance, calculating the odds of walking to the village without incident.

He glanced at his watch, marking the time. "You know where the church is at the center of town?"

She nodded.

"Good," he said. "Get to your car and drive back to the village. I'll meet you there in one hour."

Dario watched her retreat through camp, then began walking south, navigating low-lying mounds and grasses tall enough to mask his departure. Most of the onsite activity took place to the north and west of the pyramid, which meant he only had to worry about those people Doctor Christophe had stationed to keep their eyes on the fence separating the property from adjacent fields.

He kept low to the ground, watching carefully where he put his feet; it wasn't uncommon to find snakes—some pretty big ones, too—slithering through these hills.

After a few minutes, Dario came to a gravel service road. He crouched in the grasses, waiting for an opportunity to cross, when an excursion vehicle sped around a corner some fifty yards away. He backed off, unsure whether the driver had seen him. The vehicle careened past, kicking up a cloud of dust and shooting a few loose stones at him. Once it was safely out of sight, he ran across the road.

The short grass on this side wouldn't hide him, so his only recourse was to run toward the fence as fast as he could.

He arrived at the chain-link fence and sank his fingers into the holes, hoisting himself up, fueled by adrenaline.

Dario was nearly at the top when he heard shouts. He lifted his head to see a security guard running toward him from the gate where the service road exited the site. Dario hurtled over the fence and hit the ground hard.

The gun, he thought, realizing he had let go of it in the fall. A glance behind him confirmed that it had landed in the grass on the other side of the fence. There was no time to retrieve it; the guard's shouts were getting louder and would soon draw a lot of attention.

Finally free of the compound, Dario sprinted toward the main avenue leading into town. Instead of sticking to the main road, he aimed toward the back of a group of outlying homes.

Dario slowed once he reached their shade, even stopping entirely at one point to catch his breath. He continued into town, making sure to keep his distance from the main streets.

I shouldn't have chosen to meet at the church. It's too public.

He crept toward the central square only two blocks away from the church. He could see its small courtyard from the safety of a narrow alley, and it was teeming with passersby.

Dario breathed a sigh when he saw Elisabeth standing next to the church's gates, her back pressed against a stole pillar.

"Elisabeth!" Dario called.

Elisabeth's head snapped. Eventually she spotted him, waving as nondescriptly as he dared from the relative safety of his hiding place.

Instead of walking straight toward him, she crossed the street and made her way around the block, losing herself in the foot traffic.

Smart girl, Dario told himself. He doubled back and headed for the street behind him to intercept her. Five minutes later, she stepped into the alley where he waited.

"What's going on?" she asked in a low voice.

"I was seen leaving camp."

"What kind of security force does the site employ?"

Dario adjusted his glasses. "A small one, but this town is the only place they'll need to search. Where else would I run?"

"Good point, and I'm afraid we have to hide out a while longer. The plan is to meet my associate at the church at nightfall."

Dario searched the roofs of the nearby buildings. A few would make perfect hiding places and still offer a good view of the church's courtyard.

*   *   *

"Dario, I need an explanation," Elisabeth said.

The short Italian man continued his search for a suitable roof without answering.

"You said something about a god in the caverns beneath the city," she said. "What did you mean?"

"I wouldn't use the word 'god.' There is a creature down there, though, and it wields powers I can't explain."

"What kind of powers?"

He swallowed hard. "It killed my friend and possessed her body."

When his voice broke, Elisabeth realized he hadn't just discovered something rare and powerful; he had undergone a trauma. She could relate to losing someone, but she didn't want to compare tragedies. These were his experiences, his emotions.

"We discovered an enclosure in the caverns in an area we believe is directly below the ancient city," he said after a long wait. "The creature was trapped inside a metallic barrier. Rhea knew better than to go inside, but Doctor Christophe went anyway. I couldn't just leave him behind, but I wish I had. Rhea would still be alive."

Dario stopped just beneath a ladder that led to the roof of the building next to them. He seemed to shrug off the powerful emotions, his mind returning to the task at hand.

"This will suffice," he said, pulling on the rungs to ensure they were well-secured.

The roof was flat and made of corrugated tin which sprang oddly when she stepped on it. She walked across its surface, feeling the heat of the sun radiate off the reflective material. Together, they knelt at the edge of the roof, resting their arms on a raised stone edifice which created an illusion of height on three sides of the building.

Several armed men prowled the street below, having scared the normal populace away.

Members of the security detail, Elisabeth thought.

According to her watch, it was only six o'clock. Brighton still had another two hours before their agreed-upon meeting. Hopefully the armed men would disperse, or Brighton would recognize the danger and seek cover.

Dario sank down next to her so that his head was below the wall. She followed suit.

They waited quietly, watching as the sun crept lower and lower in the western sky.

"I know what it feels like to lose someone," Elisabeth finally ventured. "I wish I could tell you that the pain goes away, but mine hasn't."

Dario managed a smile—a very slight one. "Is it strange that I find that a little bit comforting?"

"No, not strange at all."

The conversation proceeded slowly, but bit by bit he shared the complete tale of what had transpired. He did his best to answer her questions, but none of his answers satisfied her curiosity. What kind of creature was Ohia?

The description of the barrier sounded eerily similar to the story Brighton had told her about his trip under the pyramids with Emery and Ira. Was there a connection between Giza and Tiahuanaco?

Periodically, they popped their heads up to look down into the main square. Seven o'clock came, and then eight. Brighton did not appear.

"He may be hiding," Dario mused. "Do you have any other way of contacting him?"

Elisabeth bit her lip. Brighton didn't have a cell phone. He had a computer, but even if he somehow had a way of accessing his email, Elisabeth didn't have the means of sending him a message. She, too, had left her cell phone behind, for fear of being tracked with it. A wise precaution at the time, but now a crippling inconvenience.

Nine o'clock came and went, and still there was no sign of him.

NINETEEN

Lake Titicaca, Bolivia
JULY 22

Brighton held on for dear life as Ricky drove his claptrap car over a twisting trail. He was grateful it hadn't rained in a few days, which would have turned this bumpy path into a mud pit. They flew over the crest of one small hill after another, Brighton clutching his seat. Wind rushed past them into the open-roofed, open-sided car. A shallow windshield provided minimal protection from rocks, insects, and the occasional low-flying bird.

Ricky laughed at Brighton's white-knuckled response but didn't slow down.

"How much farther?" Brighton shouted over the wind.

"Couple of minutes!"

Brighton held his breath as they climbed the final hill and sped toward the bright blue expanse of Lake Titicaca. The lake's southern shores were largely unadorned, free of trees and buildings. The neighboring fields ended abruptly at narrow beaches. Small grassy islands dotted the lake.

Ricky raced along the shoreline until a small wooden hut appeared just a stone's throw from the water. He stopped the car and swung himself out onto the hard-packed earth where the trail ended.

The grass around the car was torn up and rutted from drivers coming to the dead end and turning around. The grass was high, like everywhere Brighton had seen on the Altiplano, but for a trampled swath that led from the road to the hut's front door.

The hut looked as though it had seen many repairs since its first construction. The wood siding had rotted in several places, split and weatherworn. Patches had been covered over with ragged shingles which had likely torn loose from the roof during storms. Two windows faced the front, the first with a jagged crack in its pane and the second with nothing to cover it save a sheet of warped plywood. Remnants of red paint persisted here and there, but for the most part the color had faded into depressing shades of gray and brown.

Ricky climbed the front steps, which groaned loudly under his weight. Brighton followed, worried he might fall through at any moment.

The stench of ammonia assaulted Brighton the instant the front door creaked open. His hand flew to cover his nose, but the odor still seeped through. He coughed and squeezed his watering eyes shut.

He took a few minutes to acclimate before opening his eyes again to take in his surroundings. There seemed to be just two rooms, and Ricky was standing squarely in the center of this one. Stained plywood covered the inside of the windows, ensuring perpetual night for the hut's lone occupant, an old woman with long, knotted gray hair that fell to her knees. She sat in a rocking chair that had been bolted to the floor. Her wrinkles were so deep that they nearly concealed her eyes; they stared at him in such bewilderment that he thought she might never have seen a white man before.

Ricky spoke to her in Spanish. In response, her head wavered; it could have been a nod or a head shake, Brighton couldn't tell which. When Ricky spoke again, Brighton thought he heard "Jason" mixed in.

"I told her who you are," Ricky said, gesturing for him to sit.

Brighton looked behind him and found a short wooden stool. He lowered himself down on it circumspectly.

As Brighton watched, Ricky handed his grandmother a mug filled with a thick, potent liquid. Its steamy scent rose into the air and wafted toward him, mixing with ammonia on the way over.

"Ask her your questions," Ricky said. "I will translate."

Before Brighton could reply, the grandmother leaned forward and spoke. Words spilled out of her as effortlessly as the liquid over the rim of the mug that shook in her bony, arthritic hands.

"She's speaking of the old gods," Ricky said after the old woman settled back into her chair, a grim look on her face. "One in particular calls to her when she lets her guard down. It was asleep, but now it has come alive."

"Does it have a name?" Brighton asked.

Ricky translated the question, and she shook her head.

"The ancient peoples called him 'the bringer of life and death,'" Ricky told him. He swallowed, shifting uncomfortably. "They fed him their own blood. And the blood of their enemies."

"What does he want?" Brighton asked.

The old woman's eyes darkened and she let out a sickening laugh. The deep, rumbling sound made Brighton's skin crawl.

*   *   *

The sun had been down for over an hour and only sparse pools of light around the church courtyard lit the dark streets. Clouds neutralized the starlight, making it difficult to determine if the square was still guarded. Dario thought it was; Doctor Christophe wouldn't have given up so easily, especially if he had help from the government.

Elisabeth shivered next to him, her knees pulled up to her chest.

"I don't think he's coming," Dario said.

"He said he was just going to kill time before I came back. Explore the village," Elisabeth said in frustration.

"He may have gotten into trouble."

"We should look for him."

Dario sighed. "And then get the hell out of here."

Elisabeth fell silent, leaving only the sounds of the gusting wind and her chattering teeth.

Dario felt grateful to her for helping his escape, but he dreaded what might come next. They wanted different things. If Elisabeth was hell-bent on staying, Dario would have to abandon her. He had vowed to never again tangle with the god behind the barrier—a promise he had to keep.

"We can't leave," she finally said. "I haven't gotten what I came for."

Dario hung his head. "I already told you about the underground caverns. What more do you need?"

"To see them for myself."

"You do what you like," he said, "but I'm getting as far away from here as possible."

"How? You tried once before and got dragged back."

Dario set his jaw. "We'll drive. Head west, cross into Peru."

"Dario, I believe everything you told me about what you found. But I need to see it for myself. I have my own mystery to solve." Elisabeth fell quiet again. "You wouldn't understand. It sounds insane when I say it out loud."

Dario wanted to laugh. What could sound more insane than the existence of an ancient god beneath the ruins? A god who was capable of possessing dead bodies?

"Tell me anyway."

Another pause, even longer this time.

"My friend who was supposed to meet us here was contacted by a spirit while visiting Stonehenge," Elisabeth said. "I believe that spirit to be the ghost of my former lover, who died at an ancient site very much like this one."

Dario cracked a smile, despite his best efforts not to. Perhaps she was more unhinged than he'd given her credit for.

"I told you it was crazy," she said.

"Your former lover? You're right. It does sound insane."

Elisabeth leaned forward and raised her hand as though to slap him. She restrained herself. "Anyway, there's more to the story, but none of it sounds more plausible."

"Why do you think you'll find answers in Tiahuanaco?"

"Because something strange is going on. Something… energetic." She shivered again and pulled in her knees even closer to keep warm. "It's happening all over the world at certain 'hotspots,' most of which seem to converge on the sites of ancient megalithic structures. Now, Emery is trying to reach me, trying to leave me a message."

"Emery?"

"That was his name. My lover."

The look of determination in her eyes convinced him that she wouldn't be dissuaded. She had come a long way chasing a dim hope, and she wasn't going to be turned back.

Nonetheless, he had to try.

"That doesn't explain why you came to Tiahuanaco," he said. "If so many of these hotspots have become active, why choose this one?"

"Because Noam Sheply came here, and Sheply works for a man who knows a lot about what's going on. He sent Sheply here for a reason."

"Well, if you're looking for a friendly ghost, you've come to the wrong place." Dario took her hand and squeezed it; her skin was cold and clammy. "The spirit down there has already killed two people, one of whom I cared about more than I can say. If you go down there, you'll be next. I can't let you do this!"

"All you need to do is tell me where to go," she said.

"Please, listen to someone who knows firsthand—"

Elisabeth jerked her hand free and used the stone ledge they were leaning against to get to her feet. He followed her, coming to the edge of the roof and looking down into the alley below.

"What more can I say?" Dario asked, a note of desperation creeping into his voice. "How can I convince you?"

All he got from her in response were hollow eyes and down-turned lips. Without another word, he watched her climb down, possibly to her own doom.

*   *   *

Elisabeth stumbled through the underbrush, the sparse lights of the village fading behind her. She maintained a straight path north, drawn by the babbling sound of running water. The river wasn't far, and once she reached it she needed only follow its course.

What the hell are you doing? a voice inside her demanded. *Turn around, for god's sake. Turn around and see reason.*

But her feet kept moving. Thoughtlessly. Mechanically.

I wasn't supposed to be doing this on my own. Brighton was supposed to be here.

She certainly didn't need him, but they'd had an agreement. She couldn't imagine what had held him up—or at least, she didn't want to. And even if he had come, he might have tried to dissuade her. He didn't believe like she did.

Soon she arrived at the bank of the river, its murmuring waters invisible in the darkness but loud in her ears. She could smell it, the freshness pouring down from the mountains, slicing through the soft soil of the plateau.

She turned east and picked up her pace, keeping her head down. Dario had warned her not to tread too close to the water, where the bank was soft.

A light shone up ahead. She slowed, eventually stopping when she came upon two sources of light. One shone up from the ground, the light dissipating into the sky. The second aimed down from the top of a wooden pole, the light wavering as it twisted in the wind.

Well, she certainly couldn't miss the entrance, as she had feared. But the fact that it was so well-marked also meant it was monitored. Elisabeth glanced around, but saw no one. She continued walking, albeit more slowly. She took short, measured steps, careful not to make noise.

As Elisabeth approached, she saw that the light attached to the pole swung freely from a hook. An extension cord was wrapped around the pole, beating against it arrhythmically. She made out the sound of a low rumble; the hum coughed and sputtered, a telltale sign of a working generator somewhere in the caverns below.

A working generator meant people, and yet there was no one in sight.

Elisabeth crept closer still, anxiety rolling over her in waves. This was possibly the eeriest sight she'd ever laid eyes on—the swinging light, a beacon in otherwise pitch blackness, creaking in the wind, over an abandoned tunnel. And it was *cold*.

Placing one foot in front of another, she soon found herself at the edge of a square opening, the stone lid that had covered it now pushed aside. She looked into the hole and was blinded by the floodlight aimed right into her eyes. She put a hand over her face and leaned back, seeing spots.

She looked again, this time careful to avoid looking straight into the beam. A wooden-runged ladder leaned against the edges of the opening to ease traffic in and out.

Elisabeth gripped the moist, earthen edges of the hole and perched in hesitation.

Perhaps it's best not to overthink it.

That was bad advice, but it would do. She swung herself around and climbed down the ladder.

The ceiling of the cavern rose to enormous heights. This tunnel was tall enough to accommodate a man twenty to thirty feet tall. Looking up at the ceiling, its heights lost to darkness, left her feeling very small, very exposed.

The musty smell was strong, mixed with the faint aroma of gasoline. A generator rested on four rusty legs about ten feet into the cavern. Its motor churned, causing the machine to vibrate noisily. One extension cord snaked its way topside, and a second, this one bright yellow, ran along the wall of the tunnel. She noted the fixture-like stone globes protruding from the wall on metallic struts. They didn't seem to serve any purpose except to hold up the cord. Ahead, a string of electrical lanterns hung from the cord, lighting the way. She would have liked to examine the fixtures more carefully, but there wasn't time. If someone were to approach from either direction, there would be no darkness to hide in.

The long cavern continued in a straight trajectory. The flat stone walls were unadorned, except for the occasional gallery of carved faces, their features exaggerated and deranged; those open eyes and mocking smiles only contributed to her sense of vulnerability.

Elisabeth sped up, scurrying beneath the cord. She had feared getting lost, but this yellow cord pointed the way more surely than any trail of breadcrumbs.

The intersection seemed to come out of nowhere. Elisabeth turned to take a long look in each direction. The lanterns down the cross-corridor were spaced farther apart, resulting in pools of darkness between them. She dreaded the shadows and walked through them more quickly; even her heart beat faster.

While in the depths of just such a shadow, she heard a low muttering sound up ahead. The air was still and quiet. It could have been anything, drops of water trickling down from the ceiling or pebbles skittering to the ground. Or it could have been voices.

The voices were confirmed when she got to the next spoke and peeked around the corner of the stone wall. Far down the corridor, a figure stood silhouetted against a bright surface. Was that the metallic barrier Dario had told her about?

Elisabeth froze, her heart racing as she tried to figure out what to do next.

A moment later, the decision was taken out of her hands.

*   *   *

Dario sat on the edge of the hole in the riverbank, measuring the consequences of descending into it. On the one hand, Elisabeth needed help; he didn't want to abandon her, but he seemed physically incapable of moving. All his logic was defied by the mental image of Rhea Dunford, her blond hair and blue eyes almost ethereal in their beauty.

You're not remembering her the way she was, he told himself. *She was beautiful, yes, but she didn't have an ethereal bone in her body.*

Memory had done away with all her imperfections, leaving behind a golden-haired martyr who had fallen prey to his own inability to leave well enough alone.

Even that wasn't fair. The facts of what had happened that dark night were firmly etched in his mind, and yet he'd gotten so good at twisting them that he could almost convince himself Rhea was still alive, waiting for him at the end of the cavern. He had never been a good liar, but lying to himself required somewhat less aptitude.

One thing he knew for sure: Rhea wouldn't have hesitated to rescue him. She was gone now, but he now had an opportunity to pay back the karmic debt. He wouldn't be able to live with himself if another person died due to his inaction. Put that way, what choice did he have? He gripped the ladder, his courage surging, and began his descent.

The brightened passage bore almost no resemblance to the hellish tunnel he had picked his way through four days ago. It almost felt like another place entirely. Almost. He steeled himself to the reality of what waited for him at the end of his path.

Dario hurried through the tunnels, guided by instinct. Despite his ambivalence, he was running by the time he arrived at the crosscorridor. He surged ahead, unmindful of the gaps in lantern light.

"Ah, it's you," a man's voice said.

Dario stopped cold. The voice was distant, yet clearly audible. At first he thought it was the creature, but then he recognized the man's voice.

Arriving at the spoke, Dario stopped upon seeing Elisabeth, her back to him, standing in the middle of the corridor, not far from where they'd found Jorge. Over her shoulder, he saw Noam Sheply.

"I should have known I'd run into you here," Sheply said, raising his voice to be heard over the distance remaining between them.

Elisabeth stepped toward him.

Dario rushed to catch her. "Elisabeth!"

She spun around, her face overcome with surprise. "Dario? I thought—"

"As much as I hate and fear this place," Dario said. "I couldn't let you come alone."

She opened her mouth to say something, but before any sound came out another voice filled the corridor. It was Rhea, but not really Rhea. The voice had lost everything that had marked it uniquely hers; it was now devoid of compassion, devoid of warmth, devoid of every kind of beauty.

"You know these two?" it asked.

"I know the woman," Sheply tossed over his shoulder to the disembodied voice. "I've never seen the man."

"You've forgotten me," Dario said as he reached Elisabeth's side, "but I remember you."

Sheply stared at him without a hint of recognition.

"Herculaneum," Elisabeth prompted. "Does that ring any bells?"

Sheply snapped his fingers. "Yes, the site coordinator. Dario Katsulas. You'll have to forgive me, Dario, we only met the one time."

"Once was plenty," Dario said.

"Elisabeth has not been saying very kind things about me, huh?" Sheply sighed dramatically. "She could never be counted on to keep her personal and professional worlds separate."

"That's a charming fiction," Elisabeth said. "Well, not that charming."

"The man was here before," the creature intoned. *"He tried to run from me."*

Elisabeth was walking toward the barrier, and Dario followed along behind her. He would not run this time.

"A man cannot run forever. His past catches up."

Sheply grinned. "Wise words, Ohia."

Elisabeth arrived at the barrier. "Why do you stand here, outside the barrier?" she asked Sheply. "Could it be that you're afraid of what's inside?"

"Only fools rush in," Sheply told her. "Ohia and I are getting to know one another. Have been, in fact, for a couple of days now. The son of Samhazai has much to say."

"Yes. Together, we have many plans for this world."

Dario cringed, remembering Christophe's promise to him: that Ohia was to make himself known. Whatever that meant.

"You are welcome, the man called Dario and the woman Elisabeth. It would be easier to make plans face to face. You have my invitation to enter."

Elisabeth approached the barrier and gave it a solid knock with her fist. "I'm ready when you are."

"The woman Elisabeth is very bold."

Dario didn't know where her boldness came from, but he was certain it would soon get her killed if she wasn't more careful.

"What can I say? I'm eager to get on with things." Elisabeth turned on her heel to eye Sheply. "You, Noam? Surely you feel the same way."

Sheply hesitated. The Englishman tried to cover it up, but his mask slipped for an instant and his fear became apparent

He hasn't been getting to know the creature, Dario thought. *He's been stalling it.* He wanted to laugh. Sheply might be a bad guy, but he was clearly a pragmatist.

"Elisabeth," Dario said quietly, "perhaps you could discover what it is you came for from the safety of the tunnel."

"Dario is angry that I took the body of his friend," the voice said, almost regretfully.

"You're damned right I'm angry."

Elisabeth raised an eyebrow at him. "And you're the one who told me to treat the being with caution?"

Dario shrugged. "He started it."

She gave him a slight smile, then returned her attention to the barrier. "Ohia, I have business with you."

"What business?"

"I, too, have a friend. He was killed by a being called Mahaway."

The silence following Elisabeth's statement went on and on. She placed her hands on her hips, waiting for an answer. There didn't seem to be one coming. "Did you hear me, Ohia?"

"Yes. I knew one called Mahaway."

Dario took her by the hand, déjà vu shooting through him like a volt of electricity. Who was Mahaway? Elisabeth hadn't mentioned the name earlier, and there had been plenty of opportunities. "Elisabeth, perhaps we should discuss this in private."

Elisabeth shook him loose. "No, I'm here now and I want answers."

Sheply, meanwhile, stood back in amazement. "Elisabeth, what are you doing?"

"What do you know about Mahaway?" she called toward the voice.

"Much. Very much, Elisabeth, but I insist we speak face to face."

"Very well."

Dario wanted to grab her and pull her bodily from the cavern. One glance toward Sheply told him the man would probably lend a hand; the concern on his face spoke volumes about his feelings for Elisabeth. He evidently didn't want to see her dead any more than Dario did.

But Dario had a suspicion that ten men couldn't have dragged Elisabeth away from that barrier. Not ten, not twenty.

*   *   *

The old woman's dark eyes began to glow as Brighton watched. Light poured off her, collecting into a vague halo around her head.

"What's happening?" Brighton asked, turning to Ricky.

The woman's grandson had gotten down on his knees, not in reverence but to get a better view. "I believe the god speaks. She listens."

Ricky reached out and placed his hand atop the old woman's, which were now folded tightly in her lap.

She slapped him away and released a burst of Spanish.

"There is more than one presence," Ricky translated, his voice shaking with fear. "The god and … another."

A strong wind swept through the room and knocked Brighton over. He hit the floor, his face pressed against the dirt-covered floorboards. He grunted and tried to push himself back up, but a force pinned him down.

"It's manifesting," Ricky whispered.

Brighton bared his teeth and pushed with all his might against the unseen force. Nothing happened.

There's someone watching you, he told himself.

He stopped pushing.

A hand tapped Brighton on the shoulder and he spun around. Breathing heavily, he found himself face to face with Ricky, a look of wild terror writ large over the young man's face.

"Are you … fine?" Ricky asked.

Brighton nodded, massaging his neck. The pressure on his back had been strong, stronger than a man could apply on his own. He swept his eyes from one corner of the hut to the other. He studied the old woman warily; her eyes still glowed and a smile appeared on her face.

He could feel eyes on him as sharp as blades, and they didn't belong to Ricky or the old woman. Someone *was* watching him, he realized.

Someone familiar, he thought. *The same someone who watched you at Stonehenge.*

"Who are you?" he called into the room.

Ricky backed away, worried and scared. Brighton couldn't blame him for it.

The presence gave no answer to his question, though it remained nearby—moving around the room. In front of him, behind him… he wasn't imagining it.

The old woman spoke.

"It's been looking for you," Ricky translated.

Brighton turned in a slow circle. "Who are you? Show yourself!"

The old woman laughed, a hard, spine-chilling sound that could have ground diamonds to dust.

"And now I have found you."

Brighton turned again to face the woman and realized that the voice had come from her lips, not Ricky's.

"We have much to discuss, you and I," she grated.

"Tell me your name," Brighton said.

Her eyes flashed. "There will be plenty of time for that…" The woman snapped her head and looked to her right. There was nothing there but a boarded-up window.

"I want to know why you've been haunting me," Brighton said.

"There is another," she said into the emptiness.

Brighton glanced at Ricky, who was now huddled in the corner, shaking in terror.

"Another spirit?" Brighton asked. "You mean, a third?"

The woman looked at him again, smiling wide and exposing rotten teeth. "I have been called away. Another seeks my attention. I must go to her."

TWENTY

Tiahuanaco, Bolivia

JULY 22

The interior chamber hadn't changed much since Dario's last visit; the mysterious machine stood in all its glory, the glass bulb-like protrusion pointed at the ceiling, its delicate filaments glittering in the beam of a flashlight Sheply carried.

He heard both Elisabeth and Sheply gasp at the machine. They began to circle it, inspecting it with wide eyes. Dario's eyes were fixed elsewhere.

His heart leapt in his chest to see Rhea emerging from the darkness, her hands on her hips. She wore the same clothing, now with a large, red-stained rip over her chest. The gruesome wound gaped through the torn fabric, so much worse than when he'd last seen it. Dario's stomach heaved as he realized that the creature inhabiting

Rhea's body had dug its fingers into the cavity to remove the bullet.

Small, blotchy lesions had appeared on her skin. The sores looked fresh, and Dario recognized them as the beginnings of decomposition.

"You shall excuse my appearance," the creature spoke, stopping just outside the pool of Sheply's light. *"This body festers and decays. I shall soon require a new one."*

Dario took a backward step.

The creature noticed. *"Fear not. For the time being, this form is acceptable."* It turned to regard Elisabeth. *"You have many questions."*

"Yes," Elisabeth said, leaving the machine behind and advancing on the creature. "Will you answer honestly?"

The creature bowed Rhea's head.

Dario narrowed his eyes at this newfound grace and courtesy.

"Tell me what you know of Mahaway."

Together, the creature and Elisabeth walked a short distance. They spoke in hushed tones that Dario couldn't make out.

"This is remarkable," Sheply said, coming to stand next to him. His eyes remained fixed on the machine. "Do you know what it is?"

Dario looked up the long length of glass tube. "An electrical device of some kind, I suspect. Perhaps a lamp?"

"You're not far wrong. It's a Dendera light."

"A what?"

"A device just like this was discovered drawn on the walls of a tomb in the Egyptian city of Dendera." Sheply spared a glance at Elisabeth, who had turned her back toward them. "I once read a paper about it, written by one Emery Wörtlich."

"Emery," Dario said, drawing from his memory. "Emery was the name of Elisabeth's former lover, the man who was killed."

"One and the same. Emery was a close friend of mine once." Sheply lifted a hand and dragged his fingers along the sides of the glass bulb. "He was ridiculed for believing a device such as this existed in Ancient Egypt. The arguments against it were vast and unrelenting… I still can't believe Emery was right all this time, but this…" Sheply paused, retracting his hand and making it into a fist. "This is exactly how Emery described it."

Dario frowned. "And what does it do?"

"Well, Emery believed it was more than a lamp, and that the Egyptians themselves were not responsible for building it."

"If it wasn't the Egyptians—"

"Their gods, Mr. Katsulas. Emery believed they were real." Sheply drew a long breath, inspecting the lower portions of the machine, where the bulb seemed to connect to a socket of some kind. "He believed it wasn't a lamp, but a generator."

"It doesn't look like a generator," Dario said, "but that's what Ohia called it as well."

"Emery claimed it was a piece of technology designed to transmit an electrical signal. Like a radio, if you will, and one could turn the dial to the correct frequency to harness its power."

"Sounds space-age to me."

"Indeed, that was the consensus. Poor Emery never quite lived it down."

*   *   *

"Tell me what you know of Mahaway."

Elisabeth walked next to the creature—essentially, a reanimated corpse—with halting steps. Dario had been right to fear it, and yet she couldn't allow fear to rule her. She buried her mounting terror, found a place deep inside her and stuffed it down.

"Mahaway was alive until recently," she said. "He was discovered under the ocean, in a pyramid."

Ohia stopped and faced her. Elisabeth could imagine the body it possessed had once been very beautiful, but after five days rotting in this tomb, it gave off a putrid smell.

"Mahaway was a fool," Ohia said. *"His father and mine were of the Grigori. They were great allies until Mahaway's father betrayed all. He led a sect devoted to returning the creation science."*

"You mean, the Book of Creation?"

"It could be called that. After our fathers were imprisoned, Mahaway stole the… Book of Creation, intending to—" Ohia broke off, twisting its host's face into a ghoulish smile. *"But you came not for a history lesson. You have a different purpose."*

Elisabeth's heart quickened again. She leaned against the stone wall, steadying herself. "Yes."

Ohia's eyes shifted away from her. *"We are not alone in this place. We have been joined by a roaming spirit. It has come… to commune with you, Elisabeth. You know this spirit?"*

She looked around the room. "I don't see it," she said, excitement in her voice.

"It is not for the eyes to see, but for the heart to feel."

With those words, she felt something brush against her. She jumped back, her hand flying to her neck. It had felt almost like fingers… or warm breath against flesh.

A definite presence surrounded her, hovering over her like a cloud of vapor, and a finger of that invisible vapor made contact with her, grazing her arm, her neck, the skin behind her ear…

"Elisabeth."

Elisabeth started at the voice that had come from Ohia, a lower, deeper voice. Familiar. Affectionate.

She trembled, stepping backward even while feeling the impulse to approach.

Could it be?

"Elisabeth, say something."

She couldn't believe it. She had hoped for this, had clung to the remote possibility, but deep down she had always known it would end in disappointment.

But how, then, to explain this…

"Emery," she whispered. It was part-question, part-statement.

The being nodded. The being? The creature? Her dear Emery? All of those things, perhaps, and also a woman, a stranger—a dead stranger with a gunshot wound through her chest.

A thousand questions crowded in. How was this possible? Why was he here? What did he want from her?

"We always had lousy timing," she said instead. The words tumbled out. "You're dead."

She/he/it smiled. *He,* she decided. It was a *he.*

"You are dead, right?" she clarified. As silly a question as it was, she had to voice it.

"I am."

She shuddered, and tears appeared in her eyes. She tried to wipe them away with the back of her hand, but new tears took their place and escaped down her cheeks.

Pull yourself together, Elisabeth.

*   *   *

Several flat stone surfaces stuck out from the base of the machine. One in particular reminded Dario of a computer keyboard, with slightly raised squares and rectangles that could have stood in for buttons.

"Look at this," Sheply said. The man knelt over a slab of gold-plated rock that served as the machine's base.

The creators of the machine had bordered the edges of the slab with a series of carvings.

"Is it decorative?" Dario asked.

Sheply peered up at him, a look of wonder on his face. "Mr. Katsulas, I believe we are looking at the first and only example of written language ever discovered in Tiahuanaco."

"That's not possible."

"And a spirit that possesses dead bodies is?"

Dario got down next to him. "Point taken."

Sheply was right; the writing was comprised of simple straight lines, most of them vertical, though some formed parts of more elaborate characters.

"What do you think it says?" Dario asked.

"One would hope it provides an explanation for the machine's function." Sheply followed the passage of text as it wormed its way around the stone. He stopped halfway along the length of stone, where a heavier than usual vertical line divided the text in two halves. "I think it begins here."

"Do you have a pen?" Dario asked.

Sheply dug one out of his pocket, handing it over.

Dario uncapped the pen and indicated a sequence of about thirty characters at the beginning of the message. "These here are repeated along each side, you see?"

Dario pushed the sleeve of his shirt as far up his elbow as it would go and began to copy the letters on the inside of his arm.

"We can bring in a language specialist to document this," Sheply said.

Dario did not stop writing. "Doctor Christophe will want to—"

"You don't get it. Doctor Christophe isn't in charge anymore."

Sheply hoisted himself up, gripping the edge of the keyboard-like stone.

A low-frequency hum filled the room as Sheply got to his feet.

Dario's eyes shot up. He turned in a circle, trying to identify the source of the hum, which seemed to come from everywhere at once.

"What did you do?" Dario demanded.

"I didn't do a thing."

But the glow emanating from that keyboard-like stone put the lie to Sheply's statement.

*   *   *

A persistent humming sound pulled Elisabeth's attention away from the creature in front of her. She turned to shout at the men for cutting in on—

Her shout stuck in her throat and all anger flew out of her mind. A bright yellow glow shone from the machine, reflecting off the faces of Sheply and Dario, who appeared to be in shock.

The mysterious machine was in the process of powering up.

"It's happened."

Elisabeth glanced back at the creature. Emery had gone, replaced again by Ohia. Its eyes were wide with excitement.

The hum grew louder and deeper.

"What's happening?" Elisabeth asked.

"The machine seems to be activating." Dario pointed to a slab of rock which was glowing yellow, the laws of physics be damned.

Sheply placed his hand on the yellow panel, but nothing happened. "Emery believed it was a generator."

"Look."

Ohia stepped toward them, a trembling finger pointed at the glass bulb. Within it, the filament had turned bright orange.

"Gentlemen." Elisabeth had to shout to be heard over the noise, which got higher and louder by the second. "I suggest we make it stop."

Sheply pounded the glowing stone. "I would if I could!"

The widest smile Elisabeth had ever seen broke across Ohia's face. The being closed its eyes and raised its hands to the machine as though enraptured.

Dario stared at Ohia's sudden state of bliss. "Whatever's going on, the creature wants it to happen. If you ask me, that can't be a good sign."

Elisabeth turned on Ohia. "Tell us what the machine is."

"Your colleague was correct. It is a generator."

"What does it power?"

"Oh, a great many things. The lights, for one."

On cue, golden light poured out from the dozen corridors leading into the central chamber. Those stone globe fixtures along the walls of the caverns pulsed with the same bright light that came from the panel on the machine.

Sheply let out a startled cry and doubled over, both his hands clamped over his eyes. His mouth gaped in a painful grimace.

"Don't look directly at the filament," Dario said.

Instinct almost made her glance toward the enormous glass bulb, but Dario's warning registered just in time. She twisted her gaze away. The machine's blinding intensity gave her few safe places to look besides the floor.

"Can you shut it off?" Elisabeth shouted at Ohia.

Ohia stood directly in front of the machine, head back and arms spread wide as though welcoming a dear old friend.

"Almost time, almost!"

Before Elisabeth could ask what it was almost time for, the ambient light flashed. She let out a cry and slammed her fists over her eyes. For a moment, she could only see the blood-red backs of her own eyelids.

The red soon faded to orange, from orange to grey, and from grey to black. Even once blackness returned, Elisabeth waited, counting to ten before peeking an eye open.

The once-dark chamber was bathed in dull light. Previously unseen globes of light decorated the upper walls. Only a soft glow escaped the machine's glass bulb.

Elisabeth brushed her hands together. The hairs on her arms stood straight, as though affected by static electricity. She detected a faint hum in the air. Was this the generator's doing? How did it work? How could stone produce light?

Dario opened his eyes and oriented himself. Sheply stood nearby blinking fast, his hand pressed against the side of his head.

Ohia leaned against the side of the machine. It breathed heavily, smiling in elation.

"I have waited more than a thousand years for this." It turned to them as if just remembering they were there. *"You do not know what you have done."*

Ohia stepped away from the machine and turned its eyes hungrily toward the ceiling. *"Ah, I see you have left me a gift."*

The body it inhabited sagged and fell to the ground like a sack of potatoes. Dario rushed to the dead woman's side and cradled her body in his arms.

But that woman was long gone.

And now, Elisabeth thought grimly, *so too is Ohia.*

*   *   *

For several minutes, Brighton waited for the old woman to speak, but a brooding silence settled over the hut. The spirit that had spoken through the woman's body had gone and didn't seem to be in a hurry to get back.

Ricky had forced himself to his feet and was now at his grand-mother's side, making sure she was okay.

"How is she?" Brighton asked.

Ricky glanced at him. "She's alive, she's breathing."

Suddenly, the old woman's back straightened. She pushed Ricky's hands away and began to chatter.

"Is it her?" Brighton took a step closer. "Or is it the spirit who was here?"

"It's her," Ricky said, relief flooding his voice. "There were two spirits, she says. One was speaking to her over a great distance, and another was in the room with us. That second one had a name."

He paused, then asked her to repeat herself.

"What was the name?" Brighton asked.

"Em–er–y," the old woman said, stumbling over the exotic word. It needed no translation.

"Do you know that name?" Ricky asked.

Brighton ran a nervous finger through his hair and laughed. It wasn't possible. He had seen Emery Wörtlich die right in front of his eyes.

No.

Just no.

Yet how could he deny what he had witnessed?

"I knew a man named Emery," Brighton finally said, his voice as quiet as he could make it. "But he died a long time ago."

Ricky nodded. "This is not the first time the dead have spoken to my grandmother. She says the spirit was drawn to you in a powerful way. A very strong connection."

"Did the spirit leave a message for me?"

Ricky asked the question to his grandmother. In reply, she shook her head.

"It departed too quickly," Ricky said. "Something drew it away."

"I have to go," Brighton said, backing toward the door. He had missed his eight o'clock appointment with Elisabeth by a few hours. He had to make sure she was alright.

Ricky remained at his grandmother's side, smoothing her bristly grey hair and whispering to her. Brighton regretted that anyone was forced to live this way, in squalor and in contact with such supernatural terrors. But the woman looked around the hut with hard, steely eyes, not at all troubled by what had transpired.

"Go," Ricky called to him. "I want to stay with her for a few minutes."

Brighton reached for the doorknob, his heart rate returning to normal.

Despite all the trouble he'd gone through, he realized he didn't know much more now than he had before. All he had learned was that Elisabeth might not have been as crazy as he supposed; Wörtlich might indeed be trying to contact him. But for what purpose?

The stars shone unusually bright, as though someone had cranked the power behind them and they were surging as a result.

A cool breeze blew off the lake. In the distance, waves lapped against the shore in a lazy push-and-pull rhythm, punctuated by the chirping of crickets. He shivered as he stepped down the creaky steps onto the path and glanced at the low-hanging moon.

He stopped, a strange tingling sensation running up and down his spine. He squinted and focused on the car.

Something's not right. I'm being watched again.

He backed away, though he didn't think the hut provided any safety. If this spirit was determined to reach him, it would find a way.

A shadow appeared from around the side of the hut and headed toward him, brushing through the tall grasses on its way up from the lakeshore.

Who would be waiting down by the water at this time of night? he asked himself. He thought about calling for Ricky, but something stopped him, giving him pause.

As Brighton's eyes adjusted to the darkness, he made out the figure of a short man with the uneven gait of advanced age.

"Who are you?" Brighton called, curiosity winning over caution. His voice echoed as it skipped across the rolling surface of the lake.

The man laughed. "You don't recognize me."

Brighton stumbled and fell to his right knee. That voice was more than merely familiar, and this time it hadn't come from a dead man.

"Sorry I'm late," Ira Binyamin said. "I lost track of time."

TWENTY-ONE

Lake Titicaca, Bolivia
JULY 23

The rest of the world had aged a year and a half, but Ira Binyamin hadn't aged a day. He wore the same tweed jacket atop a blue sweater Brighton remembered from the last time they'd seen each other, on a deep-rutted roadway on the island of Tubuai.

Ira helped Brighton to his feet, holding the young man's hand in an iron grip. Brighton politely extricated himself from the man's hold and stepped back.

"I'm fine," Brighton gasped, catching his breath. "You just took me by—" He sat down, feeling the seat of his pants hit the damp earth. "You took me by—"

He brought a hand to his head, steadying himself as the world spun around him.

"What the hell, Ira? I mean, seriously, damn it. Where have you *been?*" He blinked, tears moistening the corners of his eyes. "You told me… you *promised* me you'd be there, that you'd help. Do you know what kind of year I've had?"

Ira sat on the path but didn't say anything.

"Wörtlich was right about you." Brighton wiped his eyes. He would not cry in front of Ira. "You decide what the people around you need to know, then withhold everything but the bare minimum. Who gave you that authority?"

"You've done alright."

Brighton barked out a laugh as the memories of one crisis after another flitted before his eyes.

The two sat in aloof silence for several minutes, the stars shining and the crickets chirping and the waves rolling onto shore.

"You aren't wet," Brighton murmured.

"Wet?"

"You came up from the lake. I take it you weren't down there for a late-night swim."

"I should think not."

"Seriously, where were you all this time?" Brighton asked. "Don't give me the runaround. I think I deserve a straightforward answer."

"Why do you assume what you've gone through is somehow more profound than what others have gone through?"

Brighton felt so enraged he had to laugh. "Okay, Ira, I'll play along. I can admit that I'm self-centered if you'll do the same. Let's trade our stories of woe. You start. I insist."

Ira rested his hand against Brighton's knee. "I've missed you, Sherwood. What do you want to know?"

"I want to know what happened to the Book of Creation."

Ira arched his eyebrows. "And if you don't like the answer?"

"I can decide that for myself."

"What you don't know, you can't share with others. With your consent or against it." Ira took a long breath, seeming to taste the air as though it were a great delicacy. "Very well. I returned the Book to its owner, where it was meant to be all along. It's safe."

"To its owner?" Brighton asked with a frown. "You're right. I don't like that answer."

Feeling somewhat more composed, Brighton pushed himself to his feet, then helped the rabbi up. Brighton continued walking toward the car. When he got there, he placed his hand on the sun-faded hood and turned to find the rabbi approaching slowly, hands in his pockets.

"Once something is in your memory, it is possible to access it," Brighton said, the words that had haunted him for so many months springing to mind.

A smile curved the edges of Ira's lips. "You remember."

"It takes discipline and action," Brighton continued to recite. "It takes patience. It does not happen by accident. It happens through intention."

Ira's smile grew wider.

"So, you remember saying those words." Brighton's voice dripped with sarcasm.

"Of course I do," the rabbi said. "Those words changed my life, just as I believe they can change yours."

Brighton swallowed, tilted his head, and forced back a fresh round of tears. A few slipped through.

Ira noticed. "I'm sorry I couldn't be here for you."

"Ira, I've been so very alone. I had no one!"

Ira came forward and stood in front of him. Brighton shifted away, but the back of his knees buckled against the car's bumper. He was cornered.

"You were never alone," Ira assured him.

That's a lie, Brighton thought, though he stopped the words from reaching his lips.

"There's a lot of power in those words," Ira said. "They were first spoken to me by my mentor, a man named Aaron. With those words, my life took on more purpose and direction than I ever could have imagined."

"You're talking about Aaron Roth."

Ira drew a quick breath. "How do you know about—"

"Because I went looking for you. And I found Aaron, on his deathbed." Brighton watched as Ira's surprise turned to dismay. "He's gone, Ira."

Ira turned toward the lake. He said something, speaking quietly, a murmur.

"Ira?" Brighton called.

The old man peered over his shoulder, as though remembering where he stood. "The secrets of the ancients must be protected. The secrets of the deep, the secrets of Jehovah ... "

"Ira, I don't know what that means."

Ira sighed. "There will be time for explanations later."

"Why always later, and never now?"

Just then, Brighton heard the hut's door creak shut. Ricky walked toward them, car keys swinging around his index finger. The Bolivian man stopped short.

"Who is that?" Ricky asked.

Brighton glanced toward the car; Ira had gotten into the front seat.

There will *be time for explanation,* Brighton thought. *I'll make sure of that.*

*   *   *

In the hours before dawn, a pall settled over Tiahuanaco. Elisabeth sat in a fold-up chair in the cafeteria tent. Dario sat next to her, his head lowered. Sheply rested at a nearby table, rubbing his sightless eyes and cursing under his breath. Much of the camp was still asleep, blissfully unaware of their nocturnal activities.

Elisabeth pushed back her chair and approached Sheply, who didn't look up. "Noam?"

She put her hand on his shoulder and sat next to him. He stiffened at her touch but didn't pull away.

"Noam, how are you feeling?" she asked.

He stopped muttering. "Stupid question. Stupid, stupid question."

"Can you see anything at all?" she asked, trying again.

"Nothing."

"Not even light?"

"Maybe a bit, around the edges."

"That's a good sign," she said. "It means your vision could still come back."

Sheply grunted and Elisabeth fell silent. Perhaps now wasn't the best time to talk him out of feeling sorry for himself.

The tent flap burst open and a tall man in a brown coat swept into the cafeteria.

"We couldn't find him," the man barked.

Elisabeth's heart fell. Guy, the man Dario had left up on the pyramid, was missing.

That was the gift Ohia mentioned, she thought. *We shouldn't have left Guy atop the pyramid. I should have insisted—*

"I had no way of knowing what would happen," Dario said, lifting his eyes to the newcomer. "Doctor, that machine in the tunnels... we must have done something to activate it."

Doctor Christophe, Elisabeth realized. This man in the brown coat was the site director.

"Well, he's gone," Doctor Christophe said, leaning forward and resting his knuckles on the table. "Ohia is gone. This is a disaster. We could have controlled him, learned from him. Now what?"

"What about those men from the government?" Dario asked.

"They're demanding to know what happened." The site director's eyes rested on Sheply, who stared blankly ahead. "Doctor Sheply, did you at least learn anything?"

"Dario's right," Sheply said in a humorless voice. "The machine is responsible for the creature's escape. It must have some connection with the barrier. But it will take time to understand how it works."

"We'll begin studying the machine right away," Christophe said. "Perhaps there's a way to trap him again."

Elisabeth couldn't believe what she was hearing. "Are you joking? We'll probably never find him, never mind find a way to control him."

Sheply pushed himself up, groping the edge of his chair to steady himself. "I'm returning to Egypt. There's nothing more I can do here."

"But your employer," Christophe began. "He must—"

"Doctor Christophe, you have no idea who I work for," Sheply interrupted. "It's laughable that you imagine you have any authority at all."

Christophe blanched, his face alternating between anger and surprise. He looked to be on the verge of protesting, but then thought better of it. Setting his jaw, he marched out with all the dignity he could muster.

"Is he gone?" Sheply asked a moment later.

Elisabeth turned to him, a very slight smile on her face. "You know perfectly well that he is."

"Elisabeth, it may take me a while to grow accustomed to this new reality." Sheply rubbed his eyes again. "I keep thinking I can somehow will my vision to return. But it doesn't work that way."

She truly did feel sorry for him. They had known each other for sixteen years and had a long history. Blindness was a terrible fate.

"Elisabeth, could I speak to you in private?" Dario asked quietly.

Sheply reached out a hand, groping for her arm. He didn't come close to touching her. "Don't shut me out, Elisabeth. I'm as much a part of this as you are."

"We aren't friends, Noam. Surely you must understand that."

"Are we not?" Unexpectedly, his voice held genuine sadness. "I thought we were."

Elisabeth felt a pang upon realizing that he really believed she was the nearest thing he might have to a friend.

But she couldn't let her emotions get in the way of what had to be done. She and Noam weren't just unfriendly; they were on opposite sides of a conflict.

She took Dario aside, far enough away that Sheply couldn't overhear. "What is it?" she asked.

Dario showed her the markings he had made on the inside of his arm. "Before the machine activated, I scribbled this down."

She squinted at the thin, shaky pen lines. "Scribbled from where?"

"From the machine," he explained. "It's less than half the message. I wasn't able to get it all down in time."

"What do you think it means?"

"I have no idea, and there aren't any language specialists here with the expertise to translate it. As far as we know, this could be an entirely new form of language."

She hung her head. "I hope not. This may be our only clue about Ohia's whereabouts."

"Do you think we'll be able to figure out where he went?"

Elisabeth didn't answer. It didn't seem likely.

"It's not a good idea to chase after Ohia," Dario said. "All I want to do is get the hell out of here and never look back."

"That would be selfish. Ohia is powerful, Dario. If we do nothing, a lot of other innocent people could get hurt. I know you don't want that."

Yet chasing Ohia was, in its own way, just as selfish. Her motivation had less to do with saving innocents than with contacting Emery. He'd been about to tell her something before the machine turned on—something important enough to seek her out from beyond the grave. She had to know what it was.

The tent flap opened and Doctor Christophe stalked inside, this time with two Bolivian men at his back. He pointed to Dario and Elisabeth.

"Take them into custody," Christophe said.

Dario surprised Elisabeth by placing himself between her and the Bolivian men, who stopped their advance.

"Under whose authority?" Dario asked.

"The government of Bolivia," Christophe said. "You'll be taken to La Paz and debriefed."

"You mean interrogated."

"As long as you answer all questions to our satisfaction, it won't matter what you choose to call it."

Christophe nodded to the Bolivian men, who took it as a cue to seize Dario. Dario tensed, as though he was going to put up a fight, but then his shoulders relaxed and he allowed himself to be led away.

"Place them in the holding area," Christophe said as one of the Bolivians grabbed Elisabeth by the shoulder.

Sheply's loud chuckle stole their attention just as they were about to leave the tent.

"It sounds like you could use a friend right about now, Elisabeth," the Englishman said in a mocking tone.

The urge to wrest free and kick him in the face was strong... just not strong enough to break out of the Bolivian man's hold.

"You are free to go, Mr. Sheply," Christophe said.

"My freedom was never in your hands," Sheply reminded him coldly. "But I will go. My employer will want to hear about what's happened."

A moment later, Elisabeth was force-marched through the quiet tent city, the obnoxious sound of Sheply's laugh ringing in her ears.

Wherever you are, Mr. Brighton, I hope you're doing better than I am.

TWENTY-TWO

Tiahuanaco, Bolivia
JULY 23

The lights of Tiwanaku twinkled on the horizon as the weather-beaten car carrying Brighton, Ira, and bright-eyed Ricky came over the top of a grassy hill.

Brighton was relieved when they came to a blessed rest along the same street they had started out from earlier in the day. He got out and felt his shoes sink into a low drift of sand which had swept across the street, forming a ridge.

Ira had been characteristically quiet during the drive. It had drained every reserve of forbearance for Brighton to contain his endless questions until he and the rabbi were alone; he would keep poor Ricky out of all this madness if at all possible—at least to the degree that Ricky could be spared after witnessing that business with his grandmother.

"Where are you going next?" Ricky asked, closing his car door behind him.

Ira's eyes turned to Brighton, silently asking the same question. Could it be that Ira didn't have a plan? Was Brighton in the proverbial driver's seat this time around? He felt a mixture of relief, delight, and fear at the prospect.

"To La Paz," Brighton lied. The less Ricky knew, the better. There weren't many places to stay in the village and most of Tiahuanaco's tourist traffic flowed to and from the capital—though if Ricky was savvy he would know better than to peg Brighton as a tourist.

But maybe it was time to stop concerning himself with what Ricky thought.

Ricky got back into his car, settling in behind the steering wheel. His eyes watched them through the rearview mirror as he drove away.

"Where are we really going?" Ira asked as Brighton led them down the dusty street. Gravel crunched underfoot.

"Oh, we are headed back to La Paz," Brighton assured him. "We just have a few things to take care of first."

"Nothing has changed, I see."

As they approached the church, Brighton explained why he had come to Tiahuanaco—and with whom. Ira seemed troubled when he learned of Elisabeth's involvement in this venture.

"What is her motivation for helping you?" Ira asked.

Brighton hesitated. Ira wouldn't be comfortable with the truth, but Brighton respected him too much to withhold it.

"She believes…" How to put this? "She believes Wörtlich's spirit is reaching out to us."

Ira didn't react with any of the disbelief Brighton had expected. *I must remember to stop underestimating him.*

"You believe this as well?" Ira asked.

"Not at first. But I've had a visitation of my own." A lump formed in Brighton's throat. That sounded ominous. Perhaps appropriately so. "While I was at Stonehenge, I had a dream in which Wörtlich came to me."

"Sometimes a dream is just a dream."

Brighton stared at him incredulously. "And sometimes dreams are enormously significant, as you well know!"

"Wörtlich is gone, Sherwood. We can't bring him back."

Rage rose up in Brighton. "You think I don't know that? You think I could ever forget what happened at Tubuai?"

He wanted Ira to raise his voice, to fight back. Instead Ira responded with his customary patience and patriarchal compassion.

"Of course not," Ira said. "I apologize if I upset you. Nonetheless, Wörtlich couldn't have appeared to you, in any form."

Brighton took a deep breath and tried to relax. Outbursts, even if Ira deserved them, wouldn't help the situation.

"Elisabeth is convinced," Brighton said, "and what I just saw at the lake seems to corroborate her theory. Something was definitely possessing that old woman. It was like nothing I've ever seen, and it made me question my default position on the existence of ghosts."

"I think that's understandable."

Maddeningly, that was all Ira said until they arrived at the church.

Brighton walked to the middle of the courtyard and turned in a circle, searching the darkness around them.

"Elisabeth was supposed to meet me here," he said. "But that was hours ago."

Ira steadied himself on the stone wall around the courtyard. "Then we can wait."

"Ira, we can't just wait. She might be in trouble." Brighton paused.

"And don't say a word about meditation and that damned imaginary river of yours. There's a time for waiting around and hoping for the best, and then there's a time for action. What kind of time do you think this is?"

The words came out more bitterly than Brighton had intended.

Before Ira had a chance to answer, the quiet was interrupted by the roar of an approaching car. A few seconds later, Ricky's car stopped on the road outside the church.

"Get in," Ricky called. "Something has happened at the dig site I think you'll be interested in."

Brighton's concern for Elisabeth grew toward panic. The smug look on Ira's face only made it worse.

As always, Ira had been right.

Ricky quickly caught them up on the rumors circulating through the village, despite the late hour. Combined with increased activity at the ruins, there had been a flash of light so intense that it had appeared to seep up from out of the ground. Brighton figured its occurrence on the same day as Elisabeth's visit to the camp couldn't be a coincidence.

"We should rest before doing anything," Ira said.

Brighton's hand froze in the act of rubbing his eyes. "Rest is a luxury we can't afford."

Ira sighed serenely. "The night is almost through. Even an hour or two of rest will improve our chances of success in the morning."

Ricky gestured down the darkened street. "Come with me. I have a small apartment where you can lie down."

Brighton begrudgingly followed them back into the car.

The apartment was as small as advertised, not much more substantial than the cabin belonging to Ricky's grandmother. It was located above a corner shop and had only a single window facing the street. Ricky owned a couch, but no bed. He invited Brighton to lie down on it, but Brighton deferred to Ira. The rabbi insisted he would sleep well enough on the floor.

*   *   *

Brighton's dreams progressed languidly despite his recent harrowing experiences. Vague recollections of former friends and acquaintances—notably a girl named Rachel whose memory afflicted him with feelings of shame and regret—drifted among them.

At one point, he strolled through the countryside of his childhood home in Virginia. His parents had owned a farm on the eastern slopes of the Blue Ridge Mountains. The nearest neighbors lived a half-mile away on either side, and a tiny ribbon of gravel road in the distance offered the only evidence of civilization. He walked along a fence, his fingers grazing the chipped whitewashed wood, counting the posts just as he had done when he was a child. Night was falling and he expected his mother's voice to waft down from the house, calling him to dinner. The call never came.

The fence ended on the cusp of a steep embankment, a creek burbling happily in the gully below. Brighton wasn't supposed to climb down there—a house rule he dared not break—but today he felt adventurous. He took a few cautious steps before lowering himself to the ground and sliding the rest of his way on his butt, not concerning himself with the green stains that undoubtedly now slashed the backside of his khaki shorts. He would get an earful for that!

He clambered over a couple of car-sized slabs of bedrock sticking out of the loamy earth. Water had long flowed over them, smoothing their surface until they were more slippery than fish scales. He pressed down onto the soles of his runners, trying to establish a cleaner grip, but instead he caught a tiny patch of moss and slipped. His whole body sailed through the air for a moment, but just a moment, before hitting the water with a loud splash. He cried out from the pain of landing on a bed of pebbles.

He remained still for what felt like several minutes, eyes pointed up at fluffy clouds speeding across a purple sky. He was suddenly wet, cold, and certain he'd broken something.

My left arm, he remembered. *It was in a cast for two months, in the height of summer.*

And that was when he recognized the dream, that none of this was real. Or rather, that it wasn't real anymore. The events had happened twenty-five years ago, on the last Saturday before school ended. The broken arm had prevented him from going to a softball tournament with the rest of his school friends; he would never forget the bitterness he'd felt over the loss. He hadn't made the team the following year. He often wondered if things would have gone differently if he'd been able to finish out the season—

"Nothing would have changed," a voice spoke softly.

Brighton wanted to turn his head, to see who had spoken, but he didn't dare move his left side. His arm was pinned between two rocks.

"What are you talking about?" Brighton asked.

"Softball. If you had not broken your arm, you still would not have made the team. It would not have made a difference. You would be exactly the same man you are today. Now, get up. Your arm is fine."

Wörtlich.

"It's you," Brighton said weakly, testing his arm. He expected a sharp jab of pain all the way up to his shoulder, but he felt nothing.

He turned his head, looking in all directions, but he couldn't see anyone.

"Yes. It is me."

Brighton searched in the direction of the voice. Darkness covered the trees, the evening shadows already long and deep. Something moved in the darkness, a figure standing just beyond the trees.

"Doctor Wörtlich?" Brighton's voice was filled with incredulity.

It's only a dream, he told himself. *There's no such things as ghosts.*

He got to his feet, water collecting in his sneakers, and climbed onto the narrow strip of level grass alongside the creek. Behind him, the house became visible atop a rise. He wouldn't go back there.

This was a dream; he could go anywhere he wanted. He followed the creek's course south, venturing into parts of the landscape his teenage self had never visited on foot, for fear of the consequences.

The gorge deepened to the point that he doubted his ability to scramble up its sides. Not far ahead was an old washed-out bridge. He remembered when the road had closed three springs earlier, when the creek flooded worse than it ever had before.

"Mr. Brighton, you are ignoring me. Do I frighten you?"

Brighton's back stiffened and he couldn't help surveying the top of the ridge. There was no one there, yet the voice sounded close enough that it may as well have been whispered in his ear.

I'm not afraid. I just don't believe in ghosts.

"Say it aloud, my friend," the voice said. "It will make you feel better."

The same dark, indistinct figure he'd seen earlier now stood above him, at the edge of the washed-out bridge. At this distance, it was barely distinguishable from the trees.

"I'm not afraid," Brighton said, taking the voice's advice. "I am *not* afraid."

"And I am glad to hear it. You never before struck me as a coward."

That didn't quite sound like the Wörtlich he knew.

Brighton began walking toward the bridge. "You sound bitter."

"Being killed would have that effect on anyone." Wörtlich's accent was strong, perhaps even stronger than Brighton remembered. "I apologize for my appearance. It takes a great deal of effort to exert myself, even here, at a hotspot."

Why did he find it so hard to believe this was really happening? The dream felt real. Why should he fear Wörtlich's appearance? Even Ira had demonstrated a similar technique.

"Have you come to me with a message?" Brighton asked.

"Mr. Brighton, why do you reduce me to the role of messenger?" The voice—Wörtlich's voice?—struck him as disappointed. "I was much more to you once."

Brighton hesitated. "Then you really are here?"

Wörtlich let out a long laugh. "Yes. I am, indeed, really here."

A wave of nausea overcame Brighton and he felt the need to sit down, but there was nothing convenient to rest upon.

"If you want someplace to sit, Mr. Brighton, might I suggest a chair?"

"There is no chair."

"Not yet," Wörtlich said. "But this is a dream. Simply create one."

Brighton didn't understand how that worked, but Ira had certainly exhibited such mastery over the dream world. He squeezed his eyes shut and focused, certain nothing would come of the effort.

Except it did. When Brighton opened his eyes again, a lawn chair, just like the one he had imagined, appeared on the grass.

"You could have chosen something more comfortable," Wörtlich remarked.

Brighton fell into the chair. His heart raced, and he could do nothing to control it. He couldn't believe he hadn't woken up from the strain, but then he decided he didn't want to wake up. When would he have another experience like this?

"Elisabeth was right," Brighton said quietly. "You are alive."

"Well, not alive. But something near enough to it that the truth is of no consequence."

Brighton's heart beat faster at the thrill of truly hearing the professor's voice again. He and Wörtlich had been little more than colleagues, but absence certainly had made the heart grow fonder.

"I feel silly asking this," Brighton said, considering his words, "but are you a ghost?"

"Does it matter what I am?"

"Maybe not," he conceded. "But if it takes so much effort to show yourself, you must have an important reason for doing so."

"That much is true." A long pause. "I have a message."

Brighton stood and continued walking toward the bridge, wanting to get a closer look at Wörtlich's apparition. "But why appear to me? Why not Elisabeth?"

"I tried. We were interrupted."

The sun dipped below the trees, casting the entire gorge in shadow. Brighton squinted at the figure on the bridge, but it was getting harder to see.

"Time is running short," Wörtlich said. "You must come and find me at Olmolungring."

Brighton quickened his pace, his feet dipping into the water's edge. "Olmo… I'm sorry. What did you say?"

"Olmolungring. It is so beautiful here, a marvelous place."

He felt his mind drifting. As the light faded, it became more and more difficult to concentrate. Brighton fought to hold on to the dream, though he could feel it slipping from his fingers.

"Come quickly. It may soon be too late for me to be restored."

Olmolungring. Olmolungring. I must not forget it…

He managed a final upward glance at the bridge, but Wörtlich was no longer standing on its edge—and a moment later the world around Brighton collapsed, darkening and twisting as he was sucked out of the vision.

"Sherwood," Ira called to him. "Sherwood, I need you to listen to me. Wake up."

Brighton groaned as he opened his eyes to the grey, featureless world of Ricky's apartment…

…except that wasn't where he was. Aside from Ira, and Ricky just over the rabbi's shoulder, this was not the same place he had fallen asleep.

"Where am I?" Brighton asked, sitting up. He sat on the ground, a river flowing past him. This river was ten times wider than the slow-winding creek that ran past his family's farm.

Ira helped him to his feet. "You were in a daze. I fell asleep myself, and when I awoke you were halfway down the stairs. Ricky and I followed you here."

Brighton took a long look around, his eyes adjusting to the early morning light. A towering ridge of mountains rose on the other side of the river, and behind Ira shone the lights of the village.

"And where is 'here'?" Brighton asked.

"We're at the river," Ira said. "You were sleepwalking."

"Why didn't you wake me?"

Ira hesitated, looking uncomfortable. "I tried. Nothing worked."

Brighton peered in the direction he had been walking. Where had he been going?

"I'm just glad you're awake," Ira said, expressing his relief. "You had me worried."

Frowning, Brighton looked the rabbi in the eye. "Rabbi, you were wrong. Wörtlich spoke to me."

Ira let out a long breath. "Sherwood, we've been over this."

"No," Brighton insisted, raising the intensity of his voice if not the volume. "Wörtlich *is* back, and he came bearing a message."

TWENTY-THREE

Tiahuanaco, Bolivia
JULY 23

Dario was sick to death of tents. A month in Tiahuanaco had led him to despise camp life. He hated everything about it—the work, the food, the people, the endless stretches of beige canvas. All the excitement he'd felt at coming to a new country and facing new challenges was dead. This godforsaken place had utterly betrayed him.

"How much time do you think we have?" Marco asked.

Dario opened his eyes, only now realizing he had dozed off. Dawn was on the way, filling the tent with diffused light.

"I'm not sure they'll be taking you at all," Elisabeth said, huddled on the hard ground on the other side of the tent. "The doctor only mentioned taking Dario and me to La Paz."

"They'll take Marco, too," Dario assured them. "They can't leave him behind after what he's seen."

Both pairs of eyes turned to him.

Elisabeth sighed. "I suppose you're right."

Marco's face fell and he looked totally defeated. Dario had no words to cheer him up; these were grim circumstances.

"Can I get another look at those symbols on your arm?" Elisabeth asked Dario in an obvious attempt to change the subject.

Dario couldn't think of any better way to pass the time. He pushed himself up and crossed over to them, rolling back the sleeve of his shirt and displaying the pen markings which were already faded and blurry from sweat.

Marco moved in for a closer look, reminding Dario that the Bolivian man knew nothing of the runes.

Elisabeth studied them, but ultimately brushed back her matted curls and looked away. "They may as well be chicken scratches."

But Marco's eyes had fixed on them.

"What is it?" Dario asked.

"They're runes," Marco said.

Dario prevented himself from smacking the man across the head. "Well, I can see that. Do you have any other insights?"

Perhaps Marco was too preoccupied to notice Dario's irritation, because he didn't react, except to say, "I think I've seen this kind of writing before."

That was enough to catch Elisabeth's attention. She leaned back in to hear what Marco had to say.

"A few years ago, I travelled to Panama to complete a research project on the Kuna, one of the region's indigenous tribes. I know very little about their language, except that it originated long before the Spanish came. I saw many examples of it. Its pictographic written form dates back centuries. The people I was with were trying to answer the question of why the Kunga learned to read and write while the Incas, and the even earlier residents of Tiahuanaco, both much larger civilizations, never bothered with written language at all."

Dario glanced down at the runic scribblings on his arm. "But these aren't pictographic, Marco. What's the connection?"

"Amongst the early Kuna documents, most of which were found on rock faces and tablets, I saw runic characters much like these. They were notable because they were so different from everything else found in the region." Marco met Dario's gaze. "As far as I know, the mystery has never been explained."

"Perhaps it could be accounted for by understanding that the indigenous civilizations were guided by shared gods," Elisabeth suggested. "Living gods, like Ohia."

Marco managed a slight nod. "Perhaps. I can't help you translate it, though. I doubt anybody could."

"Then we're no closer," Dario said, disappointed.

The tent flap opened and a dark-skinned youth poked his head in. "Come with me."

"I suppose three escapes from this camp in one week would be one too many," Dario murmured under his breath.

This time, Doctor Christophe wasn't taking any chances. More muscle waited for them outside—virtually the camp's entire private security force.

The dark-skinned youth who had come to get them also had the distinction of leading this veritable platoon of guards. Only now did Dario note that he wore army fatigues. Christophe hadn't bluffed; they really were being taken into custody by the government.

The procession drew a lot of attention, but Dario no longer cared about what his former colleagues thought of him.

Let them speculate.

A white van waited in the parking area. From the passenger window, an elderly man watched them with an inscrutable expression—one of those damned government men Doctor Christophe was so proud to have hosted.

The man in army fatigues opened the back door of the van and held it wide, waiting for the camp security escorts to load them. Dario briefly considered making a run for it, but where would he go? The parking lot was too exposed. Resigned, he allowed himself to be pulled into the van.

The army man got in last. He closed the doors behind them, shutting them in the dark, windowless interior. He and Elisabeth sat next to each other on a wooden bench. Marco and the army man sat across from them.

Dario wondered at the lack of restraints as the van pulled out of the parking area and headed for the road. Their jailers didn't seem worried about escape attempts, a handful of which Dario was already busy devising; carried out to their logical extremes, none had happy endings.

The silence was deep for the first few minutes, and indeed, what was there to say? Dario had no doubt these men would ask a lot of questions in the coming days, and work hard to elicit answers.

When they were a few miles away from camp, the army man exhaled a long breath. Dario had failed to notice, but the man had been holding it in.

"Is anyone following us?" the man asked.

The driver turned his head to the left and checked the side-view mirror. "No. I think we've gotten away."

Dario looked from one man to the other in confusion. The army man actually let out a smile and wiped some sweat off his forehead.

"You're not from the government, are you?" Marco said.

The army man let out the quiet laugh of a nervous man.

Just then, Elisabeth's hand gripped Dario's, taking him by surprise. Her mouth opened in a wide grin as she surveyed the side of the driver's face.

"I should have known!" she exclaimed. "After hearing all your stories of close calls and narrow escapes, I shouldn't have doubted you'd come to the rescue."

Dario traded confused looks with Marco. "Elisabeth, do you know these people?"

Elisabeth turned to him, her grin no less effusive. "I'd like to introduce you to a friend of mine. Dario Katsulas, meet Sherwood Brighton."

"Good to meet you, Dario," Brighton said far more happily than their circumstances dictated.

Dario knew he should feel excited, grateful for their reprieve. Instead he just felt exhausted. "I suppose this is the associate you mentioned," he said to Elisabeth.

"That's right," she said.

The van slowed, and Dario leaned forward to look out the front window. They had come to the intersection with the main highway. Instead of turning east, as he expected, the van turned west.

"We aren't going to La Paz?" Elisabeth asked.

"It's safer to head for Peru," Brighton said.

Dario felt himself relax. "Your associate is right. I was recaptured when I tried to fly out of La Paz. Escaping that way won't have gotten any easier over the last couple of days. Peru makes sense, assuming we can get across the border."

"I don't think we have to worry about that." Brighton sounded assured of that fact. "I have a magic passport."

"A what?" Elisabeth asked.

Brighton shrugged. "It's a long story."

"I promised my uncle I would return his van tomorrow evening," said the young man in army fatigues.

"We're only heading as far as Juliaca," Brighton told the man. "That'll give you plenty of time to get back. No one needs to know you were involved with any of this."

Elisabeth sat forward. "How did you know we were awaiting transport?"

"News has been flowing out of the camp like water from a sieve," Brighton said.

"And where are we going after Juliaca?" Elisabeth asked.

The van fell silent. Dario frankly didn't care where they were going, so long as it was far away.

"Have any of you ever heard of a place called Olmolungring?" Brighton asked.

Once again, no one said anything.

But then Dario realized he *had* read that name before, in one of the texts from the Herculaneum library.

"Where did you hear that name?" Dario asked Brighton.

Brighton shrugged. "From an old friend."

Elisabeth's hand touched his leg. "Dario, what do you know?"

"Not very much." He let out a long yawn. "But we have four hours to talk all about it."

TWENTY-FOUR

Islamabad, Pakistan

JULY 25

From the air, Islamabad looked like a triangular patchwork quilt. Contrary to Brighton's expectations, Pakistan's capital city was quintessentially modern. Having been established in 1960, the terrain had been carved over time into neat grids, each square organized into symmetrical thoroughfares and neighborhoods, the perfection of which stood in sharp contrast to the rolling foothills of the western Himalayas.

Once through customs and safely deposited in the terminal, the group made their way outside. They'd been forced to leave their belongings behind, and thus skipped the crowd of fellow passengers gathering around the baggage carousel.

Brighton stepped onto boiling hot pavement. The sun burned

down through a cloudless sky, the daytime temperature soaring well into the low hundreds. The heat was even more relentless than the humidity he had barely tolerated in England.

He felt bad for Ira, who was perhaps too old to put up with the rigors of travel and extreme weather. Ira, however, seemed blissfully unaware of his limitations; he stood back from the others, his feet just inside the shade of the terminal's overhanging roof. He watched with serene eyes as cars whizzed by the loading zone, honking, dodging in and out of fast-moving lanes, and passing within inches of each other.

Brighton didn't look forward to the coming drive, but the sooner they left the city, the better.

Dario sidled up next to him. "This isn't what I expected."

"What did you expect?"

"Don't get me wrong, but a crowd of women in burkas."

Brighton and Dario had spent the last day getting to know each other. Brighton had been relieved to discover that he liked the Italian man; they may have grown up on opposite sides of the world, but they had pursued similar careers and shared tastes in a lot of areas—food, film, books... even women. Dario was about the same age as him, had a comparable education, and was as skeptical of these mystical pursuits as Brighton had once been. Brighton could imagine them becoming friends, something he sorely missed.

The trip had been one of the most exhausting he had endured. They'd waited in Juliaca for seven interminable hours before boarding a plane to Lima, and thirty-three hours later—and no less than four flights—they had finally landed in Islamabad.

The one positive aspect to the long transit was that they'd had time to work out where they were going. In Lima, they had pulled together a cluster of uncomfortable plastic airport chairs and discussed their situation.

"We have to find the place Wörtlich told me about," Brighton said. He tried to sound confident, but his voice betrayed the uncertainty that had been building in him ever since Tiahuanaco. He had been so sure Wörtlich had contacted him, had given him a mission. But had it perhaps been nothing more than his own imagination?

"Olmolungring," Dario had said slowly, his accent lingering over the strange word. "Some of my college friends dabbled in Buddhism, and they often talked about a spiritual realm called Olmoliq. I can't tell you much about it, but I know it has something to do with the legend of Shamballa. An ancient lost city in the mountains of Tibet."

This information had prompted Elisabeth to get in touch with a friend of hers well-versed in Buddhism and other forms of Far East mysticism, who confirmed the connection between the two legends, except advised them to aim farther west than Tibet.

"Gayle tells me there's a hotspot in Kashmir," Elisabeth explained. "According to her, it's strongest in the Karakoram Range, near the Pakistan-China border."

Brighton didn't need to consult a map to be filled with dread. The remote Karakoram region featured some of the highest elevations on earth, and the unstable political situation only made it more daunting.

And yet here they were, a long day and a half later, speeding down Islamabad's main expressway, their jeep's climate control laboring against the oppressive midday heat as the four spires of the Faisal Mosque loomed on the horizon. The mosque's gleaming white supports stood in sharp contrast to the forested hills beyond.

Their GPS told them the Karakoram region was an eleven-hour drive north. On the way out of the city, they decided to stop at a sprawling market just long enough to buy key supplies. When Brighton volunteered to go, Ira insisted on accompanying him.

The market was crowded despite the heat. Merchants called out to them as they passed, though for the most part Brighton kept his head down. Everywhere he looked were colorful displays—fruits and vegetables, cuts of meat, jewelry and trinkets, clothing, even one booth featuring rolls of beautifully patterned, hand-embroidered prayer rugs.

Ira stopped in front of a stall featuring baskets of fresh fruit. He gestured for a bag, then filled it with bananas, bunches of grapes, and oranges. As he made his selections, Brighton fished around in his pocket for the rupees he had gotten at the airport currency exchange.

"The Karakoram is a big area," Brighton said as they moved on. "Reminds me of our trip to Antarctica, when we had no idea where we were going."

Ira was quiet as they approached another stall. Here, they picked up a dozen chapatti, stuffed with rice, lentils, and mutton curry.

Brighton decided to try again. "Ira, if you can help us narrow the search area, just say so."

"I'm not sure it's a good idea."

"Why the hell not?"

Ira raised an eyebrow. "Perhaps it would be best to keep your voice down."

"Over this din?"

"You never know who could be listening."

Brighton knew better than to argue. It was true; they were on precarious footing. There hadn't been time to cover their tracks.

They picked up some grilled kebabs and continued walking.

"Give me a straight answer," Brighton said. "Do you know where we should be going?"

Ira gave him a long, hard look. "This isn't like our search for the Book of Creation. I don't believe Wörtlich's ghost exists. Therefore, how can we find it?"

"Lagati once said you don't need to believe something exists to find it."

"He said that to you?"

"To Wörtlich, actually."

Ira looked away. "Well, you shouldn't believe everything you hear. Especially from men like Lagati. They'll tell you anything to get what they want."

"But Lagati was right about the Book," Brighton argued. "Wörtlich didn't believe it existed, and yet he *did* find it. If Wörtlich was wrong before, who's to say you can't be wrong now? You're not infallible, Ira."

"Sometimes I'm wrong, yes," Ira said with sadness in his eyes. Wherever that sadness came from, a lot of pain went with it.

After filling their bags with food, Brighton located a brass compass, a coiled rope, and a box of matches. The last item they purchased was a folding knife in a brown leather sheath. Ira didn't want to take it, but Brighton insisted. Who knew what awaited them in the mountains?

*   *   *

Every time Dario looked in Elisabeth's direction, he saw a glow in her eyes. She'd had the same look the first time they'd met, in a small meeting room in Ercolano nearly two years ago. Then, the excitement had centered around the index discovery, but this glow was different. It was personal. Dario couldn't wrap his head around it, but perhaps there was a chance the man she loved wasn't as dead and gone as she had supposed.

He hadn't truly loved Rhea. He might have come to love her, in time. Nonetheless, he would have given almost anything to bring her back, so he understood Elisabeth's zeal.

When Brighton and Ira returned from the market, Dario dove into a bag of fruit, snatching an overripe apple. Elisabeth offered him a few torn-off wedges of dry naan bread to go with it. He'd had better tasting meals, but after a long day of travel it more than satisfied. That apple tasted of freedom and relief.

Brighton got behind the wheel and started the engine. Cool air hit Dario in the face; he breathed it in and sagged back in his seat.

He napped for a few hours, waking intermittently and catching the sights through the window. The only conversation revolved around navigation. The GPS, from what he could gather, stubbornly refused to show them the way out of the city, forcing them to find their own route.

When he woke, this time for good, Dario saw that they were cruising through sparsely treed foothills along a highway. Sheep and goats watched them from behind wire fences, but never for more than a moment or two before returning to their business. There weren't many people or buildings along this lonely stretch of road. If Dario hadn't known better, he might have believed they were driving through the Italian countryside where he'd grown up.

He wanted to ask where they were, but Brighton and Ira were busy snapping at each other.

"Why do you insist on bringing out the worst in me?" Brighton seethed, his hands gripping the wheel.

Ira, somewhat slower in speech, took a moment to compose a response. "I'm not capable of bringing out anything in you that isn't already there."

That only infuriated Brighton further.

Dario had the impression Brighton didn't realize how openly he was broadcasting his emotions. In any event, the two shared an unusual dynamic, something like long friendship mixed with loathing.

Ira was a tough nut to crack. The older man wore his humility—and perhaps a dose of piety—on his sleeve. He was also sly. His eyes indicated a man whose mind was constantly at work, a man of fierce intelligence and unflappable conviction. Dario thought it might be a grating combination.

"Can't you just tell us where we're supposed to go?" Brighton demanded.

This time, Ira answered more quickly. "I don't have magic powers, Sherwood."

"That's not the way it seemed when we were looking for the Book of Creation."

"I can't account for the way you perceived me." Ira turned to look out the window.

"Then how did you know so much?"

"Through prayer, study, and meditation," Ira said. "Those are three skills you'd do well to master. I can help you, if you're willing. You've already taken the first steps."

"Do you really think this is the time to learn how to meditate?" Brighton's voice dripped with sarcasm. "Sure, Ira, let's do that. I'll just pull over onto this gravel shoulder. We can all hold hands and connect with that Jewish God of yours."

If Dario had known Brighton better, he would have jumped in, but they were barely acquaintances. Dario looked to Elisabeth, silently urging her to say something. She kept her head down, staring at the floor.

"Do you know what happened between them?" he asked Elisabeth in a low voice.

Elisabeth brushed aside a tangle of brown curls. "Ira betrayed him, I gather. Abandoned him somewhere. I actually don't think they've known each other that long."

Dario sat forward. "Really? In my experience, that level of resentment takes years to accumulate."

Her bright green eyes lost focus for a minute and she went back to looking at the floor. Had he touched on a sore spot? He shut up, not wanting to pry.

Brighton and Ira soon ran out of things to argue about, plunging the jeep into a silence no one was eager to break.

"Where are we now?" Dario ventured sometime later. He had tried to discern some clues from the signs along the road, but the few he saw were written in Arabic.

"Heading toward Mansehra," Brighton called over his shoulder while Ira consulted a map he'd found in the glove compartment. "We're a half-hour out, assuming we don't run into any trouble."

"Are we expecting trouble?" Dario asked.

"No," Brighton said. "But it'll come whether we expect it or not."

"We're near the border of the disputed Kashmir region," Ira said, almost offhandedly. "We'll want to maintain a low profile. The territorial dispute here is as bitter as it gets."

As bitter as the dispute raging between Brighton and Ira? Instead Dario said, "What happens if we don't?"

Elisabeth sighed. "Then we risk getting beheaded by one side or another."

Dario couldn't tell if she was joking.

The Karakoram Highway deposited them on the outskirts of Mansehra, a sea of low-lying buildings dotting steep green hills. Snowy peaks were visible to the north and east. The traffic was light as they looped past the city.

"The main highway detours hundreds of miles to the west from here," Ira said, eyes on the map. "I suggest we follow it, but it could add a day to the journey."

"In that case, no," Elisabeth said. "Sherwood, didn't you tell me Emery instructed us to come quickly?"

Brighton answered without taking his eyes off the road. "He certainly implied a time limit. He told me it wasn't too late for him to be restored."

"What does that even mean?" Dario asked.

Nobody answered for nearly a minute.

What have I gotten myself into? Dario wondered. *These people don't even have a plan.*

"We should take the safer road," Ira maintained.

"Let me see." Elisabeth held out her hand and Ira passed her the map. It only took her a moment to orient herself. "There's another road that takes a straighter path to the Chinese border. That's where we're going, isn't it?"

Dario craned over to see for himself. A jagged red line cut from Mansehra, connecting back with Karakoram Highway after a long detour. The shorter route would cut hundreds of miles off the journey.

"Some of those back roads are little more than dirt trails," Ira said. "The passes are barely navigable."

"He may be right," Dario said.

Elisabeth shot Ira a dark look. "And if Emery is beyond recovery by the time we get there, you'll be responsible." She tapped Brighton on the shoulder. "We'll take the shorter route."

They stopped on the far side of town to replenish their gas. Dario watched as Elisabeth slipped out a headscarf she had purchased at the airport. She wrapped it around her neck and face as though she'd done it a hundred times. No doubt she had, having spent so much time in Egypt.

Dario took a bathroom break, purchased a bottle of some kind of tea, and returned to the jeep. Ira was stretching his legs and doing his part to be inconspicuous.

"I guess you're looking forward to getting out of here," Dario said.

Ira cast him a placid look. "Why? It's very beautiful."

Dario could think of a dozen reasons to feel out of place in this backwater. Not thirty minutes ago, they'd driven through the city where Osama bin Laden had been killed. Dario had felt unsafe just walking to and from the bathroom, but perhaps that said more about his own insecurities.

"I don't even know what I'm doing here," Dario said to Brighton when the young man returned from paying for gas.

"You can't go home again."

"That's just an expression," Dario said. He placed his hand against the side of the jeep and pulled it away; after all these hours under the midday sun, it burned to the touch.

"No, it's not. I know exactly what you're going through, but you literally can't go home. Not now, anyway. Home is the first place they'll look."

Dario hoisted himself back into the jeep. "I still don't know exactly who *they* are. The Bolivian government?"

"Much worse," Brighton said. "The man who Sheply works for is one of the richest and most dangerous men in the world. Have you ever heard of Raff Lagati?"

Dario gasped. "You can't be serious."

"I wish it was all a joke, but I've been on the run from Lagati for well over a year. I don't see any end in sight."

Dario felt particularly discouraged as they continued north.

The mountains loomed ever closer as they rose out of the foothills, on approach toward the low pass at Bisian. Ira assured them that a series of more dangerous passes lay ahead, but this one was relatively tame. The pavement was smooth, though the switchbacks required some tight turns. Steep cliffs and thin ribbons of terraced farmland surrounded them—and everywhere he looked, his eyes met green, in every possible hue.

Once over the pass, they dropped into a new valley, marked by the swift-flowing Kunhar River and a ridge of snow-covered mountains. The road cut through the farm-dotted hillsides, surrounded on all sides by steep inclines. The terraces got narrower and rose higher on this side of the pass. The image reminded Dario of pictures of the Peruvian Andes he'd seen back in grade school. Men in white worked the fields, some of them at high enough altitudes that they appeared as nothing but specks to Dario's eyes.

"How much farther are we driving today?" Elisabeth asked as they snaked their way through yet another in a long series of small mountain towns.

"Depends on the weather," Brighton said. Grey clouds had formed, darkening the pristine landscape between them and the mountaintops. The occasional raindrop hit the windshield, portending more to come. "We may stop in Naran. There are tourist lodges in the area, and this is peak season."

Dario certainly liked the sound of a lodge. It would be a welcome change from the tents in Tiahuanaco. He'd managed to spend a few minutes at the airport splashing water on his face, but that hardly touched the grime and sweat accumulating beneath his ragged clothes. When he'd put these camp clothes on, he hadn't imagined traveling halfway around the world in them.

So it was that a smile lit his face as the downpour began. The jeep's wiper blades couldn't keep up with the force of rain that swept over them. As they entered Naran, he closed his eyes and listened to the pelting rain, anticipating a long, hot shower.

TWENTY-FIVE

Naran, Pakistan
JULY 25

As far as Elisabeth was concerned, the town of Naran, situated in the heart of the Kaghan Valley, was the most beautiful retreat on earth. The setting sun hovered just over jagged peaks, and below them the stony landscape exploded with the brightest blues and greens she could imagine. The town stretched out like a ribbon through the narrow valley, confined by the steep slopes on either side. The Kunhar churned relentlessly over the mass of eroded rocks littering its rapid-strewn course.

Being surrounded by such natural splendor made it easy to forget the urgency of their mission. She didn't know why Emery had sent them here, to one of the most remote and difficult places to reach on earth, but she hoped to get a direct answer soon.

Elisabeth longed to speak with Emery again—even *see* him, if such a thing were possible. Sherwood had seen him. Surely he would show himself to her, after everything they had been through, after their long separation.

You sound like a lovesick teenager, she told herself. *Get a grip on yourself.*

Naran had dozens of hotels, from the very high-end to something no more sophisticated than a Motel 6. Against all odds, Ira directed them to a small inn with a vacancy. With the town so crowded, she had feared they wouldn't find a room. This place had two.

Maybe Ira really *did* have magic powers.

Holding her headscarf in place, she practically ran toward the front door of the quaint little building. The inn was a strange combination of European and Asian architecture. Its front borrowed heavily from the style of Alps chalets, though the red roof swept upward at the fringes like a Japanese temple.

Inside, a sign proclaimed the name of the inn: Gateway to the Heavens. Elisabeth couldn't imagine a more apt description. The small but elegant front room had a fireplace that dominated one wall, opposite a wooden desk where Ira stood conversing with a slim, gaunt man Elisabeth presumed was the proprietor. His cheekbones stuck out, straining against his papery skin.

Elisabeth reluctantly arranged for payment. They hadn't withdrawn enough cash in Islamabad, and now she resorted to using credit. The risk was grave, potentially giving away their location if anyone was looking for it.

The gaunt man led them to their rooms, both of which faced the river. Even with the doors and windows closed, the sound of rushing water filled their ears. Before leaving, he looked Elisabeth up and down, appraising her. She flushed red at the unwanted attention and turned away, relieved when he finally left them alone.

"If you don't mind, I'd like to clean up," Elisabeth told the men.

The men nodded, then fell into a murmured conversation. Part of Elisabeth wished they would hold off their plans until she was ready to join in, but the larger part yearned for a shower—or better yet, a long, soaking bath, perhaps with a glass of wine, if one happened to be available.

As luck would have it, the bathroom was almost as luxurious as the one in her new home in Provo. Soft blue tiles covered the floor, with thick mats atop them. The carpeted mats felt warm under her feet as she undressed and sat on the edge of the bathtub. She adjusted the taps, then stood and looked at herself in the mirror as the tub filled with water.

Her figure wasn't what it once was. As she stared at herself, the sound of running water faded into the background and her thoughts turned back to an earlier time, another hotel encounter. Emery had waited outside while she prepared herself for what she had hoped would be their first night together. Her eyes closed as the emotions swept over her anew—the excitement, the anticipation, the danger of knowing she wasn't his wife.

That night had turned to disappointment, like so many other nights she had spent with Emery, though it had led to their year together in Egypt. So much of her life revolved around that year, travelling through the country, visiting site after site as Emery pursued his literalist theories. She'd nursed hopes that their love would blossom, and it very nearly had. Except for the work. With Emery, it always came back to the work. He couldn't get past it, couldn't let it go. Yes, they had been together, slept together, but there was always distance, an unscalable wall she had never been able to understand.

A splash brought her back. She turned off the taps, the water having risen nearly to the edge of the tub. She reached down into the steaming water and unplugged the stopper, waiting for some of the excess water to drain. The heat turned her skin red.

She lowered herself into the tub slowly, her body acclimating to the temperature. Her eyes fluttered closed as she settled in and draped her arms over the porcelain ledges. Steam filled the room like a cloud, beads of water clinging to every surface. Sweat dimpled her forehead, then slithered down her cheeks until it joined the water in rhythmic drops.

"You're looking for Shamballa?" Gayle had asked on the other end of the phone.

Elisabeth kept her eyes closed as she pictured the passenger lounge in Lima. A modern-art mosaic filled the wall opposite her, its tiny tiles adding up to a depiction of brown-skinned Incans gazing at the setting sun over distant peaks. Her chair had been uncomfortable. Hard and plastic, unyielding.

She had narrowed her eyes, shutting out the men's stares. She'd gotten up and moved away, hoping to gain some privacy.

"I take it you know something." Elisabeth had heard of Shamballa, but it didn't hold much significance to her.

Gayle chuckled. "The term is Sanskrit, and it means peace and tranquility. Happiness. But it's not an emotion, it's a kingdom. Travelers have searched for it for hundreds of years. Hitler and Stalin were said to have sent competing expeditions. The Buddhists practically structured their entire religion around it."

"But what is it? Why is it important?"

"It's a spiritual realm, part of this world, but also part of another. The land around it is hidden, perhaps behind an interdimensional portal, but within it can be found the secret to unity and human enlightenment. If you find Shamballa, it is said that you will find a brotherhood of mystics, powerful beings known as 'adepts' who labor on our behalf, with the ability to restore peace and goodness to the fallen world."

Elisabeth sighed. "That's what I was afraid of."

"Afraid?"

"Do you really believe such a place exists? If there was a kingdom up in the mountains, it would have been found by now."

"Except for the interdim—"

"The interdimensional portal, yes, yes. Gayle, how can you expect me to take any of this seriously?"

There was a long pause. "Because you're looking for someone, and you'll find him there."

Her blood had run cold at that. She hadn't mentioned anything about Emery. Gayle couldn't have known.

"Elisabeth," Gayle said after a period of long silence during which Elisabeth worried they'd been disconnected. "The brotherhood I mentioned, they're not human."

Of course they aren't.

"They're the Starseed people, visitors from other worlds, and they have been influencing humanity since the dawn of time. "

Elisabeth wanted to hang up or tell Gayle just how ridiculous she sounded. But she couldn't. Emery Wörtlich may have died, but he wasn't gone, and he was drawing them to Shamballa. Not only that, but they had seen firsthand evidence of spirits. Maybe they *were* dealing with these so-called adepts.

"Shamballa," Elisabeth had whispered, hyperaware of the people walking through the terminal around her. She turned to the wall and spoke in her lowest voice. "How do we find it? Tibet is a big area."

"There's a reason no one has found it," Gayle replied. "It's not where everywhere thinks it is."

There was a knock at the bathroom door, wrenching Elisabeth back to the present.

"We're going to the other room to sleep," Brighton's voice called. "You can stay in this one by yourself, if you're comfortable with that."

"Yes, thank you," she said, her voice hoarse. "If I need you, I'll know where to find you."

The swish of footsteps against carpet marked the men's departure, leaving her with only the gentle lapping of water against the side of the tub.

Elisabeth used her toes to claw the stopper out of the drain. The bathwater immediately receded. Standing carefully, she stepped out of the bath. She dried herself with a plush towel, hugging her breasts tightly.

She tiptoed to the door, peeking out to ensure the men had really gone. When she saw the empty room, she walked to the edge of the bed and sat. The room was cool, so she pulled back the covers and slipped beneath them. She lay down, her head falling into a host of pillows. Gateway to the heavens, indeed. She would sleep well tonight.

She continued to replay her conversation with Gayle as the last of the daylight faded. A beam of pale starlight poured in through the window above the bed, bathing her in its glow.

If this supposed hotspot was the strongest there was, it made sense Emery would wait there.

How strong is it? I wonder if we're close enough already, she thought, feeling herself drift off. She reached out the tendrils of her thoughts. They radiated out from her body like wisps of energy.

Emery, can you sense me?

If he was there, she had no way of knowing it. She redoubled her effort, imagining those tendrils stretching as far as they would go, probing the darkness.

Emery! I need you. If you're there, give me a sign.

She stilled her thoughts, seeking absolute silence. She heard only the rushing of the river outside.

Saddened by the lack of response, she fell asleep.

* * *

Brighton took off all his clothes except his underwear and dropped them in the bathtub, where Dario and Ira's clothes already swirled in murky water. Brighton sighed, then got down on his knees and emptied the tub, pulling out each article of clothing and wringing it dry.

When he left the bathroom, he found Ira asleep on the couch, his legs propped up on the overstuffed armrest. Brighton was glad to have a break from the constant war between them, but even in sleep, Ira's pious snores filled Brighton with hostility.

He glanced out the patio door and saw Dario sitting in one of two wrought-iron chairs, his body draped in a white blanket. Brighton pulled the comforter off the bed and wrapped it around himself before joining Dario outside. The evening air was bracing and he snuggled into the blanket, wishing not for the first time that they'd brought a change of clothes.

"It's not enough to simply point the jeep toward the Chinese border," Dario said after Brighton had settled into a chair.

Brighton breathed deeply of the mountain air. "I know."

"You say this Wörtlich fellow sent you here to recover his spirit." Dario's voice was flat, like he didn't believe a word of it. "What does that entail? Let's say we do find this Olmolungring place—or Shamballa, or whatever you call it. What then?"

"We'll find Wörtlich, of course."

Dario put his bare feet up on a circular glass table. "But there must be more to it than that. Don't forget—Wörtlich is dead."

"Not *really* dead."

"I'm talking physically dead. He doesn't have a body, right? Presumably he's a spirit, and I've just about had my fill of spirits. The last one I met went on a rampage and killed four colleagues."

"Wörtlich isn't like that."

Dario shivered against the cold. "I see. So, he's a friendly ghost? Either way, he doesn't have a body, and I bet the reason we're going all this way is to give him one."

Brighton closed his eyes and conjured up an image of Wörtlich's face. The archaeologist had been an intense man, but he had also been kind. Was it possible he was now involved in a scheme to possess one of them?

"No," Brighton said. "You didn't know him, but he would never do what you're suggesting."

"Then how are you planning to restore him? Surely he'll need a body."

"We'll cross that bridge when we come to it."

Dario barked out a laugh. "No thank you. I think we'll cross it now, if it's all the same to you. I've been through this song and dance before."

"You have nothing to be afraid about," Brighton said. "The question of a body is premature. Our first concern should be finding Shamballa, which people have been trying to locate for thousands of years. It won't be easy."

"It sounds impossible."

Brighton smiled. "Not with Wörtlich's help. He appears to me in dreams and gives me guidance. I can feel that we're on the right track." He stood and stretched. "Speaking of sleep, aren't you tired? You've been up more than twenty hours."

"Every time I try to sleep, I have nightmares of Tiahuanaco."

Brighton patted his new friend on the shoulder. "The nightmare will end, Dario. You'll see."

"I wish I had your confidence."

Brighton went inside and set out the clothes to dry. After pouring himself a glass of water, he made his way to the bed and lay down. As his eyes slipped shut, he wondered where he'd find himself upon awakening.

TWENTY-SIX

Naran, Pakistan

JULY 26

After a quick breakfast of bread and fruit, Dario went outside to wait by the jeep. The sun had dawned to a clear sky, but he couldn't shake the alpine chill. It had crept under his skin the moment he'd sloughed off his blanket that morning.

Dario's stomach churned with trepidation of the day ahead while Brighton was positively chipper. The man's happiness struck Dario as bizarre. This slow march up the Himalayan slopes felt to Dario like a funeral dirge.

Within an hour of waking, the jeep was parked at the town's only service station. Dario pumped gas while Brighton and Elisabeth went inside to pay. The gas pump had no display to indicate how much the fill was costing him, which Dario thought strange.

The streets were quiet at this early hour, and only one other vehicle had parked at the station. A man with brown hair and sunglasses sat in the driver's seat of a dark blue sedan. The stranger seemed to watch him, though the sunglasses made it hard to tell what exactly he was looking at.

You're imagining things, Dario told himself. *This town is full of tourists. No reason to think he's anything more sinister than that.*

Soon they were back on the road, armed with a map and directions. The highway continued north, winding up through the valley to Babusar Pass, which was open but risky, no matter that it was high summer. The innkeeper had warned against attempting the crossing without a guide. Even Ira advised them to turn back, but they couldn't be dissuaded.

Babusar was only sixty kilometers away, but the service station attendant had warned Brighton that the difficult climb would take the entire morning—perhaps longer, depending on the weather. At that altitude, storms could come from nowhere and settle in for long periods.

Muttering sounds floated back to Dario from the front seat and he leaned forward to hear where it was coming from. With his eyes closed, Ira moved his lips to a cadence and rhythm Dario didn't understand.

"I think he's praying for a storm," Dario whispered to Elisabeth.

Elisabeth rolled her eyes. "The man has a few screws loose. From how Sherwood described him, I would have expected him to be more helpful."

The farther up the road they travelled, the clearer and bluer the midday sky became. Evidently, God wasn't listening to his faithful servant this morning.

Other obstacles presented themselves. The road had flooded out in two places. At the first stop, water cascaded down the mountainside and over pavement, following its course around two switchbacks before running off the road's edge and cascading into the Kunhar. The traffic came to a standstill. Brighton waited half an hour before losing patience and creeping around the stopped vehicles. The jeep easily crossed the flooded lanes.

The second flooded-out section was worse, and they could only wait for the water to clear on its own. A short conversation with some of the locals revealed that this was a common occurrence.

After a while, Dario had to get out of the vehicle and walk around. So much time in the back seat of the jeep made him both jumpy and claustrophobic.

The views were breathtaking. The road ahead steered away from the river it had followed so closely since Naran. Barricades were in place to prevent landslides, but Dario imagined those, too, were anticipated. Dario didn't mind the wait—he was more worried about what lay ahead—but Elisabeth was especially impatient. She tried to nap in the back seat, but fifteen minutes later she stormed out of the jeep.

"Are you alright?" Dario asked, going after her.

Elisabeth rubbed her eyes. "I was up and down all night, hoping for a message from Emery. You know, the way he's been appearing to Sherwood." She paused, fastening him with an expectant stare. "How about you? Did you get anything?"

"No, of course not." Dario felt surprised she even had to ask. "Why would he contact me?"

"I don't know. It doesn't make sense that he'd contact Brighton when I'm right here, and yet that's the truth of it."

Dario held his tongue. There didn't seem any point in trying to convince her how ridiculous it was to go haring off into the middle of nowhere on the instructions of a dead man.

Once the water had drained sufficiently for them to cross, they got moving again. In the miles ahead, low crops sprouted from narrow strips of terraced farmland that rose as high as the tree line and stopped. The tree line loomed a lot closer now than it had back in Naran.

They didn't stop in the village and bypassed a couple of scenic overlooks. A handful of tourists had stopped at each, snapping photos of the view back down the valley.

Ten minutes later, the jeep lurched over the end of the pavement. From here on, the road became a wide but stony path that forced Brighton to cut their speed in half. The jeep shook as they passed over deep ruts in the roadway; it felt like trying to drive over the ridges of a washboard. After five relentless minutes, Dario had to feel his teeth to make sure none had jostled loose.

Just as Dario's stomach was on the verge of revolt, they swung around the corner of a tall ridge and were confronted with a long expanse of sparkling water. The shores were covered in velvety grass and seemingly every possible variety of wildflower, scattered with boulders. The scene reminded Dario of a graveyard, the boulders akin to unevenly spaced headstones.

"Are these the Kunhar headwaters?" Elisabeth asked as they crossed a rickety bridge built from uneven planks.

"Not according to the map," Brighton said. "The river just meets a natural dam when it hooks around this corner."

They approached a makeshift parking area where a number of vehicles had pulled over to take in the views. There were vans, compact cars, a motorcycle, and… a dark blue sedan.

"I'd like to stretch my legs," Ira called from the passenger seat.

"No," Dario said without hesitation. "I really don't think that's a good idea."

Brighton sped up as they drove past. "Dario's right. I want to get over the pass by lunchtime."

But Ira insisted on taking a break, and Brighton gave in. The jeep pulled over to the side of the road. Both Ira and Elisabeth jumped out, though they walked up the road in opposite directions.

Dario stared out the back window, half-expecting that blue sedan to come creeping around the corner at any moment.

"There was a dark blue sedan parked at the service station this morning," Dario said. "I think I just saw the same car back by the lake."

Brighton rolled down his window. "The lake seemed like a popular tourist destination. It makes sense we wouldn't have been the only people headed up this way from Naran."

That did nothing to ease Dario's anxiety. "I suppose you're right, though I'm surprised."

"You're surprised that I'm right?"

"Sorry. I mean that I'm surprised you would make that argument. You've been looking over your shoulder for over a year now. I would have expected you to be more suspicious."

Brighton smiled good-naturedly. "There's a big difference between suspicion and delusion."

Irritation bubbled up in Dario, though he kept it from showing. He was *not* delusional.

Through the windshield, Dario could see that Ira had turned around and was on his way back.

"I've been thinking some more about what you said last night," Brighton said. "We do need a better plan. I think it's safe to assume this road isn't going to take us up to the gates of Shamballa."

"If it even exists," Dario noted.

"It does." Brighton's tone brooked no argument. "The highway will take us to Gilgit, which is the capital city of Pakistan's northern territories. We'll find some leads there."

"How do you know?"

Brighton peered toward Ira. "Ira knows a trick, like a meditation. Something to try when you're lost and looking for guidance. I can ask him to try it."

That was the first semi-kind word Brighton had said about the old man since they'd landed in Pakistan. After their constant bickering, it came as a small shock.

The door next to Dario swung open and Elisabeth climbed in. She pulled off her headscarf and dropped it onto the seat between them.

"I heard from Wörtlich again last night," Brighton continued. "He told me we're headed in the right direction."

Elisabeth turned her head so fast that her hair blurred. "What?"

"I heard from Wörtlich."

"I thought he was only accessible to us at hotspots," she said, trembling.

Brighton frowned. "Yes, but the one here is very strong. He must be able to broadcast his consciousness farther than normal."

Without saying another word, Elisabeth threw open the door and got out, slamming it behind her.

"What was that about?" Brighton asked.

Dario let out a long sigh. "Jealousy."

*   *   *

Brighton's first glacier sighting came not ten minutes after they got back on the road. The mass of ice filled a crevice between cliff faces, extending to within a stone's throw of the road's rocky shoulder. Light snow began to fall a short time later, the flakes drifting lazily out of an increasingly cloudy sky. The windshield wipers swept them aside.

Splotchy carpets of yellow and red moss replaced the trees and grass. Brighton thought these dreary slopes almost lifeless, until he spotted movement on the other side of the river. A second look confirmed it was a large cat of some kind. Perhaps a leopard.

Dario spotted it, too, and pointed it out. Everyone craned to see out the windows, except Brighton, whose fingers gripped the steering wheel all the harder. His good mood faded the higher they drove. He wanted to get to the top of this pass, then down the other side. This was no place to linger.

The road was as rough as ever, but fortunately straight, with few hairpin turns. The altitude increased noticeably as the road branched from the river, which before long was a hundred feet below and no wider than a stream.

The snow came faster, joined by a thick fog that made the roadway hard to see. Brighton slowed but didn't stop, despite Ira's urging to pull over and wait out the storm.

Shortly thereafter, the fog dissipated and they found themselves again under a clear blue sky. Brighton gasped; they had reached the pass, and all around them snow-covered mountains poked upward through the cloud cover—clouds that hovered *below* them.

The road took a final turn before reaching its apex. As they started their long descent, the surrounding hills flattened, but this soon changed for the worse. While the way up had been mostly straight, the way down was steep and twisty. Brighton kept one foot firmly on the brake at all times, half-convinced they were going to lose traction in the loose shale and slide over the edge of a cliff. No one in the jeep said a word for the next half-hour, which Brighton was grateful for, especially when the snow returned at full force.

He hardly breathed until they hit a mile-long stretch of straight road. They were by no means at the bottom of the valley, but he felt they had left the worst behind them. He had counted twenty-eight switchbacks.

To his great disappointment, the road didn't improve. If anything, it got worse, passing at several points between cliff walls barely six feet apart, just wide enough for the jeep to squeeze through. Brighton was relieved they had chosen the jeep. He was also glad they faced snow and not rain, which would have transformed this rocky roadway into impassable mud. The potholes and ruts became deeper with every mile. No matter how slow he drove, they were constantly jostled up and down, side to side, straining against their seatbelts. Brighton could feel the belt cutting into his abdomen from the tension.

They all let out a whoop of joy—even Elisabeth, whose emotional temperature had cooled somewhat—when the sky cleared and revealed a gleam of dry pavement around the next bend. Phantom turbulence persisted in Brighton's gut, however, for the next twenty miles.

Up ahead, a sign greeted them: "Welcome to Pakistani Kashmir."

Ira dug through the glove compartment for the map. "It looks like we passed into the disputed territory at the top of the pass."

"Not sure why anyone would want this place," Brighton said under his breath.

He was forced to take back his words when they reached the town of Chilas, a high-altitude oasis of color. Cultivated fields broken up by a network of snaking canals lay between the village and the banks of the Indus River. How refreshing to be back in a flat, open space!

Brighton turned off the highway at the first opportunity and came to a stop on a street fronted by a whitewashed building he supposed was a mosque. He put his head down on the steering wheel and rested for several minutes.

"There were moments when I didn't think we were going to stay on the road," Brighton said through clenched teeth.

Ira put a hand on Brighton's shoulder, which Brighton promptly shrugged away.

"Sherwood, I was praying for you," Ira said.

Nothing Ira said could have been better calculated to enrage Brighton. He sat up straight and turned to the smug rabbi. "Is that your way of saying 'I told you so'?"

Ira balked. "Whatever the path we took, we've arrived. Safely, I might add. What difference does it make if I asked for divine assistance?"

"Because I didn't need it," Brighton said.

"Maybe I should take the wheel," Dario suggested dryly.

Brighton undid his seatbelt and retreated to the backseat without argument. He closed his eyes and tried to relax as they cruised through the bowl-like valley; fields on either side sported crops of a dozen colors waving in the breeze.

He reopened his eyes when they merged back onto the Karakoram Highway. The highway was wider and smoother than even the best portions of the road from Naran, and had signs marking distances. Gilgit awaited them a hundred and thirty kilometers up the road, but now that they were on a real highway, Brighton felt certain the time would pass more quickly.

And pass it did. Soon Brighton felt an insistent tap on his shoulder. He blinked twice and found himself looking into Elisabeth's green eyes.

"We're here," she said, a hint of her earlier annoyance still evident in her voice.

They had parked at another service station. Dario was getting gas.

"Gilgit?" Brighton asked. Noting Elisabeth's nod, he looked out the window and saw that they had landed in the midst of a bustling city.

"Did you have a good nap?"

He sat up and rubbed his eyes. "I think so."

"I don't suppose you heard from Emery again," she said sullenly.

Her annoyance was understandable. Why had Wörtlich chosen to reach out to him instead of her? There had to be a reason.

"No," he said. "How about you?"

That single question, the acknowledgement that she was just as invested—if not more so—in Wörtlich's recovery, worked wonders. Her features relaxed.

"I guess now we'll see how well Ira's meditation works," she said as she stepped outside, headscarf in hand.

Still feeling a bit groggy, Brighton got out and looked around. Where was Ira?

He wandered around what passed for a convenience store a couple of times before spotting Ira cross-legged on the ground, his back against a wooden fencepost. The rabbi had closed his eyes and his mouth moved.

He's meditating, Brighton realized. *Searching for Wörtlich. Coming up with a plan of action.*

Brighton approached the older man but stopped far enough away so as not to disturb him. Ira whispered in prayer, but the language wasn't English. Hebrew, perhaps?

At last, Ira came to the end of his prayer and opened his eyes. They immediately swung around to stare at Brighton.

"Why do you use prayer as a solution to every problem?" Brighton asked, making an effort to keep a civil tone. "You say you don't have magic powers, but don't you use prayer as though it were magic?"

Ira patted the ground and Brighton sat beside him. "In time, you will understand."

"I don't think *you* understand how patronizing that sounds."

Brighton wished he didn't feel so angry at Ira. His day certainly hadn't started out that way; he had woken up feeling refreshed to be on a mission again, to be traveling with friends. He had once counted Ira among those friends.

A year and a half ago, Ira had changed his life. Brighton had been directionless until his encounter with Ira and Wörtlich. Despite the ordeals of the intervening period—months on the run, hopping from one country to another, never staying in one place too long—his life had taken on purpose. Ira and Wörtlich had been mentors, even though they had shared only a short time together.

"You talk a good game," Brighton said, "but you have a way of making everything far more difficult than it needs to be. You're keeping secrets."

"I am," Ira said solemnly. "There are truths you aren't ready for. Other truths I am prevented from revealing under any circumstances. Even if I did, they wouldn't do any good."

"I wish you'd let me be the judge of that." Brighton leaned in. "Can I at least ask you some questions?"

"Of course."

"You were just meditating. Were you doing that thing with the river, the thing you taught me in Antarctica?"

"In a manner of speaking," Ira said.

"There. See, this is exactly what I'm talking about. That wasn't a straight answer."

"There are nuances to prayers and meditations you don't understand. Yes, I was meditating, communing with the creator. But it wasn't the same as the river meditation."

Brighton brushed away Ira's hand. "Can you use your abilities to help us find Wörtlich?"

"As I've told you before, Wörtlich is dead."

"Then why did you come back?"

Ira blinked, as though the answer were obvious. "I came for you."

Brighton felt certain he was supposed to take that with love and appreciation, but instead he felt demeaned. He didn't need a chaperone or a fairy godfather.

Brighton really wanted to stand up and walk away from Ira, possibly forever. He was rapidly losing patience in Ira's circumspect answers, to the point that he thought he might be better off puzzling things out on his own.

"Tell me about Aaron Roth," Brighton said, somehow wishing this conversation was over while still wanting answers. "You taught at seminary together?"

Ira licked his dry lips. "Did he tell you that?"

"Yes. He knew things about me. Things I never told him. It's like he was expecting me."

Ira laughed. "That sounds very much like the Aaron I knew. He was one of my best friends, you know."

Brighton found it odd to hear Ira speak in such humanizing terms.

"He told me that I was important," Brighton continued, "that I was a beacon of light in a dark place."

A veil of serenity fell over Ira's face. He looked very pleased. "He was right about you, Sherwood. I've seen it in you for a long time. What else did he say?"

"Something about a black awakening. Do you know what it means?"

"I have an idea."

Brighton fell silent, waiting for Ira to elaborate. Ira took a while, as usual, and when he continued he avoided a direct answer.

"Aaron taught me most of what I know," Ira said, "including the memory technique I showed you. You remember?"

"Of course I remember. I've tried to duplicate it."

"Even under Aaron's tutelage, it took me years to master." Ira drew a long breath. His chest trembled from the effort, perhaps because of the altitude. "I should have worked harder to pass it on to you."

"Then why did you go? We could have worked together, travelled side by side."

"I had to return the Book," Ira said. "I couldn't risk it falling into the wrong hands."

"Into Lagati's hands?"

Ira sighed. "Not just his. I could barely trust myself with it. Even Emery Wörtlich would have ultimately used the Book for the wrong purposes if he'd had the opportunity. I know that's difficult for you to hear, but it's the truth."

"You always underestimated Wörtlich," Brighton said. "He was a good man in search of the truth."

"Being a good and honest seeker doesn't inoculate a man from the dangers of selfish pursuits. The Book has the ability to bestow the ultimate creative power on anyone who studies it. Its allure is unmatched. Even I have been tempted."

"Okay, so you secured the Book," Brighton said. "But why not return sooner? Ira, those were desperate times. I needed your help!"

"I came as soon as I could. And you *did* have help."

Brighton heard his name being called and he looked up over the fence. Dario leaned against the jeep, waving them back.

"Time to go," Brighton said, standing up.

"Sherwood, I'm not finished. I have more to say."

Brighton had to stop himself from doing a double-take. Had he heard right? Had Ira actually been offering to tell him *more?*

"Not now," Brighton said, a mean-spirited smile coming to his lips. It felt good for the shoe to be on the other foot.

*   *   *

"I'm going in to pay," Elisabeth called to Dario, who stood next to the jeep with the gasoline nozzle in his hand.

The inside of the station was much cleaner than the exterior had suggested, with its peeling paint and overgrown weeds. Coolers lined one of the walls, peddling selections from teas to sodas. Ice cream treats and fresh fruit hid among the snacks, but the most succulent selections lay under a row of heat lamps—golden brown samosas and pakoras with curry dipping sauces. She breathed in the aroma of steamed onions and lentils. The temptation proved too great to resist, so she placed a handful of samosas into a brown paper bag and carried them to the cashier.

She regretted that she didn't speak a word of either Urdu or Shina, the two main languages in this part of the country, but she attempted English and found to her relief that the man behind the counter understood just enough to get by.

When she turned, she discovered a tall white man running in from the back door. He stopped in front of her, trembling.

"Excuse me," he said in English, "are you travelling with a gentleman in his sixties or seventies?"

Her defenses shot up. Was he talking about Ira? Speaking to a male stranger like this was a risky venture, so she offered a simple nod.

"I just saw him staggering," the man said, pointing toward the back door. "He may be having a heart attack."

Elisabeth dropped her bag of samosas and rushed out the door. She stopped on a patch of gravel and tried to spot Ira. She saw no one around, though a blue sedan idled next to the door.

Before she could make a dash back into the store, or even let out a scream, the stranger grabbed her and slapped a sweaty hand over her mouth. She tried to wrestle free, but his grip proved too strong. He shoved her inside the back of the car and slammed the door.

She dove for the handle, but it was locked. *Damn it, this is not happening…*

"Elisabeth, calm down," she heard Noam Sheply say. "You're being hysterical."

She froze and then turned toward Sheply, who lounged next to her on the grey seat cushions. One arm rested in his lap and the other was draped over the seat behind her.

"Let me go, Noam. It doesn't matter what you say, I won't help you."

Sheply's eyes fixed somewhere just north of her face, and she remembered that he had lost his vision. She was going to have to get used to that.

"Then it's a good thing I didn't come for your help," he said. "Tell me, how did our relationship come to be so adversarial?"

"I'd hesitate to define it as a relationship."

Elisabeth found it disconcerting to focus on Sheply's expressionless eyes, which had lost so much of their vibrancy. They stared blankly.

"We have a very intimate relationship," Sheply said. At least his voice still held its usual charming inflections. "You can run from it all you want, but we both know the truth."

"I hate you, Noam."

There it was: the naked truth. She expected him to react poorly, but instead he smiled.

"Hate is one of the most intimate emotions of all." His left hand groped forward and found hers after two swipes through empty air. "Elisabeth, what are you doing in Pakistan?"

She shook his hand loose. "The real question is how you knew where to find me."

"Please, give me some credit. I've gotten quite good at chasing after your card purchases. That's how I finally got to Brighton."

"You always have been a creep, first and foremost. I've thought so for fifteen years."

Well, *that* got a rise out of him. "Open your eyes, Elisabeth! I'm blind, and still I perceive the situation more clearly than you ever could. Put aside your preconceptions for a few minutes and consider that I may have your best interests at heart." He backed away from her, giving her space. "I'm not working for Lagati anymore. After what happened to me, my life will never be the same."

"I don't believe you."

He let out an exasperated breath. "You are, no contest, the most stubborn woman I have ever known. I no longer have any reason to lie to you. In fact, I regret that I ever did."

"If you're not here to track us down for Lagati, what are you doing?" Elisabeth dropped her voice. Sheply always played an angle, and this was no different.

"I came because I care for you."

"Now I *really* don't believe you."

The driver's door opened and the stranger from the convenience store got in.

"Who's that?" Elisabeth asked.

"Without my sight, I can't travel without assistance," Sheply said, rubbing at his eyes. "It's a huge inconvenience."

"Noam, I'll ask you one more time. Let me go."

Sheply sighed. "Then go."

A moment later, Elisabeth heard the click of the doors unlocking. She glanced toward the driver, whose finger withdrew from the unlock button on the center console.

"I won't hold you against your will," Sheply said, "but I will give you a warning. Even though I'm not here on Lagati's behalf, I'm certain somebody else is. Lagati wants to get his hands on Brighton, and even more so on Ira. You'll have to run a lot farther than Pakistan to escape his reach."

Even if every other word was a lie, Elisabeth knew from experience that these were true.

"If I was still working for Lagati, I would have cornered you back in Naran," Sheply added.

Elisabeth put her hand on the door handle. Before squeezing it, she turned back. "What did you mean when you said you cared for me?"

"I haven't exactly been circumspect."

"I'm going to get out of this car and leave with the people I came with. I want you to drive in the opposite direction."

Elisabeth didn't know how, but Sheply's eyes managed to zero in on her. "Can't do it. In the coming days, you will need my help. Whatever else you may think, I want you to know how important you are to me."

To her own disgust, this time she knew he meant it.

TWENTY-SEVEN

Hunza Valley, Pakistan
JULY 27

Elisabeth was a bundle of nerves as they travelled north of Gilgit the next morning, with Brighton driving. Sheply's words lingered in her ears as the miles passed. She worried what would happen if she told the others about her encounter with Sheply. Ira would leap at the opportunity to turn them around, and so might Dario.

Once again, she focused all her energy on trying to contact Emery but didn't make a connection. Her only solace came from the fact that Brighton hadn't contacted him the previous night, either, nor had Ira been able to contribute.

"Stop," Dario suddenly called. He sat forward in the passenger seat, his eyes narrowed. "You see those signs on the road ahead? The highway is blocked."

He was right. A few minutes later, they saw workers in yellow vests on the road. Traffic was backed up so far that they couldn't see what went on up ahead. A half-hour later, they inched about halfway to the front of the line before stopping again.

"Must be construction," Brighton said.

Elisabeth pulled a banana from their bag of snacks. "If that's true, the construction must go on for miles," she said whilst peeling thick greenish skin from the fruit. Between bites, she scanned the line of cars behind them for the blue sedan. It was nowhere in sight.

When they finally pulled up to the front of the line, they saw that an immense landslide had deposited enough rock over the highway to form a new mountain all on its own. The landslide looked like a recent development, but not so recent that road crews hadn't managed to blast a rough pathway overtop it.

"That's a hell of a natural disaster," Brighton commented to a worker through his open window. A dozen workers walked past like army patrols.

Elisabeth put a hand on Brighton's shoulder from the backseat. "Sherwood, mind your own business. You don't even know if they speak English."

But apparently this one did. The worker came up to the jeep and rested his arm against its metal frame.

"Where are you coming from?" A heavy Indian inflection accented the worker's words.

"Gilgit," Brighton said.

The worker looked surprised. "Nobody told you about the lake?"

Elisabeth rolled down her window, too. "What lake?"

The worker gave her only the shortest glance before returning his attention to Brighton. Women were little more than chattel to some of these backward people. Not all of them, she conceded, but clearly this one wouldn't give her the same respect as he would a man.

"An earthquake brought down this landslide in March," the contemptible worker said. "There used to be a small town under all this rock. One hundred people were killed."

Elisabeth's anger subsided. Perhaps the world had more important crises than the disrespect of an ignorant boor.

The worker looked back toward the wall of rock. "The landslide dammed the river, creating a twelve-mile-long lake on the other side."

"So the road's washed out?" Brighton asked.

"Six entire towns were washed out." The worker spoke dispassionately, despite describing one of the more horrifying catastrophes Elisabeth had heard of. "The ferry will take you across."

Without another word, the worker moved on.

Thirty minutes later, they were waved forward. The jeep rolled off the pavement and onto a ramp of packed dirt, sand, and rock. This new road proved a steep climb. Once on top, it was still a significant drive to get to the edge of the lake.

Elisabeth gasped. The sun sparkled off the surface of clear, blue water that stretched as far as the eye could see. The height of the landslide indicated that the lake was very deep. Cliffs of granite rose around the edges, ensuring there was no shore to speak of. The lake truly seemed a horrifying marvel.

A small ferry with only eight spots for cars awaited them. Brighton drove up a wide gangplank and brought the jeep to a stop on the ferry's deck. He shut off the engine.

Still no sign of Sheply, Elisabeth mused as she got out of the car and got a good look around.

She walked to the railing and peered into the crystal clear water. The tip of her headscarf dangled over the side. She acted quickly to prevent it from unspooling into the depths below.

"There were two hundred dead," Dario said, coming to stand next to her. "I overheard a couple of the other passengers. They came specifically to see this place."

"It *is* beautiful," Elisabeth allowed.

"Pretty eerie, if you ask me. Feels more like a funeral barge than a cruise."

The air had stilled and the only sound was the gentle lapping of water against the side of the ferry.

The farthest extent of the lake succumbed at last to a short shore upon which stood a town cut in half by encroaching waters. Rooftops protruded from the surface of the lake in places, suggesting the slow speed at which the water had crept since the disaster struck. The town had constructed a makeshift harbor—a single wharf just large enough to accommodate the width of the ferry. They took the long way around instead of aiming straight for the landing, perhaps to avoid unseen hazards in the shallow water.

The muffled blast of a horn prompted the passengers to return to their vehicles. As usual, Ira had remained next to the jeep, sitting on the deck. His eyes fluttered open at the horn's low thrum, but Elisabeth got the impression they had otherwise been closed for the duration of the ferry ride. Perhaps he'd been saying a prayer for the fallen men, women, and children of the Hunza Valley. Did the Islamic God hear Jewish prayers?

A small sign on the edge of the wharf marked the name of the town twice—once in Arabic, and below it, in smaller lettering, "Shishkat."

Shishkat was submerged on three sides, with only a narrow wooden bridge connecting it to the Karakoram Highway, which emerged from the lakebed and continued blithely on its way. They drove toward the road, passing a grove of half-swallowed trees whose green tips seemed to be standing on tiptoes.

The jeep struggled toward the bridge, shaking as Brighton tried to pick up speed. He suddenly geared down and pulled to the side of the road.

"What's wrong?" Elisabeth asked.

"Not sure. Mud, I think."

Sure enough, mud caked the bottom of the jeep. It would have taken some time to clean it out in the best of circumstances, which these weren't; the only tools at their disposal were the tips of their boots.

The same predicament had afflicted another set of travelers. A similar jeep stopped behind them, brown sludge bursting from its rear wheel casings. A man and woman got out, hands on hips, to survey their situation.

"Are you English speakers?" the man said when he spotted Elisabeth and company trying to dislodge packed mud by foot. His accent pegged him as South African.

Brighton glanced up. "Sure are."

The man dug through the backseat, then held up a long wooden pole with a metallic pick on the end. He grinned.

"When you travel up here, it's best to come prepared!" The man held out the tool toward Brighton, who took it. "The name's Carter. I didn't expect to run into fellow tourists this far up the road, especially since the earthquake. Where are you headed?"

Brighton didn't hesitate. "We're trying to see how close we can get to the Chinese border."

Carter gestured to his wife. "We're going to stay in town for a little while and get something to eat. You're welcome to join us."

They all looked at each other, gauging interest in the invitation. After reaching a silent consensus, Brighton nodded. "As long as it's only for a little while."

After dislodging the mud, Ira and Dario began walking in the direction of Shishkat with the South African couple.

Elisabeth pulled Brighton aside. "Sherwood, I don't think we should linger here."

"We have to eat," Brighton reminded her. "Are you suspicious of them?"

Elisabeth watched Carter and his wife, who had fallen into step with Ira and Dario. Hadn't Sheply said Lagati would send someone for them?

With a loud splash, the ferry loaded up a single southbound car and began its long trek back to the other side of the lake.

"Come on," Brighton said.

Against her better judgment, she followed.

*   *   *

Carter seemed to know his way around the small town, enough that Brighton discerned that he and his wife, Marilyn, had visited here before. The couple chose a café with a view of the lake. The deluge had skulked up to within a block of its front door.

"You should have no trouble finding your way up to China," Carter said. "The nearest checkpoint is three miles into Chinese territory. I don't know what you're expecting to find, but there isn't much there aside from sheep and goats. And mountains, of course, but that goes without saying. Heard it's the highest paved mountain pass in the world."

The altitude didn't concern Brighton, but he was relieved to hear the road would be paved, haunted as he still was by their transit of Babusar Pass.

They ate a meal of rice and thin strips of tough lamb. Brighton was hungry enough that he didn't mind. He finished quickly and pushed his plate aside.

"Why are you heading up to the border?" Marilyn asked once

they had finished eating.

"We've never been there," Elisabeth said stiffly. "Isn't that reason enough?"

Marilyn shrugged. "I suppose. There are better reasons, though." She paused, exchanging a look with her husband. "More likely ones."

Brighton took a sip of tea from a ceramic mug. "Like what?"

"You'll have to excuse me for saying so, but you're an odd group," Carter said, conspicuously not answering the question. "Are you family?"

"Just friends on vacation," Dario said. And a good thing, too, for it was more plausible than the answer Brighton had been about to offer—that they were colleagues. That would only have raised more questions about their jobs, their assignment, and so on.

"Not many people venture this far north except commercial trucks, and precious few of those," Carter said. "On the Chinese side, there aren't any towns for hundreds of miles, and the air is drier than sawdust. Not something most tourists are clamoring to see."

"Oh, just tell him," Marilyn said. "They obviously won't admit it."

Brighton's hackles rose. Just what were they not going to admit?

"You're here to see the spacecraft, aren't you?" Carter said, his eyes moving across the faces of his fellow travelers.

Dario nearly spit out a mouthful of water. "Spacecraft?" he said once the water had securely passed down his throat.

Marilyn broke into a laugh. "Well, so much for that theory. Looks like we're the only alien chasers here."

"You probably think we're out of our minds," Carter said, smiling.

"As someone who's been called crazy more times than I'd like in the last few days," Elisabeth said, "my preference would be to keep an open mind."

Brighton turned back to Carter. "I think you'll find we're a receptive audience. Tell us about these spacecraft."

"They appear in the sky above the mountains," Marilyn said, planting her elbows on the table. "All the locals know about them. They're definitely ships, and they're fast."

"They rise out of the ridges on the far side of Mount Khunjerab, right on the border," Carter said. "According to stories, there are deep cracks in the earth on the far side of the mountain. Ships rise out of them."

Marilyn nodded eagerly. "The earth shakes almost constantly. Aliens live beneath these mountains, and we're not the only people who think so. A steady trickle of alien chasers come here. If you ask me, the earthquake that created Lake Hunza is further proof. The quakes aren't natural."

"Sherwood, could I speak with you in private?" Ira said in a soft voice.

Brighton drew his brows together and appraised the rabbi. He'd almost managed to forget Ira was there at all. "Now, Ira? It has to be right now?"

"Yes, I believe it does."

"My apologies," Brighton said to Carter and Marilyn. "Our friend doesn't always have the best timing."

Brighton pushed his chair away and followed Ira out of the restaurant, their shoes creaking over the terracotta floor. Brighton turned back to the table before going outside. All eyes were staring at them. And why not? Ira's interruption was quite mysterious.

Outside, a row of wooden chairs faced the lapping waters. The wind had picked up, lifting the rabbi's thin wisps of hair in asymmetrical puffs.

"What is it, Ira?"

Ira sat down. His normally serene face was distinctly agitated. "I told you we still had things to talk about."

"Yes, but I didn't think you were going to spring it on me in the middle of lunch," Brighton said. For Ira to have grown this twitchy, he had to have something major on his mind that he couldn't say in front of the others. "Does this have something to do with alien spacecraft?"

Ira hesitated, and that alone sent a tingle down Brighton's spine. He'd been half-joking.

"I suspect the spacecraft are real," Ira allowed. "But I wouldn't go so far as to say I believe in aliens."

"Then I don't understand."

"No, you don't."

Brighton felt deeply hurt by those words; they felt like an indictment of all the myriad things Brighton didn't understand, perhaps even those things Brighton wasn't "ready" to learn. He swallowed the hurt so Ira wouldn't get the satisfaction of seeing it. This wasn't the sweet, gentle, wise Ira he remembered.

"Ira, if there's something I don't understand, it's your fault for not teaching it to me."

"Perhaps so," Ira said with an edge in his voice. "Yet you do understand the truth about the Nephilim, and you haven't been careful enough."

"I managed to not be caught for over a year. I think that's pretty damned careful."

"You've been studying the past, but it's the present you should be more concerned about. The Nephilim are active in this world. Today."

"Well, I haven't had much to go on!" Brighton shouted, finally letting his anger out. He reveled in it. "I did the best I could, no thanks to you. Wörtlich may be dead, but even he's been a better help. I need a partner I can depend on."

"Elisabeth has been a good help, albeit a flawed one. Perhaps this Dario fellow could play a role. Frankly, I don't know enough about him to say, but he strikes me as weak-willed." Ira paused. "I can say one thing—Emery Wörtlich isn't just dead; he's gone. You have to move on, Sherwood."

Brighton launched himself up, unable to stay seated another moment. "I think I've been moving on quite well until you came back. It's funny. I thought I needed you, but I didn't. As lost as I was, I was finally finding my way. Ever since your return, I've been trying to figure out how you fit in, and I think I've found my answer. You don't."

The look of indignation on Ira's face was too much to bear. Brighton stood and walked away from the restaurant, down a path guided by trees that burst with wide green leaves. The air was cool in the shade they provided.

Where are you going? he asked himself. *You have to face him, once and for all.*

Brighton turned, hands on his hips. "You don't belong, Ira. Do you hear me?"

"I heard you." Ira shot up, clenching and unclenching his fists. Brighton had never seen Ira behave so aggressively; he hadn't suspected Ira was even capable of it.

"Why did you come back if you weren't going to help?" Brighton asked.

"I *am* helping." Ira advanced on him. "It's just not the help you think you need."

Brighton couldn't even formulate a response. Laughter erupted from him, loud and inappropriate.

"You've been trying to bait me for days," Ira said. "The old Brighton had an open mind. What the hell happened to him?"

Coming from Ira, the mild curse struck like a right hook.

"The old Ira showed me respect!" Brighton's shout reverberated off the surface of the lake. "You treat me like a helpless sheep."

Ira grabbed him by the shoulders and shook him. "Listen to me, Sherwood. You have to listen to me—"

Brighton pushed him away with all the force he could muster. Ira tripped backward, losing his balance and crashing into a bed of weeds and fallen branches.

It took a minute before the horror of what he had done sank in. Brighton backed away slowly, one tentative step after another, until the edges of the lake lapped against the bottom of his runners.

"I never meant to hurt you," Ira said, "but I can see that I have. I'm so sorry for that. I don't know how to fix it."

"I don't know how to fix it, either," Brighton said, his defiant laughter now a distant memory.

Ira used the trunk of a nearby tree to help himself stand. "Sherwood, it may be too late to salvage our friendship, but I need you to listen. What Aaron told you is so very important. Something is coming, I can feel it, and it could be either glorious or disastrous. You will have a role in it."

The rabbi took a few slow steps away from the tree. He had a pronounced limp.

"Aaron was very convincing," Brighton said, almost in a whisper. "He was more forthcoming in the ten minutes I knew him than in all the time I've known you."

Brighton met Ira's gaze and saw the heartbreak in them. The man slumped, defeated.

"Then I have failed," Ira said. "Failed at everything."

"You're wrong about Wörtlich," Brighton said. "I've seen him. Don't you understand? I've *seen* him. He needs our help. These hotspots all around the world, they act like magnets, trapping and storing energy. But not just energy—souls, too. I believe Wörtlich's soul is trapped, and it's our job to release it. Maybe Wörtlich could even live again. I don't know, and I won't until I find Shamballa."

Wind whistled through the branches above, causing a leaf to flutter down onto Brighton's shoulder. He picked it up and studied its intricate lines, its perfect shape. He closed his fist over the leaf, feeling it crumple like a piece of tinfoil.

"You can help me or you can go," Brighton said, fixated on his closed fist.

"Freedom requires choice, Sherwood. You have to choose."

Brighton let go of the leaf, the wind grabbing its shredded remains and driving them toward the lakeshore. He watched until they vanished.

As Ira stumbled back toward the wooden chairs, sinking into one, Brighton ran back toward the restaurant. He had made his choice.

TWENTY-EIGHT

Shishkat, Pakistan
JULY 27

W here's Ira?" Elisabeth asked when Brighton came back into the restaurant.

Brighton headed straight for the bathroom, letting the door bang shut behind him. The other patrons stared, then resumed their chatter. As the minutes passed, Elisabeth half-wondered if Brighton hadn't crawled out a window and abandoned them.

"What do you suppose happened?" Elisabeth asked, straining her eyes through the grimy window next to her. "Ira's just sitting there."

Dario was already out of his chair, halfway to the door to check on Ira. Carter and Marilyn, meanwhile, stared at her in bewilderment.

"Excuse me," was all she said as she headed for the bathroom.

She rapped her knuckles against the bathroom door. "Sherwood, it's me. We need to talk."

Brighton swung the door open. "Come in."

"It's the men's room."

"I don't care," Brighton said.

Elisabeth cast a furtive glance to the restaurant, checking to see if anyone was watching. Fortunately, the other patrons' attention had returned to their food and lunch companions.

She brushed past Brighton, who closed the door behind her and locked it with a simple metal hook just above the knob.

When he turned to face her, his eyes were red—not from crying, but from rage. She backed away from the intensity of his look.

"Sherwood, tell me what happened."

Brighton swiveled to the mirror, staring at his own reflection. "Ira and I got into a fight."

"What do you mean, a fight?"

"He pushed me too far, and I pushed back."

Elisabeth came closer, touching Brighton on the shoulder. "Sherwood, he's a seventy-year-old man. Don't tell me you came to blows!"

"He'll be okay." Brighton twisted the tap and let the stream of water flow over his hands. "But we won't be, unless we move quickly. Ira made it clear that he's not going to help us. He says Wörtlich is beyond saving, that we should give up."

"But Emery has appeared to both of us," Elisabeth pointed out.

A knock sounded at the door, followed by Dario's voice. "Is everything alright in there?"

"We're fine," Brighton called back. "Just give us a minute."

Brighton tore off a yellow-dyed tissue from the box next to the sink. Wiping his hands, he turned to face Elisabeth.

"Ira's trying to slow us down, and I think he'll step up his efforts." Brighton tossed the tissue in the trashcan. "He isn't the mild-mannered rabbi he appears to be. He can get aggressive when it suits him."

Elisabeth frowned. "What are you saying?"

Brighton crossed toward the toilet and looked up at the room's sole window. His fingers searched the edges of the frosted pane. After a minute, he found what he was looking for and slid the window open.

"We're going to make a run for it," Brighton said, sizing up the opening. "Do you think we'll both fit?"

Elisabeth's mind reeled. "Wait. We're just going to leave them?"

"Yes, I think we'll fit," Brighton said as though he hadn't heard her. "Let's go. We don't have much time."

"What about Dario?"

Brighton lowered the toilet seat and clambered onto it. "Dario isn't much better than Ira. You should have heard him in Naran. He thinks that if Wörtlich's spirit even exists, it's luring us to Shamballa to steal one of our bodies."

"Emery would never do that."

"That's what I told him."

Elisabeth watched as Brighton lifted himself up and stuck his head out the window.

"It's not a long drop," Brighton said. "We'll have to go headfirst. Think you can manage it?"

Elisabeth glanced back at the door. Was Dario on the other side, worrying about them? Was it right to abandon him? Then she thought of Sheply, who had promised to come after her. And Emery, whose remaining time ticked away with every moment she deliberated in this bathroom.

"Hurry," Brighton said.

She turned back, startled to see that Brighton had already disappeared through the window. She mounted the toilet and gripped the window frame.

Outside, Brighton dusted himself off, standing in the midst of dense weeds. He extended his arms to catch her.

Gritting her teeth, she heaved herself headfirst through the opening. Her shins scraped against the bottom frame of the window, but at least Brighton kept her from tumbling out. He settled her onto the ground and she winced; her right pant was torn and a trickle of blood trailed down her leg.

"You okay?" Brighton asked.

She nodded, and together they rounded the building. Brighton unlocked the doors of the waiting jeep and they jumped in.

"Dario was right about one thing," Elisabeth said as Brighton started the engine and kicked the transmission into reverse. "If Emery has any chance of coming back, he'll need a body."

Brighton shifted gears and sped over the rutted street. "Then we'll find him one."

*   *   *

Dario reached the chair where Ira sat. The rabbi's despondent eyes stared at a grove of trees near the water's edge. Ira's hands were clutched in his lap, unmoving.

"What's happened?" Dario asked.

"I have failed." Ira's words didn't seem to be directed at Dario.

"At what?"

Ira sat forward and ran a hand over his dirt-smeared forehead. "I've failed, but I haven't given up." He turned to Dario. "Where's Sherwood?"

"Back in the restaurant."

Ira staggered to his feet and began the long hobble back to the restaurant's front door.

"You're hurt, Ira," Dario said. "Wait here. I'll get Brighton."

Dario returned to the restaurant and knocked on the bathroom door. "Is everything alright in there?"

Brighton's voice came back quickly. "We're fine. Just give us a minute."

By now, Ira had stumbled in through the threshold of the restaurant. He put his hand on the edge of a table to steady himself.

"Did you fall?" Marilyn jumped out of her chair and ran to Ira's side.

Ira shook his head. "I'll be fine. I just need a few moments to recuperate."

Marilyn raised her eyes to her husband. "Carter, he needs medical attention."

"Where's the nearest hospital?" Dario asked.

"Back in Gilgit," Carter said. "I can't speak for the quality of care, but you can be there in a couple of hours. In the meantime, we have painkillers that might help."

Ira waved away the offer, but Carter ignored him and hurried out.

"Don't worry about me," Ira said, letting go of the table. He wobbled but remained upright. "We have bigger problems. Where's Brighton and Elisabeth?"

Dario pointed to the closed door. "They're in the bathroom."

"And don't you think that's a little strange?" Ira asked.

Dario never got a chance to answer. Carter burst back into the restaurant. "Your jeep is gone," he said, out of breath.

"I was afraid of that," Ira said quietly.

Dario ran outside and stared at the empty spot where their jeep had been parked only a few minutes ago. Plumes of dust still hadn't settled on the road leading to the main highway.

A single word pounded through Dario's otherwise jumbled thoughts: *Why?*

Ira stepped up beside him, his face contorted in a mixture of sadness and frustration.

"Why would they leave us?" Dario asked, crossing his arms.

"Because we would have tried to stop them."

Dario began to pace the dusty ground, glancing up at the road where Brighton and Elisabeth had escaped.

"I've been manipulated by spirits enough in the last week to know not to trust them," Dario said, his stomach churning at the memory of Rhea's fate. "For some reason, Brighton refused to see that."

"Keep in mind," Ira said, "he's essentially hearing voices in his head, telling him what to do."

Dario tired of pacing and returned to the shade of the restaurant's front stoop. "I still don't understand who you are, Ira. What's your history with Brighton?"

Dario sat with his back against the building, feeling numb as Ira unspooled one of the strangest and most improbable stories he'd ever heard. All along, Brighton and Elisabeth had been on the trail of a race of monsters dating back to biblical times.

"Was Ohia one of these Nephilim?" Dario stumbled over the unfamiliar word.

"Yes," Ira said without hesitation. Brighton had described the rabbi as secretive and cagey, but this afternoon Ira was an open book. "Not a Nephilim in the flesh, but the spirit of one. They were giants, malevolent forces in the ancient world born of the union between angels and unwilling human women."

"You mean demons," Dario corrected.

Ira tilted his head in acknowledgement, then carefully lowered himself to join Dario on the ground. "I'm not sure that's the most constructive term. Their physical bodies died, but their spirits haunt the earth. Ohia's not the first I've encountered."

Dario's head shot up. "There have been others?"

"There was one other," Ira said. "Emery Wörtlich died confronting it."

"But if these creatures survived the death of their bodies, why not Wörtlich?"

"Wörtlich wasn't bound to this earth in the same way as the Nephilim. It's impossible for a human spirit to linger after death."

Dario closed his eyes and fought an impending headache. To his troubled mind, the tale didn't quite make sense. He'd poke a hundred holes in all this once he had the chance to think it through.

It's impossible for a human spirit to linger after death…

Implying that Rhea, too, was gone forever.

"But a spirit did contact Brighton," Dario said, hopelessness settling around him like a cloud. "He wasn't imagining that."

They heard footsteps behind them. Carter and Marilyn exited the restaurant, looking concerned.

"If you want, we can give you a lift back to Gilgit," Carter suggested.

Just then, the ferry floated across Dario's field of vision, headed for the Shishkat quay. He felt a stirring of anxiety when he saw the dark blue sedan on its deck.

"Ira, I think we've been followed," Dario whispered.

Ira didn't respond as he struggled to stand. Carter and Marilyn helped him up.

"Thank you for the kind offer," Ira told the couple, "but we'll make other arrangements."

Carter hesitated before accepting Ira's decision, but after a few moments he joined his wife and returned to their jeep.

"Did you hear me?" Dario asked once the couple had driven away. "I think we've been followed."

"I heard you."

Dario pointed to the ferry. "Do you see that blue sedan? I first spotted it back in Naran."

"I noticed it as well."

"Why didn't say you anything?"

Ira rubbed his side, which was no doubt still sore. "You're just like Sherwood, so full of questions. If there's one thing I'm known for, it's my tendency to keep things to myself. To my own detriment, it would seem."

The ferry docked and the vehicles upon it disembarked. The sedan rolled off the ramp third and followed the other cars toward the Karakoram Highway. A few moments later, Dario's heart lurched; the sedan pulled onto the Shishkat road—head toward the restaurant.

Dario scrambled to his feet and corralled Ira toward the door, but Ira resisted.

"We have to hide," Dario said.

Ira's eyed blazed with intensity. "Go inside, but watch and listen to what transpires. I may need your assistance."

"What kind of assistance?"

"Unfortunately, it may take the form of... violence."

That caught Dario off-guard. "Violence? Ira, there's a fine line between bravery and stupidity—"

"Go!"

Dario backed through the door, hiding just inside. Several other patrons in the restaurant had interrupted their meals again to stare at his and Ira's conspicuous behavior.

There's nothing I can do about that, Dario thought as he took a position behind one of the front-facing windows. From here, he had a good view of the street.

Ira stood his ground, watching with crossed arms as the sedan approached the restaurant. The vehicle came to a stop in virtually the same spot where the jeep had been parked.

The rear door of the sedan opened and a familiar man stepped out. Noam Sheply wore black sunglasses, but his uneven gait gave away his blindness. As he walked, he oriented himself by grazing the side of the car. He held his other arm out in front, warding him from unseen obstacles in his path.

"I've been expecting you, Mr. Sheply," Ira called out.

This drew Sheply's attention. The man leaned against the trunk of the sedan. "Who are you? I don't recognize your voice."

"Ira Binyamin, and we've met before."

Sheply pursed his lips, showing no surprise.

"We need your help," Ira said, "but I need to know if you're here on Lagati's business."

"No," Sheply said. "I'm done with all that. I came for Elisabeth."

The driver's door opened and a second man stepped out. He, too, wore sunglasses. His brown hair pegged him as the man Dario had seen while pumping gas in Naran.

"If you're not working for Lagati, why have you chosen to be escorted by one of Lagati's right-hand men?" Ira took a few halting steps toward the driver before addressing him. "Mr. Wendell, you are a most unwelcome surprise."

Wendell froze. "We were led to believe you had already left this place."

"Only part of our group proceeded up the highway," Ira said.

"Rabbi, you must believe me when I say I had no idea this man was on Lagati's payroll," Sheply said in a subdued voice. "I hired him to be my guide."

"Did you think Lagati would let you go?" Wendell said to him. "You are too valuable an asset."

Ira made his way back to the restaurant door. "Mr. Wendell, my business with Sheply doesn't concern you. You will leave and return to your master."

"It's in my interest to stay." Wendell glanced pointedly from Ira to Sheply. "A blind man and a lame one. I'm afraid you don't have the means to stop me."

"I believe I'll return to my lunch," Ira called from the entrance. He gave no hint of Dario's presence. "You may join me, if you wish."

Ira walked back to the table they had vacated a half-hour earlier and lowered himself into the chair. The dishes had not been cleared, so Ira refilled his water glass and took a long drink.

Dario stared at Ira in shock. *This* was the plan? Had the man finally gone senile?

Outside, Sheply and Wendell remained next to their car, not speaking. They formed a perfect silent tableau, blue sky overhead and craggy mountains behind.

Ira continued sipping his water and scooping a bit of leftover rice onto his spoon. He didn't even look up to see if his gambit was working.

At last, there was movement on the street. Wendell forged a straight path for the door without detouring to help his blind passenger.

Dario looked back to Ira for some cue, but he offered none.

This is ridiculous! What does he want me to do? "It may take the form of violence," Ira had said.

Dario's frantic eyes searched the restaurant for something—anything—he could use. How much force would be required to injure this Wendell fellow without doing him serious harm? Violence had never been one of Dario's raisons d'être.

Wendell was now more than halfway to the door. Dario guessed he had maybe ten seconds to come up with a plan.

Damn it, Ira. How did I get stuck with you?

Five seconds.

Thinking fast, Dario grabbed a wooden chair from a nearby table, ignoring the startled looks from the two men sitting there. The chair felt sturdier in his hands than he had anticipated. For these purposes, he supposed that was probably a good sign.

Two seconds. He heard Wendell's footsteps on the front stoop.

Dario raised the chair over his head. He thought he heard a shout of warning from one of the restaurant's patrons, but it came too late. Dario brought the chair down with as much force as he could muster. Its heavy seat crashed into the back of Wendell's head.

Wendell collapsed.

Dario stood over the body, adrenaline pumping through him. Had he killed him?

For a moment, nobody in the restaurant moved. Ira launched himself out of his chair and hurried across the room, moving much more nimbly than he had a few minutes ago.

"Check his pocket for keys," Ira said, already rushing out the door.

Dario did as he was told, finding the car keys on the first try.

Some of the other patrons had come to their feet. Fearing still more violence—this time, directed at him—Dario ran full-tilt toward the car.

"Get in the car," Ira said, opening the door to Sheply.

"What's going on?" Sheply asked.

Dario marveled at the oddity of seeing Sheply in such a vulnerable state. He didn't have much time to dwell on it, though; already people were gathering outside the restaurant.

"Better hurry," Dario said as he got into the passenger seat and shut the door behind him. "The natives are getting restless."

Once all three were in the car, Ira pulled out and rocketed toward the highway with more speed than Dario had thought he was capable of. The ruts in the gravel road didn't give Ira any pause; the car soared over them.

"Ira, I can't believe you made me do that," Dario said as they merged onto the highway and sped north.

Ira's hands gripped the steering wheel. "It was the simplest way."

"Someone please explain to me what's happening." Sheply's voice sounded livid. "Am I being kidnapped?"

"That depends on how you look at it," Ira tossed over his shoulder. "If we're going to stop Sherwood and Elisabeth in time, we have to hurry. Because of Wendell, Lagati will know where to look for us."

As the adrenaline eased off, the magnitude of what Dario had done hit home.

"I think I may have killed him," Dario said once they were a few miles up the road.

"I doubt it."

Dario had never been a praying man, but he hoped against hope that Ira was right.

"If Lagati catches up with us," Sheply said, "we may have cause to wish you had."

TWENTY-NINE

Mount Khunjerab, Pakistan
JULY 27

Two miles from the Chinese border, the highway leveled out onto a plateau, a startling change from the twists and turns that had brought them here. The jeep's wheels sliced through gravel as Brighton pulled over to the side of the road just past the sign marking the border.

"That's Mount Khunjerab," Brighton said, pointing to the wide and imposing peak across the plain from them. A glacier seemed to pour down off it, ending about a mile or two from the road.

He stepped outside into chilly air and hugged his arms around his chest to conserve heat.

"We should have stopped to buy coats," Elisabeth said, shivering.

Brighton opened the rear hatch, pulled out a folded brown tarp, and tossed it to her. "Use this."

Next, he removed a long floor mat that stretched across the rear of the jeep; one side was covered in a thick black carpet. He shook the stiff carpet, dislodging the dirt and pebbles that had accumulated in it. He could use it as a blanket.

"Do you think we can drive across the plain?" Elisabeth asked.

Brighton took a few moments to assess the terrain. Tall grasses and a multitude of white and yellow flowers covered the flat land. "The jeep can certainly go off-road, but I'm not sure how far."

"And once we get to the mountain?" Elisabeth's forehead creased. "Do we have any choice but to march up the side of it?"

"Nope," Brighton said. "This is the only viable approach, so I'm hoping to find a navigable trail. We know Carter and Marilyn have come this way before."

Agreeing to this plan, Brighton and Elisabeth returned to the jeep. They buckled in, bracing themselves as Brighton swerved off the shoulder. The jeep bounced over a shallow ditch full of loose stones, then proceeded to cut a path through the grassland. Brighton steered a straight course for the bottom of the Khunjerab glacier and maintained a steady speed of twenty-five kilometers per hour.

Fifteen minutes passed before the ground became too uneven for them to continue, at which point Brighton jumped out without saying a word.

He silently measured the remaining distance to the edge of the glacier. Already he could see a clear path up its southern edge, making the incline traversable. They didn't need to get to the top of the mountain, after all, just onto the main saddle from which the glacier fell. He felt certain that if they got a look at the far side of the mountain, they'd know where to go next.

Brighton shifted his feet. The mountain called to him. He

couldn't understand why he felt so convinced. Maybe he'd finally visited enough hotspots to be able to sense one when he stood on its doorstep.

"Let's go," Elisabeth said, tugging on Brighton's arm.

Together, they set off toward the glacier. Brighton spared two backward glances for the jeep, the lone bastion of civilization in a sprawling wilderness. Steeling himself, he turned one last time and left it all behind.

*   *   *

Elisabeth thought this might be one of the longest days of her life. She ached from head to toe and was forced to acknowledge that she wasn't as young as she used to be. The last time she had walked this long and hard had been with Emery in the desert outside Farafra, Egypt. In the closing days of their travels together, their relationship had strained. She had known he planned to go back to his wife, yet she fought for him. He hadn't seemed to notice. When they returned to Cairo afterward, Emery hadn't even seen her off.

Farafra was one of her worst memories, and she resented this mountain path for reminding her of it.

In most respects, this place and the Egyptian desert had nothing in common, except for the dry air that cracked her lips. The glacier shone like a diamond, reflecting sunlight into her eyes if she looked too far to the left. The sun was bright—and at this altitude, closer than ever—but it provided no warmth.

Brighton forged ahead and she struggled to keep up. Her legs screamed at her to sit and rest awhile, but Brighton didn't seem to be in the mood to slow, let alone stop. He moved like a man possessed.

Over the course of an hour, they covered more than a mile of ground, most of it steadily uphill. She thought they had made it about halfway up to the saddle, but the remaining mile looked more imposing with every footfall.

"How are you doing?" he called back to her after an especially grueling climb.

Elisabeth didn't say anything; she was too out of breath to form words. She paused, looking up to see Brighton perched on the edge of a large boulder.

"Another hour or two and we'll have a view of the backside of the mountain," Brighton called. "I want to get there while there's still light."

Elisabeth groaned, but forced her legs back into motion.

The afternoon turned to evening, then to dusk, and still they hadn't reached the top of the saddle. The one good thing was that the path was well-worn. For all appearances, people had come this way, and recently.

"We're not going to make it before sunset," Elisabeth wheezed. "It'll be dark soon. We have to find a place to rest for the night."

Up ahead, Brighton located a hollow in the side of a steep cliff. The shelter was surrounded on three sides and had a partial roof to protect them from the elements.

"This is as good a spot as any," Brighton said. He ventured as far into the hollow as the rock walls allowed, then sat down. "Can you feel the tingle in the air?"

Elisabeth quieted herself, closed her eyes, and drew steady breaths. Yes, she could feel it. The air was charged, with the faintest scent of ozone.

"Is it the hotspot?" she asked.

"I think so." Brighton waved her to come inside. "Sit down. It's been a long climb."

She didn't need prompting. Sleep would come easy tonight.

"Do you think we're safe?" Elisabeth said. "You have to expect there's all kinds of wildlife around."

Brighton didn't seem concerned. "We're too close to the hotspot for animals to bother us."

Elisabeth frowned, wondering how Brighton could be so sure of that. She didn't press him for details; the more she thought about it, the more right it felt. Whatever caused that ozone smell might also keep animals away.

The world faded into twilight and the sky exploded with stars. As tired as she felt, she wanted to stay awake to take in the view. Alas, despite her appreciation of the beauty around her, her exhaustion proved stronger. She pulled the brown tarp over her, the plastic crinkling as she wrapped a double layer around her body. To help preserve heat, she curled inward so that her head almost touched her knees. Plumes of starlight danced against her eyelids, a light wind whistled a discordant lullaby, and soon she was asleep.

That same wind woke her sometime later, its gusts having strengthened and cooled. She shivered and pulled her arms inside her shirt. Her teeth chattered as she looked around the hollow.

Brighton's missing, she realized, staring at the empty stretch of ground the young man had occupied.

She sat up and peered into the night, her eyes searching the top of the glacier. She pressed her hand against the rock and stumbled to her feet.

Starlight blanketed the path in both directions. It only took a moment to spot Brighton. He appeared as little more than a dark spot against the starry sky, standing farther up the path. No, not standing. He was walking up the path toward the saddle.

Elisabeth opened her mouth to call for him, then thought better of it. She braced herself against the wind and went after him, at first at a normal pace, and then nearly a jog.

"Sherwood?" she asked as she got closer.

Brighton didn't respond.

Was he sleepwalking? She had once heard that one shouldn't wake a sleepwalker, but she couldn't remember why.

Elisabeth got close enough to put a hand on Brighton's shoulder. Her fingers grazed the skin of his neck, but he didn't react. She pulled him by the arm, turning him around so she could get a good look at his face.

She gasped. Brighton's eyes had rolled back in his head, with only a small crescent of lens visible under each lid. The whites glared brightly at her.

"Emery?" she asked in a whisper, the wind snatching it away.

She couldn't tell whether she was imagining it, but she thought Brighton's head tilted toward her ever so slightly.

She tried again. "Emery, it's me. Elisabeth."

Brighton's head tilted further.

Her heart pounded; she could feel the rhythm in every molecule of her being, drumming madly.

It's him. He's here. He's with me.

"Emery, speak to me," she said. "We came, just like you asked. Is this Shamballa? What should we do? Where should we go?"

She draped her arms around the back of his neck, the way she had held on to him when they were alone together. She gazed up into his face—it wasn't Emery's face, but she could imagine that it was; the lines in his pockmarked cheeks, his chronic five o'clock shadow tinged with grey hairs, his strong jawline. The experience was so confusing.

"Olmolungring," Emery spoke in an almost inflectionless voice.

Elisabeth drew in a sharp breath. "Yes, Emery, we're here."

Without any warning, Brighton collapsed like a popped balloon. He sagged to his knees, then fell onto his side.

Elisabeth caught his head before it hit rock. She held him—cradled him—for several minutes, feeling his steady breath pulling in and out, in and out.

Brighton went into a fit of coughing and Elisabeth wished she had some water to offer him. Her eyes turned to the ice flow, and she realized she had an almost unlimited supply right in front of her. She set Brighton down, got to her feet, and walked to the edge of the ice. She knelt down and felt the surface; the ice was harder than rock, but when she pressed her palm against it, her body heat caused drops of water to condense against her skin. She held both hands against the ice, waited a minute, then returned to Brighton and placed her hands against his cracked lips, moistening them.

His eyes fluttered open. They were bloodshot, but it was Brighton again. Emery had left.

She felt guilty for the disappointment that roiled deep inside.

"I was somewhere else," he said. She had to lower her head toward his to make out his quiet words. "I was with Wörtlich."

"I know," Elisabeth said. "He was here."

Brighton repositioned himself, his strength returning. "Did he say anything to you?"

"Just 'Olmolungring.'"

Brighton nodded. "He said the same to me, over and over. I think we're close."

She helped him up and led him back to the hollow, where the tarp had been blown into a corner by the wind.

"It'll be dark for a couple of hours, but I won't be able to sleep again," Brighton said. "Let's keep moving."

They rolled up the tarp and floor mat, tucked them under their arms, and headed up the path, barely avoiding each other's heels in the near-darkness. The sky went from black to a dark blue in the course of the first half-hour, and soon a sliver of light appeared over the peaks to the east. The view was breathtaking, the first rays of sunlight streaming past spires of rock and ice.

Brighton stopped when he reached the top of the saddle and Elisabeth climbed up next to him. The magnificence of this vista swept over her like a wave. In the depression between three mountains was a deep cylindrical hole—a "crack in the earth," just as Carter had described it. Patches of ice and snow, and what appeared to be black, glistening rock, clung to its rim.

"Holy hell," Brighton whispered. "A part of me didn't really believe it would be here."

Holy hell, indeed. Elisabeth tried to calculate the size of the opening, but it defied measurement. The hole was probably a mile long, and half that distance wide.

"Let's go," Brighton said, immediately beginning the descent. Elisabeth followed right behind him.

*   *   *

Carsickness settled in over Dario after five hours on the road. They had spent all day searching for Brighton and Elisabeth's jeep and come up empty. There'd been no sign of them near the border crossing, so they had turned around and stopped in every town on the way back until they ended up right where they'd started.

A brilliant sunset purpled the sky as they once again approached the northernmost stretches of the highway. After snaking their way up a series of treacherous switchbacks, they emerged onto a level plain. This being their second trip to these altitudes, they knew the border station was only a few miles away.

They had grown increasingly testy with each other as the hours passed, to the point of hardly speaking. Sheply's blindness made him worse than useless in the search, and Dario didn't think Ira's aged eyes could be trusted, either. That left him to watch for signs along the highway, but he could only look in one direction at a time.

Just as he was about to give up, a glint of light drew his attention.

"Stop!" Dario shouted, pointing to the west.

Ira stopped the car along the side of the road. The wheels skidded through loose pebbles.

"What do you see?" Ira asked.

"The gleam of metal, a couple of miles over the plain, against the backdrop of that mountain." Dario squinted harder. "Could it be the jeep?"

"There's only one way to find out." Ira steered the car off the road into a tangle of wild grasses.

Dario held on for dear life as they mowed over bumpy terrain. The car's shocks couldn't keep up the punishment much longer.

"Gentlemen, I doubt my rental insurance covers off-roading," Sheply deadpanned from the back seat.

"You should have thought ahead," Dario said, straining against his seatbelt.

Dario heard a grinding sound, and then the car lurched. It sounded like they'd hit some kind of rock. Ira gunned the engine, but the wheels spun uselessly.

"I think this is as far as our ride takes us." Ira unstrapped his seatbelt and got out of the car.

Dario pushed his door open, too. He put his back into the effort as the bottom of the door scraped through a mound of dirt. The car had gotten stuck in a shallow gulley. They would need a tow truck to get back to the highway, and Dario doubted there were many available in this neck of the woods.

"They must have come this way and continued on foot," Dario said, again locating the jeep in the wilderness ahead.

"We'll have to do the same," Ira said as he helped Sheply out of the car.

From Sheply's luggage, they found enough jackets and sweaters to keep them warm as evening settled in. Dario felt grateful to be traveling with someone who'd had some foresight. With Elisabeth and Brighton, they'd carried nothing but the clothes on their backs. Sheply and Wendell had even stored a crate of bottled water in the trunk.

"I hope they stopped for supplies," Dario said as they trudged toward the jeep. "They were underdressed and didn't have much food or water left."

Their progress was frustratingly slow, with Sheply picking his way over the uneven ground and tripping over rocks.

They finally came to the jeep as the sun disappeared below the mountains.

To Dario's surprise, inside the jeep he discovered the compass, rope, matches, and knife they had purchased in Islamabad.

"Why didn't they take these with them?" Dario asked, holding up the knife in its leather sheath.

Ira flipped open the compass and waited for the needle to settle. "I think it's safe to say they're not thinking rationally, Mr. Katsulas."

"But they could die!"

Sheply leaned against the side of the jeep. "They'd better not. Elisabeth and I have unfinished business."

"I believe they're in the grip of powerful forces," Ira said. The words were melodramatic, but he delivered them without a trace of panache. "That said, I don't see much point in venturing further tonight."

They agreed with some reluctance, since tracking Brighton and Elisabeth's path would be next to impossible in the dark.

Sheply slept in the car, while Ira and Dario created space for themselves in the jeep. Ira sat in the front passenger's seat and reclined as far as it would go. Dario attempted to get comfortable in the back seat, a doomed venture. He was almost a foot too tall to stretch out all the way.

"Ira, what kind of forces are we contending with?" Dario asked amidst the chirping of crickets. "All this business of spirits and ghosts has me spooked."

Ira didn't answer, but Dario knew from the lack of snores that the rabbi hadn't fallen asleep.

"Ira?"

"Good night, Dario," Ira said in the darkness.

With those three words, Dario finally understood just how Brighton felt.

THIRTY

Mount Khunjerab, Pakistan
JULY 28

As they came down the slope, Brighton wondered how they would descend into the hole. He then noticed a wide, steel-framed staircase hugging the walls of the chasm. Fluorescent lamps lit the way, spaced five meters apart. The stairs and lights lent a military air to this "facility." Did it make sense for the ancient city of Shamballa, dreamed of by philosophers and mystics for hundreds of years, to be girded by modern infrastructure? He suspected not, and yet the evidence surrounded him on all sides.

As tired as they were, Brighton and Elisabeth descended. A landing awaited them after every fifty steps; they blew through the first few but eventually started using them for short breaks. All this downhill climbing took a toll on Brighton's shins.

When they reached the bottom, they discovered that the floor was constructed of steel. A diagonal line of jagged teeth crossed the floor, suggesting that it doubled as enormous doors that could open and close to accommodate aircraft from a hangar below. Brighton stepped onto it gingerly, half-afraid it would open at any moment.

"There," Elisabeth said, pointing to the far side of the pit from where the stairs had deposited them. A tall cavern, bracketed by steel supports, delved deeper into the ground.

"For an ancient city, this place certainly has a lot of modern touches," Elisabeth remarked, echoing Brighton's thoughts. "Are you sure this isn't a military base?"

"If this was military, we wouldn't have gotten halfway down the mountain before being apprehended," Brighton said, trying to convince himself. "I doubt the Chinese and Pakistanis are so lax on border security."

"Which suggests we're being allowed to continue." Elisabeth began walking toward the cavern entrance. "But what choice do we have? Emery has guided us this far."

Brighton fell into step behind Elisabeth as they passed into the enormous cavern. Light pooled on the ground, shining down from the same kind of lights that had illuminated the staircase.

"The cavern is of similar dimensions to the caverns I saw in Tiahuanaco," Elisabeth mused. "I wonder if they had the same builder."

For an underground passage, the cavern was surprisingly clean, as though someone swept the floor regularly and dusted the irregular protrusions of rock. Occasional doors interrupted the walls on both sides, their smooth surfaces devoid of obvious handles. To the left of the doors someone had affixed unassuming square panels plated in copper. Brighton guessed that they were fingerprint scanners.

"Where is everyone?" Brighton said. The facility had to be in use, or else how could it be so well-maintained? "There should be a veritable army of people running all this."

The swish of a door sliding open prompted Brighton to spin on his heels. A tall man came through one of the many doors and set a course straight for them. Shorter men flanked him on either side.

"I wouldn't call it an army, Mr. Brighton," the tall man said, hardly needing to raise his voice in the quiet cavern. "Please, don't bother running. You wouldn't get far."

Raff Lagati came to a stop just a few feet away. With head held high, he exuded confidence. The center of his personal magnetism could be located in those hard blue eyes that surveyed Brighton and Elisabeth with dispassionate contempt. Brighton found it difficult to look away. Lagati's gaze confirmed that he ruled over this place as the quintessential king in his castle.

Lagati gestured to his two bodyguards. They stepped forward and took away the tarp and floor mat before retreating into the depths of the cavern.

"You won't be needing those," Lagati said. "Don't look so terrified. I'm not the villain you imagine I am."

"You'll have a hard time convincing me of that," Brighton growled.

Lagati wagged a finger at him. "I'm sorry to hear you've been taking counsel from the wrong sort of people. Now that you're free of them, I'm hoping we can renew our friendship."

"Friendship?" Brighton asked. "You were paying me to do a job."

The Frenchman offered a cold smile. "I always liked you best, Mr. Brighton. We have much in common." He lifted his cool blue eyes to study Elisabeth. "I haven't been introduced to your companion."

Elisabeth took a step forward. "I know who you are, Mr. Lagati. Sherwood has told me everything."

Lagati let out a restrained snigger. "Not everything, I suspect. Or at least, plenty of the wrong things."

"What on earth are you doing here?" Brighton asked.

"Come with me and I'll explain." Lagati turned and walked back the way he had come.

Brighton felt profoundly anxious as they proceeded down the corridor. Were they prisoners? If so, Lagati was remarkably cavalier about it. He could have ordered his guards to secure them and escort them to a cell. Brighton feared they would soon learn the reason.

Lagati stopped at one of the doors and pressed his thumb against the small copper panel. The door slid open. Brighton hesitated, trying to decide whether to enter this rabbit hole voluntarily.

His curiosity got the better of him.

The impressive room they entered shouldn't have surprised him; Lagati had always appreciated spectacle, and given the age of these caverns, Brighton suspected the room hadn't been designed for the purpose it currently served.

Lagati had retrofitted the vast space into a lavish hospitality suite. Plush leather couches were arranged in circles, none near enough to each other to interfere with the feeling of intimacy they engendered. A granite-topped bar separated the open kitchen from the rest of the suite, and platters of food—open-faced sandwiches, two different kinds of soup, a selection of bread, and a golden-crisped chicken— had been set out. Tendrils of steam curled up from the chicken, which had clearly just been taken out of the oven. Lagati had known they were coming.

"Please, have something to eat. You must be famished." Lagati relaxed into one of the couches, visibly softening from the manner in which he had greeted them in the cavern. Even in this informal mode, however, he remained the undisputed master of all he surveyed.

Elisabeth was already halfway to the bar when Lagati spoke.

Brighton waited for her to finish making a plate for herself before indulging. Despite his rumbling stomach, Brighton helped himself to a single piece of bread; he was too hungry to abstain, but he didn't want to give Lagati the satisfaction of watching him gorge himself. The simple food was still warm in his hands.

Lagati raised an eyebrow at Brighton as the young man chose the couch farthest from Lagati.

A steward appeared and served them orange juice in spindly glasses. Brighton gave it an appraising sniff before venturing a sip.

"I could poison it and you would never know," Lagati said with a smile on his face.

Brighton made direct eye contact. "Is that your version of reassurance?"

Lagati shrugged. "Take it however you wish. I have nothing to gain by harming you."

For the first time, Brighton noticed the long wall opposite the door. Dark curtains draped overtop it from the ceiling, obscuring the wall's subtle concave curve. The setup suggested windows—odd, since the room was underground.

The atmosphere was quiet as Brighton and Elisabeth nibbled on their dinner.

"This might be a more efficient discussion if you ask some questions," Lagati said. "I'm sure you have many."

"You can start by telling us where we are," Elisabeth said.

"Fair enough. As I'm sure you've been able to guess, this is an immensely old facility. It may appear similar to a military base, but it wasn't built by any government or militia you know of, least of all the Pakistanis or Chinese, though they know we're here. It would be impossible to hide from them given current technology. It wasn't always like that. In fact, this base used to be very well hidden."

Brighton's heart sank. There was only one group of people—if they could properly be called people—who were capable of undertaking a project on this scale prior to the mid-twentieth century. The look Lagati proffered him confirmed it.

Lagati adjusted the throw pillows around him. "In any event, the whole world will soon know about us."

Brighton shot him a dark look. "That sounds ominous."

"Depends on one's perspective." Lagati sounded almost cheerful about it. "The strange truth is that this facility is six thousand years old, give or take a century, and it was built by the ancient gods. Mind you, we've given it some upgrades."

"The ancient gods?" Elisabeth asked.

"Yes," Lagati said. "You may have heard them called Watchers. They built this to serve as a base of operations."

Brighton turned to Elisabeth. "The way Ira told the story, the Watchers were angels who rebelled against God."

Lagati clasped his hands together. "Well, Ira was right about one thing. These angels certainly didn't work for God. The creature you refer to as God is not the benevolent force the world's religions think he is."

Lagati rose and circled the couch, making his way toward the curtains. He tugged on one of them and yanked the fabric away. In a fluid motion, the curtain pulled back to reveal a line of windows.

Brighton stood up when he realized what he was looking at.

Before them lay an immense, roughly cylindrical cavern. From its relative position, he guessed this was the main hangar located just below the steel floor they had crossed above. The size of the hangar would have mesmerized anyone, but the context in which he now viewed it was extraordinary. Row upon row of bright lights shone down upon a glistening craft shaped like a triangle that took up only a quarter of the hangar's area. Men and women dressed in blue slacks and red ball caps crawled over and around it like a colony of ants.

Brighton turned back to Lagati, slack-jawed. "Is that what I think it is?"

"I think it's safe to say yes," the Frenchman said, more than a hint of pride oozing through his disciplined manner.

Brighton couldn't seem to control himself from approaching the window, and he wasn't the only one. Elisabeth nearly pressed her nose against the glass.

"I suppose Carter and Marilyn were on to something," Elisabeth said, her lips quirking into a smile. "If that's not a spaceship, I don't know what is."

"This could have been constructed by anyone with enough money," Brighton said. "Just because it looks futuristic doesn't mean—"

"You wouldn't say that if you saw it fly," Lagati said.

Brighton returned to the nearest couch and sank into it, pointedly facing away from the windows. The ship gave him a lot to process, and staring at it wasn't helpful.

"Mr. Brighton, you look thoughtful." Lagati inched closer to him. "I do hope you'll share."

Brighton met his gaze. "Perhaps you could confirm a few things."

"Cetainly."

"For one," Brighton said, "does Noam Sheply still work for you?"

Next to him, Brighton saw Elisabeth squirm. She tried to cover it by looking up and meeting Lagati's gaze, but it was too little too late for someone as perceptive as Lagati.

"Your friend has been keeping secrets from you, Mr. Brighton." Lagati smiled; he was full of them today.

There was no mistaking the look of guilt on Elisabeth's face.

"Elisabeth, what is it?" Brighton asked.

"I'm sorry," she said softly. "I should have said something."

"Said *what?*"

Lagati's open grin laid bare his joy in their display of domestic strife.

"Sheply followed us to Pakistan," Elisabeth said. "He cornered me in Gilgit."

Brighton couldn't believe what he was hearing. "You didn't think that was important enough to mention?"

"I worried that if I told you, it would change our plans," Elisabeth said. "Besides, Sheply said he was no longer working for Lagati."

"And you believed him?" Brighton asked.

"Actually," Lagati interjected, "he was telling the truth about that."

Elisabeth turned to Lagati. "I don't understand. If he was telling the truth, why did he come after us?"

Lagati shrugged. "I believe he has an emotional attachment to you."

Elisabeth appeared stunned. She fell backward into the couch cushions, unresponsive for a minute or two.

"Regardless of his current status, you assigned Sheply to hunt me," Brighton said. "Do you deny it?"

"Hunt is a strong word. You led him on a merry search," Lagati said. "You told Sheply that you never found the Book of Creation, but that's a lie. I know that you did."

"How can you know something that isn't true?"

Lagati stood and went behind the bar. He knelt down, and Brighton heard the sound of bottles clinking together. Lagati re-emerged with a stout decanter filled with a dark brown liquid.

"I'm afraid orange juice isn't going to cut it for me," Lagati said offhandedly. "Care for something with a bit more kick? You may need it by the time we finish here." He poured the thick liquid into a tulip-shaped glass, then gestured to Elisabeth. "You look like you could use a drink."

"I'm not thirsty," Brighton said dryly.

Elisabeth ignored him. "I am."

Lagati filled another glass. "You'll like this. It's scotch whisky, unlike anything you've tried before, I guarantee."

"I don't know about that," Brighton murmured. "I've had my fair share of whisky these last few months, no thanks to you."

"I take full credit." Lagati poured a third glass and held it up to the light. "Have I mentioned that the bottle this came from cost me two hundred thousand pounds?"

Lagati placed all three glasses on a tray, balanced it on the palm of his left hand, and returned to the couches. After Elisabeth took hers, Brighton relented.

Elisabeth pounded back her drink in one shot. Her face flashed through several shades of pink before returning to its normal color.

The drink burned its way down Brighton's throat—just the way he liked it.

"Cheers," Lagati said, tipping back his own glass.

"What were we talking about?" Brighton asked, his cheeks feeling flush. He took another sip, and another, the smooth, smoky taste like a lover's caress.

Lagati put down his glass. "The Book of Creation. I'm not sure why you persist in lying to me, Mr. Brighton. You're quite transparent."

"You don't know the first thing about me."

"Is that so? You were born in the mountains of Virginia. Your mother's name was Althea, your father's Clarence. You had an older sister, but she died when she was a baby. You have only one aunt, on your father's side, who lives in Canada. You graduated a year later than you were supposed to, because you repeated the third grade. You've broken your left arm twice. You like baseball. You earned a scholarship to attend Caltech, but you deferred so you could travel for a year. Your favorite professor was Hikaru Kannasaki, but you weren't *his* favorite. You were eventually hired at the Smithsonian, returning home to Virginia."

Brighton pursed his lips. "Those are biographical details. You don't know *me*."

"You dated a waitress named Rachel and almost convinced yourself you loved her. You didn't. She's engaged now, you know, and to someone who makes a lot more money than you do."

"Don't bait me."

"Bait you? I'm answering your question. You're a heavy drinker and a wanted man in six different countries, under various aliases. You haven't seen your parents in three years, and for all they know you're dead and buried—"

"Enough."

Lagati laughed. "I trust I've proven—"

"Enough!" Brighton's chest heaved, his breath shallow. The scotch had loosened him up, and not for the better.

"You're a very angry man now," Lagati mused. "You weren't always."

"A lot's happened." Brighton took a few calming breaths. "You're responsible for most of it."

Lagati shook his head sadly. "The pressure I put you under is nothing compared to what Ira Binyamin did to you. Tell me I'm wrong."

That certainly took Brighton aback. "How do you know about that?"

"I know full well how difficult Ira can be. I thought he was out of the picture, but then he resurfaced with you in Islamabad. That took me by surprise, which happens so rarely. As hard as I've been searching for you, I've been searching threefold for Ira. Honestly, I had assumed he was killed on Tubuai, like Emery Wörtlich." Lagati paused, letting it sink in. "Yes, I know about that, too."

Elisabeth put her empty glass aside. "Sheply worked for you, and he didn't know."

"Noam Sheply was an employee, not a confidant." It sounded like a rebuke. There obviously wasn't any love lost between Lagati and Sheply. "I was looking forward to seeing Ira again. And yet here you are, Ira-less. What happened to him?"

"I wouldn't tell you if I knew," Brighton said. "But I have no idea. I've almost stopped caring."

"Only almost?"

"Old habits." Brighton polished off his drink and put down the empty glass.

"Would you like another?" Lagati offered.

Brighton wiped his mouth with his shirtsleeve. "No. As you've very impolitely revealed, I should exercise better control."

"Wise man." Lagati crossed his legs, getting comfortable. He looked like he would be content to remain on that couch for hours. "Anyway, Ira can't have gone far. He was with you at least until Gilgit."

This time Brighton didn't bother to look surprised.

"You've had us watched since the moment we landed in Pakistan," Elisabeth said. "But I thought Sheply wasn't reporting to you anymore."

"He wasn't alone," Lagati said. "Blind men don't drive cars."

Elisabeth fell silent at that, then ventured, "You said Emery Wört-lich is dead."

"No." Lagati raised a finger. "I said he was killed."

*   *   *

A quarter of the way up the mountain path, Dario didn't think Ira and Sheply were going to make it. At the halfway point, this conviction grew stronger. But three-quarters of the way up, despite slow going, he began to change his mind. Not only would they likely get to the top of the saddle over which the Khunjerab Glacier plunged, but they would get there by noon. Ira may have looked like a seventy-year-old man, but he had the endurance of a man half his age.

"This is where they spent the night," Ira said, bringing his water bottle to his lips.

Dario studied the natural hollow; it looked like a dent in the mountainside, just large enough for two people to fit.

"It would make a good spot," Dario agreed. "But they could have stopped anywhere along this path."

"No, it was here." Ira pushed a pile of scree with the sole of his shoe. "Somebody swept away the rock to make room to lie down."

Sheply cleared his throat, leaning against the side of the cliff. He did that often when Dario and Ira conversed, as though to remind them that he was still with them. Not that they were likely to forget.

"How much farther?" Sheply asked.

Dario found it hard to sympathize with the Englishman. Sheply's blindness marked him for special consideration, but he had an arrogant personality that chipped away at Dario's patience.

"Another hour or two, depending on the grade," Dario called back. Fortunately, Sheply couldn't see the frustration on Dario's face, so all he had to do was *sound* good-natured.

Dario and Ira had been taking turns guiding Sheply over the path's snags. For the next leg of the hike, Dario took a rotation. He grasped Sheply by the shoulder and pointed him in the right direction.

The hour passed slowly, and Sheply insisted they pass the time in conversation. Without the benefit of sight, he seemed to need the sensory stimulation.

"When Brighton and Elisabeth went on without you, you could have left Pakistan," Sheply said. "I don't understand why you stayed."

The pointed question gnawed at Dario as they took one careful step after another. He'd asked himself the same question. Throughout the last two weeks, he'd had many opportunities to bail. He could have chosen not to concern himself when Rhea told him about Jorge and Yasmine. That would have been the better personal decision; in the end, both of the young people had died, and so had Rhea. But on a human level, how could he have stood aside? He regretted the cost, but he would never regret the decision to get involved.

"Because I care," Dario said after a long time had passed.

"You're a better man than I," Sheply said.

Dario nodded even though Sheply wouldn't know it. "But didn't you say that you came because of Elisabeth? That must mean you care for her."

"I do care, more than she'll probably ever know. But that's the difference between you and me."

"I don't understand."

"I have feelings for Elisabeth." Sheply didn't use the word *love*. He didn't have to. "But you came out of loyalty to someone you barely know. How well did you know Elisabeth before all this trouble started?"

"Not very well," Dario admitted.

And I didn't know Jorge or Yasmine at all.

Ira strode several steps ahead of them, well within hearing range. If he had overheard their conversation, though, he didn't let on.

In the next few minutes, they reached the horizon and found themselves astride the saddle. The views from here were as stunning as Dario had grown accustomed to since arriving in the Karakoram, but it wasn't the scenery that grabbed hold of his attention and wouldn't let go.

"Do you see that opening?" Dario asked.

Ira nodded. "Yes."

The opening in the ground was wide and deep, and it certainly matched the description Carter and Marilyn had given them.

"What is it?" Sheply asked, reminding them of his continued presence.

"A hole in the earth large enough to launch a spacecraft," Dario explained. "That's where Elisabeth and Brighton went."

Without another word, Ira led the way down.

The going was much easier on this flank of Mount Khunjerab, and it helped for them to have a tangible destination in view.

They hadn't been on the move more than ten minutes, however, before Ira stopped them again.

"What is it?" Dario asked.

Ira's normally tranquil features transformed into a maze of worry lines. He searched the terrain to either side, and Dario did the same. The land appeared empty except for rock and the occasional low brush. But obviously Ira had something more perilous on his mind than a poison-leafed shrub.

"We are not alone," the rabbi said, drawing out the words.

By the time Dario turned to look behind them, trouble was upon them.

*   *   *

Elisabeth's heart thundered in her chest as she stared hard into Raff Lagati's eyes. He didn't seem like the man Brighton had described. He was calculating and intelligent, without a doubt, but he was also... pleasant. Brighton didn't trust him, but Elisabeth felt more conflicted. Sincerity rang in his words, and he spoke to them as equals.

"I want to see Emery," Elisabeth managed, her voice breaking.

"Patience," Lagati said. "Do you believe in spirits, Elisabeth?"

"I didn't used to."

"I was the same way. Science tells us there's no such thing as the human soul, and most of the time I'm one to trust science. In this case, however, there's a deeper reality that scientists have yet to grasp. The essence of a person *can* go on after physical death. My personal experience makes this undeniable. I imagine you've experienced it as well."

"Sherwood and I have both spoken to Emery."

Lagati stood up and carried his glass to the bar, setting it down on the granite top. "Before we continue, there's something I need to show you. I promise, it gets to the heart of what brought you here."

Elisabeth and Brighton came to their feet and stepped around the couches.

The same two guards they had seen earlier waited in the hall. Lagati dismissed them with a wave.

"Where are we going?" Brighton asked.

Lagati was already halfway out the door when he answered with a single word: "Shamballa."

THIRTY-ONE

Shamballa

JULY 28

The cavern Lagati guided Elisabeth and Brighton along followed a gentle arc, leading Elisabeth to believe they were circling the main hangar they had glimpsed through the windows. At one point, they passed an observation area where they saw the spacecraft again from a closer vantage. Atop the ship was a long compartment far too large to accommodate a human of average height, yet it was clearly designed for a pilot. Elisabeth guessed that the ship had been designed to be flown by one of the giants Brighton had told her about.

They didn't linger. Elisabeth should have felt disappointed when Lagati herded them away from the viewport, but the hope of reuniting with Emery exerted an even stronger pull.

The cavern ended in dozens and dozens of steps too large to easily accommodate a human's stride. Like the rest of this facility, they had been designed for beings up to thirty feet tall. Fortunately, the ordinary-sized humans who now occupied it had come up with a convenient workaround. A steel ramp over the steps allowed them to make the descent more gracefully.

The ramp deposited them on a broad landing, turned ninety degrees, then continued down the tunneling cavern. As they descended, Elisabeth couldn't shake a growing sense of claustrophobia, as if the cavern was shrinking. How deep underground were they? A hundred feet? Two hundred? For all she knew, they had burrowed through the roots of Mount Khunjerab itself.

The air became increasingly stuffy and the lights mounted to the walls hummed ever louder in the silence.

Elisabeth was about to ask how much farther they had to go when she detected a faint, metallic gleam just ahead. A chill passed through her as they got close enough to confirm its source.

A shining, metallic barrier.

Brighton practically bounded up to the barrier and pressed his hand against it. His face radiated curiosity. As for herself, she felt neither fear nor curiosity. Just as in Tiahuanaco, she focused on what awaited them inside. She would do whatever she had to. Emery *was* coming back, even if just by her sheer force of will.

The sound of footsteps approached from behind. The same pair of guards from before arrived, their shoes clipping against the steel ramp.

Lagati greeted them, then leaned in close so one of the guards could whisper something in his ear. Elisabeth watched Lagati's face for a reaction; he gave nothing away.

"I apologize," Lagati said, spreading his hands in a gesture of regret. "My attention is needed upstairs. I'll be back shortly. I encourage you to explore."

Lagati headed for the ramp, but the guards remained. The one who had whispered to Lagati took a few steps closer to them, his watchful eye glued to Brighton, who was closest to the barrier.

"Both of you, come with me," Lagati's voice called back. The guards stirred. "These are my friends, and I think they'd appreciate privacy."

The guards turned without question and followed Lagati up the ramp. Elisabeth felt nothing but relief when they were alone.

"This is Shamballa?" Brighton asked incredulously. "Wörtlich is inside there?"

Elisabeth joined him next to the barrier. "Emery, can you hear me?"

No response came, though she waited a good, long time for one.

"In Tiahuanaco, the Nephilim spoke to me from inside the barrier," Elisabeth said. "If Emery is inside, he can hear us. I'm certain of it." Then, to the barrier, she said, "Emery, we've come for you. We need your help to get inside."

Brighton hesitated. "We need the sonic key. That's how Ira managed it in Egypt."

Only then did Elisabeth realize how much larger this cavern was in relation to its Tiahuanaco equivalent. She wouldn't have been surprised if they could walk the full periphery of the barrier, which stretched out like the sides of a massive upright cylinder.

"Lagati suggested we explore," Elisabeth said. "I intend to take him up on it."

She glided over the smooth stone floor, keeping her eye on the barrier as she passed around its side. A part of her embraced the false hope of discovering some break in the barrier, some way to enter it; the larger part knew there wouldn't be one.

"Emery, I know you're here," she repeated. What was she missing? He had contacted them so many times, told them explicitly to find this place. Perhaps Lagati would have the answer. He seemed to have an answer for everything else!

She felt Brighton's hand on her shoulder.

"Don't move," he said.

Brighton walked out in front of her, peering at something in the dimly lit cavern. She followed his gaze—and then gasped.

A man's body lay propped against the side of the barrier.

They hurried closer and knelt next to the body. From the state of deterioration, this man had been dead for at least a week.

Elisabeth brushed aside her hair and got down on her knees, studying the corpse's face. After a moment, it clicked. The shock of the realization nearly caused her to stumble backwards.

"I remember him from the camp in Tiahuanaco," she whispered. "His name was Guy."

"What's he doing here?"

Elisabeth stepped back, but before she could answer she heard footsteps. Lagati hurried toward them, his guards nowhere to be found.

"Sorry for leaving you. We have a shipment due to arrive. These are busy days." Lagati glanced at Guy's corpse. "I see you've had a look around."

"I knew this man," Elisabeth said. "A week ago, he was on the other side of the world."

"So were the two of you," Lagati pointed out.

Elisabeth glanced back down at the body. "He was possessed by a spirit we encountered in South America. Why did he come here?"

"Well, Shamballa, of course," Lagati said.

"And this is Shamballa?" Elisabeth gestured around the cavern.

Lagati approached the metallic barrier and rapped it with his knuckles. "More specifically, Shamballa is inside the barrier."

"Have you heard any voices coming from it?" Elisabeth widened her eyes. "Have you been inside?"

"Oh yes, many times, to both questions." Lagati's eyes lost focus, a slow smile creeping across his lips. "The beings inside speak to me often. I come down several times a day to commune with them, and yes, they have invited me inside. It's a city, a beautiful city where the Watchers have dwelled for centuries. Ohia was separated from the rest of his kind for more than a thousand years. When he returned, I welcomed him myself."

Lagati approached Elisabeth with slow, deliberate steps. "It's virtually impossible for a man to truly die at a hotspot. Think of it as a subway system, with stops spread out all over the planet. Each is connected to Shamballa via an energy vortex, or what some people refer to as ley lines. When Wörtlich's body died, his soul was deposited in Shamballa. He's been trying to contact you, but it is difficult. He cannot maintain contact with the physical plane for long, and only with people to whom he has a strong connection. When a spirit abides in Shamballa, it is in a state of bliss. I can't imagine any spirit would willingly leave."

"But Wörtlich wants to leave," Brighton said quietly.

"This is the only place on earth where a human can enter bodily," Lagati said, "and I can attest to the fact that it takes immense mental discipline to leave again. If my spirit were inside—disembodied, as Wörtlich finds himself—I doubt I would have any desire to leave.

"Elisabeth, I don't think Wörtlich will leave willingly, but this can be your opportunity to experience real closure. You could continue living here, visiting him anytime you like. The Watchers are highly advanced, and highly sociable. They constantly seek those with whom to fellowship.

"You are fortunate to have been called." The thick timbre of Lagati's voice spoke of his unbridled passion. "Adventurers have searched for the mystical Shamballa almost since the beginning of time. That's what brought me here. I have learned so much from these beings."

"Who are they?" Elisabeth asked.

"Galactic travelers," Lagati said. "They came to our planet before intelligent life appeared. Hell, they may have created us—or at least helped us over the critical evolutionary leap. For thousands of years— maybe hundreds of thousands—ancient humanity revered them as kings and gods. In modern parlance, they call themselves 'ascended masters.' It sounds haughty, but they're a benevolent species." He stared longingly into the image of his own reflected face. "I envy Wörtlich. If I didn't have so much to do here…"

Silence fell.

"Emery," Elisabeth whispered. She once again faced the barrier and pressed both palms against it. "Why doesn't he answer me?"

"They don't always answer when I call, either," Lagati said. "Most of the time, they're not attuned to the physical plane."

"Elisabeth…"

Her head shot up. Though slightly muffled, the voice had definitely come from the barrier.

"Yes?" She gave the wall her full attention. "Emery, is that you?"

There was a long, ominous pause.

"Yes."

"I'm here," she said breathlessly. "We came, just like you asked."

"I am glad. There are no words to describe what it is like here. You must see it for yourself."

Elisabeth nodded, even knowing he couldn't see her. "Yes. Lagati has just explained it to us."

"There is so much to tell you. So much to talk about."

Her bliss was so complete that it took a few seconds to register the fact that the voice had fallen silent. The barest sound now conveyed a cacophony—her labored breath, her pant legs rubbing together, her shoes against the floor.

The next thing she heard was a full-throated tone, a note in perfect pitch—not a song exactly, but nonetheless musical. She recognized its ethereal beauty, for she had heard it before.

"I haven't come all this way to stop now," she said when the tone faded into silence.

This is it—the moment of decision.

Elisabeth reached out her to hand to Brighton. "You coming?"

With hands clasped and eyes closed, they took a step—only to be swallowed by darkness.

*   *   *

Three resounding gunshots broke through the stillness, echoing off distant mountains and boomeranging back to them. A couple of birds took flight, and rustling in the grass a few meters to Dario's left indicated rodents scrambling for cover.

Dario would have run were it not for his two vulnerable companions. He looked longingly up the path toward civilization, lamenting that he'd never find out if he could have been able to escape that way.

Two men and a red-haired woman advanced openly from hiding places farther down the slope, holding their guns aloft. That would have been threatening enough, but a second round of gunfire disclosed three additional attackers from behind, completing the ambush.

"We should have seen this coming, Ira," Dario pointed out.

"I did." Ira sighed. "We came anyway."

If they weren't on the same side, Dario might have struck Ira. Why hadn't the rabbi revealed to them the inherent risks?

Sheply's face clouded with extreme frustration. His blind, desperate eyes searched back and forth, sadly telling him nothing. Dario felt pity for him.

"Welcome to Shamballa," the woman shouted, her voice carried on a gust of wind. Her tone commanded such attention that Dario presumed she was the leader. "We've been waiting for you all morning."

"Where are Sherwood Brighton and Elisabeth Macfarlane?" Ira called back. "I have come to retrieve them."

"And we have come to retrieve you," she said. As she came closer, Dario saw that her red hair was pulled back in a ponytail. She might once have had delicate features, though they had been ravaged by vehemence and fierce determination.

Dario braced as he felt the butt of a rifle poke him in the back.

"Check them for weapons," the woman said.

Rough hands patted him down, starting from the legs and working upward. They stopped over his pants pocket, where he carried the knife they'd bought at the market three days earlier.

Dario's assailant slid the knife out of its sheath and brandished it for the others to see. They all laughed.

"How much damage do you think you could have done with that?" the woman asked playfully.

Dario wouldn't play her game. "Are you going to kill us?"

"Not all of you," the lead woman said. She nodded subtly at one of the men behind Dario and Sheply.

Sheply lurched in surprise. The man behind him seized his arms, pinning them behind his back while another man leveled the serrated blade against his throat.

"Don't move," Dario whispered to Sheply, who was trying to squirm out of his assailants' hold. "They've got the knife."

Sheply stood stock-still, perhaps feeling the sharp edge of the blade against his neck. A thin line of blood formed amidst Sheply's stubble. If Sheply moved even an inch, the knife would dig into his jugular.

"Please, let us go," Dario said, the words tumbling out of him.

The woman looked almost apologetic. "I'm afraid I can't do that." She walked forward, passing Ira and going straight to Sheply.

"I want to thank you," she said to the blind man. "If it weren't for you, I wouldn't be here." She paused, turning to Dario. "You, too, have my gratitude."

"But we've never met," Dario said.

"Haven't we?"

Dario peered harder at her, wracking his memory. He hadn't met her in Italy, and she certainly hadn't taken part in the Tiahuanaco dig. She possessed no great beauty, but he thought he would have remembered her regardless.

"No." He wasn't in the mood for riddles, though in truth he wasn't much in the mood for anything except freedom. "I've had enough mystery for one lifetime."

"Very well," the woman said. "After what's happened, I can't say I'm surprised. I've changed faces since we last encountered one another, and I've gone by many names, but you know me as Ohia."

*   *   *

Panic rose inside Brighton as he realized his feet were not on solid ground. He shivered at the thought of the great abyss around him, at the same time wondering what allowed him to float over it as though this place wasn't subject to gravity. As though it wasn't a part of planet Earth at all.

"You have come a long way," a deep male voice called to him. "I bid you welcome."

Brighton blinked. There was no light at all, not the faintest glimmer.

"Where am I?" Brighton asked.

"You are everywhere and nowhere," the voice said, most certainly not Wörtlich's. "It has been called many names. Shamballa is the most common. We are its residents."

"Lagati called you ascended masters. Are you aliens?"

There was a long pause. "The term 'aliens' connotes strangers, visitors. We are neither. We have been with you since the beginning."

"The beginning of time?"

"Time is impossible to measure." The voice sounded amused. "It is dependent on one's point of view. It does not elapse uniformly. It is perhaps the most difficult of concepts. Let us say that we have been with humanity since the birth of its collective consciousness."

An explosion of light assaulted Brighton from all sides, forcing him to slam his eyes shut. Clouds of color floated behind his eyelids. Several long moments passed before he risked opening them again.

When he did so, he found himself standing on relatively flat ground that extended a hundred or more feet all around. Baking under intense midday heat, he wiped sweat from his brow. Tall cliffs encircled him, their oppressive heights rising to blade-like pinnacles.

I've been here before, Brighton thought, remembering the dreams he had shared with Ira and Wörtlich. Ira had called this place Mount Hermon, where the Watchers had gathered to make their pact to defile humanity. But that had been only Ira's side of the story, and Ira had rarely presented balanced viewpoints.

A circle of high-backed chairs ornamented the center of this natural amphitheater. Each chair held an occupant. They appeared male, but unnaturally tall with high cheekbones and sharply contoured faces.

One of the men stood, his white robe draping down from wide, muscled shoulders. He extended a thin finger toward Brighton, his eyes an intense, glassy blue.

Brighton would never forget those eyes.

"You," Azazel hissed.

Brighton fought the urge to run. "Azazel…"

A smile turned up the edges of Azazel's lips. "You know my name."

Between the smile and those cool eyes, Brighton sensed the creature appraising him the way a snake might appraise a meal.

"I saw you in a dream," Brighton said. "You were here, on Mount Hermon."

"Not a dream. A memory. Barakel's, if I'm not mistaken."

Azazel cast a glance toward one of his silent companions. Was that Barakel, the father of the giant they had encountered on Tubuai?

"Why have you brought me here?" Brighton asked.

A second of the creatures rose. "Brought you? You have come to us."

Brighton recognized this being as well. Its name was Semyaza.

"We are the Twenty, the leaders of the Grigori," Semyaza said, gesturing to the other beings, all of whom stared at Brighton. "Our human emissary has spoken much about you."

"You mean Lagati."

Semyaza inclined his head. "Yes. He calls himself by that name."

Brighton heard an anguished cry behind him. Turning, he saw Elisabeth on the ground, her hair covering her face. She knelt on her hands and knees, groping the cold stone. He called her name, but she didn't respond. She continued to whimper, feeling the ground.

When she looked up, he got a glimpse of her face. Her eyes were shock-white. She couldn't see him, nor apparently could she hear him.

"Where is Emery Wörtlich?" Brighton demanded, returning his attention to the Grigori.

Azazel and Semyaza exchanged a glance, and Brighton thought he detected a smile on their lips.

"Your friend is not here," a third voice said. Brighton saw that it came from Barakel. "They have lied to you, lured you to this place. Your friend is long dead."

Brighton's heart lurched as a singular realization coursed through the very fabric of his body, every bone and sinew: *Ira was right. Oh God, what have I done?*

"What have you done to her?" Brighton pointed toward Elisabeth. "She has done nothing to you."

"Indeed," Azazel said in an abstracted voice. "We care nothing for her. It is you we have sought."

"Why?" The word burst out of him in outrage.

The faces Grigori stared impassively as Semyaza took several careful steps toward Brighton, stopping short of exiting the circle of chairs. "Barakel is being dramatic. We have given you incentive to find this place, just as we have given many humans. We are delighted you have come, since so few make the journey."

"In the memories I saw, you were making plans to destroy humanity," Brighton said.

"Destroy humanity?" Semyaza laughed. "You saw through Barakel's eyes, and Barakel has not provided an… objective picture. We aren't destroyers, but creators. We came to Earth to tend to it. Think of us as gardeners."

"Our goal is to nurture life throughout the galaxy," Azazel said. "We left our world tens of thousands of years ago and found Earth in a primordial state. We have made this world our own, coaxing life from its glowing embers. Six thousand years ago, however, the oldest of our kind tracked us here and purposed to put a stop to that which we had created."

Semyaza returned to his seat and sank into it. "Your people know him as Jehovah, and some of you worship him as a god. He is a manipulative, capricious, violent creature. He opposes the creation of life, so he cut us off from our creation and abandoned you to destroy yourselves by your own devices. We have been trapped in this place for thousands of years, resigned to the torture of watching cherished humanity come to the brink of destruction."

Brighton looked from Semyaza to Barakel, who seethed in anger. "What of Barakel, then?"

"Barakel has worked against us from the beginning." Azazel's eyes flashed with rage. "We set out to help humanity make the leap to a higher evolutionary plane. Humankind was created in our image; you have the capacity to be like us, if you embrace the enlightenment we offer."

Semyaza stretched out his arms. "We did make a plan, as you saw. By mingling our seed with yours, we intended to accelerate the evolutionary process. But our enemy intervened by bringing a great flood to wipe out the population, causing a lone family to survive. A family which he carefully manipulated to worship him, and which has peddled fear and hate ever since. If you search yourself, you will see the truth. Is it any wonder most of the planet has been deceived?"

"What do you need with me?" Brighton demanded.

Azazel's blue eyes raked across Brighton as the creature walked in a circle around the chairs, his fingers grazing their tops. "We need emissaries like you and the man known as Lagati to pave the way for our release."

"Our children were once great kings who oversaw human development from one corner of the globe to another," Semyaza said. "I had many sons, including one who has only recently returned to me. I long to be reunited with all of them. The flood may have destroyed their bodies, but their spirits linger on the earth, joining with the spirits of men, with whom they have the power to effect positive change. But our sons cannot intrude upon an unwilling host, for humankind are free to choose and act according to their own consciences."

They want me to join with such a spirit, Brighton realized, feeling the shock.

Behind him, Elisabeth had ceased moaning. She now waited with her back against the cliffs, her head down.

"And Elisabeth?"

"She is not a suitable candidate," Semyaza told him sadly. "Her purpose was to help guide you to us. We are grateful for her contribution to this enterprise."

"But you want to possess me," Brighton said.

Semyaza stood again and approached. This time, Brighton didn't shy away. He stood his ground as the tall being came close enough to touch. Semyaza's close-shorn brown curls caught the sun, bathing his face in warm light.

"Not possess," Semyaza told him. "You would be partners. One of my children has reached out to you for many weeks, coming to you in your sleep. His name is Abranel." Semyaza closed his eyes. "Abranel is here now. Can you sense him?"

At first, Brighton felt nothing. A light breeze passed calmly over his face, lifting the loose hairs atop his head. The sunlight fell warmly over them, and Brighton felt a deep sense of serenity.

And then he felt it—the familiar presence he had thought was Wörtlich.

Abranel. Brighton sounded out the strange name. Could this Abranel speak? Did it know his thoughts?

He winced as pain shot through his head from one ear to the other. In the aftermath, his mind began to grow muddy, sluggish. He found he had to concentrate hard to stay in the moment.

It would be so easy to give in, to do what they're asking.

"If you join with Abranel, you shall remain the man of renown you have already become," Semyaza assured him. "Once joined, you will be equipped with the wisdom of the ages."

*   *   *

Ohia. Murderer, liar, foe. Dario swung himself out of his attacker's grasp, but the man only clamped down on him harder, restraining him by the waist.

"Behave yourself," Ohia said in a sickly sweet voice. She regarded Sheply and the knife at his throat. "I could let this one bleed. Is that what you want?"

Dario took deep, calming breaths. As much as he loathed Sheply, he didn't want anyone else to die because of him.

"I can see you are sensible." Ohia stroked her chin and turned her attention to Ira. "You, old man, are a delicious prize. The Grigori have been hoping to possess you."

Ira's careful expression revealed nothing. "I have not come to assist the Grigori."

"What you have come for is unimportant. You will do what is required, or your friends will die. We have many methods to aid us in eliciting cooperation, including substances to make one pliable to our needs."

"I have a stronger mind than most," Ira said.

Dario was struck by how baldly arrogant the rabbi's statement sounded, though he didn't doubt its truth.

"You may be right," Ohia allowed, "but it may not come to that. Another plan is in motion at this very moment. Sherwood Brighton is on the cusp of making the most important decision of his life, and we have taken steps to ensure his pliancy."

"Sherwood, too, has a stronger mind than you think," Ira said.

Ohia shrugged. "How very self-assured for a man facing his doom."

Sheply let out a cry as the blade sliced into his throat, missing the jugular while allowing a noticeable stream of blood to flow down his neck. Tears formed in his eyes.

"Just kill me," Sheply pleaded in a whisper. "Get it over with."

The man holding the knife chuckled but kept his hand firmly in place.

"What are we waiting for?" Dario demanded. "Either let us go or finish us."

Ohia glanced at him. "You face two possible paths. In one, you are a prisoner, and in the other, you are dead. Are you so impatient for the end to come?"

"No," Ira said.

All eyes except Sheply's turned to him.

Ira drew himself to his full height. "There is another path."

Dario stared in shock as the rabbi lifted his palm—a palm that radiated light.

*   *   *

Semyaza's hard stare drilled into Brighton, who nearly stumbled back in avoidance of it, unable to look away.

"I'm not feeling so well," Brighton said slowly, nausea spreading through him.

"Our apologies," Semyaza said. "This place has a curious effect on human visitors. The sensation will pass."

Brighton felt unsure of himself. He had fought so hard to get to this point. Had he been wrong about the Watchers? Had Ira lied about their intentions?

Would it be so wrong to do what they wanted?

"Abranel awaits your decision, but he will not wait forever." Azazel's voice floated across the circle toward him. "It is not so hard a decision. The advantages to the joining are manifold."

Brighton sank to the ground. He just needed a moment to clear his head.

"Our offer is in harmony with your desires," Semyaza said, regarding him with dark, fathomless eyes. "You long for the joining."

"Why should I long for it?" Brighton asked weakly.

"For what it brings. Wisdom. Understanding." Semyaza crouched down to look into Brighton's eyes. "These things have been withheld from you. You put your trust in Ira Binyamin, and he betrayed you."

Brighton heard rather than saw the smooth steps of Azazel crossing toward them. "Binyamin pretended to have your best interests at heart, but his motivations have always been self-serving. He's an emissary of Jehovah, and he would have destroyed you. You were wise to part ways, to reject his influence."

The mountaintop dissolved around him, replaced by a wide, sandy beach. The setting sun's burnt orange glow reflected off the undulating surface of the ocean. The waves beat against the shore in a steady pulse.

Brighton squinted, disoriented. Semyaza and Azazel stood next to him, still dressed in flowing white robes that stopped just short of the sand; those robes were too pristine to be sullied. The rest of the Grigori waited at a distance, clustered together. Barakel loomed prominent amongst them, his lips pressed together so snugly they turned white.

"We can create any environment we wish, go anywhere, through the power of thought," Azazel said in a cheerful voice. "The same ability could be yours."

Brighton once again felt Abranel's strange but familiar presence suffusing him with warmth.

"And outside Shamballa?" Brighton asked through the headache. "Does this ability follow you wherever you go?"

Semyaza's eyes turned down in sadness. "Our abilities are unusually potent here. In the real world, we require a tool that was taken from us long ago."

Brighton thought he saw Azazel flash a look toward Barakel at the mention of this missing tool.

"Abranel is no overlord, I assure you," Semyaza continued. "If you wish him to leave after a time, he will do so. Our children do not speak the language of force."

Brighton's head pounded. He winced at the pain.

"I can see the effects are worsening." Semyaza placed a hand on Brighton's forehead. The being's smooth skin felt icy cold. "You will acclimate once the joining is complete. It's the only way for a human to remain in Shamballa for an extended time."

"Where's Elisabeth?" Brighton asked, his mind growing fuzzier by the second.

Elisabeth appeared out of thin air. She huddled in a ball, no doubt feeling the same ill effects now plaguing him. Her body turned in the air, hovering over the beach. When he saw her face, it was contorted in a silent scream.

"She's in pain," Brighton said.

"Indeed." Semyaza lifted a finger and somehow stopped her slow revolution. "We regret her discomfort."

You can stop this, he told himself. *It would be so easy. The path is so clear.*

Brighton forced himself to look into Semyaza's eyes. "Alright. Yes."

Semyaza's eyebrows shot up. "Yes?"

"I'll do it."

With those words, Abranel's invisible embrace lifted. Brighton's heart fell as the warm sensation vanished, leaving him cold. Even unjoined, Brighton had grown accustomed to the spirit's presence. He opened his mouth to ask where Abranel had gone when the warmth returned, except this time it didn't hug tight against his skin. Heat spread out from his chest.

A cry of surprise escaped Brighton's lips as he bolted to his feet. The spirit pulsed inside him. It was the most intimate sensation—like sex, only deeper and more fulfilling. Goosebumps rose on the skin of his arms, and then over the rest of him as well.

Brighton instinctively fought against Abranel. A wave of heat pounded through his skull, his thoughts panicked and frenzied.

"Open your memory," a voice said to him. Brighton realized it was coming from Abranel, deep inside his own head. *"The key is in your experiences."*

What key? he asked.

Instead of a response, reality shifted again. The beach vanished, replaced by a cold, dark place.

I've been here before…

They stood in the chamber at the bottom of the Great Pyramid's descending passage. The only source of illumination was the flashlight in Brighton's own hands. The realization that Abranel controlled Brighton's hand profoundly unsettled him. He could feel the muscles in his body expand and contract, but he had been reduced to an observer in his own skin.

"This is not it," Azazel said gruffly. He stood alongside Semyaza, stooping lest they hit their heads on the chamber's low ceiling. Brighton could no longer see the other Grigori, but somehow he knew they watched nearby.

Reality morphed again, this time into the bone field beneath the Antarctic ice sheet. Shrubs and grasses sprouted up around them, nestled into the hollows of low-lying green hills.

"No."

The Roman boathouse in Malta.

"No."

The statue of former Secretary of the Smithsonian Joseph Henry.

"No."

The beach of Tubuai, the blue-green waters of the lagoon stretching before them, tall palms whispering in the cool island breeze.

A longer pause this time, then: "No."

Brighton's mind reeled at the string of imagery flashing before his eyes like a three-dimensional slideshow.

The flashing vistas froze on a dimly lit underwater scene, and in that moment Brighton knew without a doubt what they searched for. His body turned to behold the pyramid he, Ira, and Wörtlich had encountered on the floor of the Pacific Ocean.

"Yes."

Azazel drew the word out, tasting it, relishing in its implications. The sinister smile on his face told Brighton how greatly he anticipated this moment.

Semyaza and Azazel led him on a march toward the pyramid, treading over loamy soil as though beckoned by the eerie luminescence of the capstone. Brighton wrestled with Abranel, but was as effective as trying to crush a diamond with a clenched fist. Did Abranel even notice him?

Brighton steeled himself as reality flashed yet again, this time landing them inside the King's Chamber. From the far wall came the otherworldly glow of a golden parchment.

The Book of Creation.

Azazel stepped up to the Book and gazed upon it.

"You cannot know how long I have awaited this moment," Azazel said in a voice tinged with reverence and lust.

None of this is real, Brighton wanted to say, though the words wouldn't come out. He could exert no control over his body.

Nevertheless, Azazel heard the thought. "It is enough that you were here. That you remember it."

I don't remember it. Not in such detail.

"You are not consciously aware of what is in your own mind," Azazel said. "Once something is in your memory, it is possible to access it."

Tears might have sprung to Brighton's eyes had he been capable of them. How had he so completely let Ira down? Had Ira known this was coming? Why hadn't he done more to stop Brighton, to turn him around?

What have I done? Oh Ira, what have I done?

Semyaza came to stand next to Azazel, looking down at the Book. "This is the key. We have searched so long."

Azazel's lips moved as he read quietly from the ancient script. Brighton couldn't understand the words, but they had a lyrical quality that contrasted sharply with the horror he felt in his soul.

When Azazel came to the end of his recitation, reality shifted again, back to the infinite blackness Brighton had first found himself in after stepping through the barrier. This time, a faint and distant light interrupted the darkness, no more than a single star against the vastness of space.

The light grew larger as they approached, and soon Brighton could make it out: an ancient device sitting upon a base cut from a monolithic block of gold. From it sprouted a tube of glass pointed at a forty-five-degree angle. Weak light emanated from the bulb's thin filament.

Dario and Elisabeth had described a similar device inside the barrier in Tiahuanaco. Its activation had been responsible for releasing Ohia.

Azazel recited words from the Book, and as he spoke, runic text appeared upon the sundry flat surfaces of the device's stone base. What had been featureless rock was soon covered in line after line of ancient text.

The filament's glow strengthened and soon the space around the device filled with the Grigori. As they sprang into existence, Brighton counted more than the initial twenty who had sat around the circle on Mount Hermon. They numbered in the hundreds.

"We are free!" a voice crowed, and Brighton knew it belonged to Azazel.

As soon as the Grigori had arrived, one by one they vanished.

*   *   *

Ohia let out an astonished yelp and leaped backward as the light from Ira's palm swelled. Bathed by the unearthly yellow light, the world around Dario shrank. First the sky faded from view, then the mountains, and soon Dario couldn't make out the ground beneath his feet. The ambiance was almost soundless, and even time seemed to move at a more sluggish pace, the seconds stretching into minutes.

Ira stood in the middle of the maelstrom of light, his eyes closed and hands outstretched as though in supplication. Light rippled from his hands, each wave delivering a sharp tingle that progressed to a slow burn. Dario looked down at his exposed skin and watched it redden and blister.

Shrieks of pain erupted around Dario, and then a shriek erupted from his own throat.

"Ira, stop!" Dario's words were absorbed by the storm, its chaotic squalls encircling them all, twisting and spinning in unpredictable patterns.

In the center of the chaos, the rabbi stood with his eyes gaping open in dumbfounded adulation. His hair thrashed wildly above his head in a mad, exhilarated dance.

"Ira!"

If Ira was aware of Dario's screams, he didn't show it.

The hands holding Dario let go. In a frenzy, Dario lunged at Ira, knocking him backward. The rabbi's eyes lost their exaltation in the span of a moment, replaced by turmoil.

"What have I done?" Ira whispered. "Oh Lord, what have I done..."

Somewhere in the distance, Dario heard the slow-motion throb of gunfire, and then a bullet skimmed his ear.

Dario threw himself over Ira, protecting the old man from the fresh assault.

A scream of anguish different from the others ripped through the air like a siren. Dario's head whipped around through the all-encompassing yellowness as streams of incongruent red gushed from Sheply's throat, splattering onto the ground.

No no no—

EPILOGUE

Provo, Utah
JULY 29

G ayle Voss waited for her tea kettle's distinctive scream, then lifted it from the bright orange element. A pillar of steam rose, dampening her forehead as she poured boiling water into her husband's favorite mug. She placed it on a wooden serving tray next to a glass of tap water and a handful of assorted pink and green pills.

She entered the bedroom just in time to see her husband shift under the covers. He groaned and she picked up her pace, ever-careful not to drop the tray. A hot water burn was the last thing her husband needed on top of everything else.

Gayle set the tray on the table next to their bed. By now, the water swirled dark brown from the combination of herbs she had placed in the mesh tea infuser. This concoction had done wonders in the past, but the only way to help Henry get comfortable these days was to supplement the tea with medication; she hated to go the pharmacological route, but none of the usual natural remedies proved effective anymore.

"Henry," she spoke in a soft voice. The groans faded. "I've brought another dose."

The bed sheets moved, and Henry turned to face her. His hair had gone white, the gray now a distant memory. At forty-three years old, Henry looked like a man in his eighties. His skin had turned pale and fragile, and his bright blue eyes shone like opals.

Gayle placed the pills into his shaky outstretched hand. They clattered against each other. He swallowed them down with a gulp of water, then collapsed into the pillows.

"Drink the tea while it's hot." She sat on the edge of the bed, brushing her fingers through his wispy hair.

Henry sipped at the tea, his whole body shuddering. "Have you learned anything new?"

For weeks, she had sensed a planet-wide build-up of cosmic energy. At first, the energy had come from Saturn, but other sources had now appeared. Whatever was going on, the earth was under bombardment.

The worst had come the previous day when an enormous burst of power struck, originating from somewhere on Earth. Gayle had deployed her network of sensitives to find answers. In the meantime, Henry was totally immobilized. And he wasn't the only one.

"We're getting strong signals that the surge came from Kashmir," Gayle said.

Henry pressed his lips together. Gayle watched the pain medication take effect. His shoulders relaxed, his breathing eased, and his shaking subsided. The relief wouldn't last long, unfortunately.

"That's as you expected," Henry told her. "Do you think this has something to do with Elisabeth?"

Gayle looked away. "I can't imagine it's a coincidence."

"That means she found what she was looking for."

"For better or worse," Gayle said, standing. "I wish there was more I could do, but I fear the only option is to wait and hope Elisabeth contacts us."

She smoothed the blankets and then walked to the door.

Her heart broke as her eyes lingered on her husband. Nobody had ever recorded this level of nodal activity before, not even close. She worried it would be too much for Henry to handle. If these effects persisted for another week, would he survive it?

There was only one conclusion to draw. The Starseed people were returning.

*   *   *

Janene unlocked the back door to the synagogue and stepped inside. Her hand went to the light switch, but paused halfway there. The door closed behind her, shutting out the early morning sun cresting over the trees across the street.

Voices drifted out from somewhere inside the building.

She reached inside her pocket for her cell phone, but didn't turn it on. Her finger hovered over the screen as she listened. At least two men spoke in low voices from the end of the hallway.

Call the police, she told herself. *If it's a break-in, you'll only put yourself in danger.*

But how come there hadn't been any cars nearby? And how had the thieves gotten inside? The door required a code to open, and alarms would have sounded if anyone forced their way in.

Call the police, her conscience insisted. *No need to be a hero.*

She snuck the opposite direction from the voices, so as not to alert the men down the hall.

"I'm at Temple Emmanuel, on Jefferson Street," she whispered into the phone. "I just got to work and heard voices coming from the offices. I think there's a break-in in progress."

The emergency operator told her to find a safe place to hide and not to move. Police were on the way.

Ten seconds after hanging up, however, she crept down the hallway, trying to hear what the men were saying.

"You've crossed a dangerous line," one of the men said. He was in Ira's old office. Who on earth would have gone in there, of all places? "Many have crossed it before. Have you not learned from their examples?"

"There have been no examples in recent memory," the second voice hissed.

"But it's exactly what we have been charged with preventing!"

"I knew the risks."

"You knew, but you didn't heed. There will be consequences."

A long pause settled in. "I understand."

Janene had to restrain herself from jumping up and down and sprinting into the room. She would have recognized that voice anywhere. Ira Binyamin had come back!

She remained rooted to the spot, however, somehow aware that this wouldn't be a good time to interrupt.

"I met Sherwood Brighton," the first voice said. "He came to see me."

"Yes, I know," Ira said.

"You were right about his importance. He is destined for big things."

"Even now?"

"Now more than ever, Ira. It's not the first time history has turned on the fate of a single individual."

"I helped him as much as I could, though he refused to see that," Ira said. "Just two weeks ago, Trevor intervened in his escape from England. He was never alone, not ever."

Janene's head swiveled at the sound of insistent knocking at the back door.

"Police!" someone shouted.

Panicking, Janene jumped from her hiding place and met two officers at the door. Even after hearing her explanation, they insisted on searching the building to rule out suspicious activity.

Janene nodded, her pleading eyes going back to the hallway. Why had Ira and the other man not come out of the office? The police had been loud enough to wake the dead.

"Ira!" she called, hurrying toward his office door. "I'm so sorry for—"

She stopped in the open door, her voice catching in her throat. The office looked the same as always. There was no sign anyone had been there in days, let alone in the last few minutes.

Janene sagged into the wooden chair in front of the desk.

"Ira?"

The long silence assured her that she was well and truly alone.

*   *   *

Three ships waited in the hangar. Raff Lagati stood at the window, hands in his pockets, and watched as his people unloaded cargo from the newest arrival. They lifted one chrome-covered box after another out of the ship's rear compartment. Two women in jumpsuits stacked and catalogued it all.

Lagati couldn't wait to learn what hid in those boxes. The collection so far had produced items more marvelous than he had hoped for.

The door opened and Semyaza glided into the room. "Glided"

was the best way to articulate the way the Watchers moved. Their smooth movements were concealed behind flowing white robes that gave away little of their physical builds.

At six and a half feet, Semyaza towered over him. His blue eyes complemented a head of carefully trimmed brown curls, and his fair-skinned, almost bony hands stuck out from the bottoms of long white sleeves.

"I see you would rather watch the effort than join it," Semyaza said glibly.

Lagati felt little comfort around the Watchers, and Semyaza in particular. Semyaza's hostility was only thinly veiled most of the time. Lagati appreciated the reason: after millennia of imprisonment, he would have been just as filled with righteous anger. Though misdirected, Lagati had vowed to bear the brunt of it so that the Watchers could finally strike a blow at the one who had left them to stew behind that horrible barrier.

If he really wanted to put an end to this, Jehovah should have killed them, Lagati mused.

"You have been an adequate servant," Semyaza said, "but you mustn't think too highly of yourself. Humility is an important virtue."

Lagati lowered his head. "Azazel has taught me much humility."

Semyaza cracked a smile. "Yes, he is an excellent teacher. Discipline is a mark of affection."

"Affection?"

The Watcher took him by the shoulders in a firm grip.

Lagati braced himself. He had been manhandled by these beings many times before, and it often turned violent.

"Do not think we are unappreciative of your efforts. Do you imagine we would fail to acknowledge those who freed us?" Semyaza let go of Lagati's shoulders and turned to the window. "You'll soon feel the affection of the Grigori, I assure you."

That did nothing to ease Lagati's insecurities. It hadn't been meant to.

"Come," Semyaza said. "I have something to show you."

Semyaza left the office, leading Lagati on a tour through the installation. The Watcher walked quickly, his familiarity a reminder that he and the other adepts had built this place thousands of years ago. They passed many of Semyaza's fellows along the way; they proffered Lagati a critical eye but gave him no trouble. More and more, Lagati saw that he and his people were being displaced as the Watchers made themselves at home. He had expected it, yet the transition was difficult.

They came at last to a nondescript door, which Semyaza opened with a simple flourish. The room beyond looked not unlike a modern-day apartment. Lagati recognized it as one of the spaces he and his people had refurbished upon their arrival more than three years ago.

"What are we doing here?" Lagati asked.

Semyaza walked into the middle of the room. "We've come to visit an old friend. Come out, Barakel!"

Barakel appeared out of a side room. He bore a white robe like the others, though his stature was somewhat bowed in comparison. His wrists were bound with what appeared to be a pair of handcuffs with no openings or clasps, constructed from the same metal as the barrier.

"Sit," Semyaza commanded.

Barakel lowered himself with great care onto a stark wooden chair.

"The Grigori offer rewards where rewards are due," Semyaza said to Lagati. "If it were not for Barakel and his sons, a great number of the Nephilim might have escaped Jehovah's flood. We might have had the opportunity to launch a counterstrike."

Barakel lifted his head defiantly. "I tried for peace!"

"You heard the words of Enoch," Semyaza said. "You were there."

"I didn't believe they represented the last word. He was looking for an act of contrition, which you and the others were unwilling to give."

"Contrition!" Semyaza fumed. "Our enemy is intractable! We did nothing to be contrite about."

Lagati listened to the exchange in fascination. Normally this kind of discussion would have been held privately. Was it possible he was more than a trusted servant to them?

Semyaza calmed himself and once again spoke to Lagati. "Six thousand years of imprisonment was more than enough for us, but I'm not sure it has been enough for Barakel."

"Please," Barakel pleaded. "I made a mistake, but you must allow me to atone. Jehovah has proven his unwillingness to deal fairly. I now know our cause is right. We have no choice but to fight back."

"We have no need of you now," Semyaza said. "You may yet prove useful, but for the moment you are a liability."

Barakel rose. "I must have my freedom."

"When you have earned the right to rejoin us, we will welcome you with open arms." Semyaza turned away. "For the time being, we will impose … trials."

Barakel's face lost its coloring.

"Enjoy your comfort while you have it," Semyaza said, leading Lagati back to the door.

They returned to the corridor. Semyaza waited for the door to close before taking long strides which Lagati struggled to match.

"I trust you took the lesson to heart," Semyaza said.

"I believe I have."

In short order, they returned to Lagati's office. Semyaza was the first inside, and he immediately took his place at the window. Among the dozens of stacked chrome boxes lay several long containers measuring as much as eight or nine feet. Lagati thought they looked like coffins.

"Do you have instructions for me?" Lagati asked.

Semyaza gestured to the office. "For one thing, this is no longer yours. We require your services elsewhere. Perhaps menial tasks, by your reckoning, though they must be carried out by someone we have faith in. Now, go. I know you are curious about the cargo. That will be your first responsibility."

Lagati felt a surge of excitement and walked to the door.

"Don't forget the lesson," Semyaza called after him. "For every action, there is a consequence."

When Raff Lagati left his office for the last time, he was a different man than when he had come in. But he didn't fear change. There was much to gain, and time was growing short.

ABOUT THE
AUTHORS

EVAN BRAUN is an author and professional editor who has been writing books for the last two decades. *The City of Darkness,* his second published novel, is the sequel to *The Book of Creation.* He lives in Winnipeg, Manitoba.

CLINT BYARS hails from Atlanta, Georgia, where he lives with his wife Sara and two children, Sydney and Reese. The author of *Devil Walk,* an autobiographical book chronicling his experiences with the demonic realm, Clint is also involved with Pokot Water, an international project aimed at providing clean water wells to remote regions of Kenya. He is the pastor of Forward Church.